Frances Rollin Whipper

Life and Public Services of Martin R. Delany

Sub-assistant commissioner, Bureau relief of refugees, freedmen, and of abandoned lands, and late major 104th U.S. colored troops

Frances Rollin Whipper

Life and Public Services of Martin R. Delany
Sub-assistant commissioner, Bureau relief of refugees, freedmen, and of abandoned lands, and late major 104th U.S. colored troops

ISBN/EAN: 9783337093624

Printed in Europe, USA, Canada, Australia, Japan

Cover: Foto ©Raphael Reischuk / pixelio.de

More available books at **www.hansebooks.com**

LIFE

OF

MARTIN R. DELANY.

LIFE

AND

PUBLIC SERVICES

OF

MARTIN R. DELANY,

SUB-ASSISTANT COMMISSIONER BUREAU RELIEF OF REFUGEES,
FREEDMEN, AND OF ABANDONED LANDS, AND LATE
MAJOR 104TH U. S. COLORED TROOPS.

BY

FRANK A. ROLLIN.

——"*et niger arma Memnonis.*"

BOSTON:
LEE AND SHEPARD.
1883.

STEREOTYPED AT THE
BOSTON STEREOTYPE FOUNDRY,
19 Spring Lane.

CONTENTS.

CHAPTER   PAGE

Introduction, ... 7

I. Genealogy, ... 13

II. Early Education, ... 30

III. Studying North, ... 38

IV. Moral Efforts, ... 43

V. Editorial Career, ... 48

VI. Practising Medicine, ... 68

VII. Fugitive Slave Act, ... 73

VIII. A Hiatus, ... 77

IX. Canada. — Captain John Brown, . . . 83

X. Canada Convention. — Harper's Ferry, . . 91

XI. In Europe, ... 96

XII. The International Statistical Congress and Lord
Brougham, ... 99

XIII. Return to America, ... 134

XIV. Corps d'Afrique, ... 141

XV. A Step towards the Service, ... 145

XVI. Recruiting as it was, ... 151

XVII. Changing Position, ... 155

XVIII. Private Council at Washington, ... 162

XIX. The Council-Chamber. — President Lincoln, . 166

XX. The Gold Leaf, ... 176

XXI. In the Field, ... 181
XXII. At Charleston and Fort Sumter, . . . 189
XXIII. Armée d'Afrique, ... 200
XXIV. The National Calamity, ... 203
XXV. Camp of Instruction, ... 209
XXVI. Extraordinary Messages, ... 214
XXVII. News from Richmond, ... 222
XXVIII. A New Field, ... 227
XXIX. General Sickles, ... 245
XXX. Restoring Domestic Relations, . . . 254
XXXI. General Robert K. Scott, ... 259
XXXII. The Planters and the Freedmen's Bureau, . 269
XXXIII. Domestic Economy, ... 272
XXXIV. Civil Affairs. — President Johnson, . . . 277
XXXV. Educational Interests, ... 285
XXXVI. Conclusion, ... 292

APPENDIX.

Political Writings, ... 303
African Explorations, ... 306
Reflections on the War, ... 309
The International Policy of the World towards the African Race, ... 313
Political Destiny of the Colored Race on the American Continent, ... 327

INTRODUCTION.

AT the close of every revolution in a country, there is observed an effort for the gradual and general expulsion of all that is effete, or tends to retard progress; and as the nation comes forth from its purification with its existence renewed and invigorated, a better and higher civilization is promised.

Before entering upon such an effort, it is usual to compute the aid rendered in the past struggle for national existence, and the present status of the auxiliaries in connection with it. In this manner, as the sullen roar of battle ceases, as the war cloud fades out from our sky, we are enabled to look more soberly upon the stupendous revolution, its causes and teachings, and to consider the men and new measures developed through its agency, the material with which the country is to be reconstructed.

In reviewing the history of the late civil war, it will be found, as in former revolutions, that those who were able to master its magnitude were men who, prior to the occasion, were almost wholly unknown, or claimed but a local reputation. Measures which before were deemed impracticable and inexpedient, in the progress of the war, were considered best adapted to meet the exigencies of the time. A race before persecuted, slandered, and brutalized, ostracized, socially and politically, have scattered the false theories of their enemies, and proved in every way their claim and identity to American citizenship in its every particular. While the war between sections has erased slavery from the statutes of the country, it has in no wise obliterated the inconsistent prejudice against color. Among the white Americans, since the rebellion, from the highest officer to the lowest subaltern, there is a recognized precedence for them, in view of their patriotism and valor in the hour of peril and treachery. They recognized their duty when Southerners had ignored it: for this we honor them; and none would gainsay an atom of the praise bestowed: the country had always honored and protected them at home and abroad; and in enhancing her prestige, they have added to their own as American citizens. But in the same dark hour of strife and treachery, there went forth from the despised and dusky sons of the republic a host, who, though faring differently, contributed no meagre offering to the cause of the Union. In the foremost rank of battle they stood, stimulated alone by their sublime faith in the future of their **country,** instead of being deterred by the disheartening experiences of the past. **From** their first **hour** in the rebellion **to the** last, theirs **was a** fierce, **unequal** contest; they were found enlisting, fighting, and **even dying** under circumstances **from which the bravest Saxon would** have **been justified in shrinking. For** them there was **"death in the front and destruction in the rear"**—torture and death as prisoners in the rebel **lines, and the** perils of the mob in many of the loyal cities awaiting them when seen in the United States uniform. **Despite all opposition,** they have traced their history in characters **as indestructible as** they are brilliant, to the **confusion of** their **enemies. On every** field, negro heroism **and valor have been** proved by them in **a** manner which **has established for** their race a grandeur of character in American annals, that, when read by the unprejudiced eyes of futurity, will gleam **with** increased splendor **amid their** unfavorable surroundings; while in song **and story** their deeds **of** prowess will live forever, reflecting **the** glories of Port Hudson, the crimson field **of** Olustee, and the holy memories which cluster about Fort Wagner.

Of **an army** of more than **a quarter of a** million **men,** less than a decade received promotion for their services. Lieutenant Stephen **A.** Swails, of Elmira, New York, a member of the Fifty-fourth Massachu-

setts Volunteers, had **the** honor of being first, **for**
having signally distinguished himself both at Wagner
and Olustee. Later followed the promotion of **Lieutenants** Dufree, Shorter, **James T.** Trotter, and Charles
Mitchell, from the Fifty-fifth Massachusetts Volunteers;
Lieutenants Peter Voglesang (Quartermaster), **and**
Frank Welch, from the Fifty-fourth Massachusetts Volunteers. Dr. Alexander Augusta, of Canada, had been
previously appointed **surgeon, with** the rank of major.
Besides these, several complimentary promotions were
given prior to the muster out of these **two** regiments.
None of the officers above named have been retained
in the service; one alone remains, who, during the rebellion, had attained the highest commission bestowed
on any **of** the race by the government — **that of Major**
of Infantry. Him whom the government had **chosen**
for this position we have made the subject of **this**
work. His great grasp of **mind and fine executive**
ability eminently befitted **him** for the sphere, and the
success which attends his measures renders him a distinct and conspicuous character at his post. His career
throughout life has been very remarkable. Prior **to**
his present appointment **his name was** familiar with
every advance movement relative to the colored **peo-**
ple: once **it** fell upon the ear of the terror-stricken
Virginians, in connection with John Brown, **of Osso-**
watomie; and scarcely had it been **forgotten when it**

was borne back to us from the Statistical Congress at London, encircled with the genius of Lord Brougham. To no more advantageous surroundings than were enjoyed by the masses he owes his successes; hence his achievements may be safely argued as indicative of the capability and progress of the race whose proud representative he is. The isolated and degraded position assigned the colored people precluding the possibility of gaining distinction, whenever one of their number lifts himself by the strength of his own character beyond the prescribed limits, ethnologists apologize for this violation of their established rules, charging it to some few drops of Saxon blood commingling with the African. But in the case of the individual of whom we write, he stands proudly before the country the blackest of the black, presenting in himself a giant's powers warped in chains, and evidencing in his splendid career the fallacy of the old partisan theory of negro inferiority and degradation.

In this history will be noticed certain strong characteristics peculiarly his own, which are traceable more to the circumstances of his birth than his race. Aiming to render a faithful biography of this remarkable man, we narrate minutely his singularly active and eventful life, which, in view of the narrow limits apportioned to him, will bear favorable comparison with the great Americans of our time.

CHARLESTON, S. C., October 19th, 1868.

LIFE OF MAJOR M. R. DELANY.

CHAPTER I.

GENEALOGY.

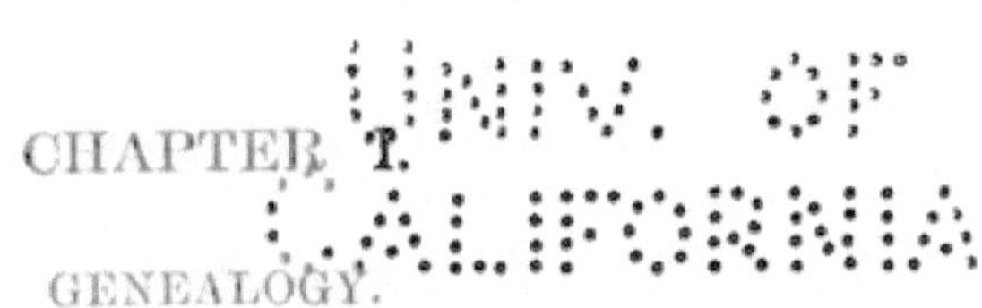

IT has always been admitted that the early slaves of America were the vanquished of the wars waged among rival tribes of Africa. Among these were kings, chiefs, and their families, accustomed to state and circumstance, consigned to slavery in accordance with the laws of their warfare. From these early slaves the colored people of the United States are descended; and some of these captive kings and princes, it naturally follows, were the progenitors of some of the colored people of this continent. Yet, in consequence of the condition assigned them by an unholy prejudice, the mere mention of a claim to a family lineage, by one of that race, is treated with derision. Despite the opposition, however, there are Americans who not only claim a regal African ancestry, but cling to it with a pride worthy of a citizen of Rome in her palmiest days. Regardless of the gloom of barbarism which encircled their ancestry, knowing that the race which now stands at the zenith of its power suffered like disadvantages, the colored people cherish **this proud** descent with all **the** strong feeling so characteristic **of them.** Prominent among **them** in this pride of race stands the subject **of this work.**

At a recent session of Congress an interrogatory **was** raised by a member of that honorable body, while **the** suffrage question was **being** agitated : " What **negro,** either ancient **or** modern, has risen up and shown his claims to a family lineage, **or** a kingdom, as have done other men through all times ? **Or** where is the negro, who, by the force of his intellect, and might of **his will and power, has** attempted to **bring** together the **scattered petty** chiefdoms south **of the** Sahara into **one grand** consolidated kingdom ? Show **me** one who has attempted any **of these, and with** all of my prejudices, **to** such will **I** accord honor." This **will temper** the criticism **to** which we render **ourselves** liable under **a state of** society where every man is supposed to stand upon **the** strength of his own merit, or fall **for** want **of** it, and where family titles are ignored, by beginning the biography of a colored man with **his** ancestry, instead of treating directly **with** himself. Since this reference **to ancestry is** not without precedent, as the histories of distinguished Americans show, **there** can be no violation **of** established rules for us to avail ourselves **of the** privilege, not in imitation **of others,** but rather with **a** view of presenting a faithful portrait **of one** representative of the race, known to **two** continents, but remarkable **in the** history of our times as the first black major in **the** United States service.

\MARTIN ROBISON DELANY, the son of Samuel and

Pati Delany, was born at Charlestown, Virginia, May 6, 1812. He was named for his godfather, a colored Baptist clergyman, who, it appeared, gave nothing beyond his name to his godson.

With the name Delany, a peculiarity illustrative of the man himself is manifested. Regarding it as not legally belonging to his family by consanguinity, and suspicious of its having been borrowed from the whites, as was the custom of those days, he expresses himself always as though it was distasteful to him, recalling associations of the servitude of his family. With these associations clinging to it, his pride revolts at retaining that which he believes originated with the oppressors of his ancestors; and though he has made it honorable in other lands besides our own, encircled it with the glory of a steadfast adherence to freedom's cause in the nation's darkest hours, and uncompromising fidelity to his race, thus constituting him. one of the brightest beacons for the rising generation, he eagerly awaits the opportunity for its erasure.

His pride of birth is traceable to his maternal as well as to his paternal grandfather, native Africans — on the father's side, pure Golah; on the mother's, Mandingo.

His father's father was a chieftain, captured with his family in war, sold to the slavers, and brought to America. He fled at one time from Virginia, where he was enslaved, taking with him his wife and two sons, born to him on this continent, and, after various wanderings, reached Little York — as Toronto, Canada, was then called — unmolested. But even there he was pursued, and "by some fiction of law, international policy, old musty treaty, cozenly understood," says Major Delany, he was brought back to the United States.

The fallen old chief afterwards is said to have lost his life in an encounter with some slaveholder, who attempted to chastise him into submission.

On his mother's side the claim receives additional strength. The story runs that her father was an African prince, from the Niger valley regions of Central Africa; was captured when young, during hostilities between the Mandingoes, Fellahtas, and Houssa, sold, and brought to America at the same time with his betrothed Graci.

His name was Shango, surnamed Peace, from that of a great African deity of protection, which is represented in their worship as a ram's head with the attribute of fire.

The form and attributes of this deity are so described as to render it probable that the idol Shango, of modern Africa, is the same to which ancient Egypt paid divine homage under the name of Jupiter Ammon. This still remaining the popular deity of all the region of Central Africa, is an evidence sufficient in itself to prove not only nativity, but descent. For in accordance with the laws of the people of that region, none took, save by inheritance, so sacred a name as Shango, and the one thus named was entitled to the chief power. From this source this American family claim their ancestry.

Shango, at an early period of his servitude in America, regained his liberty, and returned to Africa.

Whether owing to the fact that the slave system was not so thoroughly established then, — that is, had no legal existence,— or the early slaveholders had not then lost their claims to civilization, it was recognized among themselves that no African of noble birth should be continued enslaved, proofs of his claims being adduced. Thus, by virtue of his birth, Shango was enabled to return to his home. His wife, Graci, was afterwards restored to freedom by the same means. She remained in America, and died at the age of one hundred and seven, in the family of her only daughter, Pati, the mother of Major Delany.

These facts were more fully authenticated by Major Delany while on his famous exploring tour, of which we will speak hereafter. While he travelled from Golah to Central Africa, through the Niger valley regions, he recognized his opportunity, and consulted, among others, as he travelled, that learned native author, Agi, known to fame as the Rev. Samuel Crowther, D. D., created by the Church of England Bishop of Niger, the degree of Doctor of Divinity having been conferred by the University of Oxford. From all information obtained, it is satisfactorily proved, that, his grandmother having died about forty-three years ago, at the advanced age of one hundred and seven years, as before stated, then his grandfather's age, being the same as hers, would correspond with that period, which is about one hundred and fifty years, since the custom of an heir to royalty taking the name of a native deity was recognized; and, further, that his grandfather was heir to the kingdom which was then the most powerful of Central Africa, but lost his royal inheritance by the still prevailing custom of slavery and expatriation as a result of subjugation.

Some day, then, perhaps before the "star of empire westward takes its way," "the petty chiefdoms and principalities south of the Sahara" may yet be "gathered into one grand consolidated kingdom" by some negro's intellect and might.

To possess himself of the early origin of his family was in keeping with a mind so richly endowed, and soaring always far beyond the confines which the prejudices of this country apportion him. Not that he expected it to elevate him in America, knowing that custom and education are alike averse to this — scarcely allowing him to declare with freedom from derision the immortal sentence, "*I am a man*," and claiming rights legitimately belonging to its estate. For by observing his history, it may yet prove that the sequel is but the goal of his earliest determination, and not of recent conception, but nursed from his high-minded Mandingo-Golah mother, and heard in the chants of a Mandingo grandmother, depicted with all the gorgeous imagery of the tropics, as the story of their lost and *regal* inheritance. Thus becoming imbued with its spirit, it shaped itself in the dreams of his childhood, it entwined about the studies and pursuits of his youth, and, through that remarkable perseverance which characterizes him, it was realized in the full vigor of manhood to trace satisfactorily his ancestors' history on the soil of its origin.

Thus Africa and her past and future glory became entwined around every fibre of his being; and to the work of replacing her among the powers of the earth, and exalting her scattered descendants on this continent, he has devoted himself wholly, with an earnestness to which the personal sacrifices made by him through life bear witness.

Said he on one occasion, " While in America I would be a republican, strictly democratic, conforming to the letter of the law in every requirement of a republican government, in a monarchy I would as strictly conform to its requirements, having no scruples at titles, or objections to royalty, believing only in impartial and equitable laws, let that form of government be what it might; believing *that* only preferable under just laws which is best adapted to the genius of the people.

" I would not advocate monarchy in the United States, or republicanism in Europe; yet I would be either king or president consistently with the form of government in which I was called to act. But I would be neither president nor king except to promote the happiness, advance and secure the rights and liberty, of the people on the bases of justice, equality, and impartiality before the law."

Such are the principles to which he adheres. Unpopular as they are, they have not unfitted him for the duties of a republican citizen, owing to his ready adaptation to the circumstances in which he has happened to be placed for promoting the interests of his race.

For, next to his pride of birth, and almost inseparable from it, is his pride of race, which even distinguishes him from the noted colored men of the present time. This finds an apt illustration in a remark made once by the distinguished Douglass. Said he, " I thank God for making me a man simply; but Delany always thanks him for making him a *black man.*"

Doubt of his claims and criticism of his actions may be freely indulged, for even under the more favorable circumstances in a democracy like ours, they would be meted out to him; but it must be admitted it is not an ordinary occurrence, in a country like ours, with all the disadvantageous surroundings of the colored people, to find an individual lifting himself above the masses by the levers considered the most unwieldy — his faith in his race, and his deep identity with them. So completely has slavery accomplished its mission, depriving the colored people of every opportunity of profit, and every hope of emolument, confining them to the most menial occupations, engendering a timidity to advancement into the higher pursuits, unless supported by some recognized popular element, as to cause them to be at all times painfully alive to their humiliating condition, and to act as though ready to bow apologies to the public for their color. While this can hardly be charged as a fault to them, it is at best lamentable, and at the same time it is equally true, that Major Delany, in the sincerity of his belief, even unconscious of its effect, tends to the other extreme — that white men are often piqued when in contact with him, and are likely at first to be prejudiced against him.

A true radical of the old school, once in conversation with another gentleman, when the black officer's opinion on the subject on which they were conversing was quoted, rejected it, and vehemently exclaimed, "Sir, I do not believe Delany considers any white man as good as himself."

He rejects always, with the deepest scorn, the assertion of inferiority, claiming always for his race the highest susceptibility in all things, which belief he asserts with additional force since his intercourse with native Africans of the Niger valley regions, whose metaphysical reasonings and statuary designs, all circumstances considered, challenged his highest admiration, and claiming for himself, as before mentioned, a high descent.

On going to London, he made known his efforts to obtain, while in Africa, a correct knowledge of his ancestry to the distinguished Henry Ven, D. D., late tutor of mathematics and Latin and Greek in Cambridge College, now secretary of the Church Missionary Society, Salsbery Square, when the generous philanthropist at once stated that he had but one copy of Koehler's *Polyglotta Africana*, a work gotten up at great expense and labor expressly for the church publication, the price being four or five pounds sterling; but that Dr. Delany, of all living men, had a legitimate right to it, and therefore should have it; and he at once presented it to him, this being probably the only one in America. In this the high status claimed for his ancestry received additional proofs.

John Randolph of Roanoke referring always, in his pride, to his blood inherited from his Indian ancestry, as the strength upon which his great character was formed, and Martin Delany glorying in the blood transmitted to him from the dusky chiefs of Africa, cannot be considered a weakness in this country, where the Indian and the negro are entitled to the strongest consideration of the nation. For upon his parentage and race rests whatever of success and prominence our subject has achieved; they have entered so strongly into all his pursuits, and blended themselves into a most ennobling influence, that they reflect themselves in every act, and each act, marked by this strong personality, leads to the individual himself.

In personal appearance he is remarkable; seen once, **he is to** be remembered. He is of medium **height**, compactly and strongly built, with broad shoulders, upon **which** rests a head seemingly inviting, by **its** bareness, attention to the well-developed organs, with eyes sharp and piercing, seeming to take in everything at a glance at the same time, **while** will, energy, and fire are alive in every feature; the whole surmounted on a groundwork of most defiant blackness. It is frequently said **by** those best acquainted with his character, that in **order to** excite envy in him would **be for** an individual to possess less adulterated blackness, as his great boast is, that there lives **none** blacker than himself. **His** carriage, erect and independent, as if **indicative of the** man, calls attention **to** his **figure.** His wonderful powers of mental and physical **endur-**ance and great constitutional vigor, resulting in **a phy-**sique of striking elasticity, lead us to institute comparisons with the great Lord Brougham.

If there is one faculty for the cultivation of which he is more remarkable than another, it is his power of memory, almost as universal as it is tenacious, never seeming wholly **to** forget persons, names, places, or events; especially those of interest he relates with accuracy. His ready memory, always suggestive, renders him in oratory exhaustless and lengthy, but at all times interesting; especially to a promiscuous audience

he is instructive. His gestures in speaking are nervous
and rapid at first, then easy and graceful; his delivery
forcible and impressive; while his voice, deep-toned
and full, attracts his auditors, and influences them.
At all times logical, appealing more to the reason than
to the feelings, endeavoring at all times to infuse his
own enthusiasm for the glorious future of his race into
them, he appeals less to their passions than their pride.

In speaking, he is most effective when in his loftiest
flights. Losing sight of his audience, and wrapped up
in his theme, his features beaming with the beauty of
inspiration, he seems to address himself directly to the
great injustice which towers above him, no longer himself, but the spirit of some martyr-hero of his race in
the cause of right, bursting the cerements of the grave
to renew the combat on earth. To all conscious of
his life-long earnestness, and how closely the orator
and the man are allied, his efforts are not without
their effect.

He conformed to no conservatism for interest's sake,
nor compromise for the sake of party or expediency,
demanding only the rights meted out to others. His
sentiments partaking of the most uncompromising radi-
calism, years before the public were willing to listen to
such doctrine, caused his speeches and writings to be
considered impracticable and impolitic. While they
were never characterized by violent or incendiary expressions, they consequently rendered him less popular
than many others of inferior ability. He was considered impolitic for what men talked with abated breath;
when slavery had her myrmidons in church and state,
he held up, in all of its deformities, and denounced with-

·out fear or palliation, depending more upon the cause than the time to justify him. "Setting his foot always in advance of fate," his views were deemed impracticable; but, proud in the strength of his opinions, and wrapped in the consciousness of their ultimate adoption, he bided his hour.

As an advocate of moral reforms his influence finds abundant scope. His habits being as simple as they are temperate, adhering rigidly to physiological rules, they render him successful in presenting such measures. In early youth he espoused total abstinence; conforming first from principle, it afterwards became an established habit to eschew the use of liquors, or even tobacco, in any form, and from these early principles he has never been known to swerve. While his labors and sympathies are more strongly put forth in behalf of his own race, as more needful of them, yet no one exhibits a more catholic spirit, even to the enemies of his race, than Martin Delany. In his present sphere, his untiring efforts to ameliorate the condition of every class, irrespective of former condition and politics, and to advance the prosperity of an impoverished and prostrate section of our country, will render his name acceptable, not only as the able and incorruptible executive officer of the government, but as a humanitarian in its widest acceptation. To sum up his character, there will be found a strong individuality permeating it, as though aiming always to be himself in all things; possessing all the pride, fire, and generous characteristics of the true negro, without the timidity or weakness usually ascribed, as resulting from their condition in America.

There is every evidence that he possesses in an eminent degree the elements of the true soldier, and under more favorable auspices would have made a reputation worthy of record beside the great names which the late rebellion has produced. Fearless without being rash, at all times self-possessed and fully equal to emergencies, a lover of discipline; an iron will and great strength of endurance and perseverance bestowed by Nature, while she circumscribed his limits for exercising them; hence the record of his services in the late rebellion will be more of his achievements as an organizer of movements tending to advance the progress of freedom in reconstruction than of his martial accomplishments.

While the true place of the distinguished colored man is among the "self-made men" of our country, still it must be admitted that their surroundings being less favorable to insure success than white men of the same class, in proportion, their achievements are as great. And while many of this class were fostered by the Anti-slavery Society, — its patronage being always extended to the talented and meritorious of the race, — still its immediate support was never held out to him. Solely upon his own will, perseverance, and merits can be based the secret of his success wherein others have failed.

His mother was considered a most exemplary Christian, active and energetic, with quick perceptions and fine natural talents, inheriting all the finer traits of character of her Mandingo origin. The Mandingoes, from their love of traffic, are nicknamed the "Jews of Africa." An incident which is related of her shows the force of character which she transmitted to her son.

An attempt was made to **enslave** herself and children, five in all, in Virginia, where they resided. Being informed of it, she at once determined **to test or avert it.** Taking the two youngest, **she set out on foot,** with one lashed across her back, **and the other in her** arms; she walked the distance **from Charlestown to** Winchester **in** time to meet **the** court, consulted **her** lawyer, entered suit, and when all difficulties were **satisfactorily** adjusted, she returned to her children triumphant. "Some Roman lingered there," that neither the **miasma of** slavery, with which the atmosphere about **was impregnated, nor** the uncertain future of her children, could crush out; but a slow and steady **fire** burnt forever in her soul, and gleamed along **the pathway** of her youngest born to guide him to duty **in the** unequal strife of his race. **She lived long enough to** witness the overthrow **of the** oligarchy against which she had contended in Virginia. She died at **Pittsburg,** in the **family of her son, Samuel Delany, in** 1864, at the age **of ninety-six.**

This family attained great longevity, as is again shown in the father of Major Delany, who gave every indication of a hale old age, when he was carried off by the cholera which swept over Pittsburg at one time, when **he had** reached his eighty-fourth year. In life **he was known as** a man of great integrity of character, **of** acknowledged courage, and was remarkable for his great physical strength. He was well known in Martinsburg, where, for a stipulated sum, he obtained **his** freedom, thence went to Chambersburg, whither his family had preceded him. He bore a scar **on his** face, the result **of a wound,** which adds another testimony to the "bar-

barism of slavery." It was inflicted by the sheriff of
the county, who, with eight men, went to arrest him
one morning, because he had nine times torn the clothes
from off the person of one Violet, as he was endeavoring to inflict bodily punishment on him. Each time,
as he dashed the man Violet from him, he assured him
he had no wish to injure him.

The sheriff and his men, approaching, were warned by
him to keep off. He then fortified himself behind a
wagon in a lane, and, being armed with its swingle-tree,
bade defiance to the authority attempting to surround
him. The better to effect a retreat, if necessary, by
climbing backwards he raised himself to the top of
the fence, his face to his persecutors. At the moment
the top was gained, he was brought to the ground, sense-
less and bleeding, by a skilfully-directed stone. He
was then secured and taken to prison at Charlestown.

The sheriff was desirous of shooting him; but Violet,
with a view to his market value rather than appreciation of his determined courage, objected most decidedly to this, adding that he was "too good a man to be
killed." The stone was thus substituted for the bullet.
With this mark of brutality daily before the eyes of
his children, and in its train all the humiliations and
bestial associations to which their hapless race was
subjected, it is no matter of wonderment that Martin
Delany should watch every enactment concerning his
race with exactness, and his bitterness against their oppressors and abettors would sometimes outrun his sense
of the politic, or that all his efforts should, through
life, converge to the same end to contribute his aid to
root out every fibre of slavery and its concomitants.

On the 15th of March, 1843, he was married to Kate A., youngest daughter of Charles Richards, of Pittsburg, the grandfather and father of whom had been men of influence and wealth of their time. This daughter was one of the heirs to their estate, which had increased in value, as it embraced some of the best property in the city of Pittsburg, estimated at nearly two hundred and fifty thousand dollars. This was finally lost to them in 1847, simply by a turn of law, in consequence of the unwillingness of attorneys to litigate so large a claim in favor of a colored against white families.

Mrs. Delany is a fine-looking, intelligent, and appreciative lady, possessed of fine womanly sympathies, and, always entering fully into his pursuits, has contributed no little aid to his success.

With a companion whose views are so thoroughly in unison with his own, his domestic relations are prosperous and happy. Equally as zealous for the interest of her race, and self-sacrificing as himself, she encouraged and urged him on, in his most doubtful moments, — for many they were while the political horizon was darkened by the thick clouds of slavery.

While they were never possessed of means, through her management many poor fugitives and indigent persons were succored by them. She has cheerfully borne poverty when it could have been otherwise, and would forego personal comforts rather than he should fall back from the position he had taken, for pecuniary benefits for herself and children.

From this marriage eleven children were born, seven of whom are living. In the selection of the names of these children, the speciality is again evident. If the names given to children generally are intended as incentives to the formation of character, then, when they are sufficiently marked by selections from prominent characters, it may at least be indicative of the sentiments of the parents. If this is admitted, then the choice of names of these children gives unmistakable evidences of the determination of their parents that these brilliant characters should not be lost sight of, but emulated by them. While they are strictly in keeping with the father's characteristic, they being all of African affinity or consanguinity, they are nevertheless remarkable amidst such surroundings as American contingencies constantly present. The eldest is Toussaint L'Ouverture, after the first military hero and statesman of San Domingo; the second, Charles Lennox Remond, from the eloquent living declaimer; the third, Alexander Dumas, from that brilliant author of romance; the fourth, Saint Cyprian, from one of the greatest of the primitive bishops of the Christian Church; the fifth, Faustin Soulouque, after the late Emperor of Hayti; the sixth, Rameses Placido, from the good King of Egypt, "the ever-living Rameses II," and the poet and martyr of freedom to his race on the Island of Cuba; the seventh, the daughter Ethiopia Halle Amelia, the country of his race, to which is given the unequalled promise that "she should soon stretch forth her hands unto God."

CHAPTER II.

EARLY EDUCATION.

IN the recent struggle through which the nation has passed, like convulsions, sometimes, of certain portions of the physical world, old features and landmarks are swept away, and new features are apparent, developing on the surface, the existence of which very little, if anything, was heretofore known.

A class has been invoked into action, to whose sublime patience and enduring heroism the genius of poetry will turn for inspiration, while future historians, recognizing evidences of the true statesmanship which they have exhibited through the dark night of slavery, will place them amid the brightest constellations of our time. This class exhibited the same anomaly in the midst of slavery, that the slaves in a government whose doctrines taught liberty and equality to all men, and under whose banner the exile and fugitive found refuge, presented to the civilization of this century. They were an intermediate class in all the slave states, standing between the whites and the bondmen, known as the free colored; debarred from enjoying the privileges of the one, but superior in condition to the other, more, however, by sufferance than by actual law. While they were the stay of the one, they were the object of distrust to the other, and at the same time subject to the machinations and jealousies of the non-slaveholders, whom they rival in mechanical skill and trade. Prior to the rebellion these represented a fair proportion of wealth and culture, both attributable to their own thrift and energy. Unlike the same class at the North, they had but little, if any, foreign competition in the various departments of labor or trade against which to contend. Immigration not being encouraged at the South, as at the North, could not affect their progress, thus leaving all avenues open to the free colored, while they were excluded from the more liberal and learned professions. But if their faculties for accumulation were preferable to the same class North, there were influences always at work to deprive them of the fruits of their labor, either openly or covertly. On the one side were exorbitant taxes for various public charities, from the benefits of which the indigent of their race were deprived, and for public schools, to which their children were denied admittance. Business men found it in many instances impolitic to refuse requests for loans coming from influential white men, under whose protection they exercised their meagre privileges, and the payment of which it was equally impolitic to press, nor were they allowed to sue for debts.

Thus their position in the midst of a slave community was altogether precarious, as they were looked upon as a dangerous element by the slaveholders. Their lives and material prosperity standing in direct contrast to the repeated assertions of the advocates and apologists of slavery, that they would, if free, relapse into barbarism, or would burden the states in which they were found, for support. So marked and wide-spread had this class become in the Southern States, that it was a subject of general comment, but a few years before the rebellion, the almost simultaneous petitions to the various legislative bodies, to drive them from their homes, and in some of the states these were only baffled by the bribes resorted to by their victims. These continued aggressions succeeded, however, in driving large numbers to settle in the free states and the Canadas, notwithstanding the unmigratory tendency of southern races. There they remained until their listening ears caught the first note of the rebellion, as borne from Sumter's walls, and with all the holy tenderness which clusters around the national colors in the hearts of these men, they went forward to swell the Union ranks. For to them the cause was as sacred as that which inspired the crusaders of old.

There were others whose far-seeing visions, peering into futurity, beheld the balance of power held out to them, and remained awaiting the march of events not far removed, and at this time are recognized as the accepted leaders of the rising race.

Under this state of society was engendered a habitual watchfulness of public measures, making them tenacious of their rights and immunities in every community where they are found, and peculiarly sensitive to the slightest indication of encroachments, which has resulted in developing in them a foresight and sagacity not surpassed in others, whose individual status is less closely allied with political measures.

From this class sprang the honored and scholarly

Daniel E. Paine, Bishop of the African Methodist Church, — that great religious body, the power of which is destined to be felt in America, and the influence of which to be circumscribed only by the ocean. The noble Vesey, of South Carolina, who sealed his devotion to the cause of freedom with his life, was of this class. Before the walls of Petersburg, these were among the gallant soldiers who gave battle to the trained veterans of Lee, and at the ramparts of Wagner they waded to victory in blood.

Amid these uncertain surroundings was the boyhood of Martin Delany passed. In childhood the playmate of John Avis, at Charlestown, in manhood, the associate of the immortal Brown of Ossawatomie, in a measure which ultimately resulted in rendering the name of the kind-hearted Virginian historic in connection with his illustrious captive.

With all the schools closed against them in Virginia, it was not until about 1818 that his brothers and sisters ever attempted to receive instruction.

With the vast domain of Virginia at this date, teeming with school-houses, attended by thousands of colored children, and instructed by white northern teachers, as well as those of their own race, the tuition of the Delany children forms a singular contrast.

The famous New York Primer and Spelling Book was brought to them about that time by itinerant Yankee pedlers, trading in rags and old pewter, and giving in exchange for these new tin ware, school-books, and stationery. These pedlers always found it convenient and profitable, likewise, to leave their peculiar looking box wagon, to whisper into the ear of a black, "You're as much right to learn to read as these whites;" and looking at their watches, had a "snigger of time left yet to stay a little and give a lesson or so." These "didn't charge, only gim me what ye mine to." It was under such covert tuition, and with such instructors, in the humble home of Pati Delany, that the young Martin, together with his brothers and sisters, were taught to read and write.

This stealthy manner of learning, while they were unconscious of the cause, had the tendency of making them more attentive and eager, perhaps, than otherwise, for their tuition was not of long duration before the elder boys were able to read intelligently, and instruct the younger children, we are told. And after a time almost improbable had elapsed, so well arranged were the plans for imparting instruction, that the authorities, who are always so vigilant in inspecting or prying into the movements of the free blacks, "that dangerous element" of the South, were so completely baffled, that not only the smaller children were reading and spelling, but the larger boys were actually writing "passes" for the slaves of their neighborhood.

As their minds developed, all restraint was thrown aside, and the lessons given and recited heretofore in whispers, were now being recited to each other aloud. Leaving the little room in which they were accustomed to assemble, with throbbing hearts and eyes beaming with joyous anticipations to receive those early lessons, unconscious of the hair-suspended sword of southern *justice* above their innocent heads, they dared to "*play school*," like other children, under the shaded arbor of their mother's garden. This soon attracted the attention of their neighbors. Surrounded as they were by whites, it was a hazardous and "overt act." Major Delany describes the "situation" thus: "In the rear, adjoining, on the opposite street, was Downey's; on the left, adjoining, Offit's; on the right, immediately across the street from Hogan's, was the Long O'nary, where Bun's great school was kept, the largest school in the town except Heckman's Seminary." Thus the progress of Pati Delany's children was soon made the gossip of the day, and attracted thither continually curious inquirers, eager to see and hear negro children spell and read.

It chanced one day, in the midst of their recitations, their mother being absent, they were interrupted by a man inquiring the name of their parents, then of each child, taking it down in the mean time in his book. Being satisfied, he rode away. These children, unconscious of the purport of the visit, joyfully related it to their mother on her return. Great was their astonishment to see the expression of deep dejection that overshadowed the features that but a few moments before had shone with happiness as she greeted them. Her only response to their information was a long-drawn sigh, for too well she knew that visit foreboded trouble. In a few days her fears were realized. A man called at the house, and delivered a summons to her, to the effect that it was understood that she was having her children taught to read, in direct violation of law, for which she should answer before a court of justice. The devoted mother's consternation can be well pictured, when we recall the justice extended to the noble Prudence Crandell, in Connecticut, for teaching negro children to read. It followed, in her fears, that she resorted to the concealment of the books from her children; but the sole cause of offence to the majesty of Virginia's laws, the knowledge, and the insatiable thirst for further acquirement, could neither be hidden nor taken from them.

This violation of law, and the inevitable consequences, were soon bruited around the country. Neither sympathy or advice was extended to the courageous woman, whose only crime was wearing a dusky skin; but instead, the jeers and scowls which the vilest culprit receives met her on every side. Mingled with their imprecations could be remembered the significant expressions, " A wholesome lesson ! " " It will do that proud, defiant woman good ! " " She always made pretensions above a negro." Suits were constantly entered, and failed. She was persecuted by all, with one noble exception — that of Randall Brown, a banker, who often advised her to leave the place. Finally, in September, 1822, under the pretext of moving to Martinsburg, she left Charlestown for Chambersburg, Pa., where residing for fifteen years, her children were enabled to continue their studies, with " none to molest or make them afraid." There, for several years, they attended school, securing such advantages as the country schools of those days afforded.

After some time had elapsed, Delany's parents' means being limited, he was compelled to leave school. He then went to Cumberland County, about two years after he had left school, to work; but, becoming dissatisfied with his prospects, he returned to Chambersburg, to obtain the consent of his parents to go to Pittsburg, where facilities for obtaining an education were superior to those of his home. On the morning of the 29th of July, 1831, we date the first bold and determined move on his part to fit himself for the herculean task which he had marked out for himself. Alone, and on foot, the young hero set out for Pittsburg, with little or no money, and consequently few friends. Crossing the three grand ridges of the Alleghany, he soon reached Bedford. Here, employment being offered to him, he remained for one month. Never losing sight of his resolves, he now turned his face towards Pittsburg, in which city the foundation of his fame afterwards rested.

CHAPTER III.

STUDYING NORTH.

IN directing his footsteps to Pittsburg, Fortune favored the student in a degree wonderful for that time, while she chilled the energies of the man in later years. There he was compelled to labor faithfully, at whatever work his hands found to do, in order to continue his studies.

Fortunately for him, a way was opened from sources least expected at that time. Great efforts were being made by the colored people themselves, at Pittsburg, to advance their educational interests, together with other measures for the recognition of their political rights. A church was purchased from the white Methodists for a school-house, — an educational society having been previously organized, — and Rev. Louis Woodson, a colored gentleman, of fine talents, was placed at the head of it. Under the supervision of this gentleman, during the winter of 1831, his progress in the common branches were such as to warrant his promotion to the more advanced studies. It was commonly said by his friends at school, that his retentiveness of history — his favorite study — was so remarkable that he seemed to have recited from the palm of his hand.

A young student of Jefferson, seventeen miles distant, who frequently spent his vacation at Pittsburg, assisted him in his difficult studies, as they occupied the same room. While studying together, they conceived the plan for benefiting other young men of like tastes by forming an association for their intellectual and moral improvement. It soon became popular, and the Theban Literary Society was afterwards formed. Judging from the names adopted by their officers, pedantic as they are, they evince an acquaintance with the rudiments of a polite education not expected from that class under their disadvantages, the names, relative to their offices, being taken from the Greek. This was but the small beginning for wider labors. Since then they have associated with other bodies, more important in their character, yet bearing a like relation to humanity. But it was, perhaps, to the literary society of Pittsburg, resembling that formed by Franklin and his young associates, that the germ of their usefulness first came forth.

It was also about the winter of **1831–2** that the little ripple, destined to be the great anti-slavery wave, against which the ship of state would madly contend, was noticed; for, almost simultaneously with the outbreak for freedom at Southampton, Va., known as Nat Turner's Insurrection, appeared "Garrison's Thoughts on American Colonization."

Then, to the casual observer, the action of the one was a ridiculous folly; that of the other, the wild fancies of a fanatic's brain. Now, there is a dark significance in that solitary figure, looming up in the dark background of slavery as an offering on the altar of freedom,

in the home of Washington, preceded by that attempted
at Charleston with Denmark Vesey at its head, followed by the closing scene at Harper's Ferry. In each
of these there was a warning and a lesson as direct as
those which the Hebrew lawgiver received amidst the
thunders of Sinai, but by which a slavery-blinded
nation failed to profit, until the last great martyr of
Ossowåttomie was offered up.

> " When that great heart broke, 'twas a world that shook;
> From their slavish sleep a million awoke; "

when Virginia, the cradle of slavery, became its burial-
place, the Smithfield of freedom's martyrs, and the
battle-ground of a slave-founded Confederacy; while
on the other side the " fanatic " stands a witness of
the workings of the stupendous powers invoked.

The writings of Mr. Garrison, and the Southampton
insurrection, awakened much interest in many minds,
which before that time were either absorbed in selfish
speculations, and indifferent to the interest of the
nation, or despondent of ameliorating the condition.
of the black race in this country.

The young Delany, not forgetting his mother's per-
secutions, his father's humiliations in Virginia, and the
wrongs of his race generally, caught the spirit of
truth, and was fired with a high and holy purpose.
With the scene of Nat Turner's defeat and execution
before him, he consecrated himself to freedom; and,
like another Hannibal, registered his vow against
the enemies of his race. To prepare for everything
that promised success, to undergo every privation
and suffering, if necessary to accomplish this object,
was now the resolve of the young neophyte. He

began, in the right direction, to prepare himself for whatever position he should be called upon to fill, by a renewed earnestness in his studies.

To ethics and metaphysics he devoted his attention; and, while a student, so proficient was he in the essential principles of natural philosophy, as to compete successfully with a teacher in a college of respectability. His progress and attainments, under circumstances to which no people save his own race have ever been subjected, are evidences of the ambition and workings of a mind untamed by impediments which opposed it.

Then, no college or academy of note in the United States received within its walls a black student, no matter how deserving, save under obligations hereafter to be mentioned, not excepting Dartmouth, ostensibly established for Indians, nor the great, independent Harvard, of ancient pride. "At this time," said Martin Delany, "or shortly after, the *now* learned J. W. C. Pennington, D. D., who received the degree of Doctor of Divinity at the University of Heidelberg, under Prince Leopold, president, was standing either behind the door of Yale College, or perhaps on its threshold, listening to instructions given in the various branches by the professors, and considering it a privilege, as it was the closest proximity allowed him towards entering its *sacred* precincts as a student."

Such was the limited opportunity for a thorough education among the colored people, and so great was the prejudice against them while Martin Delany was endeavoring to acquire his, that it is safe to infer that no colored person, *recognized as colored,* previous to the establishment of institutions of learning under the anti-slavery agitation, ever completed a collegiate course. True it is, that a few were educated under the auspices of colonization societies, with no design of benefiting the colored people in this country, but on the condition of their leaving it for Africa.

While pursuing his studies at Pittsburg, his name was solicited and obtained by the zealous Mr. Dawes, agent of the Oberlin Collegiate Institute, at the beginning of that now famous institute. He afterwards declined going, it being then but a preparatory school, and his studies being fully equal to those prosecuted there. He, like Byron, could not understand that knowledge was less valuable, or less true as knowledge, without having the *parchment* to confirm it; while the opportunity of the great poet and that of the get-by-chance student differs; one having no formidable barriers to overcome, the other having first to struggle against oppositions, in order to create a healthy public sentiment, that others after him might gain it without the giant's task.

CHAPTER IV.

MORAL EFFORTS.

IN 1834 Major Delany was actively engaged in the organzation of several associations for the relief of the poor of the city, and for the moral elevation of his people. Among them was the first total abstinence society ever formed among the colored people; and another known as the Philanthropic Society, which, while formed ostensibly for benevolent purposes, relative to the indigent of the city, was really the foundation of one of the great links connecting the slaves with their immediate friends in the North, — known as the "Underground Railroad," — which, for long years, had baffled the slaveholders. Of its executive board he was for many years secretary.

The work contributed by this association constituted it the invaluable aid of the anti-slavery cause. Its efficiency may be judged from the fact that, while in its infancy, it is recorded that, within one year, not less than two hundred and sixty-nine persons were aided in escaping to Canada and elsewhere.

His sphere in life gave character to him, identifying him with a people and a time at once wonderful and perilous; wonderful that amid all the indignities and outrages heaped upon them, unrebuked by church or state, they did not degenerate into infidels and law-breakers, instead of being the Christian and truly law-abiding element of the republic — perilous, for the emissaries of the South instituted the fiendish spirit of mobbism, selecting either the dwellings or the business-places of the prominent colored men of the city. On one occasion, while this spirit was rife, they made an attack on the house of Mr. John B. Vashon. Major Delany, then quite a young man, but true to his principles of justice and humanity, and in view of future outrages, together with men of more mature age, called on Judge Pentland and other prominent citizens, to notify them that, though they were a law-abiding people, they did not intend to remain and be murdered in their houses without a most determined resistance to their assailants, as there was little or no assistance or protection rendered by the authorities.

This resulted in his being chosen one of the special police from among the blacks and whites appointed in conjunction with the military called out by the intrepid mayor of Pittsburg, Dr. Jonas R. McClintock. Many were the occasions on which he stood among the foremost defenders against those mobs which at that time were more frequent than desirable.

The general grievances of the colored people of the North, occasioned solely on account of caste, were a disgrace to the civilization of the age, and incompatible with the elements of our professed republicanism, which induced them to call an assemblage year after year, delegating their best talent to these, for the purpose of placing before the people the true condition of the colored people of the North, and also to devise methods of assisting the slaves of the South.

These conventions were held at an early date. As far back as 1829 we find a National Convention Meeting in Philadelphia, and where for many subsequent years they assembled; and enrolled on their list of members we find the honored names of Robert Douglass (the father of the artist), Hinton, Grice, Bowers, Burr, and Forten, together with Peck, Vashon, Shadd, and others whose names would give dignity and character to any convention.

Through a series of years these continued lifting up their voices against the existing political outrages to which they were subjected. To the last of these (about 1836) Major Delany, together with the Rev. Lewis Woodson, his former preceptor, who, being senior colleague, was chosen to represent the status of the community at large. On arriving at Philadelphia they found the Convention had been transferred to New York; and on their arrival at that point they were notified that it had been indefinitely postponed, chilling the hopes, doubtless, of our young delegate with his maiden speech trembling on his lips, the "tremendous applause" ringing in his ears, and other fancies legitimately belonging to the rôle of a young man for the first time taking his place as a representative among the elders.

About three years after, he attended the Anti-slavery Convention at Pittsburg. At this Convention were many learned divines and a president of one of the universities of Western Pennsylvania. Here he brought upon himself the censure of some of his friends for saying in the course of his argument (concerning Jewish slavery as compared with that which existed in America), that " *Onesimus was a blood-kin brother to Philemon*." This extraordinary and then entirely new ground was so unexpected and original, that while many approached, congratulating him on his able arguments, they expressed their regrets that he ventured to use such weapons, as he rendered himself liable to severe criticism from the whites. He replied that, in the course of events soon to greet them, this would become an established fact. He was not in-correct, only "imprudent," as the time had not ar-rived to proclaim such bold opinions. His fault, in most cases, is in expressing the thoughts that shape them-selves in his healthy, active brain far in advance of the time allotted by a conservative element for receiving it. He plans long before the workmen are ready or will-ing to execute. Says that friend of humanity, Wen-dell Phillips, " What world-wide benefactors these 'imprudent' men are — the Lovejoys, the Browns, the Garrisons, the saints, the martyrs! How 'prudent-ly' most men creep into nameless graves, while now and then one or two forget themselves into im-mortality."

A few years before this Delany began the study of med-icine, under the late Dr. Andrew N. McDowell, but for some cause did not continue to completion, as he entered practically upon dentistry. The knowledge acquired in surgery he made use of whenever immediate neces-sity required it. On one occasion, in 1839, he went down the Mississippi to New Orleans, thence to Texas. While at Alexandria he met with the chief of adven-turers, General Felix Houston, whose attention was attracted by witnessing him dressing the wound of a man stabbed by an intoxicated comrade. General Houston offered him a good position and protection if he would join him. He declined the offer, and continued his tour, spending several months among the slaveholding Indians of Mississippi, Louisiana, Arkansas, and Texas, viewing the "peculiar institution" as it existed in all its varied phases, — its pride and gloom, — not loving freedom less, but hating slavery more, if possible.

He watched closely the scenes through which he had passed, and the experience gained among the slaves of the south-west was carefully garnered up for future usefulness. His present post of duty on the Sea Island of South Carolina, where he executes the duties of his office with zeal and ability, while his busy brain constantly devises some new measure for the advancement and elevation of the newly-recognized people, attests this fact.

CHAPTER V.

EDITORIAL CAREER.

HE returned to Pittsburg in the midst of the presidential campaign resulting in the election of General Harrison. Finding political feeling high, as it is always on such occasions, he speedily received the infection, and threw himself forward in the political arena. Early in 1843 he became too well aware, by sad experience, of the inability of the colored people to bring their inflicted wrongs and injustices before the public, in consequence of not having a press willing at all times to espouse their cause. In many instances a paper which would publish an article derogatory to their interest on one day, if applied to on the next to publish for some colored person an answer or correction, the applicant would either be told certain expressions must be modified, the article is not respectful to the parties, or refuse entirely on the plea that "it would not be politic."

With these impediments he knew their progress would be retarded, and to this end he began unassisted a weekly sheet under the title of the Mystery, devoted to the interest and elevation of his race. Success followed the movement; the first issue in all taken was one thousand in the city; its circulation rapidly increased. For more than one year he conducted it as editor. After sustaining it solely for nine months, he transferred the proprietorship to a committee of six gentlemen, he, meanwhile, continuing as editor for nearly four years.

It was well conducted, and held no mean position in the community, especially where it originated.

The learned and lamented Dr. James McCune Smith, of New York, said " it was one of the best papers ever published among the colored people of the United States."

The editorials of his journal elicited praises even from its enemies, and were frequently transferred to their columns. His description of the great fire of 1844, in Pittsburg, which laid a great portion of that manufacturing city in ruins, was extensively quoted by papers throughout the country. The original matter, so frequently copied, was sufficient to determine the status of his paper.

During the Mexican war he bore his part in the field against the knights of the quill, for his stand against the Polk administration was so decided that on more than one occasion the subject was strongly combated.

Much good was done through the influence of that little sheet, and it is indisputable that to its influence originated the Avery Fund. Once, on the subject of female education, through the columns of his paper, he argued that " men were never raised in social position above the level of women; therefore men could not be elevated without woman's elevation; further, that among the nations of the world where women were kept in ignorance, great philosophers or statesmen failed to be produced, as a general rule. And under the then existing state of female education among the Americans of African descent, the hope of seeing them equal with the more favored class of citizens would be without proper basis.

After reading his editorial on the social requirements of the colored people, it is said that the Rev. Charles Avery determined to do something tangible for them. The reverend gentleman, after consulting some of the most prominent colored men, among whom was the Rev. John Peck, established a school for males and females. This was the first step towards that which is now known as Avery's College, at the head of which was placed, as senior professor, Martin A. Freeman, M. A. (now professor of mathematics in the University of Liberia). He was succeeded by George B. Vashon, M. A., a most accomplished scholar. The Rev. Mr. Avery did not stop in the work so well begun. He died in 1858, bequeathing in his will "one hundred and fifty thousand dollars for the education and elevation of the free colored people of the United States and Canada, one hundred and fifty thousand for the enlightenment and civilization of the African race on the continent of Africa," all in trust to the American Missionary Association of New York city; making in all a grand bequest of three hundred thousand dollars, exclusive of the college. We do not claim more than is evident — that the Mystery deserves the credit of having brought these wants before the public, and one humanitarian responded to the call most liberally.

While he was editor, on the Centennial Anniversary

of Benjamin Franklin's birthday, he received from the committee an invitation, among the editorial corps, to attend an entertainment given by the Pittsburg Typographical Society at the Exchange Hotel. . At the head of this, as president of the occasion, was an honorable ex-commissioner to Europe under President Tyler, and the position of vice-president was filled by a judge of the County Court. This mark of courtesy to him, in the days when Slavery held her carnival over the land, will serve to indicate the standing of his paper and the triumph of genius over brutal prejudice.

While editor of the Mystery, he was involved in a suit, the occasion of which will serve the double purpose of showing the estimate placed upon the merit of his paper, and the respect in which the ability and character of the man were held in Pittsburg.

It happened, in the warmth of his zeal for the freedom of the enslaved, that he, through the columns of his paper, charged a certain colored man with treachery to his race by assisting the slave-catchers, who, at that time, frequented Pennsylvania and other free states.

The accused entered a suit for *libel*, through advice, probably, of some of his accomplices, who were whites, as it is evident his calling would preclude the possibility of the individual to think himself aggrieved.

The presiding judge, before whom the case was tried, having no sympathy with abolitionists, and less with that class of negroes represented by Martin Delany, took great pains to impress upon the minds of the jury, in his charge to them, the extent of the offence of libel. After their verdict of guilty was rendered, a fine of two hundred dollars, together with the cost of prosecution, which amounted to about two hundred and fifty dollars, was imposed. In view of a fine so unusually high for that which was considered a just exposure of an evil which then existed to the detriment of one class of the inhabitants, an appeal was immediately made, by the press of Pittsburg, for a public subscription, in order that it might be borne in common, instead of allowing it to rest solely upon this faithful sentinel.

A subscription list was opened at the office of the Pittsburg Daily Despatch, which led off first in the appeal.

The chivalric governor, Joseph Ritner, was in office then — him for whom freedom's sweetest bard invoked his muse to link his name with immortality. About one week after the suit, and before the sum could be raised, the governor remitted the fine. This was occasioned through a petition originating with his able counsel, the late William E. Austin, which was signed not only by all of the lawyers of the court, but it is said by the bench of judges; thus leaving the costs only to be paid by him.

The success of this suit, however, served to embolden the slave-hunters; and again did this faithful sentinel give the alarm; but this time his language, while it unmistakably pointed to the guilty party, was carefully chosen, in order to avoid litigation. These, determined to drive him from his post, so formidable to them, still so valiantly held by him, again entered suit against him. Their former success established no precedent for the second.

In the prosecution of this case, another jurist sat in judgment, the term of the pro-slavery judge having expired. In his charge to the jury, the eminent judge, William B. McClure, made special reference to the position of the defendant, to his efforts in behalf of his race, and his usefulness in the community. Then, addressing himself more pointedly to the jury, he added, "I am well acquainted with Dr. Delany, and have a very high respect for him. I regard him as a gentleman and a very useful citizen. No Pittsburger, at least, will believe him capable of willingly doing injustice to any one, especially his own race. I cannot, myself, after a careful examination, see in this case anything to justify a verdict against the defendant." This resulted in a verdict of acquittal without the jury leaving the box.

On another occasion, he was the recipient of forensic compliment, facetiously given, because also of the source whence it emanated, and because he was not present at the court to suggest the remarks of the attorney in the midst of the pleading.

A highly respected colored man was under trial, charged with a serious offence. His counsel, an influential lawyer, Cornelius Danagh, Esq., afterwards attorney general of the state, under Governor William T. Johnson, of Pennsylvania, declared the prosecution as arising from prejudice of color against his client. The prosecution was conducted by the late Colonel Samuel W. Black, who served under General McClellan, and fell in the seven days' fight before Richmond. "They tell you," said he, in his peculiarly forcible style, "that we have brought on this prosecution through prejudice to color. I deny it: neither does the learned counsel believe it. Look at Martin Delany, of this city, whom everybody knows, and the gentleman knows only to respect him. Would any person in this community make such a charge against him? Could such a prosecution be gotten up against him? No, it could not, and the learned counsel knows it could not, and Delany is blacker than a whole generation of the color of the defendant, *boiled down to a quart.*"

It is probable that no portion of this reference to him pleased him better than that which alluded to his blackness.

While conducting the paper, another production of his elicited much discussion, and to which he still holds — that of the population of the world. He claims that two thirds are colored, and the remainder white; that there are but three original races — Mongolian, Ethiopian or African, and Caucasian or European, as yellow, black, and white, naming them in the order as given in the genealogy of Shem, Ham, and Japheth, all others being but the offspring, either pure or mixed, of the other three, as the Indian or American race of geography, being pure Mongolian, and the Malay being a mixture of the three, Mongolian, African, and Caucasian, the people of the last varying in complexion and other characteristics from pure African, through Mongolian, to pure Caucasian.

On the appearance of this article, containing the above novel declaration of the preponderance of numbers of the colored races in the world, a learned officer of the university was waited upon in the city, on one occasion, and earnestly inquired of concerning the correctness of the statement, desiring, if it were incorrect, to contradict it at once. It was never contradicted.

After the return of Mr. Frederick Douglass from England, in the summer of 1846, he visited Pittsburg, where he concluded to form a copartnership in a printing establishment with him. Disposing of his interest in the Mystery, we next find him aiding, by means of his talents and energy, the sustaining of a paper issuing from Rochester, New York, known as the North Star, the early name of the subsequent Frederick Douglass paper. To advance the interest of this, he travelled, holding meetings, and lecturing, so as to obtain subscribers, and endeavored to effect a permanent establishment of a newspaper, as a general organ of the colored people, on a secure basis, by raising an endowment for it, being convinced that this alone would insure its successful continuance.

The winter of 1848–9 found him in the eastern part of Pennsylvania, taking part in anti-slavery meetings and conventions, ably seconded by the eloquent Charles L. Remond, to whom, he says, the anti-slavery cause of New England is much indebted for the breaking down of the stupid prejudice, which once existed on the land and water transportations, against colored persons.

One of the means resorted to — so zealous were the colored people to sustain the rising North Star — was the holding of fairs in Philadelphia, supported by a number of the most influential colored ladies of that city. At the first of these, December, 1848, it was, that William and Ellen Craft, now in England, the first victims selected under the atrocious Fugitive Slave Law (enacted later), made their appearance, and under circumstances so peculiar as to become historic on both sides of the Atlantic. They were introduced by him to the visitors at the fair in an appropriate address, and in such a way that their mode of escape was carefully concealed, but which was afterwards communicated to the Liberator by an anti-slavery man. Through this their whereabouts became known to Dr. Collins, of Macon, Georgia, and as soon as the enactment was completed, a few years after, he immediately, through his agents sent north, placed all Boston under obligation to arrest them.

Hundreds of special or assistant marshals were appointed in the midst of a government which thundered her volleys of welcome to the Hungarian governor, a fugitive from Austrian tyranny! And now, in all our broad free America, there was no place of security from southern slavery for these.

For four long days these obsequious marshals, whom the slave power doubtless rewarded in after years with starvation and death in their loathsome prisons, prowled around the dwelling in which the brave Craft resided, till at length that lion-hearted reformer and ever-devoted friend of the negro, Wendell Phillips, persuaded the daring fugitive, all things being prepared, to take passage on a vessel, his wife being already on board; and thus they escaped to England, where they were received under the auspices of the Baroness Wentworth, and are now enjoying a fair share of prosperity and all the advantages of British citizenship.

During his tour in behalf of the North Star, in July, 1848, when America's sympathy yearned towards the people of Europe, in the name of whose freedom the thrones were trembling, a mob demanded his life in a village of Northern Ohio.

They first demanded of him a speech, in a derisive
manner, which he refused. In revenge they circulated
a report that he was an abolitionist and amalgama-
tionist. This had the desired effect, and soon a mob,
consisting of nearly every male in the village, and
neighboring farmers, attracted by a blazing fire which
they had kindled of store boxes and tar, in the middle
of the street, gathered, shouting, swearing, and demanding him of the proprietor of the hotel, who had
closed his doors on the appearance of the rabble.

A barrel of tar was contributed by some person, and
it was decided to saturate his clothes, set him on fire,
and let him run! Interference in his behalf was forbidden, and threats were made against the hotel
keeper, who refused to eject him. The movement to
break the doors in being threatened and attempted, the
landlord addressed them from the window to the effect
that it was his own property, and that he would not
turn any well-behaved person from his house into the
street, and if his property was injured, as was threatened, he would have redress by law. As the yells and
threats became more deafening, he saw no retreat, and
determined to yield his life as dearly as possible.
Against the entreaties and advice of the proprietor
and family, he found his way into the kitchen: seizing
there a butcher's knife and a hatchet, he returned,
and placed himself at the head of the stairs: having within his reach some chairs, he stood awaiting
the issue with all the fire of his nature aroused.

A gentleman friend travelling with him, by blood
and complexion a quadroon, was advised by Dr. Delany
to leave him by making his exit through the back door,

as he would be mistaken for a white. His friend refused to abandon him. The night was far spent; but, the clamor still continuing, the mob might have executed their fiendish purpose, had it not been for the timely arrival of one of their number, a veteran soldier, whom they called Bill. "Stop!" he exclaimed, as he came up to the spot in time to hear the final vote, "to *break into the hotel, bring the nigger out, and burn him!*" "Do you see this arm?" said he, pointing to the remaining stump of a lost arm. "I have fought in Mexico, and I am no coward; but I had rather face an army in the field than enter the room of that negro after the threats you have made in his hearing, knowing the fate that awaits him. Didn't you hear how that black fellow talked? These are educated negroes, and have travelled, and know as much as white men; and any man who knows as much as they do won't let any one force himself into their room in the night and leave it alive! You may take my word for that! Now, gentlemen, I have told you; you may do as you please, but I shan't stay to see it." During this time they stood patiently listening to Bill; and as he concluded, they shouted, "We'll take Bill's advice, and adjourn till morning." They gradually dispersed, after leaving a committee to watch and report when the *niggers* would attempt to leave. At the dawn, however, the landlord had a buggy at the door for his guests, and the few young men on the spot confined their vengeance to abusive epithets and threats if they should ever attempt to enter the town again. The mob in New York, during the war, showed the evil against which the colored people were long accustomed to contend.

One thing worthy of more than a passing notice occurred during this editorial existence, which we will relate here.

It happened that, while travelling in behalf of the paper, he stopped at Detroit, Michigan, and attended a trial in the Supreme Court, Justice John McLean presiding, before whom Dr. Comstock, a gentleman of respectability and wealth, and others of that state, were arraigned on charge of aiding and abetting the escape of a family of blacks from Kentucky, known as the Crosswaits. In the case it had been proven satisfactorily that Dr. Comstock had nothing to do with their escape. Having heard of the affair (being two or three miles distant), he came to the scene of confusion just in time to hear the threats and regrets of the defeated slave-hunter, Crossman. The doctor stood there enjoying the discomfiture, and expressed himself to a friend that he hoped "they would not be overtaken." For this Judge McLean ruled him guilty as an accomplice in the escape, stating that it was "the duty of all good citizens to do all they could to prevent it; that whether housing or feeding, supplying means or conveyances, throwing himself or other obstructions in the way, or standing quietly by with his hands in his breeches pockets, smiling consent, it was equally aiding and abetting, hindering and obstructing, in the escape of the slaves, and therefore such person was reprehensible before the law as a *particeps criminis*, and must be held to answer." This novel decision of the judge of the Supreme Court was so *startling* to him *at that time*— for, alas! decisions more wounding to the honor of the nation have since emanated from the Supreme Court — that he hastened to report to the North Star the proceedings of the trial, which he had taken down while sitting in the court-room. This publication, like a wronged and angry Nemesis, seemed to reach various points in time to be made available, especially by those attending the great Free Soil Convention at Buffalo. Everywhere was the infamous decision discussed with more or less warmth, according to the political creed of the debaters: then the reliability of the writer received some attention. The North Star may have been sufficient authority, had that correspondent who reported the McLean decision been Mr. Frederick Douglass, who had both " credit and renown." While the initials of the undersigned could be known from the title page of the paper (as the full names of each appeared as editors and proprietors), " Who is he?" became the subject of inquiry among the throng of delegates, who could not be censured for not knowing but one black man of ability and character in the United States, and supposing it to be impossible that there should be more than one.

The Mass Convention assembled outside, supposed to be forty thousand, filling the public square, hotels, and many of the streets, about six thousand of whom, occupying the great Oberlin tent, which had been obtained for the purpose, and constituting the acting body of the Mass Convention, while four hundred and fifty of the credited delegates were detailed as the executive of the great body, and assembled in a church near by, before whom all business was brought and prepared before presenting it to the body for action.

The Hon. Charles Francis Adams, late minister to

the court of St. James, was president of Mass Convention. The Hon. Salmon P. Chase, now chief justice of the United States, chairman or president of the executive body. Strange to say, in an assemblage like this, so vast and renowned, the report from the columns of the North Star found its way, and, as subsequently appeared, was the subject of weighty discussion. We give the marked circumstance. He says that "while quietly seated in the midst of the great assembly, a tall gentleman in the habiliments of a clergyman, and of a most attractive, Christian-like countenance, was for a long time observed edging his way, as well as he could, between the packed seats, now and again stooping and whispering, as if inquiring. Presently he was lost sight of for a moment: soon a gentleman behind him touched him on the shoulder, called his attention, when the gentleman in question walked towards him, stooping with the paper in his hand, pointed to the article concerning Justice McLean's decision, and inquired, " Are you Dr. M. R. Delany ? "

" I am, sir," replied he.

" Are you one of the editors of the North Star, sir ? "

"Yes, sir, I am," he answered, feeling, very likely, most uncomfortable by this attention.

" Are these your initials, and did you write this article concerning Justice McLean of the Supreme Court, in the case of Dr. Comstock and others, and the Crosswait family ? " continued his interlocutor.

" That is my article, and these are my initials, sir."

" I've but one question more to ask you. Did you hear Judge McLean deliver this decision, or did you receive the information from a third party ? " demanded the questioner.

"I sat in the court-room each day during the entire trial, and reported only what I heard, having written down everything as it occurred," returned Dr. Delany.

"That is all, sir; I am satisfied," concluded the stranger, departing from the great pavilion, and going directly across the street to the church, wherein sat the executive or business part of the convention, leaving the corresponding editor of the North Star in a most aggravated state of conjectures.

The all-important business at the church, then under consideration before them, was the nomination of a candidate for the presidency. The session was long and important. No report of the proceedings or their progress had been received during the day. Near sunset a representative of the council entered the pavilion, and announced from the stage that they would soon be ready to give the convention the result of their deliberations. Soon after there was a great move forward, and, amidst deafening applause, the Hon. Salmon P. Chase ascended the platform, and announced that, for reasons sufficiently satisfactory to the executive council, the name of Judge John McLean, of Ohio, had been dropped as a candidate for the presidency of the United States, and that of Martin Van Buren substituted; and he had been selected by the council to make this statement, from considerations of the relationship which he bore to the rejected nominee; so that his friends in the convention might understand that it was no act of political injustice by which the change was made.

Probably, apart from the executive body, none knew at the time the cause of the withdrawal of the name of the judge. Whether or not his statement, made doubly eloquent by this infamous decision, added its weight to stay the march to the presidential goal of an ambitious, soulless man, we know that he was rejected, and Martin Van Buren received the preferment. And, as Martin Delany never claimed of him a reward for the service unconsciously rendered, in the event of his election, as is customary, it is likely he was forgotten, to be remembered, however, in the better days of the nation, and by its noblest president.

From the Free Soil Convention he and a number of the colored delegates went directly to Cleveland, to attend a national convention of colored men. They assembled in the court-room, granted to them by the proper authority, the court and bar having generously adjourned for the purpose — a mark of courtesy not often, if ever, recorded at the conventions of this color. And, what was equally as remarkable, the citizens, represented by gentlemen of position, on the last day of the convention, took a vote in the house expressive of their satisfaction with the entire proceedings of the delegates.

While travelling to advance the interests of his journal, a remarkable political foresight on his part was manifested by the publication of a letter in its columns. It established for him, ever after, a character for observation of national and international polity, in which he delights to search out and compare, not at that time accorded to one of his race. This attracted the attention of many of the leading men, and their inquiries led him to a conclusion which was soon verified by action, as the following editorial letter to the North Star of February 10 1848, will show : —

Letter to the North Star.

" The recent republication of the letter of the Duke of Wellington to Sir John J. Burgoyne, a major general in the British army, respecting the dangerous exposure of the English coast to French invasion, has created quite an alarm, as well as thrown into speculation the political world. Neither is it hard for any who at all understand political economy, especially the present history of the political world, to determine the cause, at such a time as this, when ' England is at peace with all nations,' and especially in friendly relations with France, of the issue of such a document by the duke.

" Louis Philippe, King of France, is certainly, in my estimation, a great politician, having a great portion of the shrewdness, with all the intrigue, of Talleyrand, and inheriting a greater share of duplicity than most men living. And, what no monarch of France, from Louis I. to the Emperor Napoleon, was ever able to effect by political intrigue, power, and the sword, Louis Philippe is about to accomplish by duplicity, yet carried out in a manner the least to be suspected.

" It is known that France has ever desired a universal mastery, as shown by the Wellington letter, having at different periods occupied every capital in Europe, save that of England. The extension of a royal family over different kingdoms has, in Europe, ever been regarded as a most dangerous precedent, and more dreaded by rival powers than fleets and armies. For the consummation of a project of such mighty magnitude, the court at Versailles has resorted to means unparalleled, at least in modern ages. This subtle monarch, who has neither the propensity nor talents for military achievements, commenced his rapid strides to power, first by the crusade of his eldest son, the Duke of Orleans, in 1833, upon the northern nations of Africa, whom, with little or no resistance, he expected to subdue; and, this once being effected, would give a pretext for a powerful fleet to cruise in the Indian Ocean and Mediterranean Sea, and continually act as a check upon the formidable naval force of Great Britain. But, contrary to his expectations, the resistance met with from Abd-el Kader foiled and baffled that great project. In the mean time, the duke was killed, being thrown from his carriage.

"The next effort was in 1835, a demonstration upon the republic of Hayti, for which purpose an expedition was fitted out, of which his second son, Prince de Joinville, was the chief, aided by Baron Las Casses, with whom it was left optional whether that demonstration should be made by treaty or bombardment. But the prince and baron, having before their minds' eye the fate of General Le Clerc, the greatest captain and military tactician under Napoleon, considered it no disgrace to enter into friendly negotiations with the warlike republic. Leaving Hayti, without an opportunity of testing the military skill of the prince, the next attack was in 1836, upon Vera Cruz, by storming the Castle of San Juan de Ulloa. In this the squadron was quite successful, the Mexicans, under Santa Anna, being repulsed, with the loss of a leg or a foot by that chieftain.

5

"The prince hàving proved his military ability, the old king, as the first link in the great chain by which the fidelity of foreign powers was to be secured to France, manages to consummate a marriage between his son, the Prince de Joinville, and Clementina, daughter of the Emperor of Brazil. This great link being welded in order to dupe England into an indifferent observation of his rapid strides, the masterly step was to effect the union of Prince Augustus Coburg, brother to Prince Albert, husband to the Queen of England, with his second daughter. Another link being completed, he leagues in the ties of matrimony the Duke de Montpensier, his third son, to Isabella, Queen of Spain. No sooner is this effected — the last link of the great cable being complete — than the health of the Infanta Isabella becomes impaired, or she, at all events, grows weary of public life; and a proposition is at once made to abdicate the throne in favor of her spouse, Duke de Montpensier. Of course, this at once gives Spain to the crown of France, which will thereby not only hold the key of Europe, but places Cuba, the key of the western hemisphere, also in her hands.

"The last stroke of the hammer being struck, all France being upon her feet, each officer at his station, and each man at his post, Louis Philippe, looking upon his success as sure, as the crowning scene in the drama, effects the appointment of Prince de Joinville to the Lord Admiralty of the navy of France — an office of the same import and rank, but called by another name. All this is but a prelude to the design of France upon Europe. Of course England would be the first point of attack; and there is no man living more capable, and **none** who would so quickly discover and effectually foil the designs of the crafty old **monarch as the invincible** conqueror of Napoleon.

"But are we not interested deeply in these movements? Most certainly we are. England, at present, is the masterpiece of the world. Her every example is to promote the cause of freedom; and, had she possessed the same principles during the revolutionary period, in every place that she occupied, slavery would have been abolished. Hence slavery in this country could not have stood; for, the slave once tasting freedom, all the powers of earth and hell could not have reduced him again to servitude.

"But how with France? She is a slaveholding power, deeply engaged in human traffic, favoring and fostering the institution of slavery wherever she holds the power or influence; and, with the able politician and learned statesman Guizot at the helm of affairs, the cause and progress of liberty would be retarded for years.

"Yours, in behalf of our oppressed and down-trodden countrymen,

"M. R. D."

CHAPTER VI.

PRACTISING MEDICINE.

AFTER a brilliant and useful editorial career, Delany dissolved his connection with the North Star on the 1st of June, 1849. An incident in connection with this is related, which seems appropriate here, as illustrating his earnestness in behalf of the paper, though personally disinterested.

On his leaving the North Star, he was solicited, through correspondence from Ohio, to take charge of a paper in the interest of the colored people of that state. This he declined; and, after setting forth his reasons why but one newspaper as an organ of the colored people could be sustained at that time, he said, "Let that one be the North Star, with Frederick Douglass at the head."

We next find him returning to his home at Pittsburg, not for the purpose of resting upon the laurels so fairly won, but rather for recuperating his forces for the field of toil again. Here he resumed his favorite study of medicine, and, upon the strength of the preceptorship of his former instructors, Drs. Joseph P. Gazzan and Francis J. Lemoyne, he was received into the medical department of Harvard College, having been previously refused admission, on application, to the Pennsylvania University, Jefferson College, and the medical colleges of Albany and Geneva, N. Y.

After leaving Harvard, he travelled westward, and lectured on physiological subjects — the comparative anatomical and physical conformation of the cranium of the Caucasian and negro races, — besides giving class lectures. These he rendered successful. While his arguments on these subjects were in strict conformity to acknowledged scientific principles, they are also marked by his peculiar and original theories. For instance, he argues on this subject that the pigment which makes the complexion of the African black is essentially the same in properties as that which makes the ruddy complexion of the European, the African's being concentrated rouge, which is black. This he urges by illustrations considered scientifically true. He maintains that these truths will yet be acknowledged by writers on physiology.

On his return to Pittsburg, after the completion of his lecturing tour, he entered upon the duties of a physician, for which his native benevolence and scientific ardor eminently qualified him. Here he was known as a successful practitioner. His skilful treatment of the cholera, which prevailed to some extent in Pittsburg in 1854, is still remembered.

It is worthy of interest, in view of the pro-slavery spirit which brooded over every locality, to record that while there, on the occasion of the establishment of a municipal and private charity, he was selected, with other physicians, as one of the sub-committee of advisers and referees to whom applications were made by white and colored persons to enjoy its provisions.

This demonstration of courtesy on the part of the municipal authorities of Pittsburg towards one of its citizens belonging to an unpopular race was certainly an evidence of liberality hardly to be expected at that time.

He still took part in all movements relative to the advancement of his people. He held in most of these a prominent position; his long experience and life devotion to the cause of progress insured him this always.

He published a call for a national emigration convention, and, it finding favor, there assembled at Cleveland, Ohio, August, 1854, many of the eminent colored men of the northern and western states, to discuss the question of emigration. At best, emigration found but little encouragement among the people of the free states, and could hardly be called popular at the South.

Knowing the aversion held by the colored people of the country to colonization in any form, it was a matter of surprise to note the course taken by this convention. An importance was attached to this movement, so unprecedented as to constitute it a remarkable feature in their political history.

At this convention he was made president *pro tem.*, to organize, and afterwards chairman of the business committee. Before this body he read an address, entitled "The Destiny of the Colored Race in America." This production won for its author praise for its literary merit as well as for its concise and able views on the principles of government.*

Of the national board of commissioners he was made president, and the Rev. James Theodore Holley, an

* This paper will be found on p. 327.

Episcopal clergyman of New Haven, was sent to Hayti on a mission, which was satisfactorily effected.

While he presided, a correspondence was opened with many foreign countries, including the West India Islands, proposing an intercontinental and provincial convention. Among those whose advice was solicited in this new movement was Sir Edward Jordon, of Jamaica, who, while commending the propositions and measures very highly, as a stride of statesmanship, discouraged it as a policy, lest it should give alarm to her majesty's government, and, consequently, offence. Major Delany, in speaking of Sir Edward Jordon's objection, says, "The force and cause of this objection could not then be understood; but since the terrible ordeal through which the poor people of Jamaica have recently passed, under the infamous Governor Eyre, resulting in the disfranchisement of the blacks, the course of Sir Edward Jordon can now be easily comprehended. Sir Edward Jordon, premier of Jamaica for so many years, it would now appear, could not have been premier under Governor Eyre, with the power of creating measures, or enforcing policies of government, but only as a passive minister of state, with title and position, but neither authority nor power, apparently but the recipient and echo of those under whom he was called to act. Mr. Edward Jordon, the representative and champion of the rights of his race, as a prisoner in Jamaica, thirty-three years ago, thundering his defiance at his opponents through his prison bars, it is much to be feared has forgotten his race as Sir Edward Jordon, Commander of the Bath, and prime minister of the colony."

Such is the interpretation he placed upon the disapproval of Sir Edward Jordon. Happily, a change has been brought about, tending to the political advancement of the colored people, which has counteracted the necessity of such movements as were proper in the past struggle, while a portion remained enslaved.

The Rev. Mr. Holley later established a colony in Hayti, carrying thither the wealth of his splendid talents and high moral worth to add to the building up of the fortunes of his race on that island, made holy by the blood of her dusky martyred heroes.

CHAPTER VII.

FUGITIVE SLAVE ACT.

A REMARKABLE effort of this still more remarkable man is remembered, from which unmistakable evidences of the character of the individual, and that of his future line of conduct, are drawn.

It was on the occasion of the passage of that crowning triumph of the slave power, conceded by the obsequious North to them, remembered as the atrocious Fugitive Slave Act.

While this bill was under consideration, as in other dishonorable political enactments affecting the interests of the colored people, there were many persons, who, either from a desire to have peace between the two sections at any sacrifice of national honor, or from a superabundance of faith in the decisions of our lawmakers, were advising the blacks to remain passive; endeavoring to impress the belief upon them that the act could never pass, as it was too atrocious and unjust in its provisions, and that the American people would not tolerate the men who would dare vote to sanction so great an outrage on any portion of the people as that contemplated. The colored people, who never failed to enter their protest against these unjust enactments, called for public meetings.

Martin Delany, painfully alive to the magnitude of the occasion, rose in proportion to it, and, while he was not able to turn the course of the event in his favor, entered a protest which gave sublimity to his defeat. At the first appearance of the bill, with his usual foresight he saw further humiliation in store for his race,— the trampling out of the sacred rights of manhood and womanhood, the total annihilation of domestic tranquillity, and the inevitable desecration of all that was sacred to them, accompanying it in its stride. This was verified by the Dred Scot decision, which followed in its wake but a few short years after. He said that the South demanded it, and would get it, as she had never as yet, in the history of the country, failed to secure by legislation that which she demanded at the hands of the North. He held that the scheme was nothing less than a virtual rendition to slavery of every free black person in the country; or, in fact, a rendition of the free states into slavery, with the difference that while the blacks could be enslaved in the free states, they must be taken away to be held. He was instrumental in calling public meetings, and endeavored to urge, with all the strength of his fiery eloquence, the devising of some means to avert the impending danger. Forcible and truthful as his arguments were, many derided him, accusing him of being frightened; this, too, from men of experience and wisdom, whose confidence in the honor of the administration exceeded his own.

At these meetings white speakers often addressed them, some of whom advised them against being misled by rash, inconsiderate persons, who were alarmed before being hurt, being frightened by their own shadows. But as this was a shadow of such magnitude, the steady advance of which threatened to darken their political pathway, more than the shadow of an excuse must be allowed for their fright.

The bill was passed, followed by an excitement throughout the North only equalled since by that evinced at the firing on Fort Sumter. Never in the history of civilization was humanity more outraged than in that act; the Dred Scot decision was but a fitting sequel to it; one would have been incomplete without the other. "For every drop of blood drawn by the lash, the sword has avenged," said Abraham Lincoln; and for every attempt to ignore the rights of humanity there is a retributive demand awaiting individuals and nations.

There were mass meetings held throughout the North. At the first great meeting, held on the public square of Pittsburg, among the speakers loudly called for was Martin Delany. His predictions being too bitterly realized, he designedly evaded their cries, desiring some of the leading white men present first to commit themselves. This being Saturday evening, they adjourned to meet the following Monday at Alleghany City, Pa. At this meeting the mayor presided, supported by many distinguished citizens, among them the Hon. William Robinson, Jr., an ex-foreign commissioner, and the Rev. Charles Avery, the eminent philanthropist. Among the speakers who addressed them on that memorable occasion were the Hon. T. H. Howe, the recent member of Congress from Alleghany, and Hon. Charles A. Naylor, member of Congress from

Pennsylvania. Here again he was called for, and this time he responded.

It was generally conceded that his was one of the most powerful and impressive speeches of that memorable occasion. We extract the following from it. Said he, " Honorable mayor, whatever ideas of liberty I may have, have been received from reading the lives of your revolutionary fathers. I have therein learned that a man has a right to defend his castle with his life, even unto the taking of life. Sir, my house is my castle; in that castle are none but my wife and my children, as free as the angels of heaven, and whose liberty is as sacred as the pillars of God. If any man approaches that house in search of a slave,—I care not who he may be, whether constable or sheriff, magistrate or even judge of the Supreme Court—nay, let it be he who sanctioned this act to become a law, surrounded by his cabinet as his body-guard, with the Declaration of Independence waving above his head as his banner, and the constitution of his country upon his breast as his shield,—if he crosses the threshold of my door, and I do not lay him a lifeless corpse at my feet, I hope the grave may refuse my body a resting-place, and righteous Heaven my spirit a home. O, no! he cannot enter that house and we both live."

Such is a portion of the speech, remembered for its singular pathos and boldness, wrung from the lips of one whose soul was kindled with the sense of the outrages heaped upon his helpless race by a people maddened by success.

CHAPTER VIII.

A HIATUS.

HIS career thus far in life, while generally success-ful, had also its portion of failures as well as tri-umphs. Two, of a marked character, occurred about the winter of 1851-2. Their ill success seemed rather to belong to the method pursued in presenting them, than to the capability of the man to make them meritorious.

He had left Pittsburg for New York to make certain arrangements necessary for obtaining a *caveat*, preparatory to an application to the department at Washington for a patent for an invention, originally his own, for the ascending and descending of a locomotive on an inclined plane, without the aid of a stationary engine. Had he succeeded in his first plan, the second would have been satisfactory. In this piece of mechanism, he was wholly absorbed, and brought it to completion. At length he made it known to his friend, Dr. James McLune Smith, of New York. The doctor, being possessed of talents of high order, and devoted to scientific pursuits, looked favorably upon the plan, and at once proposed to take him to an extensive machine establishment in the city for consultation on the subject.

At this establishment much curiosity, if not real interest, was manifested concerning it. But the reticence which characterizes him in matters in which concealment is necessary in no wise deserting him, and as he revealed but little to the proprietor, himself an inventor, the visit and interview were of no avail.

Not disheartened by this, he applied to a distinguished patent attorney, who, on application for a *caveat* after all the arrangements necessary, abandoned the effort as being unsatisfactory, leaving the inference to be deduced by Major Delany and his friend Dr. Smith that the only cause of neglect or refusal to entertain the proposition at Washington was, that the applicant must be a citizen of the United States. His own opinion was contrary to the statement of the attorney, — he believing the right to obtain copyrights or patents as not being restricted to the citizens alone, but in the reach of any person, whether American or foreign. He made a subsequent attempt to have it patented, but finally abandoned it.

His attention and interest were drawn in another direction; for at this time adventure was at its height, and every vessel leaving the port of New York bore evidence of it. Many colored men, dissatisfied with their unrecognized condition, caught this spirit, and some embarked either for Greytown or San Juan del Norte, — this being the chief point of attraction, which was like a free city, or independent principality of Germany, but neither held obligations to the one, nor owed allegiance to the other. George Frederick, king of the Mosquitos, becoming dissatisfied with the intrusions and impositions practised by the former emigrants, Colonel Kearny, of Philadelphia, already on his way, if not at the point, said to Major Delany, "Every one seemed to breathe Central America."

While witnessing these preparations for departure to their El Dorado, he met a young friend of his, a physician of great promise, Dr. David J. Peck, *en route* for California, whom he advised to abandon the intention of going to that place, where his success would be less certain among the hundreds of white physicians from all parts, who could scarcely realize a support from their practice; but to go to Central America, where his color would be in his favor, and his advantages superior to those of the physicians there, who are mostly natives, would be preferable.

Dr. Peck heeded his counsels, and became a prominent practitioner there. From the first he was nominated for port physician, in preference to an English physician of eleven years' standing.

The black adventurers soon affiliated with the natives, and were made eligible to every civil right among them.

A committee of natives was appointed to draught resolutions for a municipal council, at the head of which was Dr. Peck as chairman. Through their influence crowds of adherents were attracted to the new policy, and a future government was decided upon as certain to organize speedily.

It was understood that the mayor should be the highest civil municipal authority, the governor the highest civil state authority, the civil and military to be united in one person, and the governor must be commander-in-chief of the military forces.

A convention was held, and a candidate nominated. An election took place (in what way it was never publicly known), and a steamer brought the intelligence, officially transmitted, that "Dr. Martin R. Delany was duly chosen and elected mayor of Greytown, civil governor of the Mosquito reservation, and commander-in-chief of the military forces of the province!" This was delivered to him by a bearer of despatches sent specially for that purpose.

An important instruction to the governor elect was, that he should bring with him his own *council of state* as the native material, although of a country abounding in mahogany and rosewood, was not suitable for "*cabinet-work.*" This, said he, was the worst feature of their choice, because such material as would be desirable was not easily obtained : they would not consent to go, being averse to emigration.

He held the belief that nothing was well tested without first giving fair trial to it; and for himself, determined to do so. To this end he travelled, for nearly eight months, in many states, until worn out, without finding the desirable material, and was compelled to abandon his designs.

By the order of Dr. Holland, the American *chargé*, the town was bombarded by Commodore Ingraham, of the United States squadron, and the embryo government disappeared from the stage forever.

While travelling on this quest he wrote and published a small work (originally designed for pamphlet form) on the condition of the colored race in America. This being published without proper revision, he having left it to another's superintendence, — for at this time

he was prosecuting his invention of the inclined plane,
and also the Central American project, — on its appearance it was nearly dashed to pieces in the storm it encountered. None criticised it so severely as himself; while
some of his friends were disposed to look favorably
upon it, as the errors it contained could not be dis-
guised, and the author was known to be aware of them.
One severe criticism, more of himself, it appeared, than
the book, he seemed to have regarded as "the unkindest
cut of all" — that of Mr. Oliver Johnson, then editor
of the Pennsylvania Freeman. To add to the list of
disasters, some person sent a copy to England to Mr.
Armisted, author of the "Negro's Friend."

He says, in speaking of Mr. Johnson's criticism of
himself, "I was poor when I wrote, weary and hungry.
This my friend Johnson did not know, else he would
not so severely have criticised me. He thought I wrote
as an author, to be seen and known of men. I wrote
not as an author, but as I travelled about from place to
place.

> Sometimes I sat, sometimes I stood,
> Writing when and where I could,
> A little here, a little there;
> 'Twas here, and there, and everywhere.

I wrote to obtain subsistence. I had travelled and
speculated until I found myself out of means."

The book was stopped by him in the midst of the
first edition of one thousand.

He always likened himself, concerning that literary
undertaking, to Gumpton Cute, a character in the play
of Uncle Tom's Cabin, who, "being on a filibustering expedition, got a little short of change." Thus failing in

all that he had designed, with the most laudable motives in view, and succeeding in that with which he neither desired nor could be satisfied — making a poor book. While he good-humoredly admits the fallacy of his moves, yet his friends, mindful of the long, wearisome months of toil and anxiety, and of high hopes wrecked, regret them, as making a void useless and unnatural in his life's history, and consider it an episode illegitimate in his rôle.

CHAPTER IX.

CANADA. — CAPTAIN JOHN BROWN.

IN February, 1856, he removed to Chatham, Kent County, Canada, where he continued the practice of medicine. While his "visiting list" gave evidence of a respectable practice, his fees were not in proportion to it. His practice embraced a great portion of those who were refugees from American slavery; hence his income here did not exceed that acquired at Pittsburg.

Here his activity found wider scope, and new fields of labor were opened to him. It was not likely that one of such marked character would remain unrecognized. He was ever suggesting measures tending to ameliorate the condition of one class or another, which resulted in gaining for him an influence only surpassed by that wielded by him at his post of duty at the South.

Once, while in Canada, an important suggestion of his being adopted, it resulted in driving both candidates — conservative and reformer — together, compelling them to offer terms for the support of the black constituency.

He took part freely in all political movements in his adopted home. For several years he was one of the principal canvassers in the hustings in the ridings of Kent for the election, and was one of the executive committee, and belonged to the private caucus of A. McKellers, Esq., member of the Provincial Parliament from Kent County.

These facts will render it conclusive that his activity was none the less in a country where the progress of his race met no resistance, but only varied in its method. Whatever prominence here, as elsewhere, was attained by him, was cast in the balance as an offering to his people.

Here were matured his plans for an organization for scientific purposes, which afterwards gave him fame in other lands. Here also was he connected with the beginning of a movement in behalf of human liberty, the most sublime in conception, and mysterious in its accomplishment, written of in modern times. The first was in 1858, when had been completed a long contemplated design of his — that of inaugurating a party of scientific men of color, to make explorations in certain portions of Africa.

In the early part of May, 1859, there sailed from New York, in the bark Mendi, owned by three colored African merchants, the first colored explorers from the United States, known as the Niger Valley Exploring Party, at the head of which was its projector, Dr. Delany. His observations he published on his return to this country, so that they need no repetition here, though an important treaty formed with the king and principal chiefs of Abeokuta we have noticed in another portion of this work. It was the importance attached to this mission, and the successful accomplishment of it, that gave him prestige, rendering him eligible to membership of the renowned International Statistical Congress of July, 1860, at London. He travelled extensively in Africa for one year.

In April, prior to his departure for Africa, while making final completions for his tour, on returning home from a professional visit in the country, Mrs. Delany informed him that an old gentleman had called to see him during his absence. She described him as having a long, white beard, very gray hair, a sad but placid countenance; in speech he was peculiarly solemn; she added, "He looked like one of the old prophets. He would neither come in nor leave his name, but promised to be back in two weeks' time." Unable to obtain any information concerning his mysterious visitor, the circumstance would have probably been forgotten, had not the visitor returned at the appointed time; and not finding him at home a second time, he left a message to the effect that he would call again "*in four days, and must see him then.*" This time the interest in the visitor was heightened, and his call was eagerly awaited. At the expiration of that time, while on the street, he recognized his visitor, by his wife's description, approaching him, accompanied by another gentleman; on the latter introducing him to the former, he exclaimed, "Not Captain John Brown, of Ossawatomie!" not thinking of the grand old hero as being east of Kansas, especially in Canada, as the papers had been giving such contradictory accounts of him during the winter and spring.

"I am, sir," was the reply; "and I have come to

Chatham expressly to see you, this being my third visit on the errand. I must see you at once, sir," he continued, with emphasis, "and that, too, in private, as I have much to do and but little time before me. If I am to do nothing here, I want to know it at once." "Going directly to the private parlor of a hotel near by," says Major Delany, "he at once revealed to me that he desired to carry out a great project in his scheme of Kansas emigration, which, to be successful, must be aided and countenanced by the influence of a general convention or council. *That* he was unable to effect in the United States, but had been advised by distinguished friends of his and mine, that, if he could but see me, his object could be attained at once. On my expressing astonishment at the conclusion to which my friends and himself had arrived, with a nervous impatience, he exclaimed, 'Why should you be surprised? Sir, the people of the Northern States are cowards; slavery has made cowards of them all. The whites are afraid of each other, and the blacks are afraid of the whites. You can effect nothing among such people,' he added, with decided emphasis. On assuring him if a council were all that was desired, he could readily obtain it, he replied, 'That is all; but that is a great deal to me. It is men I want, and not money; money I can get plentiful enough, but no men. Money can come without being seen, but men are afraid of identification with me, though they favor my measures. They are cowards, sir! Cowards!' he reiterated. He then fully revealed his designs. With these I found no fault, but fully favored and aided in getting up the convention.

"The convention, when assembled, consisted of Captain John Brown, his son Owen, eleven or twelve of his Kansas followers, all young white men, enthusiastic and able, and probably sixty or seventy colored men, whom I brought together.

"His plans were made known to them as soon as he was satisfied that the assemblage could be confided in, which conclusion he was not long in finding, for with few exceptions the whole of these were fugitive slaves, refugees in her Britannic majesty's dominion. His scheme was nothing more than this: To make Kansas, instead of Canada, the terminus of the Underground Railroad; instead of passing off the slave to Canada, to send him to Kansas, and there test, on the soil of the United States territory, whether or not the right to freedom would be maintained where no municipal power had authorized.

"He stated that he had originated a fortification so simple, that twenty men, without the aid of teams or ordnance, could build one in a day that would defy all the artillery that could be brought to bear against it. How it was constructed he would not reveal, and none knew it except his great confidential officer, Kagi (the secretary of war in his contemplated provisional government), a young lawyer of marked talents and singular demeanor."

Major Delany stated that he had proposed, as a cover to the change in the scheme, as Canada had always been known as the terminus of the Underground Railroad, and pursuit of the fugitive was made in that direction, to call it the Subterranean Pass Way, where the initials would stand S. P. W., to note the direction in which he had gone when not sent to Canada. He further stated that the idea of Harper's Ferry was never mentioned, or even hinted in that convention.

Had such been intimated, it is doubtful of its being favorably regarded. Kansas, where he had battled so valiantly for freedom, seemed the proper place for his vantage-ground, and the kind and condition of men for whom he had fought, the men with whom to fight. Hence the favor which the scheme met of making Kansas the terminus of the Subterranean Pass Way, and there fortifying with these fugitives against the Border slaveholders, for personal liberty, with which they had no right to interfere. Thus it is clearly explained that it was no design against the Union, as the slaveholders and their satraps interpreted the movement, and by this means would anticipate their designs.

This also explains the existence of the constitution for a civil government found in the carpet-bag among the effects of Captain Brown, after his capture in Virginia, so inexplicable to the slaveholders, and which proved such a nightmare to Governor Wise, and caused him, as well as many *wiser* than himself, to construe it as a contemplated overthrow of the Union. The constitution for a provisional government owes its origin to these facts.

Major Delany says, " The whole matter had been well considered, and at first a state government had been proposed, and in accordance a constitution prepared. This was presented to the convention; and here a difficulty presented itself to the minds of some present, that according to American jurisprudence, negroes, having no rights respected by white men, consequently could have no right to petition, and none to sovereignty.

"Therefore it would be mere mockery to set up a claim as a fundamental right, which in itself was null and void.

"To obviate this, and avoid the charge against them as lawless and unorganized, existing without government, it was proposed that an independent community be established within .and under the government of the United States, but without the state sovereignty of the compact, similar to the Cherokee nation of Indians, or the Mormons. To these last named, references were made, as parallel cases, at the time. The necessary changes and modification were made in the constitution, and with such it was printed.

"Captain Brown returned after a week's absence, with a printed copy of the corrected instrument, which, perhaps, was the copy found by Governor Wise."

During the time this grand old reformer of our time was preparing his plans, he often sought Major Delany, desirous of his personal coöperation in carrying forward his work. This was not possible for him to do, as his attention and time were directed entirely to the African Exploration movement, which was planned prior to his meeting Captain Brown, as before stated. But as Captain Brown desired that he should give encouragement to the plan, he consented, and became president of the permanent organization of the Subterranean Pass Way, with Mr. Isaac D. Shadd, editor of the Provincial Freeman, as secretary.

This organization was an extensive body, holding

the same relation to his movements as a state or national executive committee hold to its party principles, directing their adherence to fundamental principles.

This, he says, was the plan and purpose of the Canada Convention. Whatever changed them to Harper's Ferry was known only to Captain Brown, and perhaps to Kagi, who had the honor of being deeper in his confidence than any one else. Mr. Osborn Anderson, one of the survivors of that immortal band, and whose statement as one of the principal actors in that historical drama cannot be ignored, states that none of the men knew that Harper's Ferry was the point of attack until the order was given to march. It was Mr. Anderson whom Captain Brown delegated to receive the sword * from Colonel Washington, on that night when the Rubicon of slavery was crossed by that band of hero pioneers who confronted the slave power in its stronghold. The first sound of John Brown's rifle, reverberating along the Shenandoah, proclaimed the birth of Freedom. Already he saw the mighty host he invoked in Freedom's name. He heard their coming footfalls echoing over Virginia's hills and plains, and upon every breeze that swept her valleys was borne to him his name entwined in battle anthem. He saw in the gathering strife that either Freedom or her priest must perish, and with a giant's strength he went forward to his high and holy martyrdom, thereby inaugurating victory.

---

* This sword was a relic of the revolutionary war, presented by Frederick the Great to General Washington, and was kept in the Washington family until that time.

CHAPTER X.

CANADA CONVENTION. — HARPER'S FERRY.

IT seems remarkable that the man whom Providence had chosen to warn a guilty nation of its danger, and through whom the African race in America received the boon of freedom, which is but a prelude to the entire abolition of slavery on the western continent, should be sent first to Major Delany in Canada, through whom alone he considered himself able to perfect the plans necessary to begin the great work! Certainly the ways of Providence are beyond mortal comprehension. The extraordinary kindness of the jailer to the old hero prophet in the midst of hostile men in Virginia elicited surprise in the North, and was the subject of remark by many. To a playfellow of Martin Delany in childhood it was no matter of wonderment that he should sympathize with his helpless, way-worn prisoner, if the heart of the man were at all akin to the heart of the child. The open admiration demonstrated by the Virginia jailer for the character of his captive was a picture striking and pleasing in the midst of all the dark surroundings of that time. The man who, in the midst of hostile faces lowering with hate and fear towards him who sat beside him on his way to death, could say, " Captain Brown, you are a game man," proved himself, after his prisoner, the bravest man in Virginia that day.

In regard to the relation sustained by the brave Avis to Major Delany in childhood, it may be of interest to know that the acquaintance was renewed in after years, during the Mexican war, by the major's frequently sending him copies of the paper of which he was then editor in Pittsburg. These were duly acknowledged by Captain Avis, who recognized his name, and adverted to some of the scenes of their childhood, but cautioned him against sending them regularly, lest it should attract attention at the post-office, the paper being thoroughly anti-slavery, and taking grounds against the war, as being waged for the propagation of slavery. Hence anti-slavery sentiments were not unfamiliar to Avis. And we know not but that at some time, in that lonely prison cell, the name of Martin Delany, whom the testimony of Mr. Richard Realf before the Senate committee had made to play such a conspicuous part in the singularly significant councils at Chatham, was mentioned; and who can say it may not have been a link that had first knit the captor to the captive?

The testimony of Mr. Realf before the Senate committee appointed to investigate the Harper's Ferry affair resulted in placing Major Delany in a most cowardly light. The charges were to the effect that he, "Dr. Delany, had repeatedly urged the black men in the convention, and that all his acts and advices tended to encourage them to go with Captain Brown, to aid in an overthrow of the government, as a measure that would succeed." This is without foundation. Major Delany is remembered, by those who attended the councils at Chatham, as having objected to many propositions favored by Captain Brown, as **not** having the least chance of giving trouble to the slaveholders, except the fortification at Kansas. At one time, having objected repeatedly to certain proposed measures, the old captain sprang suddenly to his feet, and exclaimed severely, " Gentlemen, if Dr. Delany is afraid, don't let him make you all cowards!"

Dr. Delany replied immediately to this, courteously, yet decidedly. Said he, " Captain Brown does not know the man of whom he speaks : there exists no one in whose veins the blood of cowardice courses less freely ; and it must not be said, even by John Brown, of Ossawatomie." As he concluded, the old man bowed approvingly to him, then arose, and made explanations.

He accounted for Mr. Realf's discrepancies from the fact that the young man was a stranger to the country, and understood but little of its policy, and his former position in life never brought him in contact with men of such character as Mason, of Trent notoriety, and the rest of the pro-slavery committee, upon whose torturing rack he was stretched, *upon the charge of attempting to overthrow the government!*

But a few years after beheld the chairman of that committee a fugitive, a prisoner, and an exile, and Virginia the battle-ground of contending armies, one inspired by an anthem commemorating the name of him whom Virginia in her madness sacrificed to her destruction, the other endeavoring to destroy the Union in accordance with the teachings of the judges of Captain Brown and his followers.

While this stern judge of the Senate Chamber was hiding his blighted name in exile, the name of Richard Realf shone among the brightest at Lookout Mountain, as he rushed forward, amid a shower of bullets, to replace the national standard after its bearer had fallen.

These misrepresentations of Major Delany's connection with the Harper's Ferry insurrection embarrassed him greatly, at one time, while abroad, which we give, and will also show the importance attached to the Harper's Ferry invasion abroad.

While reporting on his explorations during his visit to Scotland, a letter (anonymous) was sent to Sir Culling Eardley Eardley, implicating the Major (Dr. Delany) with the "insurgents under John Brown."

Such was the effect of this insidious missive, that a whole day (Sabbath) was spent by gentlemen of the highest social and public position in discussing the matter, and considering the propriety of dropping and denouncing him.

But wisdom prevailed, and they determined to disregard the anonymous informant's advice. With this a learned ex-official of her majesty's government called upon him at his residence in Glasgow, and reported the proceedings to him. He was met with an argument from Major Delany, to which he assented, and replied that it was the same in substance as used by himself and the great-hearted Sir Culling Eardley Eardley. After passing through the scrutiny of these British statesmen, he received no further annoyance concerning this while in Europe.

Of the movement at Harper's Ferry, followed by the almost immediate execution of Captain Brown and

his devoted followers, he was ignorant, until in Abeokuta he received a copy of the New York Tribune
sent from England for him.

It was after the Canada Convention, in accordance
with designs as before stated, he embarked for Africa,
accompanied by Robert Douglass, Esq., of Philadelphia, the genius whom prejudice denied the right to
study peacefully his glorious art in the academy of his
native city, but whom the Royal Academy of England
received within its portals, and Professor Robert
Campbell, of the Philadelphia Institute for colored
youth.

CHAPTER XI.

IN EUROPE.

AFTER his expedition into Central Africa, gratified at the success of his discoveries, as well as the knowledge acquired concerning the people, among whom he found evidences of a higher civilization than that which travellers accredit them, he departed for Europe, and arrived at Liverpool May 12, 1860, where remaining for three days, he entered London on the evening of· May 15.

Here he received marked attentions from gentlemen of the highest social and public position. Three days after his arrival he was invited to meet a council of gentlemen in the parlors of Dr. Hodgkin, F. R. G. S. the Right Honorable Lord Calthorpe, M. H. M. P. C., presiding, with Lord Alfred Churchill, chairman. These councils, continuing from time to time, terminated in the great *soirée* at Whitehall, July 27, at which were invited six hundred members of Parliament, ending in the formation of the African Aid Society, numbering among its members the following personages: Rt. Hon. Lord Calthorpe, the Lord Alfred Churchill, Hon. Mr. Ashby, Thomas Bagnall, Esq., J. P., Rev. J. Baldwin Brown, B. A., Edward Bullock, Esq., George Thompson, late M. P., Sir Culling Eardley Eardley, Bart., Sir

J. H. Leake, Rear Admiral, Wm. McArthur, Esq., Rev. Samuel Morton, M. A., Jonathan Richardson, Esq., M. P., Dr. Norton Shaw, Secretary Royal Society, Rev. Thomas Mesac, M. A., Rev. Mr. Cardell, M. A., Henry Dunlop, Esq., Ex-Lord Provost of Glasgow.

He was also honored with the privilege of being present at some of the most important councils in behalf of the cause of King Victor Emmanuel, at which letters from the distinguished Garibaldi and the prime minister, Count Cavour, were read.

Besides these he was everywhere the recipient of numerous invitations, both for public and private receptions, where the most distinguished courtesy was extended to him. While in London he attended a grand *déjeûné* at the Crystal Palace, together with three hundred and fifty other guests, representing the *élite* of the world : at this presided the late Rt. Hon. Earl Stanhope, Dr. Delany being assigned a seat at the table with the foreign ambassadors and delegates.

At two brilliant gatherings at the Gallery of Art and Queen's Rooms he participated. In his hours of relaxation from business engagements connected with his explorations, he often found it convenient and profitable to make social visits. To these he refers often as fraught with interesting memories, but to none with more pleasurable recollection than a visit made to the venerable and learned astronomer, John Lee, Esq., D. C. L., where he attended the annual festival of Reform held by him in the great park of his residence at Hartwell Palace, of Elizabethan memory, and assigned by the British government to Louis XVIII. while in exile.

At these festivals the tenants and working-class gather, and partake of the advantages of traffic there offered in wares and stores, in edibles and fancy goods, as the good Dr. Lee and lady apportion for their benefit, together with the sale of these articles. They were entertained with addresses on moral and scientific subjects by distinguished speakers invited for the occasion.

This continues generally for three days, concluding with various gymnastic and muscular exercises; in some the women take part, when prizes are distributed by the doctor and his lady. On the first day of the festival a ceremony is observed, which enhances the interest of the occasion, and in this connection will serve to illustrate the elegant hospitalities extended to the African explorer. A committee, selected by their host's approval, usually meet and choose as president of the occasion some distinguished person present.. A stranger or foreigner, if present, is invariably honored with the position, and is assigned, in this event, the historic chambers once occupied by the exiled monarch of France and his queen, furnished with the ancient garniture as when occupied by them.

When the committee returned, they announced, as their choice for president, Dr. M. R. Delany, the African explorer. This was unexpected by him, but was heartily received by the guests present, some sixty-three in number, who doubtless understood it among themselves prior to its public announcement.

CHAPTER XII.

THE INTERNATIONAL STATISTICAL CONGRESS AND LORD BROUGHAM.

WHILE in London transacting business connected with the exploration, it was Delany's privilege to attain a distinction never before reached by a colored American under like auspices.

At this time he appeared more prominently before the American public, owing to his presence in that august assembly known as the International Statistical Congress, presided over by His Royal Highness Albert, Prince Consort of England.

At this Congress had convened the most intellectual and distinguished representatives of all the nations of the civilized world.* To this, by virtue of his position

* Extract from the report of the proceedings of the fourth session of the International Statistical Congress, held in London, July 16, 1860, and the five following days : —

" *Opening Meeting of the Congress.*

"At four o'clock His Royal Highness, the Prince Consort, arrived at Somerset House, attended by the Earl Spencer, the Lord Waterpark, Major General Hon. C. Grey, Colonel F. Seymour, C. B., and Lieutenant Colonel Ponsonby. His Royal Highness was received in the outer hall of King's College by the Right Hon. the President of the Board of Trade and the Right Hon.

and acknowledged scientific acquirements, he received
a royal commission, and sat, during its session, an hon-

W. Cowper, M. P., Vice-President of the Congress, the Earl of
Shaftesbury, the Earl Stanhope, Sir James Clark, Bart., Rev.
Dr. Jeff, Principal of King's College, and Dr. Guy, and the
Secretaries, Dr. Farr, Mr. Valpy, and Mr. Hammack. A guard
of honor of the Queen's (Westminster) Rifle Volunteers, with
the band of the corps, was in attendance to receive his Royal
Highness.

"Amongst the noblemen and gentlemen present were the
Honorary Vice-President, including the official delegates, His
Excellency the Count de Persigny, Ambassador of France; His
Excellency Monsieur Musurus, Ambassador Extraordinary and
Plenipotentiary of Turkey; Monsieur Sylvain Van de Weyer,
Envoy Extraordinary and Minister Penipotentiary of Belgium;
the Baron de Cetto, Envoy Extraordinary and Minister Plenipotentiary of Bavaria; the Count de Bernstorff, Envoy Extraordinary and Minister Plenipotentiary of Prussia; the Commander
de Carvalho Moreira, Envoy Extraordinary and Minister Pleni-
potentiary of Brazil; George Mifflin Dallas, Esq., Envoy Ex-
traordinary and Minister Plenipotentiary of the United States of
America; the Count Apponyi, Envoy Extraordinary and Minis-
ter Plenipotentiary of Austria; the Count de Vitzthum, Envoy
Extraordinary and Minister Plenipotentiary of Saxony; Mon-
sieur de La Rive, Envoy Extraordinary of Switzerland; Lord
Brougham, the Earl of Shaftesbury, Earl Stanhope, Lord John
Russell, M. P., Viscount Ebrington, Lord Monteagle, Lord
Wriothesley, Lord Harry Vane, M. P., the Lord Mayor, Mr.
Bouverie, M. P., Mr. Slaney, M. P., Sir John Bowring, Major
General Sir C. Paisley, Rear Admiral Fitz Roy, Colonel Sykes,
M. P., Right Hon. Joseph Napier, Right Hon. W. Hutt, M. P.,
Mr. Monckton Milnes, M. P., Sir Roderick I. Murchison, Mr.
Nassau, Senior, Mr. Pollard Urquhart, M. P., Sir F. H. Goldsmid,
Bart., M. P., the Registrar General of England, the Registrar
General of Ireland, Sir R. M. Bromley, K. C. B., Mr. Caird,
M. P., Mr. Fonblanque, Mr. Crawfurd, Mr. Newmarch, Mr.

ored member. His remarkable presence would, of itself, have attracted the attention of the Continental members; but a movement was destined to render him more conspicuous.

The value of his position in that learned gathering was doubly enhanced and appreciated by him. It was a triumphant recognition of the progress of his race, as well as of the ability of the representative. His admission into that Congress was not based upon national credentials, — for they would have been refused to him,

Edwin Chadwick, Mr. L. J. Leslie, Mr. S. Gaskell, Mr. J. Heywood, Mr. Babbage, Alderman Salomans, M. P., Mr. Mowbray Morris, Mr. T. Chambers, Mr. Lumley, Colonel Dawson, Dr. Babington, Mr. J. Glaisher, Dr. Balfour, Dr. Sutherland, Mr. Hodge, Mr. Edgar, Mr. Hastings, Mr. T. Webster, Mr. S. Redgrave, Mr. A. Redgrave, Professor Leone Levi, Dr. R. D. Thomson, Mr. H. G. Bohn, Mr. Hendricks, Sir Ranald Martin, C. B., Dr. Letheby, Dr. McWilliam, C. B., Mr. Simon, Mr. Horace Mann, Mr. Hill Williams, Mr. Panizzi, Mr. Tidd Pratt, Dr. Varrentrapp of Frankfort, Dr. Neumann of Berlin, Dr. Mühry of Hanover, Lieutenant-Colonel Kennedy, Mr. F. Purdy, Dr. Norton Shaw, Mr. A. Bonham Carter, Mr. R. Hunt, Mr. W. Clode, Chevalier Hebeler, M. Koulomzine and M. Von Bouchen of Russia, M. Chatelain of Paris, M. Carr van der Maeren, Le Chevalier Debrang, Mr. Peter Hardy, Captain Sierakowski and Professor Kapoustine of Russia, Dr. Otto Hübner, M. Coquerel, Professor Chicherin of Moscow, Dr. Bialloblotzki, Mr. J. G. Cogswell, Mr. D. V. McLean, Dr. Schwabe of Berlin, M. Villemsens of Paris, *Dr. Delany of Canada*, Mr. H. Ayres, Mr. T. Michell, M. Grigorieff of St. Petersburg, the President of the College of Physicians, the President of the College of Surgeons, Dr. Bryson, Mr. S. Brown, Mr. Jellicoe, Mr. Yates, Mr. Holland, Dr. Greenhill, Captain D. Galton, Mr. Thwaites, and a large body of gentlemen who had been specially invited to take part in the proceedings of the Congress."

—but was supported by his individual claims as the proud representative of his ancestral land.

His sterling ability won for him the friendly interest of the great Lord Brougham, who, at the first meeting, called the attention of the American minister to him, which remark, being construed offensively, resulted in the withdrawal of the American delegates, at the head of which was Judge Longstreet of Georgia. Through them and their pro-slavery partisans north and south, Major Delany acquired a popularity distasteful with the American public, to whom the circumstance was known imperfectly, and then only in a prejudicial manner. So many comments were made by the press, all tending to produce the utmost unpleasantness between the two countries, that it seemed likely to have resulted in a more disagreeable misunderstanding, but was checked by the inevitable ridicule which attached to it.

When the news of the withdrawal of the American delegates first reached the public, it was through an official source — a letter from Judge Longstreet, the American representative to the Congress. It was given to the public through Hon. Howell Cobb, of Georgia, secretary of the treasury under the Buchanan administration. And as it was only through this medium, we propose to furnish the statement of the principal personage in the affair, decisive and trustworthy, and also to reproduce the letter of Judge Longstreet, which, in view of the position occupied by them both at this time, will be of additional interest.

Delany says, —

"This is a subject upon which I never desire to en-

ter. Very seldom — I think not more than two or
three times, and then only to my most intimate friends
— have I ever related the circumstance, and always
approached it with sensitive delicacy; because to attempt to speak about it without relating the whole, is
to make it ridiculous, and leave on the mind of the
auditor the impression that there must have been on
the part of the distinguished lord a most absurd and
abrupt intrusion upon the transactions and doings of
that dignified body.

"And since Judge Longstreet withdrew from that
body immediately after the organization, and before doing anything, going home, and having nothing to report
but the cause of his delinquency or remissness, his official
report to the secretary of the treasury necessarily being concerning me, therefore I am compelled to give
the facts as to how it really transpired. And certainly
no one of the most sensitive delicacy about matters of
this kind will accuse me of dragging in extraneous matter. Indeed, it ceases to be a question of propriety,
and turns entirely upon a question of right, as to
whether or not I have the right of self-defence against
an attack by a high official of the government? Or
is it not the government which attacks me through its
foreign representative and cabinet minister? The entire affair was contrary to my desire, and by no means
flattering to me, as Judge Longstreet reported as officially follows."

We give the following from the report of the secretary of the treasury for the year ending June 30,
1860:—

Letter from A. B. Longstreet to Howell Cobb.

LONDON, July 21, 1860.

SIR: My mission to the International Congress terminated abruptly, even before the first regular meeting for the transaction of business.

At the appointed time (16th instant) a preliminary meeting was called, to appoint officers and arrange the order of business for the regular meetings. All the foreign delegates were declared to be vice-presidents, and, by invitation of the chairman, took their seats as such upon the stand. Lord Brougham was, I think, the last member of the Congress who entered the hall, and was applauded from the first glimpse of him until he took his seat; it was near and to the left of the chair. Mr. Dallas, appearing as a complimentary visitor,* was seated to the right, in a rather conspicuous position. Things thus arranged, the assembly waited the presence of his royal highness, the prince consort, who was to preside and open the meeting with an address. He soon appeared, delivered his address, and took his seat. As soon as he concluded, and the long-continued plaudits ceased, Lord Brougham rose, complimented the speech very highly and deservedly, and requested all who approved of it to hold up their hands. We did so, of course. This done, he turned to Mr. Dallas, and addressing him across the prince's table, said, "I

---

* Here, as elsewhere mentioned, Judge Longstreet is again in error, he not having remained long enough to make himself acquainted with the Congress. Mr. Dallas was not a "complimentary visitor," abstractly considered, as the judge's reference would infer, but, by general rule, an *ex-officio* member of the Congress, — a vice president, — as was every envoy extraordinary, or minister plenipotentiary to her majesty's court, and consequently had taken his seat as one of the high officials of an International (the World's) Congress, and not Great Britain's, much less England's Congress. The Congress belonged as much to Mr. Dallas as to his lordship, and, may it be permitted, even his royal highness. The great assembly simply sat by turn of appointment in Great Britain, and doubtless in time will come to the United States, especially now that they have reached the point of consummate of national justice.

call the attention of **Mr. Dallas** to the fact **that there is a negro** present (or among the delegates), and **I** hope he will have **no** scruples **on** that account." This appeal was **received** by **the** delegates with general and enthusiastic **applause.   Silence** being **restored,** the negro, **who goes by the name of** Delany, rose and **said,** "I thank your royal highness **and Lord Brougham, and** have only to say *that I am a man*."* This, **too, was** applauded warmly by the delegates.   I regarded this an ill-timed assault upon **our** country, a wanton indignity offered to our minister, and a **pointed insult** offered to me.   **I** immediately withdrew from the body.   The propriety of my course is **respectfully submitted** to my government.

What England can promise herself from exciting the ire **of the** United States, I cannot divine.   Surely there is nothing in the past history of the two countries which offers to her the least encouragement to seek contests **with** the great republic, either national or individual.   Will not her championship of the slave against his master be in full time when the slave shall complain **of his** lot and solicit **her** interference.

My reasons, more at large, for the course that I have pursued, will be found in the London Morning Chronicle, herewith transmitted, which, in its slightly-modified form, I pray you to **regard as a** part of my **report.**

I am, sir, your most obedient, humble **servant,**

A. B. LONGSTREET.

Hon. Howell Cobb, *Secretary of the Treasury.*

The American Delegate and Lord Brougham.

To the Editor of the Morning Chronicle.

Sir: After what **occurred at** the first meeting of the Statistical Congress, I withdrew immediately **from that body, intending to offer no reasons for my course, because,** from what I saw, I **judged that they would not** be worth the paper on which they **might be written.**   I reserved them, therefore, **for** my own government.   **After waiting a while to** see what comments the **papers would** make upon the opening scenes of the Congress, I commenced my despatch to **my** government; but a friend, **in** whose opinions I have great confidence, **said** he thought I ought **to** address the people here **in** vindication of **myself**. **Upon** this intimation (for it was rather an intimation than **counsel**) I sat down, and, amidst a thousand doubts **and** interruptions, **wrote** the subjoined communication. **I was** just bringing **it to a close** for the press **yesterday (Thursday),** when I received **information** that, at the **opening of the meeting** on the **day previous, Lord** Brougham had explained **his remarks** at the first **meeting,** as I would **see in a paper referred to, and the** information came with a request that I **would return to the Congress.** I read the ex- planation **in that paper and two others.** They only differ in their **reports of it, but they all concur in** making his lordship **disavow any intention to show any disrespect to the American minister or the United States; and they make** him say that he **merely meant to call** to notice an interesting or a statistical fact, **viz.: that there was a negro in** the assembly. Now, I found **myself** in a very ticklish predicament. It was not his lordship's **remarks so** much as the reception they **met with,** by all **my** asso- ciates of the Congress, that **determined me to leave it.** The signs **were** infallible that in that body I could not be received **as** an equal, either in country **or** in character, while the negro **was** received with **open arms.** They understood his **lordship as I** did. All the **papers understood** him in the **same way,** and some **of them glory in the exposure of the American** minister, and **promise themselves a rich treat when** the president shall dis- **cover in what contempt his minister is** held here. All this re- **mains precisely as it did before** his lordship's explanation. Of **course, therefore, I cannot return** to them. They would receive **me courteously, no doubt,** — possibly, **now, with** plaudits, — but **why? Not from personal respect to me or my** country, but to **avoid schism in the society — to** preserve its popularity. I am only three years removed from an Englishman (I date from **the** birth **of** my government), and I have too much English **spirit in** me to thrust myself into any company upon **charity.** Had the delegates received his lordship's remarks **with a silent smile (ill- timed as** they were), **and Dr.** Delany's response in the same **way, I never should have left the** Congress. But the plaudits came like a tempest of hail upon my half-English spirit. Nothing, then, in the piece needs qualification, but what refers to his lordship's intentions. Learning these from his own lips, I sat down to correct it in all that imputed to him, directly or impliedly, wrong intentions and wrong feelings; but I found that they were so often referred to in a vast variety of ways, so often intermingled with sentiments void against the principal, but good against the indorsers, and in all respects good against the leading spirits of Europe and the Congress, and so essential to the harmony and grammatical construction, that if I undertook to correct generally, I should hardly leave it printable or readable. And yet the piece must now appear; for if not, it will go forth to all Europe that the United States delegate took offence, pro-slavery like, at an old man's playful remark, left the Congress at the beginning, and that neither explanations nor entreaties could bring him back. I have neither time nor patience to remodel it, much less to rewrite it. I am called away to-day; I should have been off from London before. In my dilemma I have concluded to publish the piece just as I wrote it; not now as fairly representing his lordship, but as exactly representing my understanding of him when I left the Congress, and the reasons. I am at the bar now, and I am to be judged of by the reasonableness of my interpretations and of my conduct founded on them. I beg his lordship, in consideration of my situation, to indulge me in this. In return, I beg the reader to treat as revoked, and utterly null and void, every reference to his lordship that is in the slightest degree inconsistent with his explanation. I am not very far behind him in years; I have long been his debtor, and I esteem him almost reverentially; and if he is not debtor for his judicial reform bill to my native state, there is the most remarkable coincidence between the two systems that ever occurred since the world began. If he is, he ought to esteem me for my state's sake. Be this as it may, we are too old to quarrel.

A. B. Longstreet.

To the Public.

Before I terminate my first and last **visit to Europe, I deem it** due to my country and myself to leave behind me a word of comment upon a most remarkable incident of that **visit. It may be of** some service to the people on both sides of **the Atlantic.** England owes to my country much respect — to my native state a little. I came hither as a delegate (and by accident the only delegate) **from** the United States to the International Congress, now in session at this place. The appointment was made by **request of the authorities of this country. I** am a native of **the State of Georgia,** the birthplace of the two gallant Tattnalls, the **one well known to me,** the other well known to England. He **was that humane and chivalrous** commodore, who, at the **peril of his commission and his life,** rescued the captain and the **crew of Hope's** sinking ship from a watery grave at Peiho. He **has** received much praise for the deed, but not quite all that is **due** to him, **for** in yielding to his generous impulses, he forgot **that his no less** gallant brother was borne from the battle-field **at** Point Peter, severely wounded by British muskets. **What is** done in war should be, but is not, always forgotten in peace. The commodore's conduct was approved by his **government —** that government which Mr. Dallas represents at **the court of St.** James.

The Statistical **Congress convened,** a preliminary meeting was held **to appoint officers and** arrange the order of business. All **the foreign** delegates were declared to be vice-presidents, and **they** took their seats on the platform with **the** presiding officer. **Mr. Dallas, a** complimentary visitor, took **his seat** to the right **of the chair, Lord Brougham to the left. All** things being now **in readiness for the opening of the** regular meeting, his royal highness, **Prince Albert, appeared, took** the chair, and opened the meeting with that **admirable** address which has been published, and which carries its highest commendation on its **face.** As soon as **he** had concluded, and the long-resounding **plaudits ceased,** Lord Brougham rose, and after a few remarks strongly and deservedly complimentary of the address, and after calling upon all present to testify their approval of it by holding up their hands, (!) he turned to the American minister, and addressing him across the table of his royal highness, said, "I call the attention of Mr. Dallas to the fact that there is a *negro* present, and I hope he will feel no scruples on that account." This appeal to the American minister was received with general applause by the house. The colored gentleman arose, and said, "I thank his royal highness and your lordship, and have only to say *that I am a man.*" And this was received with loud applause.

Now, if the noble lord's address to the American minister was meant for pleasantry, I must be permitted to say that the time, the subject, and the place were exceedingly unpropitious to such sallies. If it was meant for sarcasm, it was equally unfortunate in conception and delivery. If it was meant for insult, it was mercilessly cruel to his lordship's heart, refinement, dignity, and moral sense. I could readily have found an apology for it in his lordship's locks and wrinkles, if it had not been so triumphantly applauded. The European delegates understood it; the colored gentleman understood it; and from the response of the latter we can collect unerringly its import. It was meant as a boastful comparison of his lordship's country with the minister's. It was meant as a cutting reflection upon that country where negroes are not admitted to the councils of white men. This is the very least and best that can be made of it, and the dignity of the American minister's character and office, his entire disconnection with slavery personally, and his peculiar position in the assembly, were no protection to his country from this humiliating assault; nay, he is selected as the vehicle of it before the assembled wisdom of Europe, who signify openly their approbation of it. All the city papers that I have seen differ from each other in their report of this matter, but they all soften its rugged features somewhat. The Times is the most correct, but at fault in making Lord Brougham preface his remarks to Mr. Dallas with, "I hope my friend, Mr. Dallas, will forgive me for reminding him," &c., and in making Dr. Delany (the colored gentleman) say to Lord Brougham, "who is always a most unflinching friend of the negro." If one or the other of these remarks were made, I did not hear it; the doctor would hardly have used the last.

Now, I take leave to say that a Briton was the last **man on** earth who should cast contemptuous reflections upon the United States, and the delegates the last men on earth who should have countenanced them. Not one of them, not a man on **all the** broad surface of Europe, can assail that country without assailing some near home-born friend of his own language and **blood,** or some kinsman by short lineage **from** a common ancestry. She spreads herself out **from the** Atlantic to the Pacific, from the Gulf to the Lakes, and through all her length and breadth she is one vast asylum for the poor, the oppressed, the downtrodden, **the persecuted of the world.   Her sons are** a multitudinous brotherhood of all climes, religions, and tongues, living together in harmony, peace, and equality, so far as these can possibly prevail within her borders. Say what you may, think as you may, sneer as you may, at her "peculiar institutions;" she is, after all, the good Samaritan of nations. Do a people cry and waste from famine? She loads her ships with supplies, and lays them at the sufferer's doors without money and without price. Do **an** oppressed people strike for liberty? You will find some of her sons under their flag. Does a wife's cry come across the **water** for help to find a noble, long-missing husband? She fits out her ships; her volunteers man them; **they search nearly to the pole;** learn the husband's fate; **disburden the wife's heart from sus-** pense, and then lie down and die from the exposure and toils of the search. Does she find a nation's sloop of war afloat, still sound but unmanned? She puts her in decent trim, and sends her to her owner in charge of her own men and at her own expense. "Bear with me." If "I am become a fool in glorying, ye have compelled me, for I ought to **have been** commended to you."

Such a nation is not to be taunted, certainly not by Great Britain. Her slavery is **a** heritage, not a creature of her own **begetting.** It was forced on her against her wishes, her prayers, and her protestations; screwed down upon her, pressed into her, until it has become so completely incorporated **with** her very **being, that it is now impossible to** eradicate it. The term

" slave property," is borrowed; it is not of her coinage. In all her slave states there are not ten men living (until very recently not one) who ever made a slave **of a free** man, counting the Hottentot a freeman. Their sin, then, is not in making slaves, but in not restoring them to liberty, in courtesy to the sensibilities of those who made them for us. Before they make this exaction of us, they surely ought to have the magnanimity of Judas, and lay the price at **our feet.** But let us look into this matter a little.

There are **about** 4,000,000 of slaves in the United States. They are worth, at a very moderate calculation, $240,000,000; but as we wish to keep within the realm of morality, we cast that **little** item aside. There they are, from a day old to one hundred years **old —** ignorant, helpless, thriftless, penniless. What would become of them if set free? They would suffer, languish, die. Does charity, does **religion,** demand of us to put them in that condition? How **are they** to live? " Support them yourselves," said a man to me once, of more *negrophilism* than brains. What would we have to support them on, **and** what obligation is there upon one class of freemen to support another? The very act of emancipation would consign nineteen twentieths of the masters to abject penury and **want. There** would be no more conscience, mercy, or remorse in the scramble between the races for the provision on hand at the date of the **act,** than there is for the means of safety among the crew of a sinking ship. **The last** year's crop of cotton was, in round numbers, **4,500,000 bales.** Three fourths of this amount goes abroad, and most **of it to** England. Will the reader take the trouble to compute the amount of shipping it takes to transport that quantity of cotton from America to Europe, the number of **hands** employed in the transportation, and the number employed in working up the raw material? Shipping, seamen, manufacturers, under-workmen, must all go by the board the first year of emancipation. Now, add to the exports 80,000 tierces of rice and 128,000 hogsheads of tobacco in the same category (nearly), and tell me if it is possible to conceive of a greater calamity that could befall the world than the immediate emancipation of the slaves of the United States. Nine millions, at least, would certainly be ruined by it (the slaves and their masters), as the first fruits of the measure; and hundreds of thousands, if not millions more, **in the free states and kingdoms**, i. e., all **who** are dependent upon cotton, rice, **and tobacco in any** way for a living, — **as its** ultimate fruits. **Will it be said** that the negroes will still produce these articles **for their own** benefit? How could they, unless the masters would **give them** the land to cultivate, implements to **till it, and** food and clothing for one year? To **do** this would cost the masters at **least** two hundred million **dollars more;** and what would become of the whites **and their dependants in the mean** time? But if the negroes had the outfit, they **would not make the fifth** part of these articles the **first year.** Look at your freedmen in the West Indies. **We regard** them as a warning, not as an encouragement. **In** the face of the thunderbolt, I would assert that our **slaves are** infinitely. healthier, holier, and happier, than your freedmen. Will it be said that **white** labor would supply their places? How could we hire white labor? And if it performed the work, where would the slaves be? But what of foreigners dependent upon those articles? Will it be said the shipping **and** labor would be turned into other channels? What other? **The** world does not produce the article, nor the wants of the world a demand **for them, if it did.** This thing **of** diverting **large** amounts of labor **and capital from one channel** into another, **is a** work of **time; it cannot be** accomplished in a day. They **who** have seen the effects of a change of fashion, simply upon many laborers, **may form some distant** idea of the consequences of turning millions of property and labor into new channels. Time may turn the sailor into a farmer, but death would overtake **him** before employment, where there **were** practised farmers **enough to** supply the demand.

Now, I could **say** much more to show the utter impracticability of emancipation in the United States, even upon the score of humanity; but enough is **said** until what is said be fairly answered. Until it is fairly answered, until some practicable **means is** pointed out of ridding ourselves of slavery, I enter **my most** solemn protest against all denunciation of our country on account **of it. It is** like denouncing a man because he carries an incurable disease; and coming from British lips, it is like stabbing a man, and, while catching his blood to work into puddings, abusing him for bleeding, and crying out all the time, "Cure yourself! cure **yourself**! or keep out of decent company!" But if abuse, vilification, sarcasm, and contempt, are to be the lot of slaveholders, let it be the lot of slaveholders alone, and of those alone who thrust themselves unbidden into the society of their betters.

Whatever his lordship did not intend by the remark, — **and I am ready to believe that he did not intend to wound, — he certainly did intend to bring to the minister's notice that England made no distinction** between men on account of their color; and herein his lordship was lamentably unfortunate, for the whole scene showed that not only he, but all his applauders, make a marked distinction between colors. Would not his lordship have had more respect for the feelings of any white man than to have made him the object of special notice — and such a notice! — to men gathered from all quarters of the world? Would his lordship's discourtesy to a white man have **been** applauded, as it was, by gentlemen of refinement and delicacy? True, it hit **Dr.** Delany's sensibilities exactly in the right place, for he returned thanks for it; but the chances were a thousand to one that it would have enkindled his indignation. "**What!**" he was likely to have said, "is it a boast of the nobility **of** England that I am admitted to a seat among white men?" His thanksgiving, too, was applauded — a thing not exactly in keeping with our **ordinary dealings** with white men. And when he proclaimed the indubitable fact, "that he was a man," again he was applauded. If any other man had arisen in the assembly, and **said** the selfsame thing, he would have been laughed at, not applauded. Again: his lordship pointed him out as a "negro," — that **was** the word, — not, as some of the gazettes have it, a "colored person," or "colored gentleman;" the Times **has it** right. Now, if he had felt a due regard for the doctor's **rank, would he** not have softened his designation, as the papers have **kindly** done for him? I am told that the doctor is **a** member of the Geographical Society, and a delegate from Canada. If so, I demand, by all the canons of courtesy, why he was not called to the stand as one of the vice-presidents, and placed right between Mr. Dallas and myself ? Here would have been a scenic representation of thrilling moral effect — more eloquent of Old England's love of freedom and contempt of mastery than all lip-compliments of all her nobles put together. Or, if that seat was too low for the doctor, why was he not placed between Lord Brougham and the chair? Had I seen him there, verily my own heart would have swelled with a compliment to noble Old England which no lips could have fitly uttered. Where was the doctor at the prince's reception? I did not see him there. To what section does he belong? I do not find him allotted to either. To how many of the entertainments has he been invited? Now, in all this, I detect a lurking feeling, ever and anon peeping out, which convinces me that the colored man is yet far, very far, below the white man in public estimation, even in Europe; and, until this is conquered, let not the European assume to lecture the American upon his duty to the slave, or upon the equality of the races. Why, if the thing is fated to us, like death, can any man of common humanity and generosity take pleasure in throwing it in our teeth? Slavery is either a blessing or a curse. If a blessing, why disturb us in the enjoyment of it? You Englishmen ought to plume yourselves upon it, for it is your benefaction. If a curse, you should not embitter it. We regard it as a blessing; why disenchant us of the delusion? You say it is a great sin. I doubt it, as I find it; and shall ever doubt, while Paul's Epistle to Philemon is universally acknowledged an inspired epistle. (See note on page 115.) But suppose it a sin; has God commissioned you to reform it? and do you think you ever will reform it by eternally sprinkling vitriol upon the master? As for your contempt, we would rather not have it, to be sure; but if you will be content with that, we will live in peace forever, for it is an article in equal store on both sides. If you cannot condescend to our company, we will not complain at giving a place to Dr. Delany, and we can beatify you with four millions precisely such. But in your intercourse with us, do not, for your own sakes, forget all the rules of delicacy, benevolence, and humanity, for every adult of us can stand up and say, "I am a man!" Farewell to thee, London, for a short time; one more brief look at thy wonders, and then farewell forever! Another visit to Liverpool; I like her better than London, because she likes my people better. "Interest!" "Cotton!" It may be so, but I am grateful for love of any kind in England. Never, in all my long, long life, did my heart-strings knit around a fair one so quickly and so closely, as they did around a lady in London, who approached me, and said, "Mr. Longstreet, I must get acquainted with you. I love your country; I have several kinsmen there." That's natural; that's woman-like. It is for man to draw favors from a country and curse her. God bless her! And God bless the family in which she said it. As Abraham, Isaac, and Jacob, slaveholders, are in heaven, I hope to get there, too. May I meet them all there! But whither am I wandering? Liverpool — another look at Liverpool, another benefice to the English Cunard line, and then farewell to Europe forever and forever!

A. B. LONGSTREET.

P. S. I forgot to mention many kind invitations that I have received from distinguished personages. I declined them all, not indifferently nor disrespectfully, but because they were obviously given to me as a member of the Congress, which I was not when they reached me, and never shall be.

NOTE. The Epistle to Philemon has been an enigma to commentators for seventeen hundred years. That it is the fruit of divine inspiration has never been questioned by Christians; and it is but a letter from Paul to a brother, pleading for a runaway slave whom he sent home to his master. Read it, and see the Christians who joined in it. In Paul's day they did not steal negroes and murder their masters. There were no Browns and Hugos in those days. Philemon was beloved of Paul, was doubtless a preacher, and had a church in his house. Is not the enigma now solved? Can we not now see why the epistle was inspired? What would become of us if we were bound to emancipate under all circumstances, or forfeit heaven? I have only hinted at the horrors of the thing.

"It was made the subject of inquiry by some as to the means by which I entered that scientific assemblage. It was through the same doorway which admitted every other member, not a delegated representative, that is, a royal commission.

"By the established usages of this annual assembly, any persons of known scientific attainments, great authorship, mechanical inventions of mathematical complication, researches and discoveries in topographical, geological, or geographical explorations, are regarded as legitimately entitled to the consideration of the royal commissioners, three of whom are always appointed by the sovereign or ruler of that country to which the succeeding Congress is assigned to meet. These commissioners have all the arrangement of the coming Congress in their hands, and issue all the commissions of special membership to those not accredited as national representative delegates.

"By courtesy, the diplomatic representatives of every nation present are *ex-officio* vice-presidents, with two specially selected vice-presidents.

"When the time drew near for the arrival of his royal highness, the Congress was organized, the members taking their seats, and the official dignitaries seated on the platform.

"The royal crimson chair, and one on either side reserved for the prince and his associates, vice-presidents, were vacant. Great demonstrations were made, which gave evidence that some important personage approached, when it was soon observed that it was the arrival of the ex-lord high chancellor of England. He was escorted to his seat on the platform.

"Soon after, music was heard, succeeded by the entry of pages, unrolling the crimson carpet, which preceded the entry of the prince president. At this the whole Congress arose to their feet, with rousing claps of applause. Ascending the platform, his royal highness stood before the chair of state, bowed, and took his seat, when immediately the Hon. George M. Dallas, the American minister, and the Right Hon. Lord Brougham, were conducted by the royal commissioners to the vacant seats on the right and left of his royal highness.

"The prince, with his usual dignity, now arose, bowed, and commenced reading one of the most profound and philosophically simple and comprehensive addresses delivered during the present century.

"In the course of his remarks, he alluded to his former preceptor, Count Vishers, paying great compliments to him. He concluded amidst suppressed applause, suggestive of a feeling which hesitated to show itself, for fear of committing an impropriety before the royal author. That great and generous-hearted gentleman, Lord Brougham, instantly arose, and addressing the Congress, said, 'I rise not to address myself to his royal highness, but to you, my lords and gentlemen of the Congress, not to permit the presence of his royal highness to restrain you from giving vent and full scope to that outburst of applause, which you are desirous of giving in approbation of that great good sense, philosophical and most extraordinary discourse, to which we have had the honor and pleasure, as well as profit, of listening.'

"Immediately taking his seat, the assemblage gave vent to rapturous applause. As it concluded, he again rose to his feet, remarking in general terms that it was a most extraordinary assemblage of the world's wisdom, and that those who were there were fortunate in being members of such a body, presided over by that great personage, the prince consort of England.

"He also made allusions to the presence of the imperial director of public works from France, the representatives from Brazil, Spain, and some other countries, as an evidence of the progress of the age; then taking his seat, and instantly arising in such a hasty manner, as though something important had been omitted, that he attracted the attention of the entire assembly; when, extending his hands almost across his Royal Highness, he remarked, 'I would remind my friend, Mr. Dallas, that there is a negro member of this Congress' (directing his hand towards me): smiling, he resumed his seat. Mr. Dallas, seeming to receive this kindly, bowed and smiled.

"Count Vishers now rose to reply to the compliments made to him by the prince; then followed the director of the public works from France, followed by the Brazilian representative, and concluding with the Spanish diplomatist.

"While I fully comprehended his lordship's interest, meaning, and its extent, the thought flashed instantly across my mind, How will this assembly take it? May it not be mistaken by some, at least, as a want of genuine respect for my presence, by the manner in which the remarks were made? And again, would not my silence be regarded as inability to comprehend a want of deference on the part of his lordship? Or should I not be accused of regarding as a compliment a disparaging allusion towards me? These thoughts passed through my mind so soon as his lordship concluded his remarks, and as soon as the minister from Spain was seated, I rose in my place, and said, —

" 'I rise, your Royal Highness, to thank his lordship, the unflinching friend of the negro, for the remarks he has made in reference to myself, and to assure your royal highness and his lordship that *I am a man.*' I then resumed my seat. The clapping of hands commenced on the stage, followed by what the London Times was pleased to call 'the wildest shouts ever manifested in so grave an assemblage.'

" So soon as the applause had subsided, the prince arose and announced the Congress adjourned, to meet at two o'clock the next day; the sections to meet in their several departments at ten, to meet the general Congress at two.

" These were my words *verbatim.* Why Judge Longstreet's sarcastic interpolations, I do not know, nor am I able to account for such manifestations.

" They were not simply British, as the learned judge complained in his singular report to the secretary of the treasury, 'because the loudest and wildest shouts' came from the Continental members. *These manifestations* I can only attribute to a spontaneous outburst of gratification to them at a scene so unexpected in all its relations, without any reference whatever to the United States. And Judge Longstreet entirely misinterpreted the interest and meaning of the manifestation.

" I take pleasure in making the correction now, as far as the generous great are concerned, that it may be favorably recorded in the history of our time, because they would not beg an interpretation at the hands of those who wilfully persist in an historic misrepresentation of that which in all diplomatic and national civility — to say nothing of generosity — should have been understood and accepted by all present.

"The next day, when the general Congress convened, on calling for the reports from the several sections, which presented the papers for ratification before that body, alphabetically arranged, and by courtesy commencing with America, it was discovered that the entire American representation, except Dr. Jarvis, from Boston, Mass., had withdrawn,— the fact being stated by the doctor, who presented the paper placed in his hands by Judge Longstreet, whose office it was to present it as head of the representation, and only direct national delegate (Dr. Jarvis being only a state delegate).   Lord Brougham, the first vice-president, who, in the absence of the royal president, filled the chair, arose, remarking, 'This reminds me of a statement made in the papers this morning, that I had designedly wounded the feelings of the American minister at this court, which I deny as farthest from my intention, as all who know me (and I appeal to the American minister himself, Mr. Dallas being a friend of mine), whether I have not uniformly stood forth as the friend of that government and people? Now, what is this "*offence*" complained of? Why, on the opening of this august assemblage (possibly the largest in number, and the most learned, that the world ever saw together from different nations, to be among whom any man might feel proud, as an evidence of his advance, civilization, and attainments), what is the fact? Why, here we see, even in this unequalled council, a son of Africa, one of that race whom we have been taught to look upon as inferior. I only alluded to this as one of the most gratifying as well as extraordinary facts of the age."

"The noble and philanthropic lord then took his seat amidst another *cause of offence*."

These are the facts of that historical incident quoted from his own writings on the subject. Whatever may have been the motive underlying the action of the southern judge besides the reasons given to the public by him, it is not our province to interfere with; but if it were his intention to bring the high-toned negro delegate, receiving the same honors accorded to the other members of the Congress, into derision, in his undignified haste his failure was most signal in Europe, as well as with most thinking persons, not governed by their prejudices, in America.*

---

* As to the insulting allusion on page 114, presented for the consideration of the British public, that the American slaveholders could " beatify them with precisely four millions such as myself," alluding to their degraded, uneducated slaves, I am admonished against retaliating in a manner which would otherwise be justifiable in view of the great changes brought about by the mistaken cherished ideas of such gentlemen as Judge Longstreet, and the consequent effects everywhere throughout the South, imploringly staring us in the face.

And in reply to the inquiry, page 114, " To what section does he belong? I do not find him allotted to either," a reply will be found in the *Transactions of the International Statistical Congress*, London, 1860; and had he remained to " belong to a section " at all, he would have been clear of the historical blunder which he is found to have made.

And finally, regarding the singular inquiry, page 114, " To

The following comment, written at the time, is from the papers of his friend, Mr. Frederick Douglas, who, towering in colossal grandeur beside the self-made heroes of our country, his eagle glance noting every pulse-throb of the great American body politic, seems a proper exponent of these indisputable facts.

" *Dallas* and *Delany.*

"Some of our American journals, to whom black in anything else than in the human heart is a standing offence, are just now 'taking on' very ruefully about what they are pleased to call a flagrant insult offered to the American minister, Mr. G. M. Dallas, by Lord Brougham, at a meeting of the International Statistical Congress, held in London. Small pots boil quick, and soon dry up, but they do boil terribly while they are at it.

"It would hardly be safe to say whereunto our present wrath would carry us, were we not somewhat restrained and held down by the onerous burdens of electing our president for the next four years. As an American, and being of the unpopular complexion, we are rather glad to see this sensitiveness. The most digusting symptoms sometimes raise hopes for the re-

how many of the entertainments has he been invited?" were I capable of either weakness or vanity in that direction, I might allude to them, as does the learned judge, page 115, but would rather refer him to those to whom he appeals, as having been complimented by, and simply conclude by the allusion that had he himself been at all the entertainments, he could not have failed to see Dr. Delany at many. The uncalled-for allusion to the reception given by his royal highness has been previously replied to.

covery of the patient, and it may be so in this case. The standing offence of the venerable and learned Lord Brougham was, that he ventured to call the attention of Mr. Dallas, the American minister plenipotentiary, to the fact that a 'negro' was an acting member of the meeting of the International Statistical Congress. This was the offence. It struck home at once. Mr. Dallas felt it. It choked him speechless. He could say nothing. The hit was palpable. It was like calling the attention of a man vain of his personal beauty to his ugly nose, or to any other deformity. Delany, determined that the nail should hold fast, rose with all his blackness, right up, as quick and as graceful as an African lion, and received the curious gaze of the scientific world. The picture was complete. Sermons in stones are nothing to this.

"Never was there a more telling rebuke administered to the pride, prejudice, and hypocrisy of a nation. It was saying, 'Mr. Dallas, we make members of the International Statistical Congress out of the sort of men you make merchandise of in America. Delany in Washington is a thing; Delany in London is a man. You despise and degrade him as a beast ; we esteem and honor him as a gentleman. Truth is of no color, Mr. Dallas, and to the eye of science, a man is not a man because of his color, but because he is a man, and nothing else.' To our thinking, there was no truth more important and significant brought before the Statistical Congress. Delany's presence in that meeting was, however, more than a rebuke to American prejudice. It was an answer to a thousand humiliating inquiries respecting the character and qualifications of

the colored race. Lord Brougham, in calling attention
to him, performed a most noble act, worthy of his life-
long advocacy of the claims of our hated and slandered
people. There was, doubtless, something of his sarcastic temper shown in the manner of his announcement
of Delany; but we doubt not there was the same genuine philanthropic motive at the bottom of his action,
which has distinguished him through life. A man covered with honor, associated with the history of his
country for more than a half century, conspicuous in
many of the mightiest transactions of the greatest nation of modern times, between eighty and ninety years
old, is not the man to indulge a low propensity to insult. He had a better motive than the humiliation of
Dallas. The cause of an outraged and much despised
race came up before him, and he was not deterred from
serving it, though it should give offence.

"But why should Americans regard the calling attention to their characteristic prejudice against the colored
race as an insult? Why do they go into a rage when
the subject is brought up in England? The black man
is no blacker in England than in America. They are
not strangers to the negro here; why should they make
strange of him there? They meet him on every corner
here; he is in their cornfields, on their plantations, in
their houses; he waits on their tables, rides in their
carriages, and accompanies them in a thousand other
relations, some of them very intimate. To point out a
negro here is no offence to anybody. Indeed, we often
offer large rewards to any who will point them out.
We are so in love with them that we will hunt them;
and of all men, our southern brethren are most

miserable when deprived of their negro associates.
Why, then, should we be offended by being asked to
look at a negro in London? We look at him in New
York, and Mr. Dallas has often been called to look at
the negro in Philadelphia.

"The answer to these questions may be this: In
America the white man sees the negro in that condition to which the white man's prejudice and injustice
assign him. He sees him a proscribed man, the victim of insult and social degradation. In that condition he has nothing against him. It is only when the
negro is seen without these limitations that his presence raises the wrath of your genuine American Christian. When poor, ignorant, hopeless, and thoughtless,
he is rather an amusement to his white fellow-citizens;
but when he bears himself like a man, conscious of the
godlike characteristics of manhood, determined to
maintain in himself the dignity of his species, he becomes an insufferable offence. This explains Mr. Dallas, and explains the American people. It explains also
the negroes themselves. It is often asked why the negroes do not rise above the generally low vocations in
which they are found? Why do they consent to spend
their lives in menial occupations? The answer is, that
it is only here that they are not opposed by the fierce
and bitter prejudice which pierces them to the quick,
the moment they attempt anything higher than is considered their place in American society. Americans
thus degrade us, and are only pleased with us when so
degraded. They tempt us on every side to live in ignorance, stupidity, and social worthlessness, by the negative advantage of their smiles; and they drive us

from all honorable exertion by meeting us with hatred and scorn the instant we attempt anything else.

" Had Mr. Delany been a mean, poor, dirty, ignorant negro, incapable of taking an honorable place among gentlemen and scholars, Mr. Dallas would have turned the specimen to the account of his country. But the article before him was a direct contradiction to his country's estimate of negro manhood. He had no use for him, and was offended when his attention was called to him.

" There was still another bitter ingredient in the cup of the American minister. Men can indulge in very mean things when among mean men, and do so without a blush. They can even boast of their meanness, glory in their shame, when among their own class, but who, when among better men, will hang their heads like sheep-stealing dogs, the moment their true character is made known. To hate a negro in America is an American boast, and is a part of American religion. Men glory in it. But to turn up your nose against the negro in Europe is not quite so easy as in America, especially in the case of a negro morally and intellectually the equal of the American minister."

Before leaving London, Delany read, by special request, a paper on his researches in Africa, before the Royal Geographical Society, and as a traveller and explorer, received the privileges extended by that body, and as such was received with due courtesy in many of the noted places dedicated to art and science, both in England and Scotland; among them, the Royal College of Surgeons, Lincoln's Inn Fields, the Hospitals, Geological and Anatomical University, Museums, and Libraries.

From a general invitation extended to the members of the Congress, and a special one to himself, by the Right Hon. Lord Brougham and Vaux, ex-lord high chancellor of England, he received his membership, and attended the Congress of the National Association for the Promotion of Social Science at Glasgow, Scotland, the September following. Here a distinguished recognition of his worth awaited him. While at this Congress he elicited expressions of a most complimentary character from Lord Brougham, who presided here with the usual dignity ascribed to him at the International Congress in the absence of his royal highness.

The following is extracted from the Report of the First Section on Judicial Statistics, by the president (Lord Brougham) and Dr. Asher: —

" I think I am authorized, not only on the part of the council of the society, but on the part of the authorities in Scotland, strongly to recommend and to invite all persons to attend that Congress. The authorities take the greatest interest in it, both at Edinburgh and at Glasgow. The magistrates of both countries, and the judges, take the greatest interest in the Congress; and I hope they will not be disappointed in having the attendance of many foreign gentlemen from different parts of the continent; and I also hope that our friend Dr. Delany will attend upon that occasion, for he will then be in the country which first laid down the maxim and the principle of law: That the moment a slave (which Dr. Delany is not, but which his ancestors were) touches British ground, his fetters fall off. That was said when that decision, which does immortal honor to the Scottish courts, was pronounced. It was a remark made in one of the arguments — ' *Quamvis ille niger, quamvis ne candidus esses.*' That remark was made by a very celebrated judge, the son of a very great mathematician, one of the greatest mathematicians that ever appeared in this country, the son of the celebrated McLaurin. I hope Dr. Delany is here. In the sanitary section, as my noble friend Lord Shaftesbury informed me before he left the room, he was of very great use, indeed, in the information which he conveyed to them, and that he made a most able speech, as Sir Roderick Murchison informs me, at the Royal Geographical Society, which he lately attended. I hope therefore, that we shall have the advantage of his attendance upon that occasion."

After the close of the Congress, he was invited to lecture on the subject of his explorations, in many parts of England and Scotland, meeting everywhere with marked success, for nearly seven months. At these lectures an appreciative audience greeted him: among them many of the *élite* of the kingdom convened, as was manifested at his reception lecture at Brighton, on the seaside, during the watering season, given in the pavilion of the Marine Palace of William IV.

At the conclusion of these, he prepared to return to Africa, having entered into obligations in England and Scotland, especially the latter place, — which in good faith are yet to be fulfilled, — when the secession of South Carolina reached Great Britain.

With almost prophetic vision he saw the great work apportioned for his race in the impending struggle.

Therefore he turned his thoughts homeward to prepare himself for his portion of it.

Hastening home from a land where he was everywhere the recipient of distinguished courtesy, in order to cast his lot with his people for good or evil fortune, he reached Canada forty-five days before the attack on Fort Sumter.

There he remained watching the progress of the rebellion, which, from the first, he foresaw, and thus expressed himself, that it would be long and desperate in its course.

The following is the speech of Dr. Delany, at the close of the International Congress:—

"I should be insensible, indeed, if I should permit this Congress to adjourn without expressing my gratitude for the cordial manner in which I have been received, from the time when I landed in this kingdom to the present moment, and in particular to the Earl of Shaftesbury, the president of the section to which I belong, as well as to every individual gentleman of that section, it matters not from what part of the world he came. I say, my lord, if I did permit this Congress to adjourn without expressing my gratitude, I should be an ingrate indeed. I am not foolish enough to suppose that it was from any individual merit of mine, but it was that outburst of expression of sympathy for my race (African), whom I represent, and who have gone the road of that singular providence of degeneration, that all other races in some time of the world's history have gone, but from which, thank God, they are now fast being regenerated. I again tender my most sincere thanks and heartfelt gratitude to those distinguished gentlemen with whom I have been privileged to associate, and by whom I have been received on terms of the most perfect equality."   (Great applause.)

We subjoin to this an extract from the Globe, published in Toronto, Canada, by which the attention of the House of Lords was called to him:—

"In the course of his remarks in asking a question in the House of Lords for the production of certain papers relating to the suppression of the slave trade, Lord Brougham said that his noble friend near him (Lord Shaftesbury) could bear testimony to the useful assistance given to the department of the Statistical Congress, over which he presided, by Dr. Delany, the negro member of the Congress.   (Lord Shaftesbury, 'Certainly.')   He had shown great talent in his addresses to the section.   He had also appeared at the general meeting over which he (Lord Brougham), in the prince consort's absence, presided."

The following extract is from page 39 of the Transactions National Asso. Prom. S. Science:—

"At our first meeting in 1857, the subject of Judicial Statistics was brought under consideration, in one of the able and useful papers read by Mr. L. Levi, and in consequence of the discussion which took place, very considerable improvements were introduced into that department of the treasury, so that, at our last Congress, hopes were entertained of such complete and regular information being afforded, as the Annual Report of the Minister of Justice presents in France.   A most important step has since been made in that direction.   The meeting of the International Statistical Congress has been held under the presidency of the prince consort, whose opening address, marked by the sound sense, the accurate information, and the general ability which distinguish all his royal highness's exertions, is in the hands of all our members. Having been requested to superintend the judicial department, and having afterwards, in his royal highness's absence, presided at the general meeting, it was a great satisfaction to find the unanimous adoption of the plan which it became my duty to report, embodying the resolutions in full detail upon the whole subject; and there was a strong recommendation unanimously passed, urging the government to appoint a permanent statistical commission. The report has been presented to the House of Lords (where, indeed, I had several years before brought forward the resolutions which formed its groundwork this year), and is now among the printed papers of the session. There were naturally present at this International Congress eminent men from various parts of the Continent; and in announcing the assembly of the present meeting, I took the liberty of inviting those distinguished foreigners, with whose presence I trust we are now honored. Among others was a negro gentleman of great respectability and talents, Dr. Delany, who had attended different departments, and in his able addresses has communicated useful information and suggestions. When inviting him to this Congress, I informed him that he would have the satisfaction of visiting the country which first declared a slave free the instant he touches British ground. Dr. Delany's forefathers were African slaves; he is himself a native of Canada.* It is truly painful to reflect that,

* His lordship is in error in regard to the birthplace, as elsewhere shown.

although his family have been free for generations, his origin being traced to one whom the crimes of white men and Christians had enslaved, he would be, in the land of trans-Atlantic liberty, incapable of enjoying any civil rights whatever, and would be treated in all respects as an alien, the iniquity of the fathers being inexorably visited, not upon their children, but upon the children of their victims, to all generations, — children whose only offence is the sufferings of their parents, whose wrongs they inherit with their hue."

"NOTE. — It was stated to Dr. Delany that he would be in the country which first pronounced the great decree of a slave's fetters falling off the moment he touched British ground. This was first decided by the courts of Scotland, in the case of Knight, a negro, 1778. In Somerset's case, 1772, the courts of England had not laid down the rule generally, but only that a negro could not be carried out of the country by his master. In the Scotch case, the printed argument was prepared by Mr. McLaurin (afterwards Lord Cleghorn, son of the celebrated mathematician), and the appropriate motto which he prefixed to his paper was : —

"'QUAMVIS ILLE NIGER, QUAMVIS TU CANDIDUS ESSES.'" Ibid. p. 53.

A most remarkable feature noticed in the position of the learned lord, in relation to Major Delany, was the occasion which he took to proclaim to him — a black man, and for the first time before such a distinguished audience — that important historic fact in legal jurisprudence, as found in note above, that it was in Scotland in 1722, the great declaration was made by

Lord Cleghorn, that the moment a slave touched British soil, he stood a freeman "by the irresistible genius of universal emancipation."

It is also worthy of record that so many long years should elapse, and he be made the first to receive the great decision from history correctly given by no less personage than the ex-high lord chancellor of England.

CHAPTER XIII.

RETURN TO AMERICA.

AS Delany was desirous of contributing his aid to the suppression of the rebellion, in various ways he offered to make his services acceptable, which being of no avail, as northern ingenuity had not yet discovered the latent powers of black muscles, he was forced to remain an unwilling looker-on while others bore the part he believed assigned to his race.

While thus unemployed, he accepted the advice of gentlemen of influence and standing, among whom were the Hon. F. S. Gregory and the Rev. Dr. Riddell, of Jersey City, Joseph B. Collins and Isaac Smith, Esqs., of New York, to make a tour through the country, and lecture on Africa and his researches there.

These lectures, beginning after the publication of his report, were exceedingly popular. They were free courses, held generally in the most prominent churches of various denominations, under the auspices of their respective pastors; his book being sold to the audience at the conclusion. These being attended by the most refined and influential of society, he took occasion always to bring forward the claims of his race to the war, endeavoring to create a popular feeling in favor of arming the blacks. For as the huge monster of rebellion began assuming its gigantic proportions with all its hideous deformities, all were admitting the absurdity of its being "put down in a few months." While many then recognized that the blast from Sumter's embattlement was but a reverberation of that which rung out so clearly upon the midnight air, a few short years back, at Harper's Ferry, they scarcely saw the blacks' identity with the issue.

To these lectures there was no impediment offered by his political enemies, on the score of color, to prevent his being heard, but on one occasion; and the cause assigned being so novel and ill-arranged we cannot help referring to the circumstance.

Being in Detroit, he was solicited by that distinguished and venerable divine, Dr. Duffield, author of "The Christian Regeneration," who offered him his church, on the following Sabbath, to deliver a lecture on any moral subject he should choose, before his congregation. The doctor accepted the invitation; but at the precise moment of leaving for the church, a gentleman called upon him, abruptly remarking, "It was not known until this moment that *you* are the person who improved the opportunity to insult the American minister at the Court of St. James. You need not come; we will not hear you!" This was of course instantly denied, with an attempted explanation; but his accuser, for some reason, persisting in the charge, and indignantly refusing to hear an explanation, abruptly withdrew. Soon after a *committee* of *gentlemen* called, stating that the church was crowded, determined to hear him and give him an opportunity to explain the impolitic charge against him. Thanking them, he peremptorily declined, lest he should compromise the excellent pastor by the accusation most certain to be made, that "the abolitionists of the church had forced a negro into it, though protested against by the other portion of the congregation." Again, that Sabbath being the first after the attack on Fort Sumter, he insisted to his friends, knowing the great issue at stake, that it was no time to divide the feelings of the people. The point was conceded by his friends, and they yielded, when one of them, a wealthy manufacturer, rented the "Murrill Hall" at his own expense, where, on the first evening, he made a satisfactory explanation of the alleged offence, and lectured for four consecutive evenings.

A few days after this, while seated in the cars, dashing along the Great Western Railway in Canada, listening to a discussion on the probabilities of the war and its result, a gentleman stepped up, addressing him by name, stated that he resided at Detroit, and was there at the time the objection was raised against having him lecture at the church, and, " although a Democrat, he did not sympathize with the issue made against him, and that it was simple justice due to him to state that the author of the charge was Colonel ——, recent charge d'affaires at the Court of R——, who made the statement as being true, he having been present at the International Congress at the time, and knew the attack on the American minister to have been of the grossest character and altogether unnecessary." This, the major says, was the first and only information he ever had of the conversion of that incident into an attack by him upon the Ameican minister.

He continued his course of lectures, and heard no

more such absurd charges, persons being perhaps too absorbed in the fearful struggle, when a nation should be born anew, and old prejudices and hatred forever **buried,** to repeat the slander.

At this time, too, there were endless speculations concerning the course and determined policy of Mr. Lincoln, who, with few exceptions, was being regarded with suspicion by the friends of the blacks as well as by **the** blacks themselves, based upon his inaugural address (to the first we allude, for the second lives forever), together with the Central American Emigration scheme, which we now recognize as a most successful *coup d'état* of **the** president. It set the opinion at rest forever that the colored people could be induced to emigrate from *their home, and this their country, en masse.*

Speculations were endless as to the tendency **of the** president's course. As it is not considered an assumption for a man of limited **means to have** an opinion **of** his own, Dr. Delany had **and** claimed **the** right, after much deliberation, to express his views concerning **the policy** of the president. Many of his friends differed widely **from him;** he held his own convictions with his usual tenacity, and endeavored to convince them. **He** thought he could discern, in the course then being pursued by Mr. Lincoln, a logical conclusion, and which, if not at first intended, would ultimately result **in accomplishing the** desires of the friends **of freedom —** emancipation to the slaves of the **South, and the freedmen's** rights as an inevitable consequence.

Said **he on one occasion,** "I thought I **could see differently from my** friends, those truly talented men,

and unswerving friends of their race. Not that I
know more than they, for I may not know as much.
But we, like white men, have our faculties and propensities, and are likely to develop them in the prosecution of our course. In this I think it may not be regarded as an unwarranted assumption or egotism to
say that in national affairs and in fundamental principles of government, I claim to be at least not far
rearward of my friends whose counsels I sought. To
inquire into the origin of races and governments, and
the rise and fall of nations, is with me a propensity I
cannot resist. This is not said for invidious comparison
with my friends, because as an orator (which I am not),
anti-slavery historian, and portrayer of black men's
wrongs, I would sink into insignificance in comparison
with Frederick Douglass, and would render myself
ridiculous were I capable of assuming to be equally
learned with Dr. James McCune Smith. While I considered him at the time of his death the most scientific
and learned colored man, as a scholar, on the American continent, yet neither scholarship and splendid
talents among black men ceased to exist with Dr.
McCune Smith, nor will end with the name of the renowned Douglass. They are more numerous, comparatively, than their opportunities warrant." He
sought his friends, to devise with them the means best
adapted to meet the demands of the hour. The subject present in his mind was that of the army. He
argued strongly, always in favor of separate organization, as the only means to give character to the colored
people, and promote their pride of race, thus crediting
them in history with deeds of their own. In this

he was afterwards supported by the late Dr. McCune Smith, and the lamented Thomas Hamilton of the Anglo-African.

On one occasion he sought Mr. Frederick Douglass at his home at Rochester, who was then restlessly impatient, as were a host of others, at the slow, undefined steps of the president. It is not for us to question whether or not those sad, patient eyes, from the beginning of the struggle, discerned, amid the mists and shadows of the future, the symbol of Union synonymous with emancipation, and, rejoicing, quietly awaited the development of events, or if it was indeed a "*military necessity*," which occasioned its promulgation. Since the many disclosures of party treachery and corruption in high places, the pureness of action which marked his career forms a striking contrast, on which the loyal heart contemplates with a pride mingled with tenderness. That a signal providence directed his course, beset as he was by false counsellors and foes, who hesitated at no measures which subserved their purposes, it is evident. The fiery trials and perplexities through which he passed but purified him for the halo of martyrdom which ultimately encircled his furrowed brow, enshrining him forever in the nation's innermost heart.

Before his departure from Rochester he had the satisfaction of hearing Mr. Douglass express himself more favorably editorially in his able journal, and this before it went to press. Said he, " It was to this change of opinion in my great-hearted friend that we date the correspondence with the Hon. Montgomery Blair, asking the aid of his great influence in behalf of the pres-

ident in putting down the rebellion, and which resulted in a special official request for Mr. Douglass to visit
Washington, and his subsequent conference with the
president and cabinet, including the able secretary
of war."

An incident is related in connection with his many
arguments in behalf of the government, believing its
policy ultimately tended to emancipation. In conversation once on this subject with some of his friends,
there was present an accomplished European lady,
who professed no respect for the Americanism of that
date, and was by no means favorably impressed with
President Lincoln's course. He sought to disarm her
of her prejudices against the administration, as his faith
was in the power behind the throne, which was greater
than the throne itself. She suddenly turned from his
theories, telling him he did not comprehend the great
questions involved in the issue of the war. Before he
could recover from this abrupt stroke, Mr. Douglass
came to his aid, which timely relief saved him from a
most terrible rout. Said Mr. Douglass, "Madam, you
do not know the gentleman with whom you are conversing; if there be one man among us to whose opinion I would yield on the subject of government generally, that man is the gentleman now before you."

CHAPTER XIV.

CORPS D'AFRIQUE.

AS early as **October, 1861, Dr.** Delany, when *en route* to Chicago, stopped at Adrian, Michigan, **for** the purpose of seeing President Mahan, of the Michigan College. The subject **of the** war, which was then being earnestly waged, instantly became the theme of conversation, and the rôle of the **colored** American **as an** actor on **its** board **was the principal** feature therein. How and **what to do to** obtain admission **to** the **service, was the** question **to which** Dr. Delany demanded a solution. **He stated that it** had become inseparable with **his** daily existence, **almost** absorbing **everything** else, and nothing **would** content him but entering **the** service; he cared not how, provided his admission **recognized the** rights **of** his race **to do so.**

To this President Mahan assented, and expressed himself as willing to sacrifice his high social position **and** literary **worth for the** cause **of his** country and humanity. He further expressed **himself** as being willing and ready to enter the service on conditions **that should** be specified, he having received a military education **in** his youth.

He proposed to apply to President Lincoln for a major general's commission, with authority to raise a division of blacks. Dr. Delany at once proposed that the application be made specially for a corps d'Afrique for signal service from the white division of the army. This was prior to the application of Dr. Gloucester to Mr. Lincoln for such an organization for Major General Fremont, or the order to General N. P. Banks.

His main reason in urging the corps d'Afrique was, he claimed, with his usual pride of race, that the origin and dress of the Zouaves d'Afrique were strictly *African.*

To President Mahan, on that occasion, he gave the following history of their formation: —

"That it was during the Algerine war waged by the Duc d'Orleans, eldest son of Louis Philippe, against Abdel-Kader, the Arab, the Zouave obtained that fame which recommended it to civilized nations.

"The French had their three grand armies of ten thousand; the struggle had been long, desperate, and costly to the French, both in men and materials of war, and the campaign began to wane, till

> ' A Moorish king went up and down,
>   Through Granada's royal town,'

and the services of the African warriors were tendered to the Duc d'Orleans by an African prince.

"When, in a terrible charge, the duke, receiving a shot through the thigh, was unhorsed, and fell bleeding to the ground, the desperate Arabs, amid the wild shouts of their leaders, charged on their steeds with open mouths and distended nostrils, their javelins drawn for the fatal thrust, those faithful black Zouaves, eighteen hundred, mounted upon jet stallions, rushed to the conflict, in turn charging, and turned the front of their antagonists with double-edged sabres, cut through the ranks **of the** shrieking enemy, covered the duke with their shields, **and** bore him **away in** triumph from the field.

"**It was** for services such as these in **a** long and bloody struggle, that could not have been brought to a close without such aid, that the African Zouaves, who **served in the** Algerine war, were taken **as veteran** troops with **the** French to Europe, **and** their dress and tactics introduced as a part of the military service of **the French.**

"It was observed years ago by persons visiting Hayti, without their comprehending **it** closely, perhaps, that the soldiers of that island had peculiar tactics, — 'throwing themselves upon the earth,' and, **as one** writer observed, turning upon their backs, then upon their sides, so swiftly that it was hard to determine what they were, all the time keeping up a continual 'load and fire.' **This** was, doubtless, nothing but the original Zouave tactics introduced long years **ago** by native Africans among these people."

Before leaving, President Mahan proposed **to** make the application, as previously agreed upon between them, and, if successful, to give Dr. Delany an appointment compatible with his desires. **The** latter proposed to avoid encroaching **on** army regulations as then being the policy; that he should receive the position **of** private medical adviser and confidential **bearer** of despatches, which would **not** interfere with any official position of army officers, and at the same time giving him the opportunity **of** being near the general's person, to obtain the military experience he desired, which he knew would render him of service in the event of the government accepting the aid of the colored troops, by admitting those fitted to proper positions.

With this understanding he left President Mahan, confident, if it was possible for his desires to be accomplished, that all endeavors would be used. Instead of hearing of the success of his plans, he soon saw them fade before him, like a dream before awakened realities, by seeing the order published giving authority to Major General N. P. Banks to raise a corps d'Afrique immediately for the service.

But this did not prevent him from looking to a brighter prospect for his race.

"As this placed us fairly in the war," he said, "thanking God, I became satisfied, and took courage."

Thus, while it proved an individual failure for his plans, as it was a gain to his race, it was as to himself, and his unselfish nature received fresh stimulant to labor to promote further recognition for them.

CHAPTER XV.

A STEP TOWARDS THE SERVICE.

WHILE completing his last lectures of the course in Chicago, the order was granted by the department to raise the famous Fifty-fourth Massachusetts Volunteers, whose fame is enhanced by the gorious burial of its brave young commander with his dusky guards, and the memories of Forts Wagner and Olustee.

For this regiment he received the appointment of acting assistant agent, under Charles L. Remond and Charles H. Langston, Esq., for recruiting, and acting examining surgeon for the post of Chicago, from Major George L. Stearns, chairman of the military committee, being authorized by Governor John A. Andrew, of Massachusetts.

His eldest son, then but eighteen years of age, at school in Canada, wrote to him for permission to join that regiment. In granting the request, it drew from him a reply worthy of his heart and head.

After the regiment was filled, he applied by letter to the war department at Washington for the appointment as surgeon to the blacks in the army. He received the usual polite reply, that "the letter was received and on file under consideration." Hearing nothing of his application, after a considerable time had elapsed, he was advised by his friends to write again by way of a *reminder*, and was on the point of doing so, when the news flashed over the wires that Dr. Augusta of Canada had been appointed as surgeon in the army, with the rank of *major*. Neither did this second defeat dishearten him, for it was a realization partly of his plans of seeing a black of representative rank in the army. He then concluded to abandon the sending of a second application to the department, fearing to embarrass the government in such appointment, and by this retard the progress of the cause he was endeavoring to advance.

Meanwhile Rhode Island had been ordered to raise the heavy artillery; and eighteen hundred black men, afterwards increased to twenty-five hundred, were required for this service. Some of his friends had pushed forward his claims in this direction to the authorities. He was visited at his home in Canada concerning the recruiting, and made agent under a commissioned captain in the service to superintend the recruiting of this arm of the service.

Establishing himself at Detroit, Michigan, removing thence to Chicago, he soon found himself borne smoothly along on the wave of success. His efforts were seconded by the most influential colored people of the place: among them we find the name of Mr. John Jones, the wealthiest colored resident of the state, who entered intimately into his confidence, bringing all his influence to bear in assisting the government to put down the rebellion.

So satisfactory was his course in the West to the authorities of Rhode Island, that the captain under whom he served was relieved, and he then placed in entire charge, and its accompanying responsibilities, *without the military commission*, however, or even rank given by *courtesy*, as the country was not up to that at the time.

Orders at this time were sent to him concerning a change about to be made in relation to the pay and recruiting of the men, which, while it would have resulted in increasing his own pay, would greatly have reduced the bounty — twenty-two dollars a man. To this proposed injustice he instantly refused to lend his influence. And he soon received a telegram to the effect that he was relieved. He then demanded a settlement for his past services. Not being answered, he sent a messenger to Governor Smith, who at once summoned him to Rhode Island. At Providence he met his excellency and Major Sanford, U. S. mustering officer, who, together with the governor, the past difficulty being satisfactorily settled, united in recommending his appointment to the military authorities of Connecticut, that state having at the time a quota to fill of five thousand. An official of that state was telegraphed, who contracted with him to superintend the recruiting. He retained his former quarters at Chicago, but was afterwards compelled to remove to Cleveland, Ohio, in consequence of an abrupt interruption on the part of the authorities of that city and the State of Illinois. He complained of affairs being badly conducted, and after a most unsatisfactory official visit to New Haven, occasioned by the absence of Governor Buckingham, he resigned, with a loss of about three thousand dollars to himself.

He immediately went west, and opened an independent recruiting station, witnessing, he says, "with unutterable disgust, the hateful mercenary recruiting trade of selling men in the highest market, and denounced them, whether black or white.

The legitimate quotas in a few country districts of Western Pennsylvania, New York, and Ohio, he aided in filling, "persistently refusing," he says, "the offers made for men, by a class who prowled the country under various names and pretended military titles, with a shudder and a scout, despising the man who would sell his brethren for a price." So great were his fears lest imposition or intrigue be practised on the men, and his promise be made void, that he invariably accompanied them to their destination.

The most interesting epoch in his recruiting career was when he was called upon, by the military committee of one of the districts of Western Ohio, to contract to fill their quota of two thousand five hundred men, under the new act of Congress. The office of the committee was at Cleveland, Ohio. He consented to negotiate for them, provided that *he was commissioned a state officer* under the new act regulating the appointment of state officers in recruiting. The committee suggested first to make sure of the choice and contract; then they would have whereon to base an application to the governor. This course was complied with, and the application then made to the governor, who expressed himself to the effect that he regarded the proposal *too novel to find favor at Washington, as a black man could never have been designed or intended in the new recruiting order.* He further intimated

that the authorities at Washington would be consulted
as to whether or not such an appointment would be
acceptable to them. "Governor Brough," said he,
" that arm which shall be the most successful in putting
down this wicked rebellion, is the arm which will be
at present most acceptable to the people of the United
States and the authorities at Washington, be that a
white or black arm." The governor, smiling, he continues, replied that he did not dispute it, adding that
he thought I might leave for my destination, and regard the commission as certain to be forwarded with
documents for other state officers.

After a short visit to his home, he engaged his examining surgeon, an accomplished colored gentleman, who
had been with him in the Rhode Island and Connecticut recruiting service, returned, and arrived at Nashville, where in two days, he received his commission
from the governor.

At Nashville the famous letter (famous at least to
those whom it concerned) of Major General Sherman,
then at Atlanta, Georgia, to Lieutenant Colonel John A.
Spooner, provost marshal general and commissioner
from Massachusetts for Tennessee, Mississippi, and
Georgia, was under consideration and discussion. He
writes of it, "Great was the consternation produced
among 'government agents' there; and such were the
offers made to me by parties for 'partnership, division
of profits, and the like,' that I was constrained to have
on hand but the one answer for all. Gentlemen, I have an
honorable appointment. I cannot and will not sell my
brethren for a price, nor my birthright for a mess of
pottage." Worn out by these actions, and disgusted,

he left the place, going directly to Ohio, where after a few weeks spent in Galliopolis and Portsmouth, " I became convinced," he said, " that the business of recruiting had reached such a state of demoralization that no honorable man, except *a U. S. commissioned officer*, could *continue it successfully* without jeopardizing his own reputation." He returned home, gaining nothing but experience by his commission.

CHAPTER XVI.

RECRUITING AS IT WAS.

WE take the following, on the subject of recruiting, with its light and shadows as viewed by him. Whatever of good or evil was entailed in his regulations, with him the responsibility rested. He says, " On entering this service, there was no guide, no precedent; but every one, however ignorant, assumed and pursued a course, in many instances, unjust to the recruit, and detrimental to the service, and at once dishonorable, but subservient to his own selfish ends. This was apparent, and at once made the object of attention. For instance, the Fifty-fourth Massachusetts Volunteers were raised by special provision by the citizens or private contributions, as was understood, allowing each enlisted man fifty dollars bounty, which at that time was twenty-five dollars more than was being given by most of the states, perhaps by any other state. It was then understood the bounties of the Fifty-fourth were not appropriated by the state funds. The states which afterwards raised colored troops did so from state appropriations. Rhode Island, being the next to Massachusetts in this movement, appropriated three hundred dollars bounty to the men." It was in the service of the latter state he acknowledged receiving the experience necessary to comprehend the entire system of recruiting. "For," said he, "in the service of Massachusetts, I was employed under my distinguished friends, Charles L. Remond and C. H. Langston, Esqs. My duty was to receive and execute orders and instructions, not to give them. In the Rhode Island service, being engaged to manage, my position and duties were quite different.

"The states which gave colored troops to the service made special arrangements for recruiting them, for the simple reason that necessarily a great part of them had to come from other places than the state which organized them. The provisions made for recruiting white soldiers could not be successfully applied in the case of the colored.

"These were points of importance, — of great importance, — because they involve principles of justice to all concerned.

"Rhode Island, for instance, paid two hundred and fifty dollars bounty to the men in raising the heavy artillery, leaving a residue of fifty dollars for all expenses incurred — salaries of officers, agents, sub-agents, subsistence of recruits till mustered in, transportation — a heavy item of expense, when it is remembered that the greater portion of these men were from the States of Kentucky, Tennessee, and Missouri, where the agents had actually to go to get them, and when obtained in Kentucky and Missouri, for the most part, it cost from ten to twenty-five dollars each to get across the river to the Indiana or Illinois side. It will be readily understood, by an experienced business man or financier, that these immense expenses could not be kept up and the recruits be justly dealt with.

"Again, Connecticut appropriated three hundred dollars bounty to the men, and I was probably the first who received an appointment, by contract, to manage her recruiting in the Western States. The first proposition in meeting the military authorities was to fix the bounties, impressing upon the gentlemen the fact that bounties, being merely awards, were large or small, according to circumstances; that all freedmen who voluntarily presented themselves for enlistment, it follows, should and would receive the three hundred dollars, because no extra or special expenses were incurred. All who had to be subsisted, and sent from the West in Indiana and Illinois, should receive two hundred and fifty dollars, and in all cases where slaves would have to be obtained in the slave states, with all the risks and expenses, one hundred dollars was ample pay. When such men as the brave Voglesang, the intrepid Lennox, and the sons of Frederick Douglass, and my own son, received but fifty dollars, regarding it as ample, their patriotism inducing them to join without bounty. Besides this, those recruited from the slave states received their liberty *de facto*, which they never would have attempted without our agency.

"This I considered justice, and so established it as a system of recruiting. If there had not been a dollar, instead of being a hundred, to give as a bounty to a single slave, or to the sons of the distinguished Douglass, and my own, I should have acted as I did — put my own son in the army, endeavor to get the bondman in, for the purpose of overthrowing the infamous system of slavery and the rebellion.

"On returning from Connecticut, I consulted my

distinguished friend, the Rev. Mr. Garnet, in regard to the system I had adopted, of which he highly approved, as '*coming from ourselves, concerning ourselves.*'

"All this, however, neither covers, defends, nor tolerates in any degree the reprehensible and most shameful impositions continually practised, by various methods of deceptions under the pretext of recruiting. What I defend is a legitimate system laid down, to be strictly conformed to the letter. Whatever was promised to the recruit he should have received, and this should have been fixed and enforced by the proper authorities, and not left optional with a stolid set of human brokers."

CHAPTER XVII.

CHANGING POSITION.

THE appointment of the black major of infantry, at
the time of its public announcement, created considerable discussion. As the causes leading to it have
never yet been publicly known, to gratify a legitimate curiosity, we will give it, beginning with the
materials with which he wrought out the claims of his
people to the national consideration. Like every intelligent observer of events, he had noted that while
the rebellion had progressed considerably, the status
of the colored people had shown no decided change.
The policy of the army relative to the slaves was
vague and undefined, and, in many instances, brutal,
while the fidelity and devotion of these blacks to the
Union army find no parallel in modern times away
from the pages of romance. No overdrawn picture, but
abounding with truthful figures, while from its background arise countless suggestions to the nation, was
that gracefully presented by Major Nichols in his
"Story of the Great March," when he said, "The negroes all tell the general that the falsehoods of the
rebel papers never deceived them, and that they believed his 'retreats' sure victories; that they would
serve the Union cause in any way, and in all ways, that

they could — as soldiers, as drivers, or pioneers. Indeed, the faith, earnestness, and heroism of the black men are among the grandest developments of this war. When I think of the universal testimony of our escaped soldiers, who enter our lines every day, that, in the hundreds of miles which they traverse on their way, they never ask the poor slave in vain for help; that the poorest negro hides and shelters them, and shares the last crumb with them, — all this impresses me with a weight of obligation and a love for them that stir the very depths of my soul."

Yet these services were not sufficient to save the bondman from being returned to his abject condition. This is familiar to all, especially in the early record of the army of the Potomac; and for a long time during the war these humiliating scenes were being enacted, either openly or under some constitutional disguise.

The word "contraband" had been spoken into history by the great radical convert; but neither that, nor the reticence of the president concerning the status of the blacks seeking the Union lines, gave light to the dark, deplorable situation.

The president was cognizant of these acts, as he at one time stated; but apportioning to himself but limited powers under the constitution, he hesitated to proceed beyond these limits, unless he had the support of the people. Silently he awaited the time when the country, aroused to its honor and best interest, would cast out from it this ghoul that had sustained itself on the life-blood of the nation. He at last issued his Emancipation Proclamation; yet this could not accomplish everything. After the capture of Chattanooga, a valiant commander wrote to Major-General Palmer in Kentucky, "Send the rebel sympathizers and their negroes down the river, out of the country, and let them seek a clime more congenial for themselves and their peculiar institution." Thus, whether displayed in military parade around Washington, or in cautious reconnoitrings on the banks of the Mississippi, or in the brilliant engagement of Chickamauga, to the terrible three days' struggle but glorious harvest of Gettysburg, the policy of the mighty armies of the Union converged to the same object — to ignore the negro's claims, and send the slave back to his master.

Delany viewed the moral bearing of this tendency upon the future of his people; he felt that in these repeated acts of injustice the energies of the blacks were fast being chilled.

On this subject he frequently expressed himself, and persistently urged measures then untouched as the only means which would insure success. He said when he made known his plans to his always noble-hearted friend, Frederick Douglass, he gave him encouragement, adding that he was no soldier himself, but had given two sons to the war.

There were others to whom he made these measures known, though not the plans by which he intended placing them before the president, among them we find the names of John Jones, Esq., of Detroit, his colleague "in office," Dr. Amos Aray, once associated with him, Mr. George Vosburg, a man of sterling worth among his people, Dr. Willis Revels, of Indianapolis, and others not unknown to fame.

In his zeal he endeavored to induce the leading

politicians among the colored people to unite upon some settled policy by which they should be governed, and to this end he addressed a letter through a paper supported by them in New York, invoking a national convention of the representative men, for the purpose of defining their position in relation to the war; but it failed to meet the general approbation.

. He saw the progress of the war producing contingencies, challenging policies, demanding of all some definite, immediate action. And the action of the president, apart from positive constitutional obligations, was based upon these. Under such circumstances, what need was most demanded *was reliable, adequate means*. These were best adapted to the desired end, and suggested by such as applied in person to the president.

He said, that " to wait upon the president at such a time to obtain anything from him could only be realized by having something, or plan, to offer the government, or it would be demonstrating an expression of Mr. Lincoln, with cap in hand, and ask, 'Mr. President, what have you to give me?' when the reply invariably was, 'Sir, what have you to offer me?'"

He saw at one time one of the possible contingencies of the war was an indication of foreign intervention. The government had its own methods and measures of meeting this event; but, aside from this, any aid would be acceptable. Where could this be found? Could it be made available? and who will offer it? were questions of importance with the government.

In view of the menacing attitude presented by two of the greatest powers of the world, with a probability of others following them, he addressed a letter on the subject to the Anglo-African, setting forth what he considered the best measure to be adopted by the colored people to the interest of the country in the event of foreign intervention. Another and most momentous contingency he viewed from his stand-point was, the probability of the south calling the blacks to arms. This event, to every intelligent observer of the times, was from the first of as much importance to the government as that of foreign intervention. It was not least among the complicated problems awaiting the solution of the nation; for while all others might be met by the general usages and laws of war, diplomacy, and force of arms, the last could only be met by measures at once unprecedented, and peculiar to the method of meeting belligerents.

To present the means of meeting these ends was certainly of vast importance to the government.

Thus, in view of the threat of Jefferson Davis to arm the blacks, as slaves to fight for the establishment of a slave confederacy, he argued that some means should be devised in order to frustrate this design.

To many of the leading colored men of the North, and the old abolitionists, this was comparatively an easy task, — having originated that great scheme known as the Underground Railroad, which, for nearly forty years had baffled the comprehension of their foes — a scheme so well devised and skilfully conducted, that from one to forty were continually being passed out of every part of the far South to Texas, Massachusetts, and Canada.

These men had the same means of reaching the

slaves, and through this medium could reach them, in order to prevent their joining their oppressors.

None expected at the beginning of the rebellion that, in its extreme weakness, the tottering Confederacy would call for aid from those its very first utterance had sought to consign to perpetual degradation. And we knew not what temptation would be held out the next hour, in order to secure the aim of the South. Therefore, can the means be made available immediately, was a matter of painful anxiety.

At length he determined on the execution of his long-designed plans. An event renewed his zeal. In January, 1865, he received a despatch from a friend to go to Indianapolis, as Governor Morton had proposed to raise two additional black regiments for the service. And this friend, to whose telegram he responded, had presented his claims to the consideration of the friends of the movement, hearing that they were determined, if possible, to secure the appointment of a black officer for the state, as acting superintendent, commissioned with the rank of captain.

But intelligence being soon after received from the secretary of war disapproving of the measure, he immediately returned to Wilberforce College, where, more fully to identify himself with the interests of the country, as well as to secure educational advantages for his children, he had previously removed his family from Canada. Thence he set out for Washington. During the time he was engaged in recruiting for the service, he had been a keen observer of measures developed in the progress of the rebellion. He had been in correspondence with many of the leading men of both races in the country, and in his own mind had been deducing measures applicable to the events transpiring relative to the colored people. Hence his presence in Washington, to see the chief magistrate, though well aware of the failure of others of his race who had preceded him there, to accomplish a satisfactory result. This consideration would have deterred many men, for among those who had sought the president were men noted for their high attainments and general popularity. Casting from him all suggestions of the impossibility of success by the strength of his character, without aid or adventitious surroundings, he struck out into a path before untrodden by others of his race.

How it was accomplished we propose to relate, as a part of the history of the great revolution, and as the crowning act of the noble president's life and his great secretary of war.

Said Dr. James McCune Smith of this movement, "Delany is a success among the colored men;" and subsequent events proved the correctness of the assertion.

11

CHAPTER XVIII.

PRIVATE COUNCIL AT WASHINGTON.

THE 6th of February, 1865, found him in Washington, for the purpose of having an interview, if possible, with President Lincoln and the secretary of war. To his friend, the Rev. Henry Highland Garnet, whose guest he was, he made known the principles on which he based his intended interview.

Mr. Garnet, living in Washington, and cognizant of every measure inaugurated among the colored people relative to the war, and remembering their ill success with the executive, at first attempted to discourage him. Mr. Garnet said to him, "Don't aim to say too much in that direction. While your position is a good one, yet I am afraid you will not see the president. So many of our men have called upon him of late, all expecting something, and coming away dissatisfied, some of them openly complaining, that I am fearful he has come to the conclusion to receive no more black visitors." To this he replied, "Mr. Garnet, I see you are mistaken in regard to my course. I am here to ask nothing of the president, but to offer him something for the government. If it suits him, and he accepts, I will take anything he may offer me in return."

His friend, still persisting, responded to him : said he,

"Doctor, I see you are on the 'right track,' but I am fearful, after all, that you will not get to see him." On Major •Delany proposing the secretary of war as a medium through which to reach the president, Mr. Garnet exclaimed, " My dear sir, you have made matters worse. I have been abroad; I have been near the persons of nobility and royalty; but I never saw personages so hard to reach as the heads of government in Washington." This information by no means deterred him. It was impossible for a host to turn Martin Delany from his task, determined as he was to continue it to the end.

He remarked to the reverend gentleman that "the mansion of every government has outer and inner doors, the outer defended by guards; the security of the inner is usually a secret, except to the inmates of the council-chamber. Across this inner lies a ponderous beam, of the finest quality, highly polished, designed only for the finest cabinet-work; it can neither be stepped over nor passed around, and none can enter except this is moved away; and he that enters is the only one to remove it at the time, which is the required passport for his admission. I can pass the outer door, through the guards, and I am persuaded that I can move this polished beam of cabinet-work, and I will do it."

Mr. Garnet, becoming convinced by his persistency, that if that strength of will and perseverance of a most untiring character, which had contributed so much to his successes on other occasions, could avail, then his friend's success in this case was certain. Turning to his lady, who was present, he said, " I believe he will do it. Go, my brother," added he, "and may God speed you to a full accomplishment of your desires." The lady's response, "Of course he will," was not without effect, coming when most needed, and ratifying a faith in perseverance.

He set himself to work to devise some means by which to gain the desired interview, and succeeded so far, that on Monday, 8th of February, he sent his card up to the president, and on the same afternoon, about three o'clock, while visiting the patent office, a message was received by him, that an audience was granted for the next morning at eight o'clock.

The auspicious morning dawned upon him, and the appointed hour found him advanced within the "outer gate." The president was absent, at the war department. But not unmindful of his engagement, he left a messenger to be sent after him.

In the appointment of Martin Delany, it was for no holiday service, or for conciliatory measures towards the colored people and their friends, for that could have been more easily and consistently effected by promoting some from among the gallant soldiers already in the service. Their heroism and endurance in the field, their discipline and manly bearing in the camp, are the nation's household stories. Familiar to all is the splendid martial fame acquired by the colored regiments of Massachusetts, while their repeated refusal, to a man, *for nearly one year*, to receive from the government less than the fulfilment of its pledges, under which they enrolled as soldiers of Massachusetts, has passed into the history of our country, furnishing an attitude of the moral sublime unparalleled amid the many glorious achievements of our war.

But the new appointment was made to carry out certain policies of the administration, which remain undeveloped in consequence of the termination of the rebellion.

If the rebellion had continued, these measures would have been developed of necessity, and like all other good measures of the war, would have been approved by a generous public sentiment. But the war having ceased, they remain on record, to the honor of the two great heads and hearts that conceived them and anticipated their adoption.

In speaking of Mr. Stanton, he says, " The secretary of war ever stood side by side with the great and good President Lincoln, in every advanced measure. He stood foremost in the cabinet in the interest of the colored people. Now that the president has passed away, I trust that the noble war minister will receive the reward due to him by a grateful people."

CHAPTER XIX.

THE COUNCIL-CHAMBER. — PRESIDENT LINCOLN.

WE give in Major Delany's own language his interview with President Lincoln.

He tells us, "On entering the executive chamber, and being introduced to his excellency, a generous grasp and shake of the hand brought me to a seat in front of him. No one could mistake the fact that an able and master spirit was before me. Serious without sadness, and pleasant withal, he was soon seated, placing himself at ease, the better to give me a patient audience. He opened the conversation first.

"'What can I do for you, sir?' he inquired.

"'Nothing, Mr. President,' I replied; 'but I've come to propose something to you, which I think will be beneficial to the nation in this critical hour of her peril.' I shall never forget the expression of his countenance and the inquiring look which he gave me when I answered him.

"'Go on, sir,' he said, as I paused through deference to him. I continued the conversation by reminding him of the full realization of arming the blacks of the South, and the ability of the blacks of the North to defeat it by complicity with those at the South, through the medium of the *Underground Railroad* — a measure known only to themselves.

"I next called his attention to the fact of the heartless and almost relentless prejudice exhibited towards the blacks by the Union army, and that something ought to be done to check this growing feeling against the slave, else nothing that we could do would avail. And if such were not expedited, all might be lost. That the blacks, in every capacity in which they had been called to act, had done their part faithfully and well. To this Mr. Lincoln readily assented. I continued: 'I would call your attention to another fact of great consideration; that is, the position of confidence in which they have been placed, when your officers have been under obligations to them, and in many instances even the army in their power. As pickets, scouts, and guides, you have trusted them, and found them faithful to the duties assigned; and it follows that if you can find them of higher qualifications, they may, with equal credit, fill higher and more important trusts.'

" ' *Certainly*,' replied the president, in his most emphatic manner. 'And what do you propose to do?' he inquired.

"I responded, 'I propose this, sir; but first permit me to say that, whatever I may desire for black men in the army, I know that there exists too much prejudice among the whites for the soldiers to serve under a black commander, or the officers to be willing to associate with him. These are facts which must be admitted, and, under the circumstances, must be regarded, as they cannot be ignored. And I propose, as a most effective remedy to prevent enrolment of the blacks

in the rebel service, and induce them to run to, instead
of from, the Union forces — the commissioning and
promotion of black men **now in the** army, according to
merit.'

"Looking at me for a moment, earnestly yet anxiously, he demanded, 'How will you remedy the great
difficulty you have just now so justly described, about
the objections of white soldiers to colored **commanders,**
and officers to colored associates?'

"I replied, 'I have the remedy, Mr. President,
which has not yet been stated; and it is the most important suggestion **of** my visit to you. And I think it
is just what is required to complete the prestige of the
Union army. I propose, sir, an army of blacks, **com-**
manded entirely by black officers, except such whites
as may volunteer **to** serve; this army to penetrate
through the heart of the South, and make conquests,
with the banner of Emancipation unfurled, proclaiming
freedom as they go, sustaining and protecting it **by**
arming the emancipated, taking them **as fresh troops,**
and leaving a few veterans among the **new** freedmen,
when occasion requires, keeping this banner unfurled
until **every slave** is free, according to the letter of your
proclamation. **I** would also take from those already in
the service all that are competent for commission officers, and establish at once in the South a camp of in-
structions. By **this we** could have in about three
months an army of forty thousand blacks in motion,
the presence of which anywhere would itself be a
power irresistible. You should have an army of
blacks, President Lincoln, commanded entirely by
blacks, **the** sight **of** which is required to give confi-

dence to the slaves, and retain them to the Union, stop foreign intervention, and speedily bring the war to a close.'

" 'This,' replied the president, 'is the very thing I have been looking and hoping for; but nobody offered it. I have thought it over and over again. I have talked about it; I hoped and prayed for it; but till now it never has been proposed. White men couldn't do this, because they are doing all in that direction now that they can; but we find, for various reasons, it does not meet the case under consideration. The blacks should go to the interior, and the whites be kept on the frontiers.'

" 'Yes, sir,' I interposed; 'they would require but little, as they could subsist on the country as they went along.'

" 'Certainly,' continued he; 'a few light artillery, with the cavalry, would comprise your principal advance, because all the siege work would be on the frontiers and waters, done by the white division of the army. Won't this be a grand thing?' he exclaimed, joyfully. He continued, 'When I issued my Emancipation Proclamation, I had this thing in contemplation. I then gave them a chance by prohibiting any interference on the part of the army; but they did not embrace it,' said he, rather sadly, accompanying the word with an emphatic gesture.

" 'But, Mr. President,' said I, 'these poor people could not read your proclamation, nor could they know anything about it, only, when they did hear, to know that they were free.'

" 'But you of the North I expected to take advantage of it,' he replied.

"'Our policy, sir,' I answered, 'was directly opposite, supposing that it met your approbation. To this end I published a letter against embarrassing or compromising the government in any manner whatever; for us to remain passive, except in case of foreign intervention, then immediately to raise the slaves to insurrection.'

"'Ah, I remember the letter,' he said, 'and thought at the time that you mistook my designs. But the effect will be better as it is, by giving character to the blacks, both North and South, as a peaceable, inoffensive people.' Suddenly turning, he said, 'Will you take command?'

"'If there be none better qualified than I am, sir, by that time I will. While it is my desire to serve, as black men we shall have to prepare ourselves, as we have had no opportunities of experience and practice in the service as officers.'

"'That matters but little, comparatively,' he replied; 'as some of the finest officers we have never studied the tactics till they entered the army as subordinates. And again,' said he, 'the tactics are easily learned, especially among your people. It is the head that we now require most — men of plans and executive ability.'

"'I thank you, Mr. President,' said I, 'for the —'

"'No — not at all,' he interrupted.

"'I will show you some letters of introduction, sir,' said I, putting my hand in my pocket to get them.

"'Not now,' he interposed; 'I know all about you. I see nothing now to be done but to give you a line of introduction to the secretary of war.'

"Just as he began writing, the cannon commenced booming.

"'Stanton is firing! listen! he **is in his glory! noble man!**' he exclaimed.

"'What is it, Mr. President?' **I asked.**

"'The firing!'

"'What is it about, sir,' I reiterated, ignorant of the cause.

"'Why, don't you know? Haven't you heard the news? Charleston is ours!' he answered, straightening up from the table on which he was writing for an instant, and then resuming it. He soon handed me a card, on which was written, —

'February 8, 1865.

'Hon. E. M. Stanton, *Secretary of War*.

'Do not fail to have an interview with this most extraordinary and intelligent black man.

'A. Lincoln.'

"This card showed he perfectly understood my views and feelings; hence he was not content that my color should make its own impression, but he expressed it with emphasis, as though a point was gained. The thing desired presented itself; not simply a man that was *black*, because these had previously presented themselves, in many delegations and committees, — men of the highest intelligence, — for various objects; but that which he had wished and hoped for, their own proposed measures matured in the council-chamber had never been fully presented to them in the person of a black man."

This, then, was what was desired to complete the plans of the president and his splendid minister, the secretary of war. The "ponderous beam," being removed, to use his figurative expression, his passport was clear to every part of the mansion. He entered the war department for the purpose of seeing the minister. As he entered, a glance revealed to him the presiding genius of the situation, surrounded by his assistants. In the room was a pressing crowd of both sexes, representing nearly every condition of life, each in turn endeavoring to reach the centre of the room, where, at an elevated desk, stood one of the greatest men of the times, and the able director of the war department.

After he had sent forward his card, he was requested by the secretary in person, to whom he was not previously unknown, to call at the department again.

He had gained the interview with the president that he wished, and the indications were brighter than his most sanguine expectations had promised. The war minister's influence alone could effect the balance.

He sought Dr. William Elder, the distinguished biographer of Dr. Kane, of Arctic memory, who was then chief of the bureau of statistics, and gave him an account of his mission to the president.

After explaining everything to the doctor, his face assuming an expression peculiar to himself, of a wholesouled satisfaction, he exclaimed, "I'll be hanged if I haven't got the thing! just the thing! Will you give me that in writing?" he asked; "I mean the points touched upon, that may be written in a letter to me."

On receiving it, in the afternoon of the same day, after he had read it, he turned to the future major, and said, "*You shall* have what you want," in like manner as he replied to a speech of Louis Kossuth, when he told him if he went to war with Austria, *he shouldn't die.*

When Delany left Dr. Elder, he was thoroughly convinced, that if the secretary of war could **be influenced** by any man, in regard **to** his mission, in none abler could he depend than **upon this true and earnest advocate of his race.**

The next call at the war department was made **the** following Monday, **the 12th** inst. His reception there, being equally as cordial as the first, seemed **already to** indicate success to his measures.

"What do **you** propose to do, doctor?" asked the secretary, as Dr. Delany began to explain to him as he did **to** the president. "I understand the whole thing, and fully comprehend your design ; I have frequently gone over the whole ground, in council with the president. What **do you** wish? What position?" He replied, —

"In any position or place whatever, **in which I may** be instrumental in promoting the measures proposed, and be of service to the country, so that I am **not subject** and subordinate to every man who holds a commission, **and, with** such, chooses to assume authority."

"Will you take the field?" asked the secretary.

"I should **like to do so** as soon **as** possible, but not until I have **had** sufficient discipline and practice in a camp of instruction, and a sufficient number of black **officers to** command each regiment," **was** the answer given.

"Of course," said the secretary, "**you** must establish your camp of instruction; and as **you have a general** knowledge of the qualified colored men of the country, I propose to commission you **at once, and** send you South to commence raising troops, to be commanded by black officers, on the principles you proposed, of which I most highly approve, to prevent all clashing or jealousy, — because of no contact to arouse prejudices. It is none of white men's business what rank a black man holds over his own people. I shall assign you to Charleston, with advices and instructions to Major General Saxton. Do you know him?" he asked. Being answered, he continued, "He is an unflinching friend of your race. You will impart to him, in detail, that which will not be written. The letter giving special instructions will be given to you — all further instructions to be obtained at the department."

Assistant Adjutant General of Volunteers Colonel C. W. Foster, at this juncture having been sent for, was instructed by the secretary of war to take him to his department, and make the necessary examination; there being no rejection, to prepare and fill out a parchment, with commission of *Major of Infantry*, the *regiment* to be left blank, to be filled by order of Major General Saxton, according to instructions to be given, and to report the next morning at eleven o'clock.

After the examination by the adjutant general, he remarked, "This is certainly an important and interesting feature of the war. And the secretary must expect much to be done by you, for he certainly holds you in high esteem."

"I hope, colonel," he replied, "that neither the honorable secretary of war nor the government will expect too much from an individual like myself. My only hope is, that I may be able to do my duty well and satisfactorily."

"I have no fears for your success," returned the colonel; "you have qualifications and ability, and must succeed, when your chances are such as they will now be. This is a great thing for **you**," he continued, "and you have now an opportunity of making yourself *any-thing that you please*, and doing for your race all that may be required at the hands of the government." He, attempting to thank the colonel for the encouraging as well as complimentary remarks, was stopped by him, saying, "I speak as I think and feel about it. The secretary has great confidence in you, and I simply wish to indorse it for your encouragement. There is nothing now to be done," he continued, "but to call to-morrow, and go with me to the war department to report finally to the secretary of war, and receive your commission from his hands." All arrangements being completed in the adjutant's department, he withdrew.

CHAPTER XX.

THE GOLD LEAF.

NO Sabbath in war times, we are told, and there was no exception in this case. The following morning (Sabbath), in accordance with the appointment, Delany reported himself at the office of the adjutant general, who accompanied him to the war department. Here the secretary, making the necessary inquiries of the adjutant, received the parchment from him. History repeated itself—the Hebrew in the palaces, the Hun in high places. At that moment the great war minister of our revolution, affixing his official signature, made an epoch in the history of a hitherto unrecognized race, and a pledge in the name of the nation to them irrevocable through all time. It seemed remarkable that in two hemispheres this man should be selected from among so many others to represent marked events in .the history of his race! Says Lamartine, " We should not despise any, for the finger of destiny marks in the soul, and not upon the brow."

So long had Delany fought against error and injustice towards his race, that it seemed almost hopeless to witness, in his day, the faintest semblance of recognition of their right in this land, and for him to be the first to receive that appointment seemed indeed to promise an age "of better metal."

While the interesting ceremony was being performed,
a major general entered the apartment, followed soon
after by Senator Ben Wade, of Ohio, now president of
the Senate, before whom the new officer was addressed
for the first time with a military title.

"Gentlemen," said the secretary, "I am just now creating a black field officer for the United States service."
Then, addressing himself directly to the new officer, he
said, "Major Delany, I take great pleasure in handing
you this commission of *Major* in the United States army. You are the first of your race who has been thus
honored by the government; therefore much depends
and will be expected of you. But I feel assured it is
safe in your hands."

"Honorable Secretary," replied the major, as the
secretary concluded his remarks, "I can assure you,
whatever be my failure to meet the expectations concerning me, on one thing you may depend, — that
this parchment will never be dishonored in my hands."

"Of this I am satisfied. God bless you! Good by."
With a hearty shake of the hand, the secretary concluded, when the first black major in the history of the
republic left the department.

If the war had not ended so soon after the major received his commission, there exists no doubt but that
his merits would have received further recognition.
It is unlikely that the government would have given
an unmeaning promotion, and thus debar him from
rising to the higher ranks of the army through the
same medium as other officers. On returning to the
office of the adjutant general, the adjutant remarked,
"Major Delany, you have now a great charge intrusted

to you, — a great responsibility, certainly, and much will be expected of you, both by your friends and others. You have now an opportunity, if the war continues, of rising in your position to the highest field rank — that of a major general."

His reply was, that he hoped to be able to perform his duty, so as to merit the approval of his government and his superior officers, and, as a matter of course, intimated courteously that further promotion would not be unacceptable to him.

The following commission is in the usual form; but, being the first on the records of our country credited to a colored American, we reproduce it here.

The Secretary of War of the United States of America.

TO ALL WHO SHALL SEE THESE PRESENTS, GREETING:

Know ye, that, reposing special trust and confidence in the patriotism, valor, fidelity, and abilities of MARTIN R. DELANY, the President does hereby appoint him Major, in the One Hundred and Fourth Regiment of United States Colored Troops, in the service of the United States, to rank as such from the day of his muster into service, by the duly appointed commissary of musters, for the command to which said regiment belongs.

He is therefore carefully and diligently to discharge the duty of Major, by doing and performing all manner of things thereunto belonging. And I do strictly charge, and require, all officers and soldiers under his command to be obedient to his orders as Major. And he is to observe and follow such orders and directions, from time to time, as he shall receive from me or the future Secretary of War, or other superior officers set over him, according to the rules and discipline of war. This appointment to continue in force during the pleasure of the President for the time being.

Given under my hand at the War Department, in the City of

Washington, D. C., this twenty-sixth day of February, in the year of our Lord one thousand eight hundred and sixty-five.

By the Secretary of War.

EDWIN M. STANTON, *Secretary of War.*

C. W. FOSTER, *Assistant Adjutant General Volunteers.*

(*Indorsement.*)

Mustered into the United States Service, February 27, 1865.

HENRY KETELLAS, *Captain 15th Infantry,*

Chief Muster and District Officer.

ADJUTANT GENERAL'S OFFICE, }
WASHINGTON, Feb. 27, 1865. }

Sir: I forward herewith **your** appointment of Major in the U. S. Colored Troops; **your receipt** and acceptance of which **you will** please acknowledge without delay, reporting at the same time **your** *age* and *residence*, **when** appointed, the *state* where *born*, and your full *name* correctly **written.** *Fill up, subscribe*, and return as soon as possible, the accompanying *oath*, **duly** and carefully *executed.*

You will report in person to Brevet Major General R. Saxton, Beaufort, South Carolina.

I am, sir, very respectfully,

Your obedient servant,

C. W. FOSTER,

Assistant Adjutant General Volunteers.

Major MARTIN R. DELANY, *U. S. Colored Troops.*

WAR DEPARTMENT, A. G. OFFICE, }
WASHINGTON, D. C., Feb. 27, 1865. }

Captain HENRY KETELLAS, 15th *U. S. Infantry,*

Commissary of Musters :

I am directed by the Secretary of War **to instruct you to mus**ter Major Martin R. Delany, U. S. Colored **Troops,** regiment into the service of the United States, for the period of three years, or during the war, as of this date.

Very respectfully, **your** obedient **servant,**

(Signed) C. W. FOSTER,

Assistant Adjutant General Volunteers.

Official copy, respectfully furnished for the information of Major Martin R. Delany, U. S. Colored Troops.

C. W. FOSTER,
Assistant Adjutant General Volunteers.

WAR DEPARTMENT, A. G. OFFICE, }
WASHINGTON, Feb. 27, 1865. }

Brevet Major General R. SAXTON, *Supt. Recruitment and*
Organization of Colored Troops, **Dept. of the**
South, Hilton Head, S. C.

General: I am directed by the Secretary of War to inform you that the bearer, *Major M. R. Delany,* U. S. Colored Troops, has been appointed for the purpose of aiding and assisting you in recruiting and organizing colored troops, and to carry out this object you will assign him to duty in the city of Charleston, S. C.

You will observe that the regiment to which Major *Delany* is appointed is not designated, although he has been mustered into service. You will cause Major *Delany* to be assigned to, and his name placed upon the rolls of, the first regiment of colored troops you may organize, with his proper rank, not, however, with a view to his duty in such regiment.

I am also directed to say, that Major *Delany* has the entire confidence of the Department.

I have the honor to be, very respectfully,
Your obedient servant,

(Signed)   C. W. FOSTER,
Assistant Adjutant General Volunteers.

Official.   C. W. FOSTER,
Assistant Adjutant General Volunteers.

CHAPTER XXI.

IN THE FIELD.

THE appointment of the black officer was received, as such advanced measures are generally, with comments of all shades. By the friends of progress it was hailed with general satisfaction.

True there was, prior to his appointment, one of *like* rank, but differing in position — that of Dr. Augusta, of Canada, who was accepted after a most rigid examination, as is customary in such cases.

But in the appointment of this field officer there existed an indisputable recognition of the claims of his race to the country. With this interpretation those who formerly hesitated in accepting the policy of the administration now upheld it with confidence. And from the golden leaf of promise, borne upon the shoulders of the first black officer, a light clear and steady seemed to shine forth, illumining with a strange, wild splendor the hitherto dark pages of his people's history, heralding the glory of the future to them.

Before he left Washington, he communicated with colored men, as far as was prudent, to make the necessary preparation in the event of a black army being organized, to be commanded by black officers. For in the Union army there were many men, from the North especially, **of fine talent and** scholastic attainments, who, from their experience **and** knowledge gained in the military campaigns, could **at once be** made available.

Certain leading spirits of the "*Underground Railroad*" **were** invoked.   Scouts *incog.* were already "**on** to Richmond," and the services of the famous Harriet Tubman, having been secured **to serve in the South,** had received **her** transportation for Charleston, **S. C.**

These arrangements being effected, he went to Cleveland, Ohio, to meet a council of his co-laborers, in order **to** enforce suitable measures by which the slave enlistment **might be** prevented, and to demoralize those **already** enrolled, as rumors had reached the North of such enlistment having been started at Richmond.

With his friend **George** Vosburg, Esq., in the lead, whom he likens always to "a flame alive, but unseen," the most active measures were instituted at this council, as their proceedings **show.**

These gave evidence that the appointment of one of their number was recognized by **them as an** appeal, though the day was far spent of the country's need for the aid of the colored men of the North, and at the first *certain sound* they hastened with their offerings.

A few days were spent at his home, preparing for his departure; and being delayed on the way by a freshet, he did not reach New York until the second day after the departure **of** the steamer for Charleston.   While it delayed the principal measures, **it gave him a** week in New **York,** in which to perfect preliminary arrangements.   Here business of importance was entered upon, and the eloquent William Howard Day, M. A., was chosen to arrange the *military policy* of the *underground railroad* relative to the *slave enlistment.*

Mr. Day, in obedience to instructions of the plans laid **down, and in anticipation of some** appointment, such as his splendid talents entitled him to, performed the task with ability and earnestness. There were others among the leading colored men who showed their appreciation of this movement; among them the learned Rev. J. W. C. Pennington, D. D., **as the following** extract from his letter, dated March 29, 1863, will show : —

"Major: Finding that our views so nearly harmonize in reference to arming the slaves, I will give you **one of** the illustrations **I use in** my lecture on the **duty of** interposing our efforts to prevent **the** rebels **from** consummating the act: 'We **have** noticed **by** *their own* papers that the rebel authorities have **many of** their great meetings in the African church in Richmond. It was there that Benjamin, the rebel secretary of state, first publicly announced the **plan** of arming the slaves. Did the pastor of that colored church and **his** congregation have the privilege of taking part **in** that meeting? **Not a bit of it.** Did they have the privilege of holding **a meeting on the** subject themselves in their own place of worship? No.

"'What was the object of the rebels in holding their **great** meetings in the African church? **W**as it because it is one of the largest buildings in the city? **No, they** had another object. That was, to *suppress any Union feelings that exist among the hundreds of slaves and free people of color who compose that congregation, and to palm off the lie to the world that they are* *friendly to the colored people, and that those people are acting freely with them.*

"'Look at the devilish impudence of this scheme of holding meetings in the African church! It is to drag the slaves and colored Christians with them into all the wickedness of the rebellion. Now, it is asked, Why we do not hear a voice from the pastor of that church and his people? The answer is obvious. They are prevented by the FORCE of CIRCUMSTANCES from speaking a word.

"'If the Son of God should enter that house, as he did the temple at Jerusalem (Mark xi. 15, 16), and thus give that congregation the right of free speech, you would soon hear a voice going out from that church, that would reach every slave in the South, telling them which way to fight. And that church will speak as soon as Grant takes Richmond! And who does not long for the day when that, the largest colored church in the United States shall be free? Who would not aid in that great forward movement of the Army of the Potomac, that will result in clearing Richmond? But in this state of facts as to that church, *we have precisely* the position of the 200,000 slaves whom the rebels are about to arm against us!

"'Let us not forget what slavery is. It is based upon the assumption, first, that the slave has no will of his own; second, that his sole business is to obey orders. Hence they will be put into the rebel army *as slaves*, to all intents and purposes, and substantially under slave discipline; they will be surrounded by circumstances which will make it far more difficult for them to escape than many think; and of course, for

the time being, they would be COMPELLED to do us
untold injury. What, then, is our duty? Our duty is
to *anticipate* the action of the rebels — organize, plan,
and go forward, and **settle** the case for our brethren.
We have no right to stand still, and presume that they
will, when armed, turn at once on our side. And it is
cruel to prejudge them in the matter. Our duty is **to**
carry out the letter and spirit of the Proclamation of
Freedom. It would be an awful state of things **to**
see the 200,000 Union **colored** soldiers confronted by
200,000 of our own race, under the rebel banner! . . .
No, this must not be. It shall not be. It **cannot be**
if we do our duty. That is, to go to our brethren, and
tell them what to do.' "

A romantic incident is related in connection with the
the Cleveland council. As Delany concluded, a moment
of intense interest and silence followed, and suddenly an
interesting girl of some fourteen years sprang to her
feet, and rushed up **to the** platform where he stood,
gently resting her hand upon his arm, and anxiously
looking up into his face, exclaimed, " O, Major Delany,
I ask one favor of you: will you spare my grandfather
when you reach **Charleston**?" Giving the name of her
grandfather in the same excited breath, she continued,
" Spare him and grandma! There sits my ma: for her
sake, if not mine, spare my dear grandpa's family."

He strove to calm her anxiety, assuring her of the
security of her grandfather's family, even if the genuine
Schemmelfening had not already had the city. His
mission was not with fire and sword for indiscriminate
slaughter, but rather to guide his brethren to liberty.

On his arrival in Charleston, the honored grandparents, unconscious of this incident, were among the earliest callers to give him welcome, and to offer him the generous civilities of their family; and these were ever after numbered among his most esteemed friends.

In expectation of a continuance of the war, he writes, " I was anxious to reach my destination, organize the black army, and see that elegant mulatto gentleman as field officer, hear his rich, deep-toned voice as he rode along the lines, giving command, or shouting in the deadly conflict, rallying the troops on to victory. Such a sight I desired to see in the cause of liberty and the Union. For William Howard Day, unobstrusive as he appears, is a brave, determined man: once aroused, he is as a panther, that knows no fear. But now that the war is ended, his aid in the battle-field will not be required. And the Union will be safe if reëstablished on the basis of righteousness, truth, and justice."

Leaving New York, and having secured the ablest workers with whom to begin the great mission intrusted to him, he arrived at Hilton Head, and in the same afternoon at Beaufort.

This beautiful little town, facing a bay of equal beauty, but of tortuous winding, never gave promise of rivalling or imitating the cities of Charleston and Savannah on either side in commercial greatness. In fact, its population was limited almost exclusively to the planters of the adjoining islands and their slaves, a few free colored families, and a less number of poor whites. The salubrity of the climate enhanced its attractions, and made it desirable as the summer residence of many of the wealthy magnates. The town was abandoned

by the entire white population at the approach of the
naval force.   Here were the headquarters of Brevet
Major General Saxton, at which Major Delany reported
himself for duty, immediately on his arrival.   Some
time afterwards, speaking of the noble general who
led, by sealed orders, the first campaign sent forth to
proclaim *emancipation*, he said that in his frequent
intercourse with him there, he was soon convinced that
the friends of his race were not confined to the executive department at Washington.   This may be considered as the general opinion uttered by him; for
among the colored people and *poor whites* of South
Carolina, General **Rufus Saxton** stood as the beloved
friend and benefactor, and esteemed among his brother
officers generally as a gentleman and soldier.

At the post, while every officer rode with a black
orderly, General Saxton's orderly *was white!*

The post was in active preparation for the flag raising at Sumter.   And on the Saturday previous to the
memorable 19th of April, the general and staff, Major
Delany accompanying the party, sailed for Charleston.

Prior to leaving Beaufort he received the following
order : —

Head Qrs. Supt. Recruitment and Organization
Colored Troops, Department of the South,
Beaufort, S. C., April 5, 1865.

Special Orders. **No. 7.**

I. *Major M. R. Delany,* United States Colored Troops, in accordance with orders received from the War Department, will
proceed without delay to Charleston, S. C., reporting in person to
Lieutenant Colonel R. P. Hutchins, 94th Ohio Volunteer Infan-

try, Recruiting Officer at that post, for the purpose of aiding in the recruitment of troops.

II. *Major Delany* will visit the freedmen of Charleston and vicinity, and urge them to enlist in the military service of the United States, reporting by letter from time to time to these headquarters the result of his labors.

        By order of   Brevet Major General R. SAXTON,

                   Gen. Supt. Rect. & O. C. P. D. S.

STUART M. TAYLOR, *Asst. Adjt. Gen.*

Major M. R. DELANY, U. S. C. T.

CHAPTER XXII.

AT CHARLESTON AND FORT SUMTER.

THE excitement attending the scenes of the evacuation of the city and its occupation by the Union forces was scarcely lulled, when it rose again on the arrival of the "black major," to whom the rumor preceding his advent had given the rank of *Major General.*

Arriving in the city on the Sabbath, when most of the people were gathered at the various places of worship, the news soon became noised about. And from the early forenoon until long after nightfall, a continuous stream of visitors poured in upon him, eager to pay their respects to him. These composed the colored residents of both sexes, representing every age and condition; nor did this cease when their curiosity became satisfied, but grew with their acquaintance and increased with time. At the time of his arrival the population of the once proud city was limited, consisting only of a few regiments of Union soldiers on duty, the former free people, the new freedmen, — a greater portion of the latter being driven from the plantations around the city, and from the upper portions of the state, — and a few white families representing the old element. An air of mournful desolation seemed to brood over the conquered city. There existed no signs of traffic, except in the sutlers' stores of the regiments.

Confederate bonds and scrip were most plenteous, and but a small amount of currency was in circulation with which to purchase the common necessaries of life. For this cause thousands were thrown upon the charity of the government for daily subsistence. Nor was it confined to the colored people; it was no uncommon sight to meet daily in the streets many of the former enemies of the government, loaded with its injustice (!) to them in the form of a huge basket of subsistence received from the quartermaster's department, and in many instances assisted by some former chattel, who in several known cases, afterwards, with true negro generosity, divided their own portion with them. Such was their position after the evacuation of the city. Never before in the history of Anglo-Saxon civilization were there such manifestations of genuine charity and forbearance towards an unscrupulous and implacable foe, as indicated by the actions of government. "I was hungry and ye gave me meat, naked and ye clothed me," were literally proven by these recipients of its immense charities. This gave promise of more converts than the sword. While the great concourse of people, gathered for rations at different places, attracted thither the curious visitor, he would turn from this to the many evidences of the unerring precision of the batteries of Morris Island, which met his gaze on every hand, suggestive of the tales of horror, and in many instances of retributive justice, through which they had so recently passed. Much property was destroyed and but few lives during the siege.

There were incidents related of marvellous escapes from the reach of these shells, and also deaths of a most appalling character on being overtaken by them, — the greater portion of the latter being colored **persons**, the innocent sharing a worse fate than the guilty.

One case of sad interest happened at midnight, while the siege was at its height, occurring in a family representing the wealth, culture, and refinement of the respectable colored citizens of the city.   The father of **this** family, a man of great mechanical genius, accumulated considerable property and established for himself a well-earned reputation as a skilful machinist throughout the state.   They were aroused one night by the noise which usually precedes the near approach of a shell, which was seen by a member of the family to fall within a few feet of the house, who, occupying the third story of the building, attempted to escape below with his wife; but before either could escape from the room, a second report was heard, followed almost immediately by the appearance of a shell entering the roof above them, crashing through the ceilings, which, in covering the latter with its *débris*, preserved her life, the fragments scattering, one of the pieces falling into the front room beneath, only disfiguring a bedstead, but not injuring its occupants, while another piece, more remorseless, taking another direction, entered the back room, burying itself in the side of an interesting boy of twelve years, the little grandson of the old gentleman.   The child, startled from its sleep by the double shock of the explosion and terrible wound, rushed from the room, exclaiming, in his agony, "Mother! mother! I am killed!"   It was eleven days of the most excruciating agony before the angel of death relieved little Weston McKenlay.   Never did Christianity and true womanhood beam more beauteously than at the moment when the mother of that child, relating the wild confusion of that night, laying aside her own personal sorrow, said, "It was God's will that the deliverance of the South should cost us all something." Major Delany, in speaking of this class of Charlestonians, as well as the colored people generally, says, "Their courtesy and natural kindness I have never seen equalled, while instances of their humanity to the Union prisoners at the risk of their own lives, speak in trumpet tones to their credit, of which the country is already cognizant." On Tuesday after his arrival, an immense gathering greeted him at Zion's Church, the largest in the city, indescribable in enthusiasm and numbers.   In the church were supposed to be upwards of three thousand, while the yard and street leading to the church were densely packed.

The resolutions passed on this memorable occasion by them we present here, embodying a testimony of their gratitude for their signal deliverance from a conflagration which threatened to involve them in a general desolation, and of their patriotism, setting aside forever the error that the sympathies of the free colored citizens were enlisted on the side of their enemies, and not that of the Union, for many they were who participated in this meeting.   We reproduce it also as expressive of the sentiments gushing from the hearts of a people for the first time in their history holding a political meeting on the soil of Carolina, with *open doors*, with none to condemn it as "an unlawful assemblage," amenable to law for the act.

Brevet Major General Saxton, and other distinguished officers were present, and freely **took** part **in the** proceedings. Here Major Delany, for the first time, introduced the subject foremost in his mind, that of raising an armée d'Afrique, which subject met **the enthusiastic** approval of his auditors, and the movement for its organization soon became popular.

The eventful 14th of April, which **was so eagerly awaited**, came, and the earliest beams of the morning found the "City of the Sea" alive with preparations for **the** brilliant scene at Sumter, unconscious of its fearful tragic close at Washington. The city was almost deserted during the ceremony in the harbor, for all were anxious to witness the flag **in** its accustomed place, with its higher, truer symbol, placed there by the same hands which were once compelled to lower it to **a jubilant** but now conquered foe, maddened prior **to** their destruction. As the old silken bunting winged itself to **its** long-deserted staff, thousands of shouts, and prayers fervent and deep, accompanying, greeted its reappearance.

Major Delany embarked to witness the ceremony **on the** historical **steamer Planter**, with its gallant **commander**, Robert Small, **whose** deeds will live **in song and** story, whose unparalleled feat and heroic courage in the harbor of Charleston, under the bristling guns of rebel batteries, bearing comparison with **the** proudest record **of our war**, will remain, commemorative of negro strategy and valor.

On the quarter-deck **of the** steamer **the** major remained an interested **witness**. Beside him stood one, whose father, believing and loving the doctrine that all

13

men were born free and equal, and within sight of the emblem of freedom as it floated from the battlements of Sumter, dared to aim a blow by which to free his race. Betrayed before his plans were matured, the scaffold gave to Denmark Vesey and his twenty-two slave-hero compatriots in Charleston, South Carolina, in 1822, the like answer which Charlestown, Virginia, gave John Brown in 1859.

Virginia was free, and black soldiers were now quartered in the citadel of Charleston, and garrisoned Fort Sumter. The martyred reformers had not died in vain.

The excitement attending the scene continued during the week, occasioned by the presence of the distinguished company who came to participate in the restoration of the flag at Fort Sumter. There were seen the veterans of the anti-slavery cause, the inspired and dauntless apostle of liberty, William Lloyd Garrison, the time-honored Joshua Leavitt, the eloquent George Thompson of England; then the glorious young editor of the Independent, the able and accomplished orator of the day, Rev. Henry Ward Beecher, Judge Kellogg, and others, all anxious to tell the truths of freedom to these hungry souls. The colored schools paraded the streets to honor these visitors, flanked by thousands of adults, marshalled by their superintendent and assistants, and led by stirring bands discoursing martial music, the citadel square densely crowded, and the great Zion's Church packed to overflowing. There were speakers on the stands erected on the square — speakers at the church. There were shouts for liberty and for the Union, shouts for their great liberator, shouts for the army, rousing cheers for the speakers, for their loved General Saxton, and for the "black major;" the people swayed to and fro like a rolling sea.

On Saturday morning, when the visitors left, an immense concourse followed to the **wharf; the** steamer seemed loaded with floral gifts, the graceful ovation of the colored people to their friends. Cheer after cheer resounded for a parting word from them. **They were answered by** Messrs. Thompson **and** Tilton; **at last** came forth the immortal Garrison in answer to an **irresistible** call.

Major Delany, describing this parting scene at the dock, says, "The mind was forcibly carried back to the days of the young and ardent advocate of emancipation, incarcerated in **a** Baltimore prison, peering through the gates and bars, hurling defiance at his cowardly opponents, exclaiming, 'No difficulty, no dangers, shall deter me: **at the East or at the** West, **at** the **North** or at the South, wherever Providence may **call** me, my voice shall be heard **in behalf** of the perishing slave, and against the claims of his oppressors.' **Again** did the mind revert to him in after years, as a man of high integrity in the city of Boston, led as a **beast to** the slaughter, with **the** lyncher's rope around his neck, only escaping death **by** imprisonment. When exhausted, he fell **to the floor,** exclaiming, 'Never was man so glad to get into **prison** before!' And in this his last speech he was more **sublime than ever.** There he stood in the harbor **of Charleston, surrounded by the** emancipated slave, giving his **last anti-slavery** advice :—

" 'And now, my friends, I bid you farewell. I have always advocated non-resistance; but this much I say.

to you, *Come what will never do you submit again to slavery! Do anything; die first! But don't submit again to them — never again be* **slaves.** Farewell.

"When the steamer gracefully glided from the pier, the music struck up in **stirring strains,** shouts rent the air, and the masses, after gazing with tearful eyes, commenced slowly retracing their steps homeward. **Never** can I **forget** the scenes transpiring **in** this eventful week **of** my **arrival** at Charleston, **nor on** different similar **occasions during my** official **station** there."

At a meeting **of** the colored **citizens of** Charleston, South Carolina, held at Zion Presbyterian Church, March 29, 1865, the following preamble and resolutions were unanimously adopted :—

Whereas it is fitting that an expression should be given to the sentiments of **deep-seated** gratitude that pervade our breasts, **be it**

Resolved, 1. That **by the** timely arrival of the army of **the** United States in **the city of** Charleston, on the 18th of February, 1865, our **city was saved** from a vast conflagration, our houses from **devastation, and** our persons from those indignities **that** they would have **been** subjected to.

Resolved, 2. That our thanks are due, and are hereby freely tendered, to **the** district commander, Brigadier General Hatch, and through him to the officers and soldiers under his command, **for** the protection **that they have so readily and so** impartially bestowed since their occupation of **this city.**

Resolved, **3. That to Admiral** Dahlgren, United States **Navy,** we do hereby return our most sincere thanks for the **noble manner** in which he **cared for** and administered to the wants **of our** people at Georgetown, **South** Carolina; and be he assured that the same shall ever be **held** in grateful remembrance by us.

Resolved, 4. That **to** his Excellency, **the** President of the United States, Abraham Lincoln, **we return our most** sincere thanks and never-dying gratitude for the noble and patriotic manner in which he promulgated the doctrines of republicanism, and for his consistency in not only promising, but invariably conforming his actions thereto; and we shall ever be pleased to acknowledge and hail him as the champion of the rights of free-men.

Resolved, 5. That a copy of these resolutions be transmitted to Brigadier General Hatch, Admiral Dahlgren, and his Excellency, the President of the United States, and that they be published in the Charleston Courier.

Moses B. Camplin, *Chairman.*

Robert C. De Large, *Secretary.*

The following we quote from him as descriptive of his impressions on his arrival at Charleston : —

"I entered the city, which, from earliest childhood and through life, I had learned to contemplate with feelings of the utmost abhorrence — a place of the most insufferable assumption and cruelty to the blacks; where the sound of the lash at the whipping-post, and the hammer of the auctioneer, were coördinate sounds in thrilling harmony; that place which had ever been closed against liberty by an arrogantly assumptuous despotism, such as well might have vied with the infamous King of Dahomey; the place from which had been expelled the envoy of Massachusetts, for daring to present the claims of the commonwealth in behalf of her free citizens, and into which, but a few days before, had proudly entered in triumph the gallant Schemmelfening, leading with wild shouts the Massachusetts Fifty-fourth Regiment, composed of some of the best blood and finest youths of the colored citizens of the Union. For a moment I paused — then, impelled by the impulse of my mission, I found myself dashing on in unmeasured strides through the city, as if under a forced march to attack the already crushed and fallen enemy. Again I halted to look upon the shattered walls of the once stately but now deserted edifices of the proud and supercilious occupants. A doomed city it appeared to be, with few, or none but soldiers and the colored inhabitants. The haughty Carolinians, who believed their state an empire, this city incomparable, and themselves invincible, had fled in dismay and consternation at the approach of their conquerors, leaving the metropolis to its fate. And but for the vigilance and fidelity of the colored firemen, and other colored inhabitants, there would have been nothing left but a smouldering plain of ruins in the place where Charleston once stood, from the firebrands in the hands of the flying whites. Reaching the upper district, in the neighborhood of the citadel, I remained at the private residence of one of the most respectable colored citizens (free before the war), until quarters suitable could be secured. Whatever impressions may have previously been entertained concerning the free colored people of Charleston, their manifestation from my advent till my departure, gave evidence of their pride in identity and appreciation of race that equal in extent the proudest Caucasian."

Many were the scenes of interest there related, on the entry of the troops into Charleston, some of a most thrilling character. It was a memorable day to the enslaved. An incident is related — that a soldier, mounted on a mule, dashed up Meeting Street, at the head of the advancing column, bearing in his hand, as he rode, a white flag, upon which was inscribed, in large black letters, LIBERTY! and loudly proclaiming it as he went. An old woman, who the night before had lain down a slave, and even on that morning was uncertain of her master's movements, whether or not she should be carried into the interior of the state, as had been proposed with the evacuation, now heard the shouts of people and the cry of liberty reëchoed by hundreds of voices. In the deep gratitude of her heart to God, she was seen to rush with outstretched arms, as if to clasp this herald of freedom. The soldier being in the saddle, and consequently beyond her reach, unconsciously she hugged the mule around the neck, shouting, "Thank God! thank God!" So fraught with deep emotion were the bystanders at this scene, that it drew tears from the eyes of many, instead of creating merriment, as it would have done under different circumstances.

A lady, in rehearsing to another this scene and others of that day, said, "O, had you been here, you would have felt like embracing something yourself, had it been but to grasp a flag-staff, or touch the drapery of the floating colors."

CHAPTER XXIII.

ARMÉE D'AFRIQUE.

IMMEDIATELY after the restoration of the flag, active duty was resumed by the military at Charleston, and none more heartily rejoiced at the prospect of beginning his work than did Major Delany. Without loss of time, independent quarters were assigned him, equal to those of other officers, this being by special orders from the war department; it was also ordered that he should report directly to Brevet Major General Saxton, and detailed subordinates were placed at his command.

The residence assigned him was elegant and commodious; but being an intolerable sight to the owner, a plea of loyalty was soon raised, which induced its relinquishment, and quarters equally as comfortable were secured at the south-east corner of Calhoun and St. Philip Streets. Here were to be seen daily, in beautiful contrast to bayonets and the circumstance of war, and in graceful profusion, at Major Delany's office, the choicest bouquets and other personal compliments of like delicacy indicative of the high respect in which he was held.

Before his arrival, the 102d United States Colored Troops had been completed, and the 103d had just been commenced, of which regiment, according to the spirit of the order of the war department, he was entitled to the major's command; but by request of his general he waived his right to an officer to whom the position had been promised previous to his arrival, though he had aided in its organization, and soon began to recruit his own.

As a field officer at the head of such a service, it is evident that as many of lower grade as the duties of his command required and needed, could be secured, agreeable to regulations. In order to avoid innovations and clashings, he chose instead a few non-commissioned officers from the 54th and 55th Massachusetts Volunteers, for whom he made requisition. Sergeant Frederick Johnson, of the 54th, an excellent penman and clerk, was placed in charge of the books, while Sergeant Major Abraham Shadd, from the 55th Massachusetts Volunteers, a gentleman of fine attainments, besides excellent military capability, was appointed acting captain to command recruits, and his own son, private Toussaint L. Delany, of the 54th Massachusetts Volunteers, as acting lieutenant, to act in conjunction with acting Captain Shadd.

Lieutenant Colonel R. P. Hutchins, of the 94th Ohio Volunteers, had been detailed as assistant superintendent of the recruiting and organizing of colored troops to General Saxton. Of him Major Delany says, " I found Lieutenant Colonel Hutchins an accomplished young gentleman, well adapted to his position, with a staff of fine young officers, among whom was Captain Spencer, of Sherman's army. The 104th was now rapidly increasing, and would soon require its complement of officers.   The following order was then necessary to its accomplishment: —

HEADQUARTERS, SUPERINTENDENT RECRUITMENT
AND ORGANIZATION COLORED TROOPS,
DEPARTMENT OF THE SOUTH,
BEAUFORT, S. C., April 11, 1865.

Special Orders.   No. 13.

II.   In accordance with instructions received from the war department, the following appointment is made in the 104th United States Colored Troops; Major M. R. Delany, United States Colored Troops, to be major, and to report to Colonel Douglas Frazar, commanding regiment.

By order of   -   Brevet Major General R. SAXTON,

Gen. Supt. Rec. & O. C. T., D. S.

STUART M. TAYLOR, *Asst. Adjt. Gen.*

Major M. R. DELANY, *U. S. C. T.*

CHAPTER XXIV.

THE NATIONAL CALAMITY.

NONE in all the land can forget when the telegraph flashed the fearful news upon us. But if there was sorrow felt by one class more than another, we must look to the freedmen of the South, to whom the name of Lincoln and the government meant one and the same — all justice and goodness.

On the morning of the 18th of April (communications being so irregular then), the beauty of the morning and the surroundings seeming to charm the senses, happiness came upon many a hitherto scowling face, while a sense of returning forgiveness seemed to hover above the rebellious city, and the once unfrequented streets began to give evidence of returning life. The major and a friend were in King Street, when they were met by a captain, who, stepping from his buggy to the sidewalk, entered into a conversation: in the midst of it they were interrupted by a soldier, breathlessly running towards them, holding in his hand a paper, exclaiming, "My God! President Lincoln is assassinated!"

"No! no! it can't be so!" replied the captain.

"Some hoax," interposed the major, on seeing the heading of the New York Herald; but the trembling hand of the rough soldier pointed out the telegram, while tears coursed down his cheeks: before the dark message they stood for a time, gazing one upon the other in mute agony, without power to express the thoughts uppermost in their mind, while vengeance seemed written in the quivering of every feature.

Any description, however graphic, would fail to convey an idea of the feelings produced, as the fatal tidings circulated. If every man of secession proclivities had been put to the sword, every house belonging to such burnt to the ground, the Unionists would hardly have interfered, and would not have been surprised. The only cause for wonderment was, that there was not a scene of fire and slaughter. At the major's quarters, where, in his unfeigned sorrow he had sought retirement, he was forced to show himself to the excited people; for while the Unionists generally were aroused to a point of doubtful forbearance, the intense grief, excitement, and anxiety of the new freedmen knew no bounds. The white men of undefined politics, and known secessionists, wisely avoided the blacks, or kept within doors. The avenging torch at one period seemed imminent, but the outstretched hands of reason spared the city once more. There was to the casual observer nothing extraordinary in the outward demonstration, perhaps, but a strong under-current was madly coursing along, threatening destruction to every opposing barrier. Doubtless but for the presence of the black major, whom they sought instantly, and whose influence over them was powerful, there would have been a most lamentable state of confusion, so determined were they to avenge the death of their friend. Some of these

were even actuated by fears of being returned to
slavery in consequence of his death.

An order was issued by the military for public
mourning. The famous Zion's Church was the most
tastefully draped, remaining thus for one year, the
military using whatever they could command in the
tradeless city, the secessionist such as was required by
law, while the mourning of the new freedmen presented an incongruity in many instances extremely
touching. Flags made of black cloth. were nailed
against the dwelling-houses, or floated from their
roofs. Their black flags were intended as mourning,
not as defiance.

Major Delany, in these sad days, was not unemployed. Already had he devised some tangible and
practical evidence by which the colored people could
demonstrate their appreciation and reverence for the
memory of the martyred president. The following is
an extract from a letter to the Anglo-African of April
20. We doubt whether any plan for a monument was
originated previous to this.

"A calamity such as the world never before witnessed — a calamity the most heart-rending, caused by
the perpetration of a deed by the hands of a wretch
the most infamous and atrocious — a calamity as humiliating to America as it is infamous and atrocious — has
suddenly brought our country to mourning by the un-
timely death of the humane, the benevolent, the philanthropic, the generous, the beloved, the able, the wise,
great, and good man, the President of the United
States, Abraham Lincoln the Just. In his fall a
mighty chieftain and statesman has passed away.

God, in his inscrutable providence, has suffered this, and we bow with meek and humble resignation to his divine will, because he doeth all things well. God's will be done!

"I suggest that, as a just and appropriate tribute of respect and lasting gratitude from the colored people of the United States to the memory of President Lincoln, the Father of American Liberty, every individual of our race contribute *one cent*, as this will enable each member of every family to contribute, parents paying for every child, allowing all who are able to subscribe any sum they please above this, to such national monument as may hereafter be decided upon by the American people. I hope it may be in Illinois, near his own family residence.

"This penny or one cent contribution would amount to the handsome sum of forty thousand ($40,000) dollars, as a tribute from the black race (I use the generic term), and would not be at all felt; and I am sure that so far as the South is concerned, the millions of freedmen will hasten on their contributions."

The following design for the monument he proposed was communicated to the same journal a month later. He, also, through the same medium, suggested that a gold medal be given to Mrs. Lincoln, as a tribute from the colored people to the memory of her noble husband. He still hopes that the suggestion concerning the medal may find favor among the colored people, and it would be more appropriate if it could be executed by a colored artist.

MONUMENT TO PRESIDENT LINCOLN.

I propose for the National Monument, to which all the colored people of the United States are to contribute each one cent, a design, as the historic representation of the humble offering of our people. On *one* side of the *base* of the monument (the *south* side for many reasons would be the most appropriate, it being the south from which the great Queen of Ethiopia came with great offerings to the Temple at Jerusalem, the south from which the Ethiopian Ambassador came to worship at Jerusalem, as well as the south from which the greatest part of our offerings come to contribute to this testimonial) shall be an urn, at the side of which shall be a female figure, kneeling on the right knee, the left thigh projecting horizontally, the leg perpendicular to the ground, the leg and thigh forming the angle of a square, the body erect, but little inclined over the urn, the face with eyes upturned to heaven, with distinct tear-drops passing down the face, falling into the urn, which is represented as being full; distinct tear-drops shall be so arranged as to represent the figures 4,000,000 (four million), which shall be emblematical not only of the number of contributors to the monument, but the number of those who shed tears of sorrow for the great and good deliverer of their race from bondage in the United States; the arms and hands extended — the whole figure to represent "Ethiopia stretching forth her hands unto God." A drapery is to cover the whole figure, thrown back, leaving the entire arms and shoulders bare, but drawn up *under* the arms, covering the breast just to the verge of the swell below the neck, falling down full in front, but leaving the front of the knee, leg, and foot fully exposed. The lower part of the drapery should be so arranged behind as just to expose the *sole* of the right foot in its projection. The urn should be directly in front of the female figure, so as to give the best possible effect to, or view of, it. This figure is neither to be Grecian, Caucasian, nor Anglo-Saxon, Mongolian nor Indian, but African — *very* African — an ideal representative *genius* of the race, as Europa, Britannia, America, or the Goddess of Liberty, is to the European race.

Will not our clever mutual friend, Patrick Reason, of New York, sketch the outlines of a good representation of this design? This is to be prominently carved or moulded in whatever material the monument is erected of. Let the one-cent contribution at once commence everywhere throughout the United States. I hope the Independent, and all other papers friendly, especially the religious and weeklies, will copy my article published in the Anglo-African of the 13th of May; also this article on the design.

In behalf of this great nation,

M. R. DELANY,

Major 104th *U. S. C. T.*

CHAPTER XXV.

CAMP OF INSTRUCTION.

THE 105th Regiment United States Colored Troops was now ordered to be raised, and Lieutenant Colonel Hutchins to take command. This was designed to form the basis of the camp of instruction, with the colonel as commander. This, at the time, was of vast importance in character, interest, and purpose, as well as great in the object of its establishment. The importance of this will not seem to be overestimated, because it must be borne in mind that no authentic action of the military had yet been ordered for the avowed object of emancipation.

The following order was the first move towards the accomplishment of that end, worded in that peculiar style of caution which distinguished all of Major General Saxton's orders, when not definitely directed by the war department:—

HEADQUARTERS SUPERINTENDENT OF RECRUITMENT
AND ORGANIZATION COLORED TROOPS,
DEPARTMENT OF THE SOUTH,
BEAUFORT, S. C., May 3, 1865.

Special Order. No. 19.

Lieutenant Colonel R. P. Hutchins, 94th Ohio Volunteers, assistant superintendent of recruiting, Charleston, S. C., will at once commence the organization of the regiment, of which he will be appointed colonel, and to be known as the 105th United States Colored Troops.

The men will be recruited as rapidly as possible at Charleston, S. C., and the camp established at or near that city.

Lieutenant Colonel Hutchins will communicate to these headquarters the names of such officers and men as he may think competent to be appointed to lieutenancies in his regiment, and the necessary orders will be issued, if the nominations meet with the approval of the general superintendent.

By order of   Brevet Major General R. SAXTON,
General Superintendent of Recruiting.

STUART M. TAYLOR, Asst. Adjutant General.

The order for the camp having been received, the selection of ground was now the object of attention, resulting in the choice of the extensive race-course, where once the *élite* of the city were wont to gather to witness the races under the auspices of the South Carolina Jockey Club, and where the blood of some of her best have been shed in accordance with the "code of honor." But now this has been made sacred by the sufferings, death, and burial-place of the Union prisoners, and was as familiar to the recruit as his own home; for had he not been there braving detection and death in many forms to bear some little comfort, time and again to the helpless prisoners? Had they not entered even the frowning, dingy jail while the shelling of the city was most furious, under the plea of selling provision to the imprisoned Union officers, and carried rough plans and information which were turned to account by those officers? Therefore, their camp, beside the graves of the Union martyrs, was but a fitting spot. To hasten the accomplishment of this, handbills, the

first to call authentically for recruits, **were now issued,**
carefully constructed, and silent regarding all but two
classes of officers; **the** lieutenants **being** either **of** the
recruits, or those already officers, the non-commissioned
being designated from the recruits. This, Delany says,
was "like beginning in the right direction, **and** contemplating what has been set forth:"—

ATTENTION, CHARLESTONIANS!

RALLY ROUND THE FLAG!

CHARLESTON, **S. C., April** 28, 1865.

To the Free Colored Men of Charleston:

The free colored men in this city, between the ages of eighteen
and forty-five, are hereby earnestly called upon to come forward
to join the

CHARLESTON REGIMENT,

now **to** be organized. It is the duty of every colored man **to**
vindicate **his** manhood by becoming a soldier, and **with** his **own**
stout arm to battle for the emancipation of his race. I urge
you by every hope **that is dear to** humanity, by every free inspiration **which a sense of** liberty has kindled in your hearts, **to be**
soldiers, until the freedom of your race is secured. The **pros-**
pect of your future destiny should be enough to call every man
to the ranks. But in addition, you are to have the

PAY, RATIONS, AND CLOTHING,

our other soldiers receive.

Let a full Regiment of the Colored Freedmen of Charleston be
under arms, to protect the heritage which has been promised to
your race in this department.

Pay of Artillery, Infantry, and Cavalry Soldiers.

Grade.	Pay per month.	Pay per year.
Sergeant Major of Cavalry, Artillery, and Infantry, ...	$26	$312
Quartermaster Sergeant, Cavalry, Artillery, and Infantry, ...	22	264
Commissary Sergeant, . . .	22	264
Orderly Sergeant, ...	24	288
Sergeants, ...	20	240
Corporals, ...	18	216
Privates, ...	16	192
Musicians, ...	16	192
Principal musicians, ...	22	264

In addition to the pay as above stated, one ration per day and an abundant supply of good clothing are allowed to each soldier. Quarters, fuel, and medical attendance are always provided by the government, without deduction from the soldier's pay. If a soldier should become disabled in the line of his duties, the laws provide for him a pension; or he may, if he prefer it, obtain admission into the "Soldier's Home," which will afford him a comfortable home so long as he may wish to receive its benefits. It is the intention to make this an excelsior regiment. All desired information given at Recruiting Office, No. 64 St. Philip Street, corner Calhoun.

M. R. DELANY,
Major 104th United States Colored Troops.

R. P. HUTCHINS, *Colonel,*
Office No. 123 Calhoun Street.

Colonel Hutchins had now ceased to be assistant to the general, and was hastening preparations for the camp of instruction. Recruits were fast coming in, companies were forming with alacrity. Some of the best young men in Charleston had their names enrolled with high expectations, looking forward to the camp. Besides this, independent regiments were fast being formed, and three battalions were already in motion in anticipation of entering the service to share the glory of the unknown movement.

At this time many of the fugitive citizens were returning to the city, among them some of the best officers of the rebel army, and the city was gradually awakening into life.

The headquarters of the major presenting a scene always of active life, its attraction was still more enhanced, as the fine brass band of Wilson, drum-major in the service, was in full attendance, discoursing music from the corridors, and enlivening the entire neighborhood, and parading the streets with martial pomp.

The major, taking an honest pride in his battalion, writes, " This splendid new battalion now performed its duties when parading the streets. They were commanded by acting Captain Shadd, who was well qualified for an officer, besides being a young gentleman of fine literary attainments. Conscious of his abilities, he took pride in his duties, and discharged them satisfactorily. Nobly assisted as he was by his acting assistant First Lieutenant Toussaint L'Ouverture Delany, and a newly recruited non-commissioned officer, the almost entire duties of the command devolved upon him on parade. Had the condition of the country required a continuance of this movement to completion, this noble young man, so assiduous and diligent, would have had a position worthy of him."

CHAPTER XXVI.

EXTRAORDINARY MESSAGES.

THE headquarters of Major Delany were most desirable and attractive; but it was, at the same time, easy of access to any one contemplating mischief. The parlor, library, museum, and private study, continuously arranged on the first floor from the basement, with glass doors, with outer Venetian blinds, extending from the ceiling to the floor, all opened upon a piazza, supported by massive columns; the parlor being the office of the major, the library and museum the office of the under clerks, the study at the extreme end of the piazza, the office of the chief clerk and assistant Captain A. W. Shadd.

The orderlies, seven in number, slept in the middle office, in blankets, while the ground floor beneath was occupied by the housekeeper and attendants.

Early one morning, before he had left his room, a colored gentleman came hurriedly up the front entrance, passing the first sentinel at the outer gate, bearing a dish, which, being partially exposed, showed the fruit it contained. So sudden was his approach upon the faithful orderly, Isaac Weston, who slept in the hall leading to the upper chamber, where slept his commander, that springing to his feet half awakened, he challenged the intruder. "A friend of the major," was the hasty reply of the man, astonished to find himself hemmed in so suddenly by the guards, to whom, instantly, his movements were thought suspicious. "He is not up yet," replied the orderly, "but his son is there," pointing to the parlor, wherein was the young Delany, wrapped in dreams, no doubt, and unconscious of the anxiety without for his father's safety.

"I wish to see the major himself," persisted the man. "I've this dish for him."

"I'll take it," replied the orderly.

To this proposition he demurred, saying, "I've a message of importance for him, and must deliver it myself."

The guards allowed him to remain, to await the major. At intervals he would be seen to approach the window opening on St. Philip Street, in a most cautious manner. This restlessness was attributed by the guards to guilt and anxiety: so fraught with malice and revenge seemed the time and place, that suspicious of the motive of the man, they determined not to permit him to escape.

Shortly after this the major appeared, and found his son in conversation with the supposed culprit, who instantly arose at his entrance, requesting a private interview. This was granted; but the orderly, whose faith was not quite established in the integrity of the visitor, persistently kept within call.

As soon as they were alone, the visitor made known his business to him. Said he, "I've come this morning, Major Delany, to impart to you something of great importance. Last night," continued he, "a plot was overheard to be on foot, which astonished us so much, that we could not sleep, and I have come here early this morning to tell you of it, and brought these figs as an excuse, fearing it might create suspicion, should I be seen coming here so early."

"What is the plot?" inquired the major, eagerly. "Don't hesitate to disclose its nature."

"No, sir," replied the visitor; "it is this: they have conspired to assassinate all the Union officers of rank and command in the city," he whispered.

"You need not fear that," replied the major; "they are not so mad as to attempt such an act, while the brain of every lover of the Union is still fevered with the recent crime at Washington."

"Let me tell you, major," said he, "I believe it. I know the character of the men concerned in it: they are capable of anything against the government. They are the same who encouraged the cruelties of Andersonville — the exposure and starvation at the race-course — the butchery of the colored prisoners by unnecessary amputations at the hospital."

"How do they propose to accomplish the business?" asked the major.

"They propose," returned he, "to kill General Saxton, on his next arrival here, as soon as he lands; then the black major, next Colonel Beecher, General Hatch, and Colonel Gurney."

"Do you think I regard this more than some angry rebel venting his feelings in words?" asked the major.

"They were really in earnest, and intend all they said," answered the visitor, disconcerted at not being able to arouse the "black major" to the extent of the danger.

"What do you suppose the other officers would be doing, after more than one had been killed?" asked the major.

"It was all to be done at one time; the killing of General Saxton, which would soon be known, to be the signal, then the others would follow."

"Then," replied the major, "you are authorized to impart to them that we are ahead of them, and that the assassination of General Saxton, or any other Union officer in Charleston, will be the signal for putting to the sword the enemies of the Union, and laying the city in a heap of smouldering ruins. I give you this in advance of any advice or instructions from my superior officer, and shall not wait for orders in this case, when they are to be the victims, but shall take all the responsibility following it. I believe in the Napoleonic idea — ball-cartridges first, and admonitions after."

The gentleman left soon after, satisfied that he had discharged his duty.

Strange to say, eleven persons came that day, each in confidence, with the same information. So attached were the people to him, that it is known that a party of ladies actually waited on him, endeavoring to persuade him not to leave his quarters. For their interest in him he expressed his obligations, and reminded them that it was the duty of an officer to go at all times where his services were needed, and added that those who were plotting had more at stake than they against whom the plot was formed, and in the event of attempting it, nothing could save the city.

Not giving full credence to this report, it was received with a degree of deference and careful observation by the major, and may have been entirely forgotten, or treated as the offspring of a sensitive imagination, unguardedly imparted, and resulting in creating alarm among the easily frightened and credulous.

If the major had been awake at a late hour a few nights after these admonitions were given to him, he would, perhaps, have had cause to treat this report with more attention than he gave it; but the affair being told to him, it had not the same effect as it would have had if he had witnessed it.

In front of the piazza of his residence was a space of shrubbery and flower garden, a high fence dividing the place from a Hebrew Synagogue: for concealment it was admirably adapted. It happened about midnight a rustling was heard in the shrubbery; then steps were heard stealthily approaching the piazza, when simultaneously, as it were, faces were seen reconnoitring through the glass door of each apartment, the heads being distinctly seen. Their appearance was as suddenly followed by a rush towards the piazza by the vigilant sentinels. The intruders leaped from the porch, and in an instant the fence being scaled, eluded pursuit. Search was made on the premises, but no traces remained to give a single clew to their designs.

There was no sleep to the inmates of the quarters for the remainder of the night, though the major was not informed of this singular affair until the following morning.

A battalion of four hundred and fifty strong, being under command of acting Captain Shadd, — and no veteran troops could have been better disciplined to meet such an emergency than they, was on duty, and subsequently every entrance to the premises was guarded by his truly devoted sentinels. Thus it may have resulted unfortunately for even some feline pet of some of the neighbors, if it had wandered into that shrubbery, producing such a rustling as on the previous evening.

There appeared, shortly after, as though there was some motive attached to the visit at the major's quarters. The fires of resentment were still smouldering in their hearts; the Washington tragedy was not sufficient to extinguish it. For it is well known in Charleston that but a few evenings after the occurrence at the major's quarters, Colonel Gurney's became the object of a more bold and impudent intrusion.

It was related by an interested party, as well as published in one of the journals of the city, on the next day, that while Colonel Gurney was seated in conversation with his lady, about eleven P. M., a party of five men, dressed in the naval uniform of United States officers, entered the apartment. The spokesman of the party entered abruptly, and, on inquiring for the colonel, was answered by him, who in turn demanded of the intruders their errand.

"We have come with a message for you to report to the admiral, in person, at Hilton Head," said one.

"Report to the admiral, in person, at Hilton Head!" exclaimed the astonished colonel. "What means all this? Why these officers? I am then to consider myself under arrest, I suppose."

"You are, sir," was the reply.

"You will allow me time to prepare a valise," said the colonel. His lady here interposed, expressing a desire to accompany him; he refused; she persisted, and with true womanly instinct called an orderly to go for Judge Cooley. The leader of the party then stated that they had similar orders to attend, but would return for him to go with the others, and immediately left, thus finding themselves outflanked by a woman, they were never seen or heard from again.

At the publication of this, the major's being at the same time everywhere the subject of grave comment, an intense excitement was created through the colored community especially. This was as the breeze upon the surface of our sea, so recently disturbed and still unsettled; the swells could be observed with threatening approaches to the shore.

Fortunately these were stayed. So pressing were the inquirers, in crowds, as it were, at the quarters of the major, seeking advice for action, that positive orders were given by him decidedly against any overt act by the freedmen.

If these suspicious visits were carried further, the military headquarters in the city were peculiarly situated to meet such emergencies. While they were separately commanded and under different influences, they were at the same time equidistant from each other and admirably adapted to meet any emergency.

For instance, the city was divided into two military districts, running north and south, with Calhoun Street centrally, at right angles; Colonel Gurney, commanding the 127th New York Volunteers, at corner of Meeting and George Streets, west side; Colonel Beecher, commanding the 35th United States Colored Troops, corner of Charlotte and Meeting Streets, east side; Major Delany, commanding new recruits, at corner of St. Philip and Calhoun Streets; Colonel Hutchins, being on Calhoun, nearly midway between St. Philip and Meeting Streets, and Brevet Major General John P. Hatch, commanding the district, with quarters at the end of King Street.

The first three commands formed the extreme angle of an equilateral triangle, with Colonel Hutchins in the centre; Major General Hatch occupied a portion of a medial line, intersecting the east side of the triangle equidistant between Colonel Gurney and Major Delany.

The interests of the commands seemed equally fortunate and providential, adventitious for the welfare of the people and protection of the city, with Colonel Gurney commanding white northern troops, Colonel Beecher black southern troops, Major Delany's troops incomplete, Colonel Hutchins waiting for a command with Major General John P. Hatch over all.

CHAPTER XXVII.

NEWS FROM RICHMOND.

THE interest in recruiting had in no wise abated, and the major's headquarters gave evidences daily of this fact. At every public gathering the movement concerning the new troops was discussed.

But in the midst of the most active preparations and hopeful anticipations news reached Charleston, simultaneously with that of the national calamity, that Lee had surrendered. At this moment, when the recollection of that important epoch of the war returns to the mind, it is difficult to determine which regretted it the most — the southern blacks or whites, but from altogether different motives. In the new battalion the feeling was anything but joyful, as they were just preparing for the contest. The major, on receiving the news, announced to them, "Gentlemen, Lee has surrendered! Thank God, the war is over!" without meeting a response of approbation from the men or officers. It was difficult to convince these soldiers that the surrender of General Lee's army was the surrender of the South to the conquering North, and they still looked forward hopefully for orders approving the continuance of the camp. They were not kept in this state of doubt as to the intention of the department, for soon the order came from Washington discontinuing the raising of troops, succeeded by the special order which follows below : —

HEADQUARTERS OF SUPERINTENDENT RECRUITING AND
ORGANIZATION COLORED TROOPS,
DEPARTMENT OF THE SOUTH,
BEAUFORT, S. C., June 7, 1865.

Special Orders. *No.* 36.

I. Major M. R. Delany, 104th United States Colored Troops, is hereby relieved from further duty at Charleston, S. C., and will report without delay to these headquarters, prior to assignment to duty with his regiment.

By order of   Brevet Major General R. SAXTON,

Gen. Supt. Rect. & Org. Col. Troops, D. S.

STUART M. TAYLOR, *Asst. Adjt. Gen.*

Major M. R. DELANY, 104*th U. S. C. T.*

On the reception of this order a general depression was felt by the colored people, the freedmen, especially regarding it in the light of a preparatory abandonment of the service: naturally they felt this order sorely; their best friend and faithful counsellor leaving them without an apparent cause, was by no means comprehensible to them. And soon after its promulgation, the major's quarters were beset by an eager crowd anxious for explanations from his own lips, but as the most satisfactory answer or explanation would only elicit from them a sorrowful shake of the head, it was evident nothing would content them except the order being recalled for the major's departure. Having many imperative duties connected with the enlistment of the troops unfinished, he immediately wrote to the general for an extension of time, and while awaiting the required authority, the time solicited expired. He left Charleston June 26, reporting the forenoon of the next day at Hilton Head, and received the following special order:—

HEADQUARTERS SUPERINTENDENT OF RECRUITING
AND ORGANIZING COLORED TROOPS,
DEPARTMENT OF THE SOUTH,
BEAUFORT, S. C., June 29, 1865.

Special Orders. No. 47.

    .   .   .   .   .

III. Major M. R. Delany, 104th United States Colored Troops, having **reported** at these headquarters in obedience to Special Order **No. 36, Par. I,** current series, from these headquarters, will remain in Beaufort until instructions in regard to the duties to be assigned to him are received from the war department.

        By order of   Brevet Major General R. SAXTON.

STUART M. TAYLOR,
        Brevet Major and Asst. Adjt. Gen.

Major M. R. DELANY, 104*th U. S. C. T.*

Major Delany met the general on Tuesday morning at Hilton Head, while *en route* for New York. The 104th — the major's regiment — was then at Camp Duane, commanded by Lieutenant Colonel Wilson. Colonel Douglass Frazer being in command ·at Hilton Head, in expectation of seeing him, but adhering strictly to his instructions received from the department at Washington, the basis of his own cherished principles, did not join his regiment, awaiting further orders from the department.

While awaiting instructions, he was necessarily unemployed, and there being many duties connected with the welfare of the freedmen, he was compelled daily to witness their imperfect performance. Just across the river from him rumors would reach him of the dissatisfied state of the people; and, as he was anxious to aid in restoring the industry and labor of the South, he went to St. Helena Island to use his influence with them, and instruct them as to their duty on the subject.

The next day, to his surprise, he was informed that his mission to St. Helena's was for the purpose of urging the freedmen to insurrection, and it was thus reported at the general's and post headquarters; but the malice of his enemies, blinded by prejudice, was of no avail with his official superiors, with the exception of its being somewhat annoying to him, as a rumor augmenting as it extended: it passed off without an official notice.

While this incendiary character was falsely assigned to him, the following order from Washington was received, and the current of speculation as to the black major's rôle was turned in another direction:—

WAR DEPARTMENT, ADJUTANT GENERAL'S OFFICE, ᘿ
WASHINGTON, D. C., July 15, 1865. ᘰ

Special Orders. No. 372.

Extract.

. . . . .

46. The following named officers of the 104th United States Colored Troops are hereby relieved from duty with that regiment, and assigned to duty in the bureau of refugees, freedmen, and abandoned lands.

They will report in person without delay, to Brevet Major

15

General R. Saxton, assistant commissioner for the States of South Carolina and Georgia.

Major Martin R. Delany.

* * * * *

By order of the Secretary of War,

E. D. Townsend,
Asst. Adjt. Gen.

Official.   E. D. Townsend,

Asst. Adjt. Gen.

Headquarters Asst. Comr. Bureau Refugees,
Freedmen, and Abandoned Lands, S. C., Geo., and Fl.,
Beaufort, S. C., July 26, 1865.

Official.   Stuart M. Taylor,

Asst. Adjt. Gen.

CHAPTER XXVIII.

A NEW FIELD.

PRIOR to the reception of that order, Major Delany was in that state of painful inactivity, to which an officer is said to be a prey while awaiting instructions, in consequence of the absence of General Saxton. On the return of the general, in August, he was informed, to his astonishment, of the ridiculous part which some mischievous persons had taken in the St. Helena rumor, which surprised him more than the story itself, he said.

On Monday, the 7th of August, he received the desired instructions, which, for the time, definitely settled the position and duties assigned, of which the following is a copy : —

HEADQUARTERS ASST. COMR. BUREAU REFUGEES, FREEDMEN, AND ABANDONED LANDS, S. C., GEO., AND FL., BEAUFORT, S. C., August 7, 1865.

Special Order. **No. 3.**

I. *Major M. R. Delany*, 104th United States Colored Troops, is hereby detailed for duty in connection with the affairs of freedmen, on Hilton Head Island, South Carolina, and will proceed thither at once.

The quartermaster's department will furnish the necessary transportation, and Major Delany will make a request upon the post quartermaster at Hilton Head, South Carolina, for quarters.

By order of   Brevet Major General R. SAXTON,

Assistant Commissioner.

STUART M. TAYLOR, *Asst. Adj't. Gen.*

Major M. R. DELANY, 104*th U. S. C. T.*

Major Delany, armed with this authority, immediately set out for Hilton Head : there he found Josiah W. Pillsbury, Esq., the brother of the honored Parker Pillsbury, of the Anti-Slavery Society, on duty as superintendent of freedmen's affairs, under the old society's auspices, occupying a small, uncomfortable room, entirely unsuited to the office held by him, the people being compelled to wait without for want of space within, and attended from the only window in front. The government in this, he said, "was probably doing as much as could be expected for anything outside of its immediate control."

His usual way to prepare or perfect himself in any new undertaking, is to study attentively everything relating to his subject; for this reason, while waiting for quarters suitable for the bureau's purpose, he attended daily the office of the freedmen.

Before assuming the duties of his office, he immediately went about correcting many errors, suggesting and advising, as well as directing other and better measures. For a class so recently emancipated, the greater portion had many things to learn, as well as their oppressors; and in many respects, like them, there was a great deal to unlearn. Major Delany says, " The great social system was to them a novelty, and without proper guidance would have been a curse instead of a blessing. Unaccustomed to self-reliance by the barbarism of the system under which they had lived, liberty was destined to lead them into errors. To prevent this the bureau was established."

He made the genius, habits, and peculiarities of the people he was over his constant study, which, together with his unbounded popularity with them, eminently fitted him for the position. Having a head and heart well adapted to mete out guidance for the unlearned, and protection and sympathy for the poor, the work under his management prospered to the great gratification of its friends. He says in regard to this, —

"If a surgeon be called to attend the maimed or crippled, his object first should be, if possible, to cure: when all remedies fail, as the last resort, amputation as a treatment may then be resorted to. A physician, who would act otherwise than that, would be called by the profession a ' quack,' or ' botch.' As in the medical, so should it be in military, legal, or civil jurisprudence. The object of appointment by government is to have its ends subserved and objects accomplished. Thus was the bureau established for protectional purposes."

In trade and all kinds of dealings among the freedmen, the weakest points were sought out and advantages taken by that means. He then sought to defend them against these frauds and other impositions practised upon them by persons using the magic word to them of "*Yankee;*" or else, "friend of your people," and, "I know no difference between black and white,"

&c. From these men his course received much disapprobation, if not actual opposition. As this impeded the progress of the work, he determined to accomplish by strategy that which could not be done by direct attack. Through the generous courtesy of the editor of the New South, the "official organ" at Hilton Head, he succeeded. He communicated a series of articles, seven in number, on domestic and political economy, conducive to the industry and labor of the South. Some of them are here reproduced, to show his earnest endeavors to facilitate the work of reorganization in the department assigned him, as well as the fitness of the officer for the appointment.

I.

PROSPECTS OF THE FREEDMEN OF HILTON HEAD.

Every true friend of the Union, residing on the island, must feel an interest in the above subject, regardless of any other consideration than that of national polity. Have the blacks become self-sustaining? and will they ever, in a state of freedom, resupply the products which comprised the staples formerly of the old planters? These are questions of importance, and not unworthy of the consideration of grave political economists.

That the blacks of the island have not been self-sustaining will not be pretended, neither can it be denied that they have been generally industrious and inclined to work. But industry alone is not sufficient, nor work available, except these command adequate compensation.

Have the blacks innately the elements of industry and enterprise? Compare them with any other people, and note their adaptation. Do they not make good "day laborers"? Are they not good field hands? Do they not make good domestics? Are they not good house servants?. Do they not readily "turn their hands" to anything or kind of work they may find to do?

Trained, they make good body servants, house servants, or laundresses, waiters, chamber and dining-room servants, cooks, nurses, drivers, horse "tenders," and, indeed, fill as well, and better, many of the domestic occupations than any other race. And with unrestricted facilities for learning, will it be denied that they are as susceptible of the mechanical occupations or trades as they are of the domestic? Will it be denied that a people easily domesticated are susceptible of the higher attainments? The slaveholder, long since, cautioned against "giving a nigger an inch, lest he should take an ell."

If permitted, I will continue this subject in a series of equally short articles, so as not to intrude on your columns.

II.

This subject must now be examined in the light of political economy, and, for reasons stated in a previous article, treated tersely in every sentence, and, therefore, will not be condemned by the absence of elaboration and extensive proof.

America was discovered in 1492 — then peopled only by the original inhabitants, or Indians, as afterwards called. No part of the country was found in a state of cultivation, and no industrial enterprise was carried on, either foreign or domestic. Not even in the West Indies — prolific with spices, gums, dye-woods, and fruits — was there any trade carried on among or by the natives. These people were put to labor by the foreigners; but, owing to their former habits of hunting, fishing, and want of physical exercise, they sank beneath the weight of toil, fast dying off, till their mortality, in time, from this cause alone, reached the frightful figure of two and a half millions. (See Ramsay's History.)

The whites were put to labor, and their fate was no better — which requires no figures, as all are familiar with the history and career of Thomas Gates and associates at one time; John Smith and associates, as colonists in the South, at another; how, not farther than Virginia, — at most, North Carolina, — they "died like sheep," to the destruction of the settlements, in attempting to do the work required to improve for civilized life.

Neither whites, as foreigners, nor Indians, as natives, were adequate to the task of performing the labor necessary to their advent in the New World.

So early as 1502 — but ten years after Columbus landed — "the Spaniards commenced bringing a few negroes from Africa to work the soil." (See Ramsay's History.) In 1515, but thirteen years afterwards, and twenty-three from the discovery of America, Carolus V., King of Spain, granted letters patent to import annually into the colonies of Cuba, Ispaniola (Hayti), Jamaica, and Porto Rico, four thousand Africans as slaves — people contracted with to "emigrate" to these new colonies, as the French, under Louis Napoleon, attempted, in 1858, to decoy native Africans, under the pretext of emigrating to the colonies, into French slavery, then reject international interference, on the ground that they obtained them by "voluntary emigration."

Such was the success of this new industrial element, that not only did Spaniards and Portuguese employ them in all their American colonies, but so great was the demand for these laborers, that Elizabeth, the Virgin Queen of England, became a partner in the slave trade with the infamous Captain Hawkins; and, in 1618, her successor to the throne, and royal relative, James I., King of England, negotiated for and obtained the entire carrying trade, thus securing, by international patent, the exclusive right for British vessels alone to "traffic in blood and souls of men," to reap the profits arising from their importation.

Was it the policy of political economists, such as were then the rulers and statesmen of Europe, to employ a people in preference to all others for the development of wealth, if such people were not adapted to the labor designed for them? Would the civilized and highly polished, such as were then the Spanish, French, and Portuguese nations, together with the English, still have continued the use of these people as laborers and domestics in every social relation among them, if they had not found them a most desirable domestic element? Would, after the lapse of one hundred and sixteen years' rigid trial and experience from their first importation, the King of England have been able — whatever his avarice as an individual — to have effected so great a diplomatic treaty, as the consent from all the civilized nations having interests here to people their colonies with a race if that race had been worthless as laborers, and deficient as an industrial element? Would, in the year of the grace of Jesus Christ, and the light of the highest civilization, after the lapse of two hundred and twenty years from James's treaty, the most powerful and enlightened monarchy have come near the crisis of its political career in its determination to continue the system, and for two hundred and forty-seven years the most powerful and enlightened republic that ever the world saw have distracted the harmony of the nations of the earth, and driven itself to the verge of destruction by the mad determination of one half of the people and leading states, to perpetuate the service of this race as essential to the development of the agricultural wealth of the land? After these centuries of trial and experience, would these people have been continually sought after, had they not proven to be superior to all others as laborers in the kind of work assigned them? Let political economists answer.

V.

As shown in my last article, these people are the lineal descendants of an industrious, hardy race of men — those whom the most powerful and accomplished statesmen and political economists of the great states of Europe, after years of trial and rigid experience, decided upon and selected as the element best adapted to develop in a strange and foreign clime — a new world of unbroken soil and dense, impenetrable forests — the industry and labor necessary to the new life. This cannot and will not be attempted to be denied without ignoring all historical authority, though presented in a different light — and may I not say motive? — from that in which history has ever given it.

These people are of those to retain whom in her power the great British nation was agitated to the point, at as late a period as 1837–8, of shattering the basis of its political foundation; and, within the last four years, the genius of the American government was spurned, assaulted, and trampled upon, and had come well nigh its final dissolution by full one half of the states, people, and statesmen inaugurating a civil war, the most stupendous on record, for no other purpose than retaining them as laborers. Does any intelligent person doubt the utility of such a people? Can such a people now be worthless in the country? Does any enlightened, reflecting person believe it? I think not.

But this is an experiment. Have we no precedent, no example? What of the British colonies of the West Indies and South America? Let impartial history and dispassionate, intelligent investigation answer. The land in the colonies was owned by wealthy capitalists and gentlemen who resided in Europe. The "proprietors," or planters, were occupants of the land, who owned the slaves that worked it, having borrowed the capital with which to purchase them at the Cuba markets or barracoons and supply the plantations. In security for this, mortgages were held by those in Europe on "all estate, real and personal," belonging to the planters, who paid a liberal interest on the loans.

When the opposition in the British Parliament, led by Tories, who were the representatives of the capitalists, yielded to the Emancipation Bill, it was only on condition of an appropriation of twenty millions of pounds sterling, or one hundred millions of dollars, as remuneration to the planters for their slaves set free. This proposition was so moderate as to surprise and astonish the intelligent in state affairs on both sides of the ocean, as the sum proposed only amounted to the penurious price of about one hundred and twenty dollars apiece, when men and women were then bringing at the barracoons in Cuba from five to six hundred dollars apiece in cash; and the average of men, women, and children, according to their estimate of black mankind, were " worth " four hundred and fifty dollars. Of course the tutored colonial laborer would be worth still more.

After the passage of the Act of Emancipation by the Imperial Parliament, the complaint was wafted back by the breeze of every passing wind, that the planters in the colonies were impoverished by emancipation, and dishonest politicians and defeated, morose statesmen seized the opportunity to display their duplicity. "What will become of the fair colonial possessions? The lands will go back into a wilderness waste. The negroes are idle, lazy, and will not work. They are unfit for freedom, and ought to have masters. Where they do work, not half the crop is produced on the same quantity of land. What will the whites do if they don't get servants to work for them? They and their posterity must starve. The lands are lying waste for the want of occupants, and the negroes are idling their time away, and will not have them when offered **to them.** The social system in the West Indies has been ruined by the emancipation of the negroes." These, and a thousand such complaints, tingled upon the sensitive ear in every word that came from the British colonies, as the key-note of the pro-slavery British party, till caught up and reëchoed from the swift current **of the south**ern extremity of Brazil to the banks of the Potomac, the northern extremity of the slave territory of the United States. **But** alive to passing events, and true to their great trust, the philanthropists and people **soon** discovered, through their eminent representatives and statesmen in Parliament, that the whites in the colonies had never owned the lands nor the blacks which they lost by the Act of Emancipation. And when the appropriation was made by Parliament, the money remained in the vaults of the banks in Europe, being precisely the amount required to liquidate the claims of the capitalists, **and to** satisfy the mortgages held by those gentlemen against "all estates" of the **bor**rowers in the colonies, both "real and personal."

The cause of the cry and clamor must be **seen** at a **glance.** The money supposed to be intended for the colonists, small as **it** was, instead of being appropriated to them, simply went to satisfy the claims of the capitalists who resided in Great Britain, not one out of a hundred of whom had ever seen the colonies. And the lands **being** owned in Europe, and the laborers free, what was to save the white colonists from poverty? All this was well known to leading pro-slavery politicians and statesmen in Europe as well as America; but a determination to perpetuate the bondage of a people as laborers — a people so valuable as to cause them, rather than loose their grasp upon them, to boldly hazard their national integrity, and set at defiance the morality of the civilized world in holding them — caused this reprehensible imposition and moral outrage in misleading to distraction their common constituency.

VI.

Mr. Editor: This is my sixth article on the subject of the "Prospects of the Freedmen of Hilton Head" Island, which you have so generously admitted into the columns of The New South, and for which liberality towards a recently liberated people, I most heartily thank you. The time may come when they, for themselves, may be able to thank you. I hope to conclude with my next.

After what has been adduced in proof of their susceptibility, adaptation, and propensity for the vocations of the domestic and social relations of our civilization, what are their *prospects?* for that now must be the leading question, and give more concern to the philanthropist, true statesman, and Christian, than anything relating to their fitness or innate adaptation, since that I hold to be admitted, and no longer a question — at least with the intelligent inquirer.

What should be the prospects? Will not the same labor that was performed by a slave be in requisition still? Cannot he do the same work as a freedman that he once did as a slave? Are the products of slave labor preferable to free? or are the products of free labor less valuable than slave? Will not rice and cotton be in as great demand after emancipation as before it? or will these commodities cease to be used, because they cease to be produced by the labor of slaves? All these are questions pertinent, if not potent, to the important inquiry under consideration — the prospects of the freedmen of Hilton Head.

Certainly these things will be required, in demand, and labor quite as plentiful; but not one half of the negroes can be induced to work, as was proven in the West Indies, and is apparent from the comparative number who now seek their old vocations to those who formerly did the same work.

Grant this, — which is true, — and is it an objectionable feature, or does it impair the prospects of the freedman? By no means; but, on the contrary, it enhances his prospects and elevates his manhood. Here, as in the case of West India emancipation, before emancipation took place every available person — male and female — from seven years of age to decrepit old age (as field hands) was put into the field to labor.

For example, take one case to illustrate the whole. Before liberated, Juba had a wife and eight children, from seven to thirty years of age, every one of whom was at labor in the field

as a slave. When set free, the mother and all of the younger
children (consisting of five) quit the field, leaving the father and
three older sons, from twenty-five to thirty years of age, who
preferred field labor; the five children being sent to school.
The mother, now the pride of the recently-elevated freedman,
stays in her own house, to take charge, as a housewife, in her
new domestic relations — thus permanently withdrawing from
the field six tenths of the service of this family; while the husband and three sons (but four tenths) are all who remain to do
the work formerly performed by ten tenths, or the whole. Here
are more than one half who will not work in the field. Will any
one say they should? And this one example may suffice for the
most querulous on this subject. Human nature is all the same
under like circumstances. The immutable, unalterable laws
which governed or controlled the instincts or impulses of a Hannibal, Alexander, or Napoleon, are the same implanted in the
brain and breast of page or footman, be he black or white, circumstances alone making the difference in development according to the individual propensity.

As slaves, people have no choice of pursuit or vocation, but
must follow that which is chosen by the master. Slaves, like
freemen, have different tastes and desires — many doing that
which is repugnant to their choice. As slaves, they were compelled to subserve the interests of the master regardless of themselves; as freemen, as should be expected and be understood,
many changes would take place in the labor and pursuits of the
people. Some who were field hands, among the young men and
women of mature age, seek employment at other pursuits, and
choose for themselves various trades — vocations adapted to their
tastes.

Will this be charged to the worthlessness of the negro, and
made an argument against his elevation? Truth stands defiant
in the pathway of error.

VII.

I propose to conclude the subject of "The Prospects of the
Freedmen of Hilton Head" with this article, and believe that

the prospects of the one are the prospects of the whole population of freedmen throughout the South.

Political economy must stand most prominent as the leading feature of this great question of the elevation of the negro — and it is a great question — in this country, because, however humane and philanthropic, however Christian and philanthropic we may be, except we can be made to see that there is a prospective enhancement of the general wealth of the country, — a pecuniary benefit to accrue by it to society, — the best of us, whatever our pretensions, could scarcely be willing to see him elevated in the United States.

Equality of political rights being the genius of the American government, I shall not spend time with this, as great principles will take care of themselves, and must eventually prevail.

Will the negroes be able to obtain land by which to earn a livelihood? Why should they not? It is a well-known fact to the statisticians of the South that two thirds of the lands have never been cultivated. These lands being mainly owned by but three hundred and twelve thousand persons (according to Helper) — one third of which was worked by four millions of slaves, who are now freemen — what better can be done with these lands to make them available and unburdensome to the proprietors, than let them out in small tracts to the freedmen, as well as to employ a portion of the same people, who prefer it, to cultivate lands for themselves?

It is a fact— probably not so well known as it should be — in political economy, that a given amount of means divided among a greater number of persons, makes a wealthier community than the same amount held or possessed by a few.

For example, there is a community of a small country village of twenty families, the (cash) wealth of the community being fifty thousand dollars, and but one family the possessor of it; certainly the community would not be regarded as in good circumstances, much less having available means. But let this amount be possessed by ten families in sums of five thousand dollars each, would not this enhance the wealth of the community? And again, let the whole twenty families be in possession of two thousand five hundred dollars each of the fifty thousand, would not this be still a wealthier community, by placing each family in easier circumstances, and making **these** means much more available? Certainly it would. And **as to a community** or village, so to a state; and as to **a state, so to a nation.**

This is the solution to the great problem **of the** difference between the strength of the North and **the South in the late** rebellion — the North possessing **the means within itself** without requiring outside help, **almost every man** being able to **aid the** national treasury; everybody **commanding** means, whether earned by a white-wash brush **in black hands, or** wooden nutmegs in white: all had something to sustain **the integrity of the Union. It must be seen** by this that the **strength of a** country — internationally considered — depends greatly upon its wealth; the **wealth** consisting not in the **greatest amount** possessed, but the greatest available amount.

Let, then, such lands **as** belong to **the government, by** sale from direct taxation, be let or sold to these **freedmen, and** other poor loyal men of the South, in small tracts **of from** twenty to forty acres to each head of a family, **and large** landholders do the same, — the rental and sales of which **amply** rewarding them, — and there will be no difficulty in **the solution of the** problem of the future, or prospects of the **freedmen, not only** of Hilton Head, but of the whole United States.

This increase of the **wealth** of the country by the greater division of its means **is not** new to New England, nor **to the** economists of the North generally. **As** in Pennsylvania, **many** years ago, the old farmers commenced dividing their **one hundred** and one hundred and fifty acre tracts of lands **into twenty-** five acres each among their **sons and daughters, who are known** to have realized more available means **always among** them — though by far greater in numbers — than **their** parents did, who **were** comparatively few. And it is now patent **as an** historic fact, that, leaving behind them the extensive **evergreen, fertile** plains, and savannas of the South, the rebel **armies** and raiders continually sought the limited farms of the **North** to replenish their worn-out cavalry stock and exhausted commissary department — impoverished in cattle for food, and forage for horses.

In the Path Valley of Pennsylvania, on a single march of a

radius of thirty-five miles of Chambersburg, Lee's army, besides all the breadstuffs that his three thousand five hundred wagons (as they went empty for the purpose) were able to carry, captured and carried off more than six thousand head of stock, four thousand of which were horses. The wealth of that valley alone, they reported, was more than India fiction, and equal to all of the South put together. And whence this mighty available wealth of Pennsylvania? Simply by its division and possession among the many.

The Rothschilds are said to have once controlled the exchequer of England, compelling (by implication) the premier to comply with their requisition at a time of great peril to the nation, simply because it depended upon them for means; and the same functionaries are reported, during our recent struggle, to have greatly annoyed the Bank of England, by a menace of some kind, which immediately brought the institution to their terms. Whether true or false, the points are sufficiently acute to serve for illustration.

In the apportionment of small farms to the freedmen, an immense amount of means is placed at their command, and thereby a great market opened, a new source of consumption of every commodity in demand in free civilized communities. The blacks are great consumers, and four millions of a population, before barefooted, would here make a demand for the single article of shoes. The money heretofore spent in Europe by the old slaveholders would be all disbursed by these new people in their own country. Where but one cotton gin and a limited number of farming utensils were formerly required to the plantation of a thousand acres, every small farm will want a gin and farming implements, the actual valuation of which on the same tract of land would be several fold greater than the other. Huts would give place to beautiful, comfortable cottages, with all their appurtenances, fixtures, and furniture; osnaburgs and rags would give place to genteel apparel becoming a free and industrious people; and even the luxuries, as well as the general comforts, of the table would take the place of black-eye peas and fresh fish, hominy and salt pork, all of which have been mainly the products of their own labor when slaves. They would quickly prove that arduous and faithfully **fawning,** miserable volunteer advocate of the rebellion and slaveholder's rule in the United States, — the London Times, — an arrant falsifier, when it gratuitously and unbidden came to the aid of **its kith** and kin, declaring that the great **and** good President Lincoln's Emancipation Proclamation would not be **accepted** by the negroes; "that all Cuffee wanted and cared for to make him happy was his hog and his hominy;" **but they** will **neither** get land, nor **will the** old **slaveholders give them** employment. **Don't fear any such ab**surdity. There **are too many** political economists **among the** old leading slaveholders to fear the adoption of any such policy. Neither will the leading statesmen of the country, of any part, North or South, favor any such policy.

We have on record but one instance of such a course in the history of **modern** states. The silly-brained, foolhardy king of France, **Louis V.,** taking umbrage at the political course of the artisans and laborers against him, by royal decree expelled them **from the** country, **when they** flocked **into** England, which readily opened her doors to **them, transplanting from France to** England their arts and industry; **ever since** which, England, **for fabrics,** has become the "workshop of the world," **to the poverty of** France, the government of **which is sustained by borrowed** capital.

No fears of our country driving into neighboring countries **such** immense resources as emanate from the peculiar labor of these people; but when worst comes to worst, they have among **them educated freemen of** their own color North, fully competent **to lead the way,** by making negotiations with foreign states **on this continent,** which would only be too ready to receive them **and theirs.**

Place no impediment in the way of the freedman; let his right be **equally** protected and his chances **be** equally regarded, and with the facts presented to you in this series of seven articles as **the basis, he** will stand and thrive, as firmly rooted, not only **on** the soil of Hilton Head, but in all the South, — though a black, — **as** any white, or "Live Oak," as ever was grown in South Carolina, or transplanted to Columbia.

These articles were published from September to December consecutively, with two weekly exceptions, until the command of the department was assumed by Major General Daniel E. Sickles. They were form-. erly published anonymously: until then the major was not at liberty to exercise the full functions of his office as a representative of the bureau, as more would be accomplished by concealing the author's name. Feeling free from a restraint which, while it may have been enjoyed by others, was distasteful to him, at last he ventured for the first time to give official publicity to. these articles, as will be seen by the following letter: —

Triple Alliance. — The Restoration of the South. — Salvation of its Political Economy.

The restoration of the industrial prosperity of the South is certain, if fixed upon the basis of a domestic triple alliance, which the new order of things requires, invites, and demands.

Capital, land, and labor require a copartnership. The capital can be obtained in the North; the land is in the South, owned by the old planters; and the blacks have the labor. Let, then, the North supply the capital (which no doubt it will do on demand, when known to be desired on this basis), the South the land (which is ready and waiting), and the blacks will readily bring the labor, if only being assured that their services are wanted in so desirable an association of business relations, the net profits being equally shared between the three, — capital, land, and labor, — each receiving one third, of course. The *net* has reference to the expenses incurred after gathering the crop, such as transportation, storage, and commission on sales.

Upon this basis I propose to act, and make contracts between the capitalist, landholder, and laborer, and earnestly invite, and call upon all colored people, — the recent freedmen, — also capitalists and landholders within the limits of my district, to enter at once into a measure the most reasonable and just to all parties concerned, and the very best that can be adopted to meet the demands of the new order and state of society, as nothing can pay better where the blacks cannot get land for themselves.

I am at liberty to name Rev. Dr. Stoney (Episcopal clergyman), Joseph J. Stoney, Esq., Dr. Crowell, Colonel Colcock (late of the Southern army) — all the first gentlemen formerly of wealth and affluence in the State; and Major Roy, of the United States Regular Army, Inspector General of the department; Colonel Green, commanding district, and Lieutenant Colonel Clitz, commanding post, also of the regular army, each having friends interested in planting, who readily indorse this new partnership arrangement. Of course it receives the approval of Major General Saxton.

I am, sir, very respectfully,

Your most obedient servant,

M. R. Delany,

Major & A. S. A. Commissioner Bureau R. F. A. L.

Hilton Head, December 7, 1865.

The planters of the islands and upland districts, recognizing the advantages of the bureau in their midst, when conducted by an efficient officer, consulted him when occasion required.

Among them was Colonel Colcock, with whom he had, on one occasion, an extended interview, previous to the publication of the foregoing article, in which interview the following resulted: —

Hilton Head, December 8, 1865.

Major M. R. Delany, *A. S. A. C. Bureau R. F. A. L.*

Major: I wish to employ sixty laborers on my homestead place on Colleton River, and two hundred on Spring Island, and will thank you to engage them for me, on the basis of the contract which I showed you on Friday. In engaging labor, you will please give the preference to the freedmen who formerly resided on these islands, provided there is nothing objectionable in their character.

Try to arrange it so that each family will average three field hands, as I have house-room to accommodate them on that basis.

Yours respectfully,

C. J. Colcock.

Headquarters Bureau R. F. A. L.,
 Hilton Head, S. C., December 11, 1865.

Colonel C. J. Colcock, *late of the Southern Army.*

Colonel: I received your communication on Saturday last, desiring to know whether or not two hundred and sixty laborers, or cultivators, can be obtained on the basis of copartnership of capital, land, and labor, or what I term the domestic triple alliance, embracing a series of articles drawn up by yourself, as the conditions of your contract.

I reply most positively, that you may confidently rely upon such aid in your business arrangements, as the people are waiting, ready and willing, to consummate such contracts as this plan proposes, alike advantageous to all the parties interested.

I may here be permitted to suggest in this connection, that there are generosity and liberality of feeling in the North towards the South, in its present position, scarcely believed by southern people; and all the North asks is, that their neighbors be disposed to do right, and they may obtain anything in reason, financially, that is desirable.

I have taken the liberty to suggest several modifications in the articles of agreement which you present, to prevent misconstruction or ambiguity, and added one more article, which I consider important (Art. 14). I name this, that it may not be thought that you have assumed to prescribe what should suit the people, but that the injunction of frugality and economy may come from themselves, through their own representative.

I am, colonel, very respectfully, yours,

M. R. Delany,
 Major and A. S. A. C.

CHAPTER XXIX.

GENERAL SICKLES.

MAJOR DELANY was opposed openly in every advanced step he made, as stated before; hence, to accomplish any new measure of his relative to his office, he was compelled to resort to strategy. Before, oppositions of various characters were placed in his way, but he never permitted himself to be disturbed by them. He was actually forbidden to address the freedmen on public occasions concerning their rights; he spoke through the voice of the press, to the public at large, of their wrongs, and it found an echo in every loyal and generous heart. His color made him objectionable to many at that post as an officer, and his scathing denunciations of injustice rendered to the helpless and uneducated people who constantly challenged their consideration, showing him to be no mean opponent, rendered him still more objectionable.

Now he was at liberty to act freely; having an acceptable basis on which to begin his work, though late in the season, his prospect of usefulness appeared in its most promising light.

It was not long after the appearance of his "Triple Alliance Contract" that the following telegram was sent by order of the distinguished commander of the

Department of South Carolina, since of the Second Military District.

CHARLESTON, December 18, 1865.

To Major DELANY, 104*th* *U. S. C. T.*

General Sickles desires to see you at Charleston as soon as possible.

W. L. M. BURGER, *A. A. G.*

The brilliant record written in unmistakable characters by this great neophyte to Liberty, as military lawgiver of the Carolinas, vies with the glory which encircled him at Gettysburg.

When the history of these eventful times shall have been compiled, the most pleasing development of the late revolution will be noted in the invaluable service given to the cause of human rights by those who previously opposed it. The ardor of these converts gave renewed zeal to the faithful; conspicuous among these, in letters as imperishable as their deeds, will be found the name of this gallant commander.

A few days after the reception of the telegram found Major Delany reporting his presence at the quarters of Major General Sickles. Of him he wrote afterwards, "I consider the gallant general who contributed so much to the victory at Gettysburg, a most liberal-minded statesman. His massive intellect at once grasped with vivid comprehension the entire range of political economy, domestic and social relations. In this interview he reviewed the situation thoroughly, giving me the details of instructions which were embodied in an *order*." This recognition, after previous discouragements, of his earnest efforts, from sources least expected, was certainly gratifying.

The general, in giving the instructions to him, said, " I cannot go myself," pointing to the remnant of the limb which he contributed to the nation's life at Gettysburg; " it requires an active person, and one in whom I can place reliance. You will be my representative. And *I shall crush* whatever dares to oppose you in your duties," he added, rising and straightening himself upon his crutches, as is characteristic of him, and suiting a gesture to the word.

Immediately after the interview with the commanding general, Major Delany returned to his post at Hilton Head, to make arrangements for starting on his tour of inspection. In this capacity he was *de facto* the military representative from the headquarters.

The discerning general had his attention drawn on several occasions to the many abuses, both by the civil and military, of the person and property of blacks and whites. He could not fail to notice, when he assumed command of the department, that the bureau was unpopular with a large class, comprising Northerners and Southerners — its friends and officers hated; and with the exception of orders which came directly from the assistant commissioner, discouragements were placed in the way, of such nature, that the entire social arrangement was threatened with neglect. It will be remembered that at this time the status of the bureau was not definitely settled, and its authority could be, and was, disputed by any ordinary military official.

Thus, in order to check the growing evil, it was necessary that a proper inspection should be made by one familiar with the system of the bureau, and yet, in order to be respected, with a military authority; hence the appointment of Major Delany by General Sickles.

The following order was furnished him: the instructions therein given, being strictly adhered to, resulted satisfactorily, as will be shown.

HEADQUARTERS DEPARTMENT OF SOUTH CAROLINA, CHARLESTON, S. C., December 21, 1865.

Special Orders. No. 148.

IV. *Major M. R. Delany,* 104th United States Colored Infantry, will proceed at once to the Military District of Port Royal, and the Sea Islands in the Military District of Charleston, South Carolina, and inspect, and report upon the condition of the population therein, according to the instructions received from the major general commanding. Commanding officers will afford **Major** Delany **all** necessary facilities.

The **quartermaster's** department will furnish **the necessary transportation.**

By command of   Major General D. E. SICKLES.

W. L. M. BURGER, *Asst. Adjt. Gen.*

While on the eve of setting out on his tour of inspection, a report had reached Hilton Head that the negroes of Port Royal Island had matured an insurrection, to take place on Christmas night, their headquarters being Beaufort. At first no person paid sufficient attention to a rumor so silly; but finally it magnified into an alarm, which caused the major to be sought out by many of the white citizens and some of the military, and requested to take a detachment of troops, and make Beaufort his first point of inspection. This was Christmas Eve.

Believing that "the better part of valor is discretion," and to make assurance doubly sure, he at once made a requisition for a detachment of the 21st United States Colored Troops, then doing duty at the post. A part of Company E was detailed, under command of a sergeant, with other assistant non-commissioned officers. On Christmas night the transport steamer Sampson, Dennett, master, was ordered, which carried him to Beaufort, though, in consequence of a fog, he did not reach that point till five o'clock the next morning; not in time to quell an insurrection of the evening before, but in good season to learn from the "*rising inhabitants*," that among the most quiet and pleasant evenings of the year was that which had just given place to the morning; and the insurrection-haunted whites of the island could again repose in peace, until the next report would awake them.

Completing his official duties at Beaufort, the next point of importance was Edisto, where he went by advice of Major General Sickles. Here he met, at the headquarters of Captain Batchelor, commanding a detachment of United States forces, a delegation of the old planters, at the head of which was Jacob Jenkins Mikell, Esq., formerly one of the largest cotton-growers of Sea Island.

The 1st of January found him here, and he attended an immense gathering of the freedmen at their emancipation celebration. He addressed them, and in the course of his advice endeavored to disabuse their minds of the expectation of obtaining land, which he

foresaw, and believed from the course of events then transpiring, would **not be** realized. On account of this **advice** he was misrepresented by ignorant, though **well**-meaning, as well as mischievous and designing persons, the latter induced, doubtless, **by their mercenary pro**-clivities. The **people** were led to believe **that he was** opposed to their interest, and in that of **the** planters. But the greater portion of these freedmen **have** since learned whether or not his advice on that occasion **was** in their **favor or** that of others.

By the force of his genius and acquirements, as **well** as position, he had compelled the **old** planters of Carolina **to extend a** recognition to him such **as** no black **had ever before received;** so that, while visiting many **of the plantations of Edisto, so** thoroughly had slavery **done its work, that his advice to** them only served to arouse their suspicions. John's, James's, and Wadmalaw Islands were barely touched **upon; but the advice** given was strictly guarded, **in order to be** effective.

He turned towards Charleston soon after, and **re**-ported his observation to the major general commanding, and paid **his** respects to the commissioner of the Bureau of Refugees, Freedmen, and Abandoned Lands.

The detachment of troops which had accompanied **him had acted only thus** far **as a** guard of honor, he having **had no occasion,** happily, for their **service.**

While he was reporting in Charleston, the order **was** received relieving Major **General** Saxton of his **com**-mand. **The** people, not having a knowledge **of his** noble successor, Major General Robert **K.** Scott, **were** anxiously excited.

The following Sabbath, three days after the news of his removal was received, a large meeting of the colored people, indiscriminately, was called at Zion's Church, for the purpose of expressing their gratitude to the general for his steadfast adherence to their interest, and their unfeigned regret at his removal.

At this meeting the general, his family, and a part of his staff, with other military officers, including the black major, were present. The speeches and resolutions on this occasion gave evidence of their appreciation of the character of that distinguished military philanthropist; and at a subsequent meeting some testimonials were presented by the people, and the scholars of the Saxton and Morris Street Schools, in simple acknowledgment of his official services, and of their personal attachment to him.

Knowing the suspicion and dissatisfaction with which the freedmen and colored people generally in South Carolina look upon such changes respecting those whose friendship they have enjoyed, or those upon whose impartial sense of justice they are willing to abide, the days of General Saxton's removal, in remembrance of their unbounded attachment and devotion, and the scenes attending it, remain in the mind as one of the most touching reminiscences of our war.

After the great Saxton meeting, the major prepared for setting out for his post at Hilton Head. On arriving on Monday morning at the wharf, he was met by Brigadier General Bennett, with two companies of colored troops, just boarding the transport steamer Canonicus, *en route* for Mount Pleasant and Sullivan's

Island, for four companies more, on an expedition on the Ashley River, to o plantation about ten miles distant, to quell an "insurrection of the negroes." This offspring of a haunted southern mind having in hot haste reached the headquarters, the major general commanding deemed it advisable to take measures to quiet all apprehension by the presence of forces on the spot, and with his characteristic deliberation, in order to remove all unfavorable impressions as to the intentions of the military towards the freedmen, he requested that Major Delany should accompany the expedition, so that whatever action might have been necessary, his presence among them would indicate that it was executed under the most favorable circumstances.

Sending back his baggage in charge of his orderly, he embarked with the brigadier general. On reaching the plantation, they found the only evidence of an insurrection, was an attempt that had been made by some persons to effect an unjust contract, which the freedmen refused to receive, and declared their intention to abandon the place before they would submit. The military applauded their action, as there was no violence accompanying it, and their verdict, "You did right," settled everything further on the part of the aggressors. The major introduced to their consideration, and finally placed them fairly on, his system of land, labor, and capital, or triple alliance system. There being no further need of military intervention, they returned to Charleston, happy at the result of their passive victory. We would have cause for gratulations if future military expeditions into other places on similar bases of equality and right and claims settled between oppression and oppressed, rich and poor, had terminated as happily as did that.

The major, having accomplished his mission, set out that afternoon for Hilton Head, to resume his functions.

CHAPTER XXX.

RESTORING DOMESTIC RELATIONS.

ON Delany's return to his post, encouraged by the approval of the commanding general, he again turned his attention to resuscitating the lulled industrial powers of the people, by vigorously urging and aiding, in his official capacity, the reproduction of the staples which were once the traffic of the South.

The triple alliance system had now become popular, and his office was always thronged by those seeking advice, of all classes, blacks and whites, ex-slaves and ex-slaveholders.

This will be more readily comprehended when it is remembered that the freedmen had shown a determination that they would never again work for these ex-slaveholders.

In his interviews with either party, he never omitted to remind them that there existed no longer either slaves or slaveholders,—their relation to each other being essentially changed; that all were American citizens, and equal before the law ; that the war having reduced many to poverty, unless some exertion should be made, starvation would soon ensue; and this while they had the support and self-sustenance within their own reach, by a mere alliance of their efforts. It had been done before ; it could be repeated in their case. Under the old *régime*, the master supported the slave by the slave's own production, which also supported the owner ; hence the support was reciprocal by mutual dependence. The condition of each being changed, a union of interests was now required to bring prosperity to the country. The freedman was now to be a partner, having an equal share, and controlling his own affairs. This would induce him to be more self-reliant. His observation of the labor systems of other countries had given him experience. He explained in the clearest terms to them, that, throughout the world, the only established order of wealth and prosperity to a people was through the proper union of land, labor, and capital.

He frequently urged upon them that the blacks and whites were the social and political element of the South, and must continue the basis of her wealth by a union of their efforts and strength ; that the displacement of the white southern planters for northern capitalists, would not be found desirable, as it would result in substituting for the black laborers, the poor whites from the North, relatives of the rich capitalists, or immigrants, while it was desirable that northern capitalists should unite with southern proprietors, and northern mechanical skill and intelligence be incorporated among the southerners, rich and poor. By this means the South would obtain her true civilization.

On this subject the editors of the **New South**, recognizing the success of the endeavors of this indefatigable work, and justly popular officer, pay the following deserved tribute to him in the issue of January 27, which was but the public sentiment concerning his administration : —

"THE LABOR QUESTION. — We are happy to report a continued improvement in this neighborhood. The freed-people — men, women, and children — are beginning to display, not only a willingness, but an anxiety, to get to work at once, as the time for cotton-planting will soon be over. While we are writing, several hundred are congregated around Major Delany's **quarters, who acts as** medium between the employers and employees, and carefully adjusts all points of difference."

An incident relative to his simple and decisive mode of disposing of cases is related.

The case was brought up a few weeks **after his appointment** in the Bureau, by **a** former slave-owner against her ex-slave. In deciding cases in which **the** freedmen are the aggressors, whatever may be his opinion in regard to their claims **to** the consideration **of the** planters, he ignores both color **and** condition, aiming **solely to render unto** Cæsar **the things that are** Cæsar's.

An intelligent-looking middle-aged woman, accompanied by her **husband and two male** friends, entered his office, apparently laboring under great excitement, followed by an intelligent-looking black youth. The lady being politely handed **a seat, the major** inquired **her** business, judging her, from her manner of acting, to **be the complainant in** the case. About this time horses were being sold in that section at very high prices, the most ordinary commanding from one hundred to **a** hundred and seventy-five dollars. The complainant had just left the Provost Court, where a horse, her **favorite, and only remaining** property left from the late war, having been seized upon by the young lad, — a former "chattel," "Jim," — had been restored to her in conformity with a current order of the government. But Jim persistently refused to return the property, declaring in the hearing of the judge, as he left the court, he would kill the horse the moment they should attempt to take him away.

They had been advised for protection to repair to the quarters of Major Delany.

The major gave his attention to both sides, and satisfying himself as to the proceeding, he decided that the case was regular and valid, and that, the decision of the Provost Court being just, the parties should comply with its demands ordering the young man to give it up. The horse, meanwhile, stood tied to the fence, directly opposite the window where sat the major at his desk. The lady hesitated to leave the office.

"Go and take your horse, madam," said he.

"Where is the guard?" inquired the lady.

"What guard, madam?"

"The guard to protect me and my property," she answered.

"You need no protection ; you, being just from the interior, forget that hostilities have ended," said the major.

"Yes, but he'll kill the horse — he swore that he would, and I know that he'll do it."

"Take your horse, madam," said he, becoming impatient at her hesitancy, "and don't be alarmed at the idle talk of a disappointed boy."

"Major," said she, "I will not go without protection.

I know Jim well, and if you knew him as well as I do, you wouldn't talk that way; I must have a guard, or my horse will be lost, and all my trouble and expense in coming down here, and my only dependence, gone."

Turning to the woman and young man at the same time, with that stern expression that his brow sometimes assumes, said he, "Madam, do you really suppose that the power which put down the masters, compelling them to submit at discretion, is not sufficient to control one of their former slaves — an idle, babbling black boy?"

The young man, giving vent to laughter, which he evidently did to disguise his chagrin, replied, "Major, I ain't going to trouble the horse; she kin have um." The parties, being assured of this, left the office with better feelings towards each other, we trust, than when they entered.

CHAPTER XXXI.

GENERAL ROBERT K. SCOTT.

THE affairs of the Bureau promised a change in the advent of its new chief, in the person of Brevet Major General Scott. He entered upon the duties of his office in a most spirited and independent manner.

In many respects, it was thought, his administration was better adapted to the times than was the former general's. The rebels, encouraged by the smiles of their friends in high places, were fast resuming their old practices, and the status of the Bureau was scarcely recognized. General Scott having had some insight into the southern character while a prisoner in Charleston, during the war, his administration was looked upon with terror by the unrepentant chivalry of South Carolina; and it was not long before the difference was felt by them between the mild administration of West Point's accomplished soldier and that of the bluff western general.

On assuming the duties of his office, the general, accompanied by a portion of his staff, made a tour of inspection through his department, visiting every officer on duty, previous to reappointing him.

On this occasion the major's post received attention, and the satisfactory expressions of the general gave a new impetus, if possible, to both officers and laborers in their respective spheres. The plans by which he had accomplished so much in the department were submitted to his inspection, and received his indorsement.

We present here the contract written expressly for his district, and rigidly enforced by him, though in many cases all the articles signed by the contracting parties would be simply an acknowledgment of his triple alliance contract: —

Article I. This contract between Justice Goodman and the freedmen, whose names are hereunto affixed, is on the basis of an equal partnership between Capital, Land, and Labor — each receiving one third of the proceeds of the productions of the cultivated plantation of Homestead Farm, Beaufort District, South Carolina, and to continue till January 1, 1867.

Article II. Each laborer is to receive (besides the privilege of firewood, with team and vehicle to haul it, and *one acre* of land to each family) one third of all that he or she is able to produce by cultivation, clear of all expenses except those incurred in the transportation and sale of the staple, as freight and commission on storage and sales, they supporting themselves and families; the proprietor making all advances of provisions or rations on credit (if required), finding all dwellings for the contractors, supplying all farming utensils, vehicles, machinery, sufficient working stock; and no labor is to be performed by hand or by a person that can better be done by animal labor or machinery.

Article III. All restrictions and obligations legally binding contracting parties in the fulfilment of their articles of agreement are implied in this article, and all damage for injury or loss of property by carelessness is to be paid by fair and legal assessment.

Article IV. Negligence of duty in cultivation, so as to become injurious to the proprietor or other contracting parties, either by loss in the production of staple, or example in conduct or precedent, may, by investigation, cause a forfeiture of the interest of such person in their share of the crop. Any contractor taking the place of one dismissed shall succeed to all of their rights and claims on the part of the crop left by them; otherwise it shall be equally divided between those who work it.

Article V. All Thanksgiving Days, Fast Days, "holidays," and national celebration days are to be enjoyed in all cases by contractors, without being regarded as a neglect of duty or violation of contract.

Article VI. Good conduct and good behavior of the freedmen towards the proprietor, good treatment of animals, and good care of tools, utensils, &c., and good and kind treatment by the proprietor to the freedmen, will be strictly required by the authorities; and all dwellings and immediate premises of freedmen must be kept neat and clean, subject to inspection and fine for neglect by such sanitary arrangements as the government may make.

Article VII. No sutler stores will be permitted on the place, and nothing sold on account except the necessaries of life, that such as good, substantial food and working clothes, conducive to health and comfort, at cost, that no inducements may be given for spending earnings improperly. Spirituous liquors will not be permitted.

Article VIII. All accounts must be entered in a pass-book, to be kept by each family or individual for the purpose, that no advantage be taken by incorrect charges; and no account against them will be recognized except such entry be made. No tobacco charges above fifty cents a month will be recognized by the Bureau. In all cases of the loss of their account-books, then the account in the proprietor's books must be taken to date of loss, when another pass-book must be obtained, and entries of accounts made as before.

Article IX. In all cases where an accusation is made against a person, the proprietor or his agent, one of the contractors or freedmen selected by themselves, and a third person chosen by the two, — provided neither of these three is biassed or prejudiced against the accused, — shall be a competent council to investigate and acquit the accused; but in all cases where a decision is to be made to dismiss or forfeit a share of the crop, the officer of the Bureau, or some other competent officer of the government, must preside in the council of trial, and make the decision in the case. When the proprietor is biassed or prejudiced against an accused person, he must name a person to take his place in the council who shall neither be biassed nor prejudiced against the accused.

Witness our hands and signs this 17th day of February, 1866.

He still indicated, by his unflagging energy and industry, as well as equitable measures, his consciousness of the immense responsibilities resting upon him.

This only served to redouble his zeal and activity, as this trait is in consonance with his character generally. In more than one instance in other days, while the political horizon seemed to increase in gloom, the man seems to have loomed up more conspicuously in proportion to the exigency of the situation. Always actuated by his insatiable though laudable ambition, Major Delany leads an age in advance where others of his own people, possessed of abilities and acknowledged courage, would even hesitate to follow.

In his official duties so conscientiously did he perform his part, and so firm was he in his high-toned native pride, and honesty against bribery and partiality, that he received aid from many of those whose duties were not altogether in the same channel. Among them he mentions particularly his indebtedness to Major J. P. Roy, 6th United States Infantry, inspector general of the Department South, Colonel J. D. Green, 6th United States Infantry, commanding district, and Colonel, now General H. B. Clitz, 6th United States Infantry, then commanding the post at Hilton Head, now Charleston.   They facilitated and aided him in his official duties, as well as ameliorated the condition of the freedmen and suffering whites, refugees, and ex-slaveholders: all of these came under his department, and **were constantly** referred to him when not voluntarily applying. The editors of **the New South,** who took note of his movements, again make mention of him, **in their issue of the 3d of February:—**

"Major M. R. Delany, the 'black major' of the Freedmen's **Bureau,** is now on the right track.   Comprehending the situation **of affairs, he** has seized at once upon its difficulties, and **is** doing a noble work for his race.   His sympathies are, of course, with those of his own color; **but,** being a man of large experi**ence,** highly educated, and eminently conscientious, he does not **allow** prejudice to sway him one way or the other, and, consequently, he has a wonderful influence for good over the freedmen.   He tells them to go to work at once; that **labor surely** brings its own reward; and that after one more good **crop is** gathered, they will find their condition **much** better than at **pres**ent.   And he tells the planters **they** must be kind and just to their **laborers, if** they would quickly bring order **out of** chaos, **and establish** a prosperity far beyond what they **ever** dreamed **of** in the **dark** and dreadful era of slavery.

"**Our** whole community here is taking heart.   One **obstacle** after another, to thorough regeneration, is being removed.   As **the** planters succeed in procuring laborers, their credit is **im**proved, and the merchants of this place come forward **to** assist the onward movement.   Agricultural implements, seed, subsistence, and the various wants of a plantation, are being much more liberally supplied than they were a month **ago.**   We all look forward to a large measure of success the present season."

Meanwhile, the "muster out" of the major was being talked of, which was occasioned by the disbanding of his organization.   But the following telegram from the headquarters of the department quieted the rumor for at least a time.   .

HEADQUARTERS DEPARTMENT OF SOUTH CAROLINA, ?
CHARLESTON, February 3, 1866. }

To the Commanding Officer, District of Port Royal.

The major general commanding directs that Major **M. R. De**lany, 104th United States **Colored** Troops, remain, until further orders, in the performance of the duties in which **he is** now employed, by special orders from these headquarters. **He will not for** the present **rejoin his** regiment.

W. L. M. BURGER,
Asst. Adjt. Gen.

Indorsement on above Telegram.

HEADQUARTERS, DISTRICT OF PORT ROYAL, ?
SECOND SEPARATE BRIGADE, }
HILTON HEAD, S. C., February 3, 1866.)

Respectfully referred to Major Delany, 104th **U. S. C. T.**, B. R. F. & A. L., for his *information* and *guidance.*

By order of   **A. G. BENNETT,**
Lt. Col. 21st U. S. C. T., Commanding District.

CHARLES F. RICHARDS, 1st *Lt. & A. D. C.*

The interest created in his department **was** an acknowledged success. He had attempted and succeeded in organizing a system of labor in a place where it was previously almost wholly unknown — leaving **the** employee to **the** tender mercy **of** his employer, but upon **equal** terms. **He** could see order and harmony arising **out of chaos** and **discord. He** was partially satisfied, **for one of** his favorite meas**ures** was popular, originating from a black, for the good of the inhabitants of his district, blacks as well as whites.

His methods, and the successes attending, attracted the attention, as well as challenged the admiration, of the people in and around his post. A brother officer, bearing witness to his indefatigable labor, called attention to it, in his report to the commanding general of the Carolinas, which report induced the general to request the department at Washington to continue him in the service after his regiment should be mustered out.

By such recognition of his services and ability, emanating as it did from that distinguished commander, the black major received another offering at the shrine of his boundless ambition, which none knows better than himself how to value. Just in connection with this, we are reminded of an expression of a distinguished divine in regard to him. "Well for this country," said he, "that Martin Delany is not a white man, for he has the ambition of a devil." But when we reflect that the motive power of that conspicuous trait of his character is solely for the sake of his race, and utterly devoid of personal selfishness, one sees the beauty of the halo encircling his dusky brow, instead of the deformity of the cloven foot.

The following is the letter to which reference is made : —

HEADQUARTERS DEPARTMENT SOUTH CAROLINA,
CHARLESTON, S. C., January 30, 1866.

General : I have the honor to invite your attention to the following extract from a recent report of Major J. P. Roy, 6th United States Infantry, and Acting Inspector General of this department, regarding the services of Major M. R. Delany, 104th United States Colored Troops : —

"Before closing this report, I desire to bear testimony to the efficient and able manner in which Major Delany, 104th United States Colored Troops, and agent of the Freedmen's Bureau, is performing his duties. I took occasion several times during my stay to go to his office, and hear him talk and explain matters to the freedmen. Being of their own color, they naturally reposed confidence in him. Upon the labor question he entirely reflected the views of the major general commanding, and seemed in all things to give them good and sensible advice. He is doing much good, and in the event of his regiment being mustered out, I hope he may be retained as an agent of the Freedmen's Bureau."

I have also received the same satisfactory reports from other sources, and concurring in the foregoing suggestions of Major J. P. Roy, I must respectfully recommend that Major M. R. Delany be, for the present, retained in the service of the United States. I have ordered his muster out to be postponed until a reply is received to this communication.

I have the honor to remain, general,

Very respectfully, your obedient servant,

(Signed)   D. E. SICKLES,
                        Major General Commanding.

To Brig. Gen. E. D. TOWNSEND,
         A. A. G., War Dept.

HEADQUARTERS. DEPARTMENT OF SOUTH CAROLINA, ⎱
         CHARLESTON, **S. C.**, January 31, 1866. ⎰

Official.   W. L. M. BURGER,
                        Brevet Lt. Col. & A. A. G.

Copy furnished Major M. R. Delany for his information.

This was soon after followed by one demonstrative of the liberality of the major general commanding, showing the great distance he had cast from him his early Tammany Hall political education, recognizing only the true and broad republican principles of our better civilization. It redounds to his credit, and is another evidence of the impartial justice of the great secretary of war in affairs of the government, and appreciation of merit in its officers, regardless of former notions which seemed to underlie the basis of its principles. **This order is** fully explanatory **of the** retention **of** the black major in the service so long.

A report had been freely circulated by some persons that the old planters had petitioned the general to retain him, as he was "*high in their favor.*" The latter clause is admissible, **as even** among that peculiar class there are men who are liberal enough, by **virtue of** their acquirements, to **respect and** appreciate the dignified manhood and high **moral** character **of the negro** officer. The planters can **offer** no allurement **sufficient to** tempt him to their **special** interest. **They cannot** promise *power* to him, **as they are** devoid **of it,** and his own incorruptible integrity **to** the government is known to have caused him to peremptorily refuse all offers, on **the** most advantageous terms, to even enter into **any** speculations **of** cotton, **or** any other staple. The **following** order **is** sufficient to prove the falsity **of the** report.

War Department, Adjutant General's Office,
Washington, February 8, 1866.

Major General D. E. Sickles, *Comm'g Dept. of South Carolina, Headquarters, Charleston, S. C.*

General: I have respectfully to acknowledge the receipt of your letter of the 30th ultimo, recommending that Major *M. R. Delany,* 104th Regiment United States Colored Troops, be retained in service, and in reply thereto, I am directed by the *Secretary of War*, to say that this is authority for the retention of that officer in service, until further orders from the War Department.

I have the honor to be, very respectfully,

Your obedient servant,

(Signed)   C. W. FOSTER,
Asst. Adjt. Gen. Vols.

HEADQUARTERS, DEPARTMENT SOUTH CAROLINA, }
CHARLESTON, S. C., February 12, 1866.   }

Official copy.   W. L. M. BURGER,
Asst. Adjt. Gen.

CHAPTER XXXII.

THE PLANTERS AND THE FREEDMEN'S BUREAU.

AS the season for contracting with the freedmen of the islands approached, the old planters from the main land and sea islands could be seen hastening to the quarters of the "black major" for consultation with him.

The picture of the statesman warrior of St. Domingo, surrounded by the conquered and impoverished planters of the island, dictating terms to them, was again reproduced in our time, with the black officer in the foreground as the chief figure, giving law to the planters of South Carolina.

Without the assistance of the Bureau, the planters would have been unable to proceed at any time after the war, and that section of the country would have presented a most deplorable aspect. For the freedmen, in view of their past condition, were naturally suspicious of their offers, and, partly resting on the promises held out of lands being given to them, were with difficulty persuaded to accept employment from them. And the often repeated tales of cruelty, with the many evidences of glaring fraud, practised upon those who had been employed immediately after the war, helped to give an odium to the planters which threatened to interfere greatly with the reproduction

of their cotton and rice. After the establishment of
the Freedmen's Bureau by Congress, the presence of a
competent sub-commissioner, whom neither threats nor
bribes could move, supported by the strong arm of the
Bureau, could check these malpractices and adjust all
difficulties between them. And in this mediatorial
character he was placed, without the slightest devia-
tion from his principles, or assuming more to himself
than was guaranteed by his position : respected by the
planters, trusted and regarded by the freedmen with a
sentiment of pride mingled with reverence, he has, by
this means, wrought out incalculable advantages to the
cause of reconstruction, and given to these islands the
germs of a civilization previously unknown, while in
his own administration he has given to the country
abundant demonstration of the negro capability for
government.

The planters at first disliked the presence of the
Bureau in their midst; but powerless to retard its operations, and witnessing its impartial administration, and
the growing prosperity of their district, as the result,
have reconciled themselves, and some have even acknowledged it as a *success*. Thus we find the quarters
of the major visited for consultation by the representatives of a class, prior to the war, the most bitter opponents of black men's rights, and many who were conspicuous in the late rebellion, in the interest of the
confederacy. There might have been seen Colonel
Charles J. Colcock, who commanded the Confederate
cavalry at Honey Hill against General Hatch; Colonel
Jos. Stoney, Rev. James Stoney, Colonel E. M. Seabrook, who commanded at the fortification before the

capture of Hilton Head; Mr. Hayward, **J. W. Pope**, upon whose lands the batteries **were** found erected at the capture **of** Hilton Head; Major Manning Kirk, Drs. Seabrook, Kirk, and Pritchard, Ellis, and Crowell, besides many of the younger planters **of the** families of the Barnwells, Rhetts, Fripps, Elliots, and Fullers, including the young General Stephen Elliot, **who commanded at** Fort Sumter, and Jacob **Jenkins** Mikell, the famous Edisto planter of the long staple cotton. **While** the affairs of the Bureau were thus being conducted by him, General Scott divided the state into sub-districts, assigning an officer to each. Hilton Head had now been visited three times by the general, and on each occasion the quarters of the major were officially visited, previous to the following order being received, which is another indication of the satisfaction **of his** immediate commander **in** regard to **his official** conduct:—

HEADQUARTERS, STATE OF SOUTH CAROLINA,
CHARLESTON, S. C., June 11, 1866.

General Orders. No. 5.
Extract.

. . . . . .

III. The *Military Reservation of Hilton Head* and its Dependencies, known as the Islands of Hilton Head, together with Dawfuskie, Bull, and Pinckney Islands, are hereby announced as the territorial limits of, and will constitute the Bureau District of Hilton Head, with Major *M. R. Delany*, U. S. C. T., as *Sub-Assistant Commissioner*, in **charge**, with headquarters at Hilton Head.

By command of   Brevet Major General **R. K.** SCOTT.

H. W. SMITH, *Brevet Lt. Col. Ass't. Adj. Gen.*

Official.   H. W. SMITH,
Assistant Adjutant General.

CHAPTER XXXIII.

DOMESTIC ECONOMY.

AROUND Major Delany's district, there being evidence of an abundant harvest, the movements of persons designing to reap large profits, to the detriment of the freedmen, were apparent. With a view of frustrating their designs, he suggested proper measures to obviate the difficulty, which we find in his general report made to headquarters, dated March 1, 1867, for the year 1866. Therein he gave his views, showing the necessity of important changes in the industrial pursuits of the freedmen; also the measures put forward by him for their financial protection.

"It was apparent from observation and experience that the custom of renting the lands to speculators, who sub-let them to freedmen, or employed them to work at disadvantageous rates — that these poor people, at the end of the planting year, habitually came out with nothing — nay, worse than nothing, as those working them in shares having provision supplied from the stores of the speculators, or renting the lands, and obtaining them on credit from such stores. When the crops were realized, they paid them all away to these stores for the scanty mouthfuls they received on credit during cultivation — finding themselves with nothing

—in rags, and debt for "balance due" on the books of these first-hand lessees and supply speculators. And those who had a little chance of raising crops for themselves to advantage, were equally the victims of the petty brokers and cotton traders (resulting from their superior business knowledge and intelligence, and the almost entire absence of such qualifications on the part of the freedmen), their cotton being sacrificed in the market. It was evident from these facts that there could be but little or no chances for the freedmen or refugees to compete with bidders or lessees of the land, let at the highest cash price (frequently above their value in this district), except by an adoption of some measure for their protection, whereby a portion of their scanty earnings could be saved, and the lands let to them at prices suited to their means, in preference to speculators and capitalists.

"To this end I recommend the establishment of a freedmen's cotton agency, to be attended by a competent agent, where all could have their cotton deposited on consignment, culled (assorted), ginned, packed (bagged), and sold at the highest cash market value, in Charleston; they realizing the profits themselves, instead of the speculators.

"To make such an establishment profitable to them, the expenses should be as moderate as possible, and less than the usual rates of charges in commission houses. Hence, to accomplish this, a suitable building was obtained from the quartermaster's department (free of rent, of course), and those freedmen possessing footgins requested to put them up in the establishment, where they might be used in ginning the cotton brought, charging twenty **per cent**, **or one** fifth less than the market price for ginning, and receiving, when not worked by themselves, one fourth of the proceeds of the gin, the freedman who worked **receiving the** other three fourths as his compensation, thus making them self-sustaining as well as self-reliant.

"The agent supplied the bagging, and **received, as** compensation for the advances thus made, the pay for the weight **of the bag,** deducted from the price of the bag of cotton. This will be understood in mercantile circles, as bagging is always worth the price of an equal weight of cotton.

"**The** next effort, officially, was to secure **to them** the advantages of the lands at a 'first-hand' low rate, as they were now able to raise the money among themselves, by which to secure leases. To accomplish this, interviews and correspondence were had with the United States Direct Tax Commissioners, **who, being** without instructions, were awaiting **the action of Con**gress and government in relation **to the division** and assignment of **land on** the tenure of Lieutenant General **Sherman's field** order, **No.** 15. After mature consideration, as the season for planting **was** rapidly approaching, and the people clamorous and anxious to go **to** work, preparing for cultivation, I concluded to divide responsibilities with the commissioner, and let the lands to the freedmen at *one dollar* an acre, for **the** year 1867.

"They had been advised to prepare for leasing them at two dollars an acre, the leases to be made to one man on each plantation, who would receive and pay over their money, **and** see to a proper apportioning of the land. In less than three weeks from the time that notice to this effect was given, upwards of **three thousand** dollars in cash and cotton vouchers were deposited **with** the bureau to secure leases, and fourteen plantations taken with **the extreme** satisfaction of paying **back** to **each** individual *one half* of his money. This last act **of the** commissioners crowns their official doings with discretion and liberality, which should **entitle them to at** least the thanks **of the** friends of humanity, if not respectful consideration of Congress."

The action of the major in this direction was approved **and** commended by his superior officers, and resulted in proving so far successful. His duties gave indications of further extension at **this** time, by the following document, issued from the war department, and reissued from the headquarters of the assistant commissioner subsequently : —

HEADQUARTERS ASSISTANT COMMISSIONER,
BUREAU R. F. & A. L., SOUTH CAROLINA,
CHARLESTON, S. C., Feb. 19, 1867.

The following circular letter is republished for the information of officers and agents of the Bureau R. F. and A. L., in this state : —

Circular Letter.

WAR DEPARTMENT, BUREAU R. F. & A. L.,
WASHINGTON, February 12, 1867.

To Brevet Major General R. K. SCOTT,

   Assistant Commissioner, Charleston, S. C.

It has become apparent that the designation of the several officers of this Bureau should indicate the nature **of** the duty which each is to perform, and that such designation should be uniform throughout the jurisdiction of this Bureau.

Each state will **be** divided into sub-districts, **of** the proper number of counties, in the discretion of the assistant commissioner. The officers in charge of each will be empowered to exercise and perform within their respective sub-districts all the powers and duties of assistant commissioners, except such as by regulations devolve upon assistant commissioners themselves, and these officers will be designated sub-assistant commissioners.

Any officer or agent serving under the direction of the sub-assistant shall be denominated an agent, except those serving in staff department and as clerks.

All officers authorized to disburse the funds of this Bureau shall be designated disbursing officers.

Major General O. O. HOWARD,
Commissioner.

Brevet Major General R. K. SCOTT,
Assistant Commissioner.

Official.   EDWARD L. DEANE,
Brevet Major & A. A. A. Gen.

Soon after the publication of the "circular letter," the State of South Carolina, by order of the major general commanding, was divided into twenty-four sub-districts. Major Delany's administration of affairs in the spheres previously assigned him, receiving the confidence of the assistant commissioner, his province was extended, as the following order will show : —

HEADQUARTERS, ASSISTANT COMMISSIONER,
BUREAU R. F. & A. L., SOUTH CAROLINA,
CHARLESTON, S. C., February 20, 1867.

General Orders.   No. 3.

Extract.

XI. The **Sub-District** of Hilton Head will comprise the Islands of Hilton Head, Pinckney, Savage, Bull, Dawfuskie, and Long Pine : headquarters at Hilton Head; Major M. R. Delany, United States Colored Troops, sub-assistant commissioner.

By order of   Brevet Major General R. K. SCOTT,
Assistant Commissioner.

Official.   EDWARD L. DEANE,
Brevet Major & A. A. A. Gen.

CHAPTER XXXIV.

CIVIL AFFAIRS. — PRESIDENT JOHNSON.

MAJOR DELANY was fully cognizant of the exceeding delicacy of his position, filling, as he was, a position of trust and honor such as no man of his race had ever yet obtained under the general government; and how easily it could be compromised *in his case!* yet his old ardor in contributing his efforts in building up any measure, or uprooting whatever opposition presented itself in the onward march of his race, remained unabated.

Notwithstanding his position in the army, yet to every one aware of his life-long consecration to the interests of his race, there would be no hesitancy on their part to decide on which side he would be found in any matter in which he should choose between them and his position. While he studiously avoided the general discussion of politics, he was by no means indifferent to the political aspect of the times, and aided, in his position as the military official, as he had formerly done in deeds as the civilian. Thus, while in Beaufort awaiting orders, the subject of reconstruction being under popular discussion, he perceived that the claims of the colored people were evaded; and that the sacrifice of lives made in countless battle-fields by dusky warriors, that the country might be saved, was valueless and unappreciated. His moral courage urged him to remonstrate, even though his position should be compromised. To this end he addressed the following to President Johnson, which afterwards found its way into print : —

To His Excellency PRESIDENT JOHNSON :

Sir : *I propose, simply* as a black man, — one of the race most directly interested in the question of *enfranchisement* and the *exercise* of suffrage, — *a cursory view of the basis of security for perpetuating the Union.*

When the compact was formed, the British — a foreign nation — threatened the integrity and destruction of the American colonies. This outside pressure drove them together as independent states, and so long as they desired a Union, — appreciating the power of the enemy, and comprehending their own national strength, — it was sufficient security against any attempt at a dissolution or foreign subjugation.

So soon, however, as, mistaking their own strength, or designing an alliance with some other power, a portion of those states became dissatisfied with the Union, and recklessly sought its dissolution by a resort to the sword, so nearly equally divided were the two sections, that foreign intervention or an exhausting continuance of the struggle would most certainly have effected a dissolution of the Union.

But an element, heretofore latent and unthought of, — a power passive and unrecognized, — suddenly presented itself to the American mind, and its arm to the nation. This power was developed in the blacks, heretofore discarded as a national nonentity — a dreg or excrescence on the body politic. Free, without rights, or slaves, mainly, — therefore *things* constructively, — when called to the country's aid they developed a force which proved the balance precisely called for, and essentially necessary as an elementary part of the national strength. Without this force, or its equivalent, the rebellion could not have been subdued, and without it as an inseparable national element, **the Union is insecure.**

What becomes necessary, then, **to secure** and perpetuate the integrity of the Union, is simply the *enfranchisement* and recognition of the *political equality* of the power that saved the nation from destruction in **a** time of imminent peril — a recognition of the *political equality* of the **blacks with the whites in all** of their **relations as American** citizens.   **Therefore, with the elective franchise, and the exercise of suffrage in all** of the **Southern States recently** holding **slaves,** there is **no** earthly power able **to cope with** the United States **as** a military power; **consequently nothing to** endanger the national integrity.   Nor can there **ever arise** from this element the same contingency to threaten **and disturb the** quietude of **the country** as that which has just **been so happily** disposed **of.   Because,** believing themselves **sufficiently** able, either **with or without** foreign aid, the rebels drew **the** sword against their **country,** which developed a power in national means — military, financial, and statesmanship — that astonished the world, **and** brought them to submission. Hence, whatever their disposition or dissatisfaction, **the** blacks, **nor** any **other** fractional **part of the country, with the historic knowledge** before **them of its prowess, will ever be** foolhardy **enough to attempt rebellion or** secession.   **And their own** political **cal interest will ever keep** them true and faithful to the Union, **thereby securing their own** liberty, and proving a lasting safe**guard as** a **balance in** the political scale of the country.

As the fear **of the** British, **as an** outside pressure, **drove,** and **for a time kept** and **held the Union** together, so will the fear of the **loss of** liberty and **their** political **status, as** an element in this great nation, serve as the **outside pressure** *necessary* **to secure the** fidelity of the blacks **to the Union.**   And **this fidelity, unlike that** of the rebels, **need** never **be** mistrusted; **because, unlike** them, **the** blacks have before them the *proofs* of the *power* and *ability* **of the Union** to maintain unsullied the *prestige* **of** the national **integrity, even were they,** like them, **traitorously** disposed to **destroy their country, or see** it **usurped by** foreign nations.

This, sir, seems to me conclusive, and is the main point upon which I base my argument against the contingency of a future dissolution of the American Union, and in favor of its security.

I have the honor to be, sir, your most obedient servant,

M. R. DELANY,
Major 104th U. S. C. T.

PORT ROYAL ISLAND, S. C., July 25, 1866.

On another occasion from his island post he stood an interested listener to the sounds which the breeze bore up to him, telling of the plans of reconstruction towards the Southern States. Impatient, he watched for the action of the leaders of colored people themselves on this momentous question, but as yet saw no evidence of it.

In his position as an officer in the service of the government, and a civil magistrate, as all officers of the Bureau necessarily are, he was contributing a giant's help to the cause, which, in view of the limited sphere apportioned his race, rendered him an invaluable auxiliary.

The political horizon had suddenly become overcast; the rôle of the executive was changed to that of Pharaoh instead of "Moses," and he beheld with joy the general uprising of the colored people in their strength to avert the threatening ruin.

It was an occasion long to be remembered, and suggestive of a moral which should not be lost sight of by the American people. They sent from every section of the Union delegated representatives of their own race to the national capital, near the government, to "lobby" for their claims in the great American body politic, as at this time these claims were fast being evaded, if not actually ignored.

It is not yet forgotten the visit of the delegates to the president; his remarks on the occasion, with the advice to *place their cause before the people ;* or the able manner in which the noble Douglass replied to him, and the subsequent ringing appeal which he made resound through the land to reach the people.

Major Delany, anxious to identify himself with the movement, though absent from the immediate scene, showed his entire coöperation with them in the following letter, which he addressed to them : —

Bureau R. F. A. L.,
Port Royal, Hilton Head Island, S. C.,
February, 22, 1866.

To Messrs. G. T. Downing, William Whipper, Frederick Douglass, John Jones, L. H. Douglass, *and others, Colored Delegation representing the Political Interests of the Colored People of the United States, now near the Capital and Government, Washington, D. C.*

My dear Brothers : I have been watching with deep interest your movements at Washington, near the government of your country.   I need not repeat to you that which you all know, and that which we have oft repeated to each other privately, in council, and through the public journals, — we are one in interest and destiny in America.   I am with you; yea, if your intentions, designs, purposes, matter, and *manner* continue the same as those presented to the chief magistrate of the nation, then I am with you always, even to the end.   Be mild, as is the nature of your race; be respectful and deferential, as you will be; and dignified as you have been; but be determined and persevering. Your position before the saged president, and reply after you left him, challenges the admiration of the world.   At least it challenges mine, and as a brother you have it.

Do not misjudge the president, but believe, as I do, that he means to do right; that his intentions are good; that he is interested, among those of others of his fellow-citizens, in the welfare of the black man. That he loves Cæsar none the less, but Rome more. Do not expect too much of him — as black men, I mean. Do not forget that you are black and he is white. Make large allowances for this, and take this as the stand-point. Whatever we may think of ourselves, do not forget that we are far in advance of our white American fellow-citizens in that direction. Remember that men are very differently constituted, and what one will dread and shun another will boldly dare and venture; where one would succeed another might fail. Not far from where I am at present posted on the coast of South Carolina, there are several inlets, of which I will name two — Edisto and St. Helena. Of these, one pilot will shun one, and another the other, each taking his vessel easily through that which he enters; while another will not venture into either, but prefers — especially during a storm — to go outside to sea for the safety of the vessel; all reaching, timely, their destination, Hilton Head, in safety.

Here, what one shuns as a danger another regards as a point of safety; and that which one dreads another dares. What General Sherman succeeded in, General Meade might have failed in; while General Grant may have prosecuted either with success. Men must be measured and adjudged according to their temperaments and peculiar constitutional faculties.

Do not grow weary nor discouraged, neither disheartened nor impatient. Do not forget God. Think, O think how wonderfully he made himself manifest during the war. Only think how he confounded, not only the wisdom of the mighty of this land, but of the world, making them confess that he is the Lord, high over all, and most mighty. He still lives. Put your trust in him. As my soul liveth, you will reap if you faint not. Wait! "The race is not to the swift nor the battle to the strong, but he that endureth to the end." Bide your time.

Since we last met in council great changes have taken place, and much has been gained. The batttle-cry has been heard in our midst, a terrible contest of civil war has raged, and a death-struggle for national life summoned every lover of the Union to the combat. We among our fellow-citizens received the message, and eagerly obeyed the call. Our black right arms were stripped, our bosoms bared, and we **stood in** the front rank **of battle.** Slavery yielded, the yoke was broken, the manacles shattered, the shackles fell, and we stood forth a race redeemed! Instead of despair, "Glory to God!" rather let us cry. In the cause of our country you and I have done, and still are doing, our part, and a great and just nation will not be unmindful of it. God is just. Stand still and see **his salvation.**

> "Be patient in your misery;
> Be meek in your despair;
> Be patient, O be patient!
> Suffer on, suffer on!"

Your brother in the cause of **our** common country,

M. R. Delany.

Before the immediate reapers themseves could discern the whitening harvest, he had **within** sight other fields in which to lead them.

For their protection, and at the same time to facilitate the duties of the Bureau, he established a police system, each plantation **or** settlement **having its** distinct body of policemen, **not** exceeding five. **This** included **the chief, or, as called** by the freedmen, "headman," **who made choice of his** assistants, who reported, and **were responsible** to him for their action; the chief, **in** turn, monthly reporting to Major Delany. And **all** such cases as could not be settled by the chief of police were immediately reported to him at headquarters. As it **was** mutually beneficial, causing **each to respect** the right of the other, this arrangement found favor with both planters and freedmen. **It was** practically demonstrating **the** reality of the new social relation. It was designed **by him** to prove the fitness of the exslave to perform his part in the duties of the civil, **with** equal ability to that displayed in the military service of the government, while it would seem to make him more self-reliant, and desirous of controlling his own affairs as a free man.   It proved a success.

After its adoption, Brigadier General Nye, commanding the district at that time, witnessing its utility, at once approved of it.   And it continued uninterrupted through all the succeeding commands.

Their vigilance in detecting fraud and other unlawful practices, it was acknowledged, far exceeded the military police.   Nothing seemed to escape them.   Indeed, it was often said their adroitness in detection was such as might be coveted by a New York detective.

They were frequently called upon by the military authorities to accomplish work which strictly belonged to the soldier police, but in which they had failed.

It was a matter of general regret that there was no remuneration provided for these men, who had so cheerfully and faithfully served the country, aiding in establishing order where otherwise anarchy might have ensued.

CHAPTER XXXV.

EDUCATIONAL INTERESTS.

OF the military gentlemen stationed at the post of Hilton Head, the major writes thus : " In addition to these high-toned military gentlemen, already named as aiding me, and making easy as well as pleasant the duties of my office in the bureau, I with pleasure acknowledge my indebtedness to Lieutenant Colonel Thompson, Assistant Provost Marshal General, Lieutenant Colonel Bennett, 21st United States Colored Troops, and Lieutenant Colonel O. Moore, who expelled John Morgan from Ohio, Colonel Douglass Frazer, of the 104th United States Colored Troops, and Brevet Brigadier General Nye, of the 29th Maine Volunteers, all commanding at the post. Captain Henry Sharpe, of the 21st United States Colored Troops, Lieutenant Hermon, Lieutenant Tracy, 29th Maine Volunteers, and Provost Major H. E. Whitfield, 128th United States Colored Troops, Assistant Provost Judges, and Lieutenant C. F. Richards, 21st United States Colored Troops, Assistant Adjutant General Lieutenant Jones, and Lieutenant Blanchard, 21st United States Colored Troops, and that excellent gentleman, now President of Florida Land and Lumber Company, Dr. J. M. Hawkes, Surgeon 21st United States Colored

Troops. It is due, as a military courtesy, that I should make this record of the names of gentlemen who came forward at a time when most required, and aided in measures so important to the new life upon which a large portion of the political and social element of the nation was just entering.

As bearing a close relation to his official duties, we give in this connection the subjoined correspondence, being a letter of thanks from that distinguished philanthropist, the Rev. George Whipple, formerly professor of mathematics in Oberlin College, in behalf of the American Missionary Association. This, coming from such an Association, is deemed of sufficient importance to show the general character of the major in whatever position he is placed, — ever untiring in his efforts to aid the cause of humanity, and unselfish in his aim.

New York, July 5, 1867.

Major M. R. Delany, *Bureau of R. F. & A. L., Hilton Head, South Carolina.*

Dear Major: Several of our teachers have reported your attention to their interests, and many acts of kindness in ministering to their comfort.

In their behalf and at their request, and in the behalf and at the request of my associates in these rooms, I beg of you to accept our and their thanks for your oft-repeated kindnesses to them, and your continued interest in our great work. As you have given them more — "a cup of cold water" in the name of a disciple, may you receive a disciple's reward.

Permit me to add the assurance that I take great pleasure in being the agent of our friends in this matter. My cordial thanks accompany theirs.

Yours in behalf of the poor and needy,

George Whipple,
Corresponding Secretary.

The graceful reply to the letter of the Association is worthy of admiration, replete with loyalty and gratitude to the noble band, who for long years have labored without faltering for the well being of his race.

Headquarters Prov. Dist., Hilton Head,
Port Royal, S. C., July 18, 1867.

Professor George Whipple, *Cor. Sec. A. M. A.*, *53 John St.,*
New York.

My dear Sir : Your very kind letter in behalf of the teachers and your Christian associates in the rooms of your great institution was received by the last mail here.

Permit me to state that I have done nothing more, in my attentions to the excellent self-sacrificing and intelligent ladies and gentlemen continually sent to this district, to labor for the moral elevation of my once oppressed and degraded, but now, thank God, disinthralled brethren, in the new social relations which this wonderful dispensation of divine Providence has brought about in fulfilment of his promise, and the promotion of his own glory, than my simple duty. If I have done that, I shall feel satisfied and thankful.

If my acts have been worthy of their and your acceptance, I feel that I may have done something feebly in return towards repaying the long years of untiring labor, anxiety, hazard, and pecuniary loss of the Phillipses, Garrisons, Whipples, Browns, Motts, McKims, Burleighs, Wrights, Pillsburys, Fosters, Leavitts, Wilsons, Sumners, Stevenses, Hales, Wades, Giddingses, Whittiers, Parkers, Lovejoys, the Chases, Pinneys, Collinses, Cheevers, Bellows, Beechers, Stowes, Elders Mahans, Phinneys and Tappans, Rankins, Josclyns, Smiths, Goodells, and Adamses, and others of your race, for the outraged and down-trodden of mine. For this I deserve no thanks. But in my heart of hearts I not only thank you for tender, Christian-like expressions in conveying to me their sentiments, but in return for the patient endurance of yourself and such as those named, for your incessant labors for the overthrow of American slavery, the superstition and heathen regeneration and civilization of foreign lands, all of which are peopled by the colored races, your continued efforts in their behalf, and the elevation of man.

Please convey to the teachers and your Association my heart-felt gratitude for their expressions of kindness towards me, and accept for yourself, dear Professor, my highest personal regards and esteem,

M. R. Delany.

In his report to the Assistant Commissioner of the Bureau concerning the school system, the reform which he advocated was not without deliberation, as demonstrated by a circumstance in his own experience. After his failures in authorship, the Central American expedition project, and railroad improvement, in consequence of all being attempted at the same time, as if to redeem that unsuccessful period of his singularly active life of its appearance of uselessness, a position entirely new in his rôle presented itself.

The principalship of a colored school was offered to him by a committee of the seventh ward. At first he declined, as he contemplated resuming the practice of medicine, his legitimate and choice profession. But the board insisting, as the school by law was compelled to open within a week, and no teacher had been secured, he accepted on conditions that he should be relieved in one month, or so soon as a teacher could be obtained.

He took charge at once, and organized what was then one of the most unmanageable schools, a great portion of the pupils being large boys and girls. The rules laid down by the board allowed *whipping*, while they forbade suspension or dismissal of the pupils from school. To flog a pupil, he alleged, was an evidence of the incapacity for governing on the part of the teacher, and that when it was evident a pupil could not be restrained without resorting to such measures, he was unfit to be among the others.

He notified the directors of his objections to their rule. He regarded it as barbarous, rendering the school-house repulsive and objectionable, instead of being associated with pleasant and profitable memories. Therefore, if they desired him to take the school, he would conduct it in his own way.

They yielded to him in the manner of government. This resulted in binding the pupils to him by ties of sincere devotion, and he remained for thirteen months instead of the one month agreed upon at first. When he resigned, it was a source of regret among both pupils and directors. Teaching, though he loved it as a continual medium of imparting knowledge to the young, yet it was confining him to a sphere too limited for the grasp of his desires. In this capacity he will be remembered by some of the now adult inhabitants of Pittsburg, and his excellent assistant, now the wife of one of the professors of the College of Liberia.

We here insert a portion of his report bearing upon his observation of the schools of his district, and an extract from his last annual report, made to headquarters of the assistant commissioner, for the year 1867, ending the last of August, the close of the planting season. The report is replete with suggestions, and equal to the demands of the time. If the suggestions made be carried out, there would accrue a vast amount of good, rendering the laborer less dependent on others, and more frugal, whereas, in pursuing his former line of labor, he was kept at disadvantage on account of the expenses to be kept up before the sale of cotton, the staple, in the cultivation of which the freedmen use all their time, money, and labor.

Even to make this an effective and self-sustaining measure, the local habits of the occupants must be essentially changed. Instead of the former old plantation people remaining on the places as a local preference, which generally allows but an average of five (5) acres to the family, the lands must be let in portions of not less than twenty (20) acres to each family before they can be made available to their support. This would necessitate a general scattering, or greater division of the people, causing at first quite a change of places with many. To do justice to the people as an available, sociable, or domestic element, no one hundred acres of farming land should be occupied by more than five (5) families, thus allowing twenty (20) acres to the family, which, in the light of domestic or political economy, is little enough. Less than this is to place them in a position of hazardous uncertainty and anxiety, and encourage idleness and improvidence, by inducing the thriftless to settle under circumstances which must make them burdensome to the thrifty and provident. By this course the aged and otherwise needy and deserving helpless could be easily aided by their neighbors, without, as now, being over-burdensome.

It is very evident that the entire system of cultivation will have to be changed, both in the method of doing it, and more especially the produce raised, to suit and meet the change in the social system and the demands and status of these new possessors and permanent residents of small farms or gardens. Every month in the year but one (December) may be made productive of some vegetable for provision, or family use, whereby the people may be independent in subsistence. It is a settled matter that in this country cotton can only be profitably produced by extensive cultivation and large capital, under favorable circumstances; consequently it is a loss of time and labor for the freed-men to plant cotton with their limited means of land and mate-rials, as the ground to them can be put to a much more useful and profitable purpose.

I am preparing the people in this sub-district to this end, and believe that against the approaching leasing year they will be quite willing and ready to enter into the new system of habita-tion and occupancy.

During the current year there have been no rations issued in this sub-district, except two hundred (200) bushels of corn from the Southern Relief Association, and five hundred (500) bush-els of corn, and one thousand (1000) pounds of bacon, of the Congressional appropriation, assigned through the Commissary of Subsistence Bureau, Charleston.

The example and precepts of the teachers have been such as to merit my most hearty approval. But there is one custom as yet common to schools, and almost regarded as an essential part of training, and which I most heartily desire should be done away with. I refer to *whipping* children as a correction in school. It is simply a relic of ignorance, and should not be tolerated by intelligence. And while this is tolerated, teachers will resort to it as the easiest and to them least troublesome mode of correction.

A teacher either is, or is not, adapted to teaching. If proper-ly adapted, she could and should teach without whipping. If she cannot correct and control her pupils without whipping, then it only proves that she is not adapted to teaching, and all such should seek other employment. This is not a reflec-tion on any particular teacher or teachers, but a condemnation of the general customs of schools. A school-house should be made a place of the most pleasurable resort and agreeable asso-ciations to children, but certain it is that in no wise can this be the case where the great hickory, thong, leather strap, or bridle-rein meets, as it enters the school-house, the child's eye as it does the eye of the visitor, reminding one, as it must the other, of entering the presence of the old plantation overseer in waiting for his victim.

CHAPTER XXXVI.

CONCLUSION.

THE order for mustering out the remaining volunteer officers was long anticipated, and anxiously looked for by these officers, and by none more than by Major Delany, who, as sub-assistant commissioner of the Bureau district of Hilton Head would be affected by this. At last it was received, as will be seen by the following document. While upon this subject, a humorous anecdote, bearing on this subject, may be related.

While awaiting the order, about the middle of December, he visited the headquarters of the assistant commissioner at Charleston.

On entering the department of the adjutant general, a group of officers surrounded the desk of the acting adjutant, who, at the time, was reading out the names of the officers mustered out by special orders, which had just been received from the war department that morning, erasing them from the roster suspended on the wall before him, among which was his own name.

"How is this, major?" asked the chief clerk; "I do not see your name among them. Do you report regularly?"

"I do; my report for this month was sent on now more than ten days," he replied.

"How is it that you are not among these named in the special order just received?" inquired the acting assistant adjutant general, with much interest.

"I suppose," said the major, very quaintly, "that I am in the position of the old black man, a devoted Second Adventer, during the Millerite excitement, who, disposing of his earthly effects, betook himself to a cellar, with simply food and fuel sufficient to sustain him comfortably, the season being winter. While waiting, a snow storm came on, the drift completely embanking that side of the street, burying everything beneath it.

"Thus isolated, and enveloped in darkness for several days, except the light of his little fire, without the sound of a footstep or voice above, the old man believed that the final consummation of all things had taken place, and he was actually left in his tomb.

"Presently the scavengers reached his cellar door, when, first hearing footsteps, succeeded by scraping and prying, then light ushering in through the cracks as the snow was removed. Suddenly bursting up the cellar door, the old man exclaimed, 'Is de end come?' Being answered in the negative, 'O!' said he, 'I thought de end was come, an' all you white folks was gone up, an' forgot dis old black saint.' Now," concluded the major, turning to the assistant adjutant general, "I suppose de end is come, an' all you white folks is *gone up*, an' forgot dis black saint," amidst a roar of laughter among the officers.

A few days after this an order came from Washington, retaining Brevet Major General Scott in the service, as assistant commissioner, on the staff of Major General Canby, commanding the Second Military District, by whose advice and generous indorsement the retention of Major Delany was recommended to General Canby, and by which he has been retained in the service.

Thus, in addition to the established duties of his office, he is now the disbursing officer of soldiers' claims for the sub-district of Hilton Head.

This is another testimony, as exhibited by different commanders, of the ability and usefulness of this officer in retaining him. But while fully appreciating these repeated recognitions of his service to the government by these high officials, giving it the full value of its civil and political worth, construing it to a desire of recognizing the true status of the colored race as American citizens by the continuance of their only representative, as an incumbent and military officer in this prominent and honorable position of the government, Major Delany says, "By this change or modification in its jurisdiction the Bureau loses nothing, but otherwise its status and prestige is thereby enhanced.

"Previous to this an important difficulty presented itself. A large force of volunteer officers must be kept up in a time of peace, — which is contrary to the jurisprudence of all highly civilized nations, — or the volunteer officers must be mustered out, and thus leave an important arm of the war department without the necessary administrative government.

"To impose the duties of the Bureau on the officers of the regular army, would be to entail duties which they could not care to have upon them, and, therefore, for the most part, neglect. To employ civilians, would bring them directly under the military men, wholly ignorant of the details, import, and meaning of military orders and duties. To employ those who have been commissioned officers in the service, competent for the duties, would involve an expense equal, at least, to that already incurred by the volunteer officers now on duty.

"The only course left the government in carrying out the well-regulated custom of reducing the army to a true peace basis, by doing away with an independent volunteer force in time of peace, was to place the bureau under the regular army.

"This virtually places Major General O. O. Howard on the staff of General Grant; Brevet Major General R. K. Scott, and all other assistant commissioners, *de facto*, on the staffs of the major generals commanding the military districts; brings the entire volunteer officers, retained in the service, under and subject to, without being in, the regular army; and cements a perfect harmony between these two branches of the government which nothing can detract.'

"In this stride of statesmanship, will it be presumed that the American army, or the military branch of the government, has no statesmen as competent counsellors of the executive?"

Headquarters Second Military District, }
Charleston, S. C., December 4, 1867. }

General Orders. *No.* 140.

The following general orders, from the headquarters of the army, are republished for the information and guidance of all concerned.

HEADQUARTERS OF THE ARMY, ADJT. GEN. OFFICE, }
WASHINGTON, November 26, 1867. }

General Orders. No. 101.

The following orders have been received from the War Department, and will be duly executed: —

Extract.

.   .   .   .   .   .

Par. III. All volunteer officers now retained in service will be mustered out, to take effect January 1, 1868, except the commissioner and the disbursing officers of the Bureau of Refugees, Freedmen, and Abandoned Lands.

By command of   General GRANT.

E. D. TOWNSEND,
Asst. Adjt. Gen.

By command of
Brevet Major General ED. R. S. CANBY.

Official.   LOUIS V. CAZIARC,
Aid-de-Camp, Act'g Asst. Adjt. Gen.

HEADQUARTERS SECOND MILITARY DISTRICT, }
CHARLESTON, S. C., December 6, 1867. }

General Orders. No. 145.

The following arrangement of the troops in this district will be carried into effect with as little delay as possible.

Extract.

.   .   .   .   .   .

In addition to duties with which they are charged by existing orders, commanding officers of posts are designated as sub-assistant commissioners of the Bureau of Refugees, Freedmen, and Abandoned Lands, for the districts embraced within the territorial limits of their commands, and will exercise all the functions of officers of that bureau, except so far as relates to the administration and control of the funds or property of the bureau.

Extract.

.   .   .   .   .   .

All officers and agents of the bureau, who may be on duty
within the territorial limits of any post, will report to its commander, and will be governed by his instructions in all that relates to the protection of persons and property, under the laws
of the United States, the regulations of the bureau, and the
orders of the district commander. In all that relates to the
details of administration, they will report as heretofore to the
assistant commissioner for the state in which they are stationed.
The assistant commissioners for the States of North and South
Carolina, respectively, will furnish the commanders of posts
with the names and stations of the officers and agents of the
bureau on duty within the limits of their respective commands,
and with a statement of any special duties they may have been
charged with in relation to the protection of person and property. They will also, by conference or correspondence with the
post commander, determine what officers or agents of the bureau
can be relieved or discharged, and report the same to district
headquarters.

By command of

Brevet Major General ED. R. S. CANBY.

Official.   LOUIS V. CAZIARC,
Aid-de-Camp, **Act'g Asst. Adjt. Gen.**

HEADQUARTERS ASST. COMR. BUREAU REFUGEES,
FREEDMEN, AND ABANDONED LANDS, DISTRICT OF S. C.,
CHARLESTON, S. C., December 19, 1867.

Major M. R. DELANY, *Asst. Sub-Asst. Comr.*

Major : In accordance with the provisions of general orders
No. 145, C. S., Second Military District, I am directed by the
assistant commissioner to inform you that your designation and
limits of your district are as follows : —

You will hereafter be designated as Assistant Sub-Assistant
Commissioner for Hilton Head, Savage, Bull, Dawfuskie, Pinckney, and Long Pine Islands, and will report to Brevet Brigadier

General H. B. Clitz, port of Charleston, and sub-assistant commissioner, subject to existing orders and instructions.

I am, major, very respectfully,

Your most obedient servant,

EDWARD L. DEANE,

Brevet Major, A. D. C., & A. A. A. Gen.

HEADQUARTERS ASST. COMR. BUREAU REFUGEES,
FREEDMEN, AND ABANDONED LANDS, DIST. OF S. C.,
CHARLESTON, S. C., February 8, 1868.

Major M. R. DELANY, *Acting Sub-Assistant*
Commissioner, Hilton Head, S. C.

Major : The following copy of indorsement from War Department, Adjutant General's Office, dated January 28, 1868, is respectfully furnished for your information.

.   .   .   .   .   .

Respectfully returned to Major General O. O. Howard, Commissioner. Major M. R. Delany, 104th United States Colored Troops, having been reported in your letter of November 30, 1867, as on duty in the Bureau of Refugees, Freedmen, and Abandoned Lands, as a disbursing officer, was retained in service under the provisions of General Orders 101, November 26, 1867, from this office.

(Signed)   THOMAS M. VINCENT,

Asst. Adjt. Gen.

Very respectfully, your obedient servant,

H. NEIDE,

Brevet Major, 1st Lieut. 44th Infantry,
Act'g Asst. Adjt. Gen.

With this last order we will bring this volume to a close. We have endeavored to narrate the career of an individual of our time, living and still working in our midst, the extent of whose labors, and the great ability demonstrated in their execution, cannot be thoroughly understood or felt, without first having known the great struggle and anxiety entailed in its accomplishment. This we have attempted to give, but found it no easy task; therefore we have simply narrated the events of his singularly active life, allowing the reader to deduce his own comments.

At this writing, Major Delany is still in the service of the government, as sub-assistant commissioner of the Freedmen's Bureau, while many of the volunteer officers have been mustered out, under order of the department at Washington.

In his retention, is shown the recognition and the thorough appreciation of the indefatigable zeal and great ability displayed by the black officer, especially as in conjunction with his former duties others, in which greater responsibilities are entailed, are assigned to him. His efficient labors in the department render him a distinct character from his surroundings, while his administrative qualities attract the attention of friends and foes alike, as unprecedented in the history of his race in this country. While comments may vary, they unite in saying, " There is still a latent amount of greatness within the man, which has not yet been called forth."

To his lofty aspirations, and great originality of thoughts, together with his real earnestness in everything he undertakes, and his iron will to pursue to completion, we trace the secret of his success in this field.

Illustrating in his career entire personal sacrifice for the accomplishment of a grand purpose, no character has been produced by our civilization in comparison with which this remarkable man would be deemed inferior. Men have died for the freedom and elevation of the race, and thereby have contributed more to advance the cause than would their living efforts, while others have lived for it, and under circumstances where death would have been easier. Such describes Martin Delany. Nature marked him for combat and victory, and not for martyrdom. His life-long service, from which neither poverty nor dangers could deter him, his great vitality and energy under all and every circumstance, which have never abated, proclaim this truth. His life furnishes a rare enthusiasm for race not expected in the present state of American society, occasioned by his constant researches into anything relative to their history. No living man is better able to write the history of the race, to whom it has been a constant study, than he; as it is considered by the most earnest laborers in the same sphere that few, if any, among them, have so entirely consecrated themselves to the idea of race as his career shows. His religion, his writings, every step in life, is based upon this idea. His creed begins and ends with it — that the colored race can only obtain their true status as men, by relying on their own identity; that they must prove, by merit, all that white men claim; then color would cease to be an objection to their progress — that the blacks must take pride in being black, and show their claims to superior qualities, before the whites would be willing to concede them equality. This he claims as the foundation of his manhood. Upon this point Mr. Frederick Douglass once wittily remarked, "Delany stands so straight that he leans a little backward."

Such is the personal history of an individual of the

race, whose great strength of character, amid the multitudinous agencies adverse to his progress, has triumphantly demonstrated negro capability for greatness in every sphere wherein he has acted.

The late revolution has resulted in bringing the race to which he belongs into prominence. They have begun their onward march towards that higher civilization promised at the close of the war. Let no unhallowed voice be lifted to stay their progress; then, with all barriers removed, the glorious destiny promised to them can be achieved. And then our country, continuing to recognize merit alone in her children, as shown in the appointment of the black major of Carolina, will add renewed strength to her greatness. Begirt with loyal hearts and strong arms, the mission of our revolution shall embrace centuries in its march, securing the future stability of our country, and proclaiming with truthfulness the grandeur of republican institutions to the civilization of Christendom.

APPENDIX.

HAVING given thus far, in a most impartial manner, the services of Major Delany; endeavoring to concede all that rightfully belongs to him, without debarring others of their dues; claiming, as we have in this work, *for him always an advanced position;* to bear out this statement more fully, we add some selections from his published political works, which will show that his administration in a military capacity but reflected the brilliancy kindled about the civilian.

The most remarkable feature of the greater portion of the writings is, that they constitute the *present essential principles* which form the basis of the reconstruction of the South, and ultimately for the nation at large. These are definitely and significantly expressed in paragraphs 6th, 7th, 8th, 10th, 12th, 18th, and 22d of the Platform or Declaration of Sentiments, and also in his paper on the Political Destiny of the Colored Races, &c.

These are the writings to which reference has been previously made, and were presented before, and adopted by the Cleveland Convention of 1854, without modification of any kind.

On the appearance of these, numerous comments were drawn from the leading daily journals of the country. From the Pittsburg Daily Post, of October 18, 1854 (a pro-slavery paper), we quote the following : —

"Dr. M. R. Delany, of Pittsburg, was the chairman of the committee that made this report to the convention. It was, of course, adopted. If Dr. D. drafted this report, it certainly does him much credit for learning and ability, and cannot fail to establish for him a reputation for vigor and brilliancy of imagination never yet surpassed." Not being able to continue long in this vein, it concludes: "It is a vast conception, of impossible birth. The committee seem entirely to have overlooked the strength of the 'powers on the earth' that would oppose the Africanization of more than half the western hemisphere."

In their singular adaptability to the extraordinary events now challenging the highest intelligence of the land for their permanent adjustment, they will be regarded as reflecting no ordinary credit on the colored race for one of their number to adduce such thoughts as are contained in these on National Polity and Individual Rights, published as they were some thirteen years ago, hence prior to the present discussions upon the new issues. While the position he claimed and sentiments expressed are most thoroughly anti-slavery, they are unlike in their issues, and manner of presenting such, as well as far in advance of the *then* most radical, with few noble exceptions, and *now* in harmony with the requirements of the. times. Then they were looked upon as extremely impracticable measures and sentiments. Now they will testify to the fitness of the colored people for the present right they claim; as these issues, instead of finding them unprepared, as their political enemies proclaim, it has found theories promulgated by a black representative, standing in the midst of this mighty political combat, side by side with the most advanced of his white brothers on either continent.

Whatever the seeming tenor of the advice and feelings which thrill through these productions, it should be remembered they were written at a time when the present state of the country was scarcely expected to be realized, in our age, even by the radicals; penned within sight of slave renditions into bondage, when his manhood was humiliated by the legal ordeal under which the colored people of the United States were placed by that most infamous of enactments, the Fugitive Slave Law.

After the publication of his paper on the Destiny of the Colored Race in America,* a committee, selected for the purpose, sent a copy to each member of the Congress, of which Mr. Frank Blair was a member, he having acknowledged its receipt by letter to Mr. J. M. Whitfield, one of the committee, and in which he broached the subject he afterwards made the theme of his lecture which surprised the country from the boldness of the position taken. By comparing the scheme put forth during the year 1844–5, in favor of Central and South American emigration, and the brilliant effort of Mr. Frank P. Blair in its behalf, including his great lecture before the Boston Lyceum, we venture to assume that it was suggested by the paper herein presented.

* See page 327.

In the recent report of his African explorations, the following curious document we quote, as among his political works.   To the discerning historical reader it will be read with interest, while its significance will become in time more appreciable.

African Commission.

The president and officers of the General Board of Commissioners, viz., **W. H Day, A. M.**, President, Matisen **F. Bailey**, Vice-President, George **W.** Brodie, Secretary, James Madison **Bell**, Treasurer, Alfred Whipple, Auditor, Dr. Martin R. Delany, **Special** Foreign **Secretary**, Abram D. Shadd, James Henry **Harris, and** Isaac D. Shadd, the executive council **in behalf of the organization for the promotion of the political and other interests of** the colored inhabitants **of North America, particularly the United** States and Canada.

To all unto whom these **letters** may come, **greeting : The** said General Board of Commissioners, in executive council assembled, have this day chosen, and by these presents do **hereby** appoint and authorize **Dr.** Martin Robison Delany, **of Chatham** County of Kent, Province of Canada, Chief **Commissioner, and** Robert Douglass, Esq., Artist, and **Professor** Robert Campbell, Naturalist, both of Philadelphia, Pennsylvania, **one of the United States of America, to be Assistant Commissioners;** Amos Aray, Surgeon, and **James W. Prinnel,** Secretary and Commercial Reporter, both **of Kent County,** Canada West, of a scientific corps, **to be known by the name of**

The Niger Valley Exploring Party.

The object of this expedition is to make a topographical, geological, and geographical examination of the **Valley of the River** Niger, **in** Africa, and an inquiry into the state and condition of the people **of** that valley, and **other parts of** Africa, together with such other scientific **inquiries as may by them** be deemed expedient, for the purposes of science, and for general information **; and** without **any reference** to, and with the board being entirely opposed to, any emigration there as such. Provided, however, that nothing in this instrument be so construed as to interfere with the right of the commissioners to negotiate, in their own behalf, or that of any other parties or organization, for territory.

The Chief Commissioner is hereby authorized to add one or more competent commissioners to their number, it being agreed and understood that this organization is, and is to be, exempted from the pecuniary responsibility of sending out this expedition.

Dated at the office of the Executive Council, Chatham, County of Kent, Province of Canada, this thirtieth day of August, in the year of our Lord one thousand eight hundred and fifty-eight.

By the President,

WILLIAM HOWARD DAY.
ISAAC D. SHADD, Vice-President.*
GEORGE W. BRODIE, Secretary.

While the Commission is worthy of a place among his political writings, the next in order, and of equal importance, furnishing another evidence of his adaptability to circumstances, the essential characteristic to his success, as well as that which has always been the secret of the success of all men in public life, is his treaty made with the king and chiefs of Abbeokuta, in view of advancing the future prosperity of his fatherland. We give the treaty, extracted from page 35th of his "Official Report."

The Treaty.

This treaty, made between His Majesty Okukenu, Alake, Somoye, Ibashorum, Sokenu, Ogubonna, and Atambola, Chiefs, and Balaguns of Abbeokuta, on the first part, and Martin Robison Delany, and Robert Campbell, of the Niger Valley Ex-

---

* Mr. Shadd was elected Vice-President in the place of Mr. Bailey, who left the Province for New Caledonia.

ploring Party, commissioners from the African race of the United States and the Canadas, in America, on the second part, covenants:

Art. 1. That the king and chiefs, on their part, agree to grant and assign unto the said commissioners, on behalf of the African race in America, the right and privilege of settling, in common with the Egda people, on any part of the territory belonging to Abbeokuta not otherwise occupied.

Art. 2. That all matters requiring legal investigation among settlers be left to themselves, to be disposed of according to their own custom.

Art. 3. That the commissioners, on their part, also agree that the settlers shall bring with them, as an equivalent for the privileges above accorded, intelligence, education, a knowledge of the arts and sciences, agriculture, and other mechanical and industrial occupations, which they shall put into immediate operation, by improving the lands, and in other usefulavocations.

Art. 4. That the laws of the Egba people shall be strictly respected by the settlers; and, in all matters in which both parties are concerned, an equal number of commissioners, mutually agreed upon, shall be appointed, who shall have power to settle such matters.

As a pledge of our faith, and sincerity of our hearts, we each of us hereunto affix our hand and seal, this twenty-seventh day of December, Anno Domini one thousand eight hundred and fifty-nine.

His Mark, ✕ OKUKENU, ALAKE,
His Mark, ✕ SOMOYE, IBASHORUM,
His Mark, ✕ SOKENU, BALAGUN,
His Mark, ✕ OGUBONNA, BALAGUN,
His Mark, ✕ ATAMBALA, BALAGUN,
His Mark, ✕ OGUSEYE, ARIABA,
His Mark, ✕ AGTABO, BALAGUN, *O. S. O.*
His Mark, ✕ OGUDEMU, AGEOKI,
M. R. DELANY,
ROBERT CAMPBELL.

Witness, SAMUEL CROWTHER, Jun.

Attest, SAMUEL CROWTHER, Sen.

Says the report on the Niger Valley Exploration, "On the next evening, the 28th, the king, with the executive council of chiefs and elders, met at the palace in Aka, when the treaty was ratified by a unanimous approval. Such general satisfaction ran through the council, that the great chief, his highness Ogubonna, mounting his horse, then at midnight, hastened to the residence of the surgeon Crowther, aroused the father, the missionary, and author, and hastily informed him of the action of the council.

An event of revenge, from prejudice to his race, was of great personal loss to himself, occasioned by the burning of Wilberforce College, the first and only thoroughly literary institution of that capacity owned and controlled solely by the colored people of this country. This happened on the memorable night of the 14th of April, 1866; he having had in the third story of the right wing of the edifice a room as a depository of valuables, among which were his entire collection of African curiosities, collected during his tour, together with his entire European and African correspondence, and that with distinguished Americans after his return home. In this conflagration it was a loss entailed to him, never to be remedied, as these were the collections of twenty years. Besides correspondence, there were manuscripts, by which we are deprived of some of his finest productions.

The following papers are of a recent date: —

Reflections on the War.

One important fact developed during this gigantic civil war, and which could not have escaped the general and mature intelligent observer as a result of the struggle, and so contrary to concessions under the old relations of the Union, is, that no great statesmen were produced on the part of the South; although at the commencement, at the Montgomery Convention, or Provisional Congress, August, 1861, their independence was declared, and consequently must have been fully matured, not a measure was put forth of national import to sustain their cause, except the issue of the cotton bonds thrown upon the foreign market — a cheat so consistent with the Mississippi bond repudiation of Mr. Jefferson Davis, that it is not difficult to determine the source of that financial scheme, which, of itself, was an ordinary commercial measure, of every-day transaction, enlarged to meet the occasion of a " national want."

Previous to the war, it was generally conceded that by far the ablest statesmen in the service of the nation came from the South. And doubtless this may have been so, for a long period of the government, after the close of the revolutionary struggle; because, the people of the North, caring for little else than business, of personal interests, and local legislation, few men could be found among them willing to devote more than one term in Congress, or the executive departments of the government; while the policy of the South was to continue the same men as long as possible in the councils, in consequence of their domestic relations affording them ample time and leisure in their absence from home to mature their plans of ascendency.

During the revolutionary period, which may be reckoned from the Albany Continental Congress, in 1754, to the Peace Congress at Ghent, 1814, both grand political divisions, north and south of Mason and Dixon's line, show with equal brilliancy in the national forum.

After the treaty of peace with Great Britain, gradually the leading spirits passed away, either by death or withdrawal from public life, till Clay, Calhoun, Adams, and Benton appeared for many years as the only dependence of the country in questions and measures of great national import.

These master spirits continued their career till they, in turn, one by one, left the stage of action, the last terminating in 1852, by the death of Mr. Webster.

Of this galaxy, the Hons. John Quincy Adams, of the House

of Representatives, and Henry Clay, of the Senate, were the leaders of international measures; Senators Daniel Webster and Thomas H. Benton, those of national import; while Senator John C. Calhoun was especially confined to that of state rights sovereignty. During the existence of these, there were other men of note and distinction, all of whom have left the stage of action. Of the great personages above named, all, excepting Senator Benton, have held the portfolio of first minister of state; and it is notorious, that although Senator Calhoun's was under President James K. Polk, 1844, a period most auspicious for the display of statesmanship, as great and vital questions of national and international polity were prominent before the country and the world, — such as the extension of territory, and the annexation of Texas, — not a measure was put forth by Mr. Calhoun to meet the exigencies of the occasion and the times. Indeed, that senator, outside of "state sovereignty" and South Carolina, as history bears witness, as a *statesman*, was a failure.

The social polity of the North being based upon labor, and that of the South on leisure, depending on slave labor for maintenance, as an almost natural consequence, the North neglected as much as possible places of honor in the nation, — the army, and navy, — conceding these, as a matter of course, in all good faith, to its brethren of the South. In good faith the concession was certainly made, because the North then as heartily approved of slavery as the South.

Foreign intervention being permanently settled, and no longer any dread of a common enemy, the South accepted the indifference of the North, and commenced preparations for her own independence. This was probably maturing shortly after the battle of New Orleans (1815), till the election of James Buchanan, 1856; or, more historically, from the treaty of Ghent, 1814, to the Ostend Congress, in 1854.

When the civil war commenced, it was alarmingly apparent that the South had by far the best officers, the North having few trustworthy, or those of military experience. And while the army was routed, and the enemy gaining strength at home and abroad, the masterly ability of statesmanship of the North not only challenged the respect and admiration of the world by the wisdom of the great executive head of the government, but intricate questions of the greatest international policy were raised, met, sustained, and established; military and financial measures created by the ministers of state, war, and the treasury, never yet equalled by any nation.

During the time immediately succeeding the revolutionary period, — from 1815 to 1851, — with the exception of representatives from Missouri, Kentucky, Maryland, and Delaware, in the persons of Hons. Thomas H. Benton, Henry Clay, Reverdy Johnson, and John M. Clayton, every great measure of national interest was represented by gentlemen of the North. So completely had the state rights question engrossed the attention of the South, that nothing could be elicited in the halls of Congress from that side of the house, of whatever import the question, but "Old Dominion" and "first families," "South Carolina and state rights," "Georgia and negro slaves," "Alabama and cotton," "Louisiana, slaves, and sugar," "Mississippi negro traders," "Arkansas and amen with abolition," "Texas and bowie knives." These appeared to be the only rejoinders given, and arguments made for many years past, in the councils of the nation, by representatives from the South.

Absorbed entirely in the one erroneous idea of state sovereignty, thinking of nothing besides this, neither fearing nor caring for anything else, then is a degeneracy in statesmanship much to be wondered at on the part of the South? Certainly not. It is but charity to the South to admit of finding a solution of their deficiencies in the statement of these grave and important truths.

Was there any one man or measure, either in or out of the whole Southern establishment, civil or military, approaching those of the North? Not one. I am fully aware that "comparisons are odious;" that these features of observations are "in bad taste," and that it will be adjudged ungenerous to make such allusions to our fallen and subjugated fellow-countrymen. I fully appreciate the extent of the objection; but when it is remembered that many of this very class of Southerners, — the old leading politicians are straining their intellects to prove the inferiority and incapacity of my race to high social and intellectual attainments, — the objector will, at least, find an explanation, if not justification, in the strictures.

I admit there are many excellent gentlemen in the South, and many have, through the press of the country, acknowledged their approval of **the great principles of equality before the law, liberty and justice, and the natural inalienable rights of all men by birth;** but I must be permitted to place **my record,** if not **measure my steel,** against those who tauntingly dare challenge **me.** It was the Hon. Daniel **Webster, who, long years** ago, on **the** floor of the United States Senate, **on the very** subject of disparagement, told Senator Hayne, of South Carolina, in reply to his assertion, " The gentleman from Massachusetts has found *more* than his match " in debate with Senator Benton, — " Sir, where there are *blows to be received,* there must **be blows given** in return."

The International Policy of the World towards the African Race.

One of the highest pretensions set up in favor of the enslavement of the African race is its inferiority. If the Britons, Caledonians, Hibernians, **and** others of the Celtic as well as Teuton and pure Caucasian races had never been enslaved; if Caractacus, the king and proudest prince the British ever had up to that period, had **not** been led in chains, and sold by order of **Julius Cæsar, with** many other British slaves, in the public market of Rome; **if** the British nobles, long years ago, had not **written of their own** peasantry, that they were incapable of elevation; if they had not recorded and passed enactments against the Scotch and Irish, that they were innately inferior, and totally insusceptible of instruction and civilization, calling them **" hea-**then dogs, only fit for slaves of the lowest order; " if a general **system** of serfdom, known **as** the Feudal System, **had** not existed generally among the white races for ages through **all** Europe, before a black slave was ever known among the whites; if the whites had not been held in slavery many centuries longer than **were the** blacks; and finally, if Russia had not, just within the **last** three years (1864), emancipated her forty-two millions of slaves, — ten times more than the African slaves in the United States, allowing four millions to the South, — then there would be some semblance of honesty and sincerity in the continued plea of justice for ages of wrong and crime against an unoffending, helpless people.

Through all times white slavery had existed among the nations of Europe, and as civilization advanced, and the **lower classes** became more elevated, the difficulty became more apparent in perpetuating the system. What to do, and how to remedy the evil, was a question of paramount importance. To suppress the approach of civilization, and keep down the rising aspirations of **the** common people, could not be well determined. The genius **of social** and political economy were put to the test to divine the desired end to be attained. Legislative and royal decrees could **not reach it; the march of man and** the light of intellect kept in **advance of** legal injunctions.

In 624 — twelve hundred and forty-three years ago, and twelve hundred and thirty-nine before the Emancipation Proclamation of President Lincoln — the Saracens or Arabs gained access to Africa, controlling the commerce for seven **hundred and** fifty-eight years, being the only foreigners accessible to, and **holding** a friendly intercourse with, the people.

In the year 1487, Bartholomew Diaz, of Portugal, discovered the Cape of Good Hope, calling it *Cabo del Tormentoso* — " **the** Cape of Storms." **On** reporting to his sovereign the discovery, with all **of its prospects, the king cried** out, " No, let us not call it ' Cabo del Tormentoso,' but rather let us call it *Cabo del Buen Speremza!* — the Cape of Good Hope ! " And it was a good hope to Portugal, because it must be remembered that access to Africa, **by** communication with the western coast, was then **to** Europeans unknown; the only intercourse being from the north by the Barbary States, and through the interior by caravans, all of which purported to reach the eastern part of the continent by that way.

The year 1482 was an eventful period to the African **race,** and I here record, for the first time probably in which it has ever been given to the world (except the authority herein quoted), the startling facts that the enslavement of the African race was the result of a determination on the part of at least four, and probably more, of the strongest, the most enlightened and polished nations at the time, to make the African race supplant, by substituting it for European slavery. These nations were, Spain, England, France, and Portugal.

And I should not feel, whatever I may have effectually done, that my work had been more than half completed, did I not, as a wronged and outraged son of Africa, give to the world this crowning act of infamy against a people, the facts of which have ever been closely concealed, and even denied, while thousands of the world's good people have no knowledge that such facts ever transpired.

The demands for ameliorating the condition of the whites pressed heavily in all parts of Europe, as the elevated wealthy noble could not longer bear to see the ignorant poor of his kinsmen degraded. To longer deny them the right of elevation, was to disparage the genius, and degrade the whole Caucasian race. To remedy this, a race must be chosen foreign to their own, and as different as possible in external characteristics. For this dreadful purpose the African was selected as the victim of an international conspiracy. A political conspiracy of malice aforethought, prompted by avarice and the love of lucre. During the memorable events that thrilled with emotion the communities of every country in 1862, in the midst of our national struggle, the Rev. Felix, Archbishop of Orleans, France, in a pastoral, sent forth to exhort the people of France and the French Catholics of the United States to support the position taken by President Lincoln, in pronouncing his malediction against the cause of the South, said, " It is the teaching of experience that the slavery of the day — the slavery of the blacks — has an origin and a consequence equally detestable. Its origin was the Treaty, the ignoble and cruel bargain, condemned by Pius II. in 1482, by Paul III. in 1557, by Urba VIII. in 1539, by Benedict XIV. in 1741, by Gregory XVI. in 1839." His revelation should startle Christendom, and none would question the historical accuracy of the facts in the case, when coming from such a trustworthy source as the reverend and honored Archbishop of Orleans.

Objections were many and serious on the part of the common

classes to the introduction of this new people as a domestic element into European countries. But notwithstanding this, there would, doubtless, have been many sent, if a timely relief had not been afforded by the discovery of America in 1492. So lucrative became this traffic in a foreign people, running through many years, and engrossed by the most elevated, as elsewhere referred to, that in 1518, James I. made it the basis of the revenue, if not the wealth of England. The people of the New World — Spanish, English, French, Portuguese, and Dutch — made this race their "hope and expectation."

Whole fleets of merchantmen, from every nation in Europe, environed Africa, to subjugate her people. Powerful naval forces were also brought against her, and national representatives, in the persons of their emissaries, prowled along and about her entire coast, sowing the seeds of discord, and a baser corruption among those of the already corrupted natives, inciting them to war, and the devastation of their homes.

Every vestige of civilization was driven from the coast, the interior placed under fearful apprehensions, the entire social system deranged, the progress of improvement suspended, and permanent establishments abandoned. With the entire white world against her, is it not clear why Africa, in the last twelve centuries, has not kept pace with the civilization of the age? Certainly it is. But there are those who still affect to doubt the former civilization of Africa, and dispute that race as the authors of her ancient arts and sciences. Why dispute it? If the African race were not the authors, what race were? Why are not the same arts and sciences found in some other portion of the globe than Africa? Why confined to this quarter of the world? The identity of one people with another has its strongest evidence in the characteristics, habits, manners, customs, especially in moral and religious sentiments, peculiar to themselves, even after all traces by language are lost.

It is simply ridiculous for ethnologists to claim the few Bebers who are found in and about Egypt, as the remnants of the ancient Africans, and erectors of the mighty pyramids, and authors of the hieroglyphics. The present Bebers of Egypt are none other than mixed bloods of the ancient Egyptians who once inhabited it, — who were pure blacks, — and Saracens who had conquered the country by conquest B. C. 146, and without any prestige, except that inherited from the Ishmaelitish or Arab side of their ancestry — avarice and treachery.   I mean not to be unkind in stating this, but simply to paint facts in a strong light.

Certainly the general character of this (the Arabian) race of men has been known through all times.   And although they had given the world in literature the nine numerals in arithmetic, a chirography, and a religion which necessarily has some beautiful philosophy, yet there is little comparison in any of these to the literature of ancient Africa.   I believe it is not pretended that the Arabians have any peculiar order of architecture; and I hope not to be regarded uncharitable if I suspect the cunning Arab, instead of originating, as having *stolen* the nine numerals of our common arithmetic from the Alexandrian Museum, destroyed by them in the memorable conflagration.   It was clever in them to do so, and keep it to themselves; and I shall not raise the voice of envy against them.

The most striking character of the ancient Africans was their purity of morals and religion.   Their high conception and reverence of Deity was manifested and acknowledged in everything they did.   They are known in history as having been the most scrupulous of all races, and conscientious in their dealings.   In this I have reference to the Ethiopians, of whom the inhabitants of Egypt were lineal descendants by colonization or emigration down the valley of the Nile, and settlement in the territory at its mouths; being identical in all their characteristics of a " black skin and woolly hair," even as described as late as the time of Herodotus, " the father of history," the learned Grecian philosopher who travelled and resided among them during twenty-five years.

A people or race possessing in a high degree the great principles of pure ethics and true religion, a just conception of God, necessarily inherit the essential principles of the highest civilization.   And is it not a known and conceded fact by all who are at all conversant with the true character of the African, that he excels all other races in religious sentiments, and adaptation to domestic usages, wherever found?   In this I will not

even except the Caucasian race, because those characteristics
in the African are in such striking contrast to the same in the
Caucasian, that they are regarded by him as exaggerations and
extravagances. Indeed such is the susceptibility and adaptation of the African to the civilization of the times and places in
which he may be found, that the Caucasian, instead of looking
upon it in approved comparison with that which he admires in
his own race, has, by usage of a policy, become accustomed to
undervalue it as a mere "imitation." Can imitation give intellectual ability for acquirements? If it enables a parrot or split-
tongued crow to gabble words by imitation of sound without any
conception of meaning; if it enables a monkey or an ourang-ou-
tang to "come down from a tree and tie gloves on others' hands,"
to go back leaving it unable either to loosen the strings, or climb
the tree to escape the artful huntsman, in imitation of what he did
to insnare it; or "thrusting a hand into a jug of figs, grabbing
it full," and thus holding on to the figs, screams, endeavoring to
take the hand out full, until caught, not having intellect to let
go the figs; does it make him capable of high intellectual attain-
ment, such as languages, chirography, arithmetic, philosophy,
mathematics, the sciences of war, music, painting, sculpture,
political science, and polite literature?

Let the traducers of the African race, those who affect to believe that his faculties consist in mere "imitation," answer this
inquiry. Even in the Southern States, terribly crushed and
shattered as has been for centuries the true African character,
these lurking faculties for the higher attainments rising superior
to the fetters which bound the body of the possessor, would
occasionally burst forth like the sudden illumination of a brilliant meteor, startling the midnight gazer while all was en-
shrined in darkness around. Whether in the person of the distinguished orator and advocate of his race, Frederick Douglass
of Maryland, or an Ellis, the negro blacksmith linguist, or
George Madison Washington of Virginia, or Blind Tom of
Alabama, the musician and pianist, now suprising the world,
Elizabeth Greenfield of Mississippi, the celebrated "Black
Susan," — all slaves when developed, — these great truths of
African susceptibility are incontrovertible. With one more

point this treatise shall have ended. But subsequent to its completion, and very recently, a high functionary, at the head of one the greatest nations of modern times, in an elaborate argument on the subject, having seen fit to make it history, by recording, as part of an official document, the following declaration, I deem it as treacherous to the African race, to which I wholly belong, if I did not place as permanently on record an equally bold and defiant declaration — a proof to the contrary. Says this sage and statesman, —

"The peculiar qualities which should characterize any people who are fit to decide upon the management of public affairs for a great state have seldom been combined. It is the glory of white men to know that they have had these qualities in sufficient measure to build upon this continent a great political fabric, and to preserve its stability for more than ninety years, while in every other part of the world all similar experiments have failed. But if anything can be proved by known facts, if all reasoning upon evidence is not abandoned, it must be acknowledged that, in the progress of nations, negroes have shown less capacity for government than any other race of people. No independent government of any form has ever been successful in their hands. On the contrary, whenever they have been left to their own devices, they have shown a constant tendency to relapse into barbarism." Instead of the assertion, that in the progress of the nations the negro has shown less capacity for government than any other race of people, that no independent government of any form has ever been successful in their hands, I shall commend a reply to this predicate, by the proposition that the negroes were foremost in the progress of time; first who developed the highest type of civilization. National civil government and the philosophy of religion were borrowed by the white races from the negro. And if the learned jurist will go back to school-boy days, he will remember what time has evidently caused him to forget.

In the days of Egyptian greatness one dynasty existed, evidently, for more than one thousand years. This is known to Holy Writ as the government of the Pharaohs. During the reign of these princes, the sovereigns repeatedly were chosen from Egyptian and Ethiopian families. By Ethiopian families, is meant the going out of the kingdom of Ethiopia to select from a royal family the ruler, just as Great Britain goes into Germany to select from a family a sovereign for the throne.

Among these mighty princes were Menes, or Misraim, Sesostris, Osiris, and the Rameses, the last of which was the dynasty name numerically recorded I., II., III., and so on. Rameses I., the greatest of the princes, was the god-man, and none other than Jupiter-Ammon. In him was the beautiful and symbolic idea of the attributes of Deity, — the Christian's God, — first developed. The person of the Deity, Rameses I., was represented as a human being of robust proportions, having a "bushy, woolly head, with ram's horns." His position, seated on a throne of gold and ivory, ivory base and golden floor; in his left hand a sceptre, the right grasping a thunderbolt. At his side was the Phœnix, in its well-known attitude. This last symbolic attribute is sometimes, indeed generally, spoken of by writers as an " eagle with extended wings," which is evidently an error, from all the facts connected with the god Jupiter, and Rameses II., his successor; besides, the eagle was not an ideal, symbolic bird of religion in Africa. It is suggestive of combat and carnality instead of purity, the successor being styled by the ever-devoted Africans, " Rameses the Ever-living, Always-living Rameses " — his name occurring twice in the saluation.

Here, in this ideal symbol of a God, was also the identity of man; ivory representing durability, gold, purity, the sceptre, authority, and the thunderbolt, power; the ram's head, innocence, decision, and caution against too near approach. In a word, none must presume to attempt to speak face to face with the Deity, as death would be the result; as it is a well-known characteristic of a ram, while innocent as a sheep, he will instantly attack any head, man's or beast's, that approaches his.

Another beautiful symbolic attribute of Jupiter-Ammon, — Rameses I., — which afterwards personified Rameses II., was the Phœnix. This bird, like many ancient images, was allegorical or ideal. It was described as similar to an eagle, larger, and beautiful; with breast, wings, and tail of a brilliant gold tint; a crown of solid gold crest capped its head, the rest of the body covered with green. It never flew, but always walked with stately step and dignity. There was but one known to have an existence, and the beginning was never known. It produced no young, but was itself from the beginning a full-grown bird. It lived, and lived, and lived on, from generation to generation, through ages and periods, and periods and ages, till, seeming weary of life, it built a nest of fagots and brush picked up, which was long constructing; sat upon it when finished, laid a golden egg in time; the egg ignited the nest into a burning mass; the bird continuing to sit, threw up its wings and head in great excitement, and was consumed in the flames; when in the ashes was left a ball, out of the ball came forth a worm, from this worm instantly sprang another Phœnix, which lived on like the first, to transfigurate or reproduce itself again in time.

There were still other symbolic representatives of Deity among them, Rameses II. being also called Apis, and represented as an ox or a bull; while Ramesis III. was called Osiris, and represented as a dog — the ox or bull, as the attribute of patience, endurance, and strength; the dog, as faithfulness and watchfulness.

Is it not clear that much of the philosophy of our theology was borrowed from their mythology? Whence the " great white throne" upon which God sits; the "golden pavement," the " thunders" of his wrath, " Behold the Lamb of God," " Our God is a consuming fire," " No man can look upon God and live," " A self-creating God," with numerous kindred quotations which might be made from the Scriptures?

The Africans, as is well known, were great herdsmen; a great part of their wealth and available currency consisting in their live stock; every family, however limited their circumstances, having a flock of sheep or goats, and both more or less; this running through to the present day, where, in recent travels on that continent, the writer met, in the first large city, a dairyman, who, every morning, milked eighty cows, and farther in the interior, towards Soudan, the dairy which supplied him every morning milked two hundred cows. And among the higher families, as nobles, chiefs, and princes, from five to ten thousand

21

head, the property of one person or family, is commonly met with. . Dr. Livingstone speaks of meeting with kings, even in that least civilized interior region of his explorations, who possessed as many as forty thousand cattle. These herds are watched by faithful attendants, — men when large, or women when small, with the indispensable shepherd dog, which is generally black. In speaking of the riches of Job, the man of Uz, the Scriptures tell us that his cattle were on a " thousand hills."

Can it not be conceived that the God who was thus bountiful in bestowing such wealth might be symbolized by the property itself and the means of its protection? Hence Jupiter Ammon or Rameses I., as a ram or sheep; Sesostris, or Rameses II., as a bull or ox — Apis; Osiris or Rameses III. as dog or jackal.

There was also another beautiful symbolic personification in this — three persons in one. For it is a striking and remarkable fact, as must be noticed by all antiquarians, that these three persons inseparably appear, both by inscription and in statuary — Rameses, Sesostris, Osiris — sheep, ox, dog. Here are innocence, patience, faith, and charity or love, as none so loving as a dog. And how typical of the true African character!

It was shown that the authors of this beautiful and pure religious doctrine were black. This will not be disputed, when it is remembered that Moses took one of the daughters of Jethro, prince and priest of Midian, to wife, and the Scriptures inform us that she was an " Ethiopian woman;" Aaron and Miriam, the brother and sister of Moses, entering into strife with him about it. Not, as it is concluded by modern civilization, because she was black, but because she was identical with their oppressors and recent masters the objection was made.

It is very evident that the highest conception of the Jewish religion is that which was borrowed from Africa during the Israelitish bondage in Egypt, transmitted through them to the present, and devoloped in the metaphysical theology of the age.

And it will not do to call this " mummery," since later, in June, 1867, the President of the United States took part in the consecration of a hall, erected in part to the perpetuation of this African symbolic philosophy and religion.

The capital city of this great people in Africa was Thebais, commonly called Thebes, supposed to contain two millions of inhabitants, surrounded by a wall with one hundred gates, twenty-five at each point of the compass. On the occasion of his Asiatic conquest, Sesostris, or Rameses II., went out of the city with ten thousand infantry and two hundred chariots, with charioteers armed for war, from each gate at one time, having an aggregate of one million two hundred thousand warriors. The conquest of this proud and mighty prince was carried to the banks of the River Indus, conquering every nation as he passed; where he set his memorable pillars, with the peculiar inscription, " Sesostris, the king of kings, has conquered the world to the banks of the Indus; " when he evacuated the country, and returned to his own, having vindicated the prestige and dignity of his name.

Who were the builders of the everlasting pyramids, catacombs, and sculptors of the sphinxes? Were they Europeans or Caucasians, Asiatics or Mongolians? Will it be at once conceded that the authors of the symbolic mythology and hieroglyphic science are identical? Upon this point there is but one opinion. The inventors or authors of the one were the builders or architects of the other.

Among what race of men, and what country of the globe, do we find traces of these singular productions, but the African and Africa? None whatever. It is in Africa the pyramids, sphinxes, and catacombs are found; here the hieroglyphics still remain. Among the living Africans traces of their beautiful philosophy and symbolic mythology still exist. In the interior their architecture and hieroglyphics are still the subjects of their art. Through all time the arts of a people have been among the clearest evidences of identity.

Asia has her several peculiar orders of architecture, the Chinese and Japan being identical; that among the Hindoos the type of the others. Europe has her Tuscan, Doric, Ionic, Corinthian, and Composite, with Gothic, and other modifications of modern orders.

If the originators and builders of the pyramids and sphinxes had been Asiatics, is it not certain that the same architecture would have been found in Asia? of Europeans, in Europe? There is nothing more certain than it would; and the entire absence of all traces of the purely African architecture, arts, and symbolic religion and mythology among other races and in other countries than the Africans and Africa, makes it simply preposterous for the white race to claim these as productions of their own.

Would the Asiatic or the European, who had erected the architectural monuments in Africa, have lost their arts? Would they not have originated another as they returned to their original homes? Do the fixed, especially original, arts of a people leave them simply by a change of countries? Certainly not; as among the greatest advantages to be gained by emigration is the arts that are taken by the people to a country. And had the architectures of Africa been an importation, originated by or among any other people than themselves, is it not one of the most striking known to history by ages of experience, that it would have been found in some other country among the descendants of the originators and authors, and not been found in Africa alone, and peculiar to the African race? Were they Persians who had succeeded by conquest in Africa? Were they Greeks under Alexander? Were they Greeks and Romans who made their advent into Egypt with Antony? or those who fled in dismay under Pompey, after the famous defeat of Pharsalia? or Jews under tetrarch governments? Certainly not; as all of them, from the Persian to the Jewish advent, found these arts and sciences there. And is it not known to history that Egypt was the "cradle of the earliest civilization," propagating the arts and sciences, when the Grecians were an uncivilized people, covering their persons with skins and clothing, anterior to the existence of the she-wolf with Romulus the founder of Rome?

On the invasion of the Saracens, A. C. 146 years, the African library, known as the "Alexandrian Museum," was known to contain in manuscript seven hundred thousand volumes. The secretiveness of the Africans was a matter of history for ages known to the world, their arts and sciences being held as sacred, and propagated with the greatest caution. The kings and priests were the first recipients; the nobles and gentlemen the other. All Egypt and Ethiopia regarded this library as the "hope and expectation" of their countries.

The value of the collection will be estimated by remembrance of its age and manner of obtaining, printing then being unknown to the world. The age of the library, from its first collections, was coequal with the first dawn of science among them.

And had this immense fountain of knowledge been transmitted to posterity, the African would have had a history and a name. And I repeat, with emphasis, that the loss of the African library was a catastrophe unequalled in the age of the world, as bearing on the destiny of a people and a race.

But the "Museum" was made the centre of attraction; the Saracen invaders surrounded the stupendous edifice; orders were given that not a relic be preserved; the flambeau was the weapon of attack; assault and fire was the command, — when the accumulated literature, art and science, of four thousand years' collection, sent fire and smoke towards the heavens, more destructive in its consequences than the world had ever before witnessed! The African library, the depository of the earliest germs of social, civil, political, and national progress, the concentrated wisdom of ages, stood in flames! Fourteen days burning, the building in ruins, and the light of science and civilization, for generations, was extinguished, and Africa became a prey to avarice, imposture, and oppression!

So enlightened, polished, and humane were this race, that after the birth of Jesus, subsequent to the downfall of Egypt by the Saracens, the "warning of the Lord to Joseph" was to take the young child and his mother, and flee into Egypt, and be thou there until they are all dead who seek the child's life. Nor can it be denied that the African race were that which the "Spirit of the Lord" meant, because, notwithstanding Saracen subjugation in Egypt, the African polity, civilization, and humanity still prevailed. Besides, it is a historically known fact that Greeks and Jews were with the Romans in government and sentiments against this Messiah, the promised king of the Jews; all conspiring for his deposition in the event of his coming. It will also be remembered that after the crucifixion and ascension, that Africa was the only country which held prestige enough to send a national representative to "Jerusalem to worship" under the Christian doctrine, as propagated by the scattered and terror-stricken apostles; the Ethiopian eunuch, a man **of great authority**, and chief lord **of her majesty, Queen Candace's, royal** treasury.

One word **more**, and I **close a review already too elaborate; but** driven by necessity **to the defence of my race, duty compelled me to the** point where **I cease.** Would any other race than the **African,** in the symbolical statues of the sphinxes, have placed **the great** head of a *negro woman* on the majestic body of a lion, as an **ideal** representation **of** their genius?

If it be **the** "glory of the white **race to know that they have** had these qualifications **in sufficient measure to** build upon this **continent a great political** fabric," it is also the glory of the **black race to** know **that they have had** these qualities in sufficient measure to build a great political fabric long before the whites, **imparting to** them the first germs of **civilization, and** enlightening the world by **their wisdom. And the most momentous, ex-**traordinary international conspiracy **against the African race,** which this memento commenced **to expose, has never been by** convention annulled **nor abrogated, and, therefore, still** stands optional with either party to **continue or** withdraw; **it is fondly and confidently hoped will not be encouraged nor induced to continue** by **an equally extraordinary, if** not momentous, **official** denunciation against that **race, from** the executive of one **of the** most powerful nations **existing on** this **globe.**

And in behalf of **my race,** once **proud, polished, and** elevated, — at the **feet of whose philosophers the** learned and eminent of **the world sought wisdom, as did** "Herodotus, the father of his-**tory," and** others, — **may** I fondly hope that another generation **will not** pass away **till** Africa, in and by her own legitimate chil-dren, gives evidence **of** a national **regeneration,** breathing forth with fervid and holy aspirations **in** the religious sentiments of her native heart and beautiful **words of** one of **her own native** languages: *Bi-Olorum Pellu* — "the Lord has **been merciful to us."**

And in behalf of my emancipated brethren in America, may the blessings of that God, whose signal promise **must** and will be fulfilled, despite political official anathema, **rest** upon **the** devoted head and in the holy **heart** of the most eminent prelate, **Father Felix, Archbishop of** Orleans in France.

Political Destiny of the Colored Race on the American Continent.

To the Colored Inhabitants of the United States : —

Fellow-Countrymen : **The duty** assigned **us is** an important one, comprehending **all** that pertains to our destiny and that **of our posterity, present** and prospectively. And while it must **be** admitted that the **subject is** one of **the** greatest magnitude, **re-**quiring all that talents, prudence, and wisdom might adduce, **and** while it would **be folly to** pretend to give you the combined result **of these three agencies,** we shall **satisfy** ourselves with doing our **duty to the best of our** ability, **and that in the** plainest, most **simple, and** comprehensive manner.

Our object, then, shall **be** to place **before you our true position in this country** (the United States), the improbability of realizing **our desires, and the sure,** practicable, and infallible remedy for **the** evils we now endure.

We have not addressed **you as** *citizens,* — **a term** desired and ever cherished by **us,** — because such you have **never been.** We have **not addressed you as** *freemen,* because such privileges **have never been enjoyed** by **any** colored man **in** the United **States. Why, then, should we** flatter **your credulity, by** inducing you to **believe that which** neither **has now, nor never before had, an ex-**istence? Our oppressors are **ever gratified at our manifest satis-**faction, especially when that **satisfaction is founded upon false** premises ; an assumption on **our part of the enjoyment of rights** and privileges which never have **been conceded, and which, ac-**cording to the present system of the **United States policy, we** never **can enjoy.**

The *political policy* of this country was solely borrowed from, and shaped and modelled after, that of Rome. This was strikingly

the case in the establishment of immunities, and the application
of terms in their civil and legal regulations.

The term *citizen*, politically considered, is derived from the
Roman definition, which was never applied in any other sense —
cives ingenui ; which meant, one exempt from restraint of any
kind. (*Cives*, a citizen; one who might enjoy the highest honors in his own free town, — the town in which he lived, — and in
the country or commonwealth; and *ingenui*, freeborn — of GOOD
EXTRACTION.) All who were deprived of citizenship — that is,
the right of enjoying positions of honor and trust — were termed
hostes and *peregrini ;* which are public and private enemies, and
foreigners, or aliens to the country. (*Hostis*, a public, and
sometimes private, enemy; and *peregrinus*, an alien, stranger,
or foreigner.)

The Romans, from a national pride, to distinguish their inhabitants from those of other countries, termed them all "citizens," but, consequently, were under the necessity of specifying
four classes of citizens : none but the *cives ingenui* being unrestricted in their privileges. There was one class, called the *jus
quiritium*, or the wailing or *supplicating* citizen; that is, one
who was continually *moaning, complaining,* or *crying for aid
or succor.* This class might also include within themselves the
jus suffragii, who had the privilege of *voting*, but no other
privilege. They could vote for one of their superiors — the *cives
ingenui* — but not for themselves.

Such, then, is the condition, precisely, of the black and colored
inhabitants of the United States; in some of the states they an-
swering to the latter class, having the privilege of *voting*, to elevate their superiors to positions to which they need never dare
aspire or even hope to attain.

There has, of late years, been a false impression obtained, that
the privilege of *voting* constitutes, or necessarily embodies, the
rights of citizenship. A more radical error never obtained favor
among an oppressed people. Suffrage is an ambiguous term,
which admits of several definitions. But according to strict
political construction, means simply "a vote, voice, approbation." Here, then, you have the whole import of the term *suffrage.* To have the "right of suffrage," as we rather proudly

term it, is simply to have the *privilege* — there is no *right* about it — of giving our *approbation* to that which our *rulers may do*, without the privilegè, on our part, of doing the same thing. Where such privileges are granted — privileges which are now exercised in but few of the states by colored men — we have but the privilege granted of saying, in common with others, who shall, for the time being, exercise *rights*, which, in him, are conceded to be *inherent* and *inviolate:* like the indented apprentice, who is summoned to give his approbation to an act which would be fully binding without his concurrence. Where there is no *acknowledged sovereignty*, there can be no binding power; hence, the suffrage of the black man, independently of the white, would be in this country unavailable.

Much might be adduced on this point to prove the insignificance of the black man, politically considered, in this country, but we deem it wholly unnecessary at present, and consequently proceed at once to consider another feature of this important subject.

Let it then be understood, as a great principle of political economy, that no people can be free who themselves do not constitute an essential part of the *ruling element* of the country in which they live. Whether this element be founded upon a true or false, a just or an unjust basis, this position in community is necessary to personal safety. The liberty of no man is secure who controls not his own political destiny. What is true of an individual is true of a family, and that which is true of a family is also true concerning a whole people. To suppose otherwise, is that delusion which at once induces its victim, through a period of long suffering, patiently to submit to every . species of wrong; trusting against probability, and hoping against all reasonable grounds of expectation, for the granting of privileges and enjoyment of rights which never will be attained. This delusion reveals the true secret of the power which holds in peaceable subjection all the oppressed in every part of the world.

A people, to be free, must necessarily be *their own rulers;* that is, *each individual* must, in himself, embody the *essential ingredient* — so to speak — of the *sovereign principle* which composes the *true basis* of his liberty. This principle, when not exercised by himself, may, at his pleasure, be delegated to another —his true representative.

Said a great French writer, " A free agent, in a free government, should be his own governor; " that is, he must possess within himself the *acknowledged right to govern :* this constitutes him a *governor*, though he may delegate to another the power to govern himself.

No one, then, can delegate to another a power he never possessed; that is, he cannot *give an agency* in that which he never had a right. Consequently, the colored man in the United States, being deprived of the right of inherent sovereignty, cannot *confer* a franchise, because he possesses none to confer. Therefore, where there is no franchise, there can neither be *freedom* nor *safety* for the disfranchised. And it is a futile hope to suppose that the agent of another's concerns will take a proper interest in the affairs of those to whom he is under no obligations. Having no favors to ask or expect, he therefore has none to lose.

In other periods and parts of the world, as in Europe and Asia, the people being of one common, direct origin of race, though established on the presumption of difference by birth, or what was termed *blood*, yet the distinction between the superior classes and common people could only be marked by the difference in the dress and education of the two classes. To effect this, the interposition of government was necessary; consequently the costume and education of the people became a subject of legal restriction, guarding carefully against the privileges of the common people.

In Rome the patrician and plebeian were orders in the ranks of her people — all of whom were termed citizens (*cives*) — recognized by the laws of the country; their dress and education being determined by law, the better to fix the distinction. In different parts of Europe, at the present day, if not the same, the distinction among the people is similar, only on a modified, and in some kingdoms, probably more tolerant or deceptive policy.

In the United States our degradation being once — as it has in a hundred instances been done — legally determined, our color is sufficient, independently of costume, education, or other distinguishing marks, to keep up that distinction.

In Europe when an inferior is elevated to the **rank of equality** with the superior class, the law first **comes to his** aid, **which, in** its decrees, entirely destroys his identity as **an** inferior, **leaving** no trace of his former condition visible.

In the United States, among the whites, **their color** is made, by **law and custom, the mark of** distinction **and superiority**; while the color of the blacks is a **badge of degradation**, acknowledged by statute, organic **law, and the common consent of the people.**

With this view of the case, — which we hold to be **correct**, — to elevate to equality the degraded subject of law and custom, **it** can only be done, as in Europe, **by an entire** destruction **of the** identity of the former condition of the applicant. **Even were** this desirable, which we by no means admit, with the deep-seat**ed prejudices** engendered by oppression, with which we have to **contend**, ages incalculable might reasonably be expected **to** roll around before this could honorably be accomplished; otherwise, we should encourage, and at once commence, an indiscriminate concubinage and immoral **commerce of our** mothers, sisters, wives, and daughters, revolting to **think of**, and a physical curse to humanity.

If this state of things be **to succeed, then, as in Egypt**, under the dread of the inscrutable approach of the destroying angel, to appease the hatred **of our** oppressors, **as** a license **to** the passions **of every** white, let the lintel of each door of every black man be stained **with the blood of** virgin purity and unsullied matron fidelity. **Let it** be written along the cornice in capitals, **"The** *will* of the white man is the rule of my household." Remove the protection **to our** chambers **and** nurseries, that the places once sacred may henceforth become the unrestrained resort of the vagrant and rabble, always provided that the licensed commissioner of lust shall wear the indisputable impress of a *white* **skin.**

But we have fully discovered and comprehended the great political disease with which we are affected, the cause of its origin and continuance; and what is now left for us to do is to discover and apply a sovereign remedy, a healing balm to a sorely diseased body — a wrecked but not entirely shattered system. We propose for this disease a remedy. That remedy is emigration. This emigration should be well advised, and like remedies applied to remove the disease from the physical system of man, skilfully and carefully applied, within the proper time, directed to operate on that part of the system whose greatest tendency shall be to benefit the whole.

Several geographical localities have been named, among which rank the Canadas. These we do not object to as places of temporary relief, especially to the fleeing fugitive, — which, like a palliative, soothes, for the time being, the misery, — but cannot commend them as permanent places upon which to fix our destiny, and that of our children, who shall come after us. But in this connection we would most earnestly recommend to the colored people of the United States generally, to secure, by purchase, all of the land they possibly can while selling at low rates, under the British people and government; as that time may come, when, like the lands in the United States territories generally, if not as in Oregon and some other territories and states, they may be prevented entirely from settling or purchasing them, — the preference being given to the white applicant.

And here we would not deceive you by disguising the facts that, according to political tendency, the Canadas, as all British America, at no very distant day, are destined to come into the United States.

And were this not the case, the odds are against us, because the ruling element there, as in the United States, is, and ever must be, white; the population now standing, in all British America, two and a half millions of whites to but forty thousand of the black race, or sixty-one and a fraction whites to one black! — the difference being eleven times greater than in the United States, — so that colored people might never hope for anything more than to exist politically by mere sufferance; occupying a secondary position to the whites of the Canadas. The Yankees from this side of the lakes are fast settling in the Canadas, infusing, with industrious success, all the malignity and negro-hate inseparable from their very being, as Christian democrats and American advocates of equality.

Then, to be successful, our attention must be turned in a direction towards those places where the black and colored man comprise, by population, and constitute by necessity of numbers, the *ruling element* of the body politic; and where, when occasion shall require it, the issue can be made and maintained on this basis; where our political enclosure and national edifice can be reared, established, walled, and proudly defended on this great elementary principle of original identity. Upon this solid foundation rests the fabric of every substantial political structure in the world, which cannot exist without it; and so soon as a people or nation lose their original identity, just so soon must that nation or people become extinct. Powerful though they may have been, they must fall. Because the nucleus which heretofore held them together, becoming extinct, there being no longer a centre of attraction, or basis for a union of the parts, a dissolution must as naturally ensue as the result of the neutrality of the basis of adhesion among the particles of matter.

This is the secret of the eventful downfall of Egypt, Carthage, Rome, and the former Grecian states, once so powerful — a loss of original identity; and with it, a loss of interest in maintaining their fundamental principles of nationality.

This, also, is the great secret of the present strength of Great Britain, Russia, the United States, and Turkey; and the endurance of the French nation, whatever its strength and power, is attributable only to their identity as Frenchmen.

And doubtless the downfall of Hungary, brave and noble as may be her people, is mainly to be attributed to the want of identity of origin, and, consequently, a union of interests and purpose. This fact it might not have been expected would be admitted by the great Sclave in his thrilling pleas for the restoration of Hungary, when asking aid, both national and individual, to enable him to throw off the ponderous weight placed upon their shoulders by the House of Hapsburg.

Hungary consisted of three distinct "races" — as they called themselves — of people, all priding in, and claiming rights based on, their originality, — the Magyars, Celts, and Sclaves. On the encroachment of Austria, each one of these races, declaring for nationality, rose up against the House of Hapsburg, claiming the right of self-government, premised on their origin. Between the three a compromise was effected; the Magyars, being the majority, claimed the precedence. They made an effort, but for the want of a unity of interests — an identity of origin — the noble Hungarians failed. All know the result.

Nor is this the only important consideration. Were we content to remain as we are, sparsely interspersed among our white fellow-countrymen, we never might be expected to equal them in any honorable or respectable competition for a livelihood. For the reason that, according to the customs and policy of the country, we for ages would be kept in a secondary position, every situation of respectability, honor, profit, or trust, either as mechanics, clerks, teachers, jurors, councilmen, or legislators, being filled by white men, consequently our energies must become paralyzed or enervated for the want of proper encouragement.

This example upon our children, and the colored people generally, is pernicious and degrading in the extreme. And how could it otherwise be, when they see every place of respectability filled and occupied by the whites, they pandering to their vanity, and existing among them merely as a thing of conveniency?

Our friends in this and other countries, anxious for our elevation, have for years been erroneously urging us to lose our identity as a distinct race, declaring that we were the same as other people; while at the very same time their own representative was traversing the world, and propagating the doctrine in favor of a *universal Anglo-Saxon* **predominance**. The "universal brotherhood," so ably and eloquently advocated by that Polyglot Christian Apostle * of this doctrine, had established as its basis a universal acknowledgment of the Anglo-Saxon rule.

The truth is, we are not identical with the Anglo-Saxon, or any other race of the Caucasian or pure white type of the human family, and the sooner we know and acknowledge this truth the better for ourselves and posterity.

The English, French, Irish, German, Italian, Turk, Persian, Greek, Jew, and all other races, have their native or inherent

* ·Elihu Burritt.

peculiarities, and why not our race? We are not willing, therefore, at all times and under all circumstances to be moulded into various shapes of eccentricity, to suit the caprices and conveniences of every kind of people. We are not more suitable to everybody than everybody is suitable to us; therefore, no more like other people than others are like us.

We have, then, inherent traits, attributes, so to speak, and native characteristics, peculiar to our race, whether pure or mixed blood; and all that is required of us is to cultivate these, and develop them in their purity, to make them desirable and emulated by the rest of the world.

That the colored races have the highest traits of civilization, will not be disputed. They are civil, peaceable, and religious to a fault. In mathematics, sculpture and architecture, as arts and sciences, commerce and internal improvements as enterprises, the white race may probably excel; but in languages, oratory, poetry, music, and painting, as arts and sciences, and in ethics, metaphysics, theology, and legal jurisprudence, — in plain language, in the true principles of morals, correctness of thought, religion, and law or civil government, there is no doubt but the black race will yet instruct the world.

It would be duplicity longer to disguise the fact that the great issue, sooner or later, upon which must be disputed the world's destiny, will be a question of black and white, and every individual will be called upon for his identity with one or the other. The blacks and colored races are four sixths of all the population of the world; and these people are fast tending to a common cause with each other. The white races are but one third of the population of the globe, — or one of them to two of us, — and it cannot much longer continue that two thirds will passively submit to the universal domination of this one third. And it is notorious that the only progress made in territorial domain, in the last three centuries, by the whites, has been a usurpation and encroachment on the rights and native soil of some of the colored races.

The East Indies, Java, Sumatra, the Azores, Madeira, Canary, and Cape Verde Islands; Socotra, Guardifui, and the Isle of France; Algiers, Tunis, Tripoli, Barca, and Egypt in the

North, Sierra Leone in the **West, and** Cape Colony in the South of Africa; besides many other islands and possessions not herein named; **Australia, the** Ladrone **Islands,** together with **many** others of Oceanica; **the** seizure and appropriation of **a great por**tion of the Western Continent, with all its islands, **were so many encroachments of** the whites upon the rights of **the colored races. Nor are they** yet content, but, intoxicated with the success of their career, the Sandwich Islands are **now** marked **out as** the next booty to be seized in the ravages of their exterminating crusade.

We regret the necessity of stating the fact, but duty compels us to the task, that, for more than two thousand years, the determined aim of the whites has been to crush the colored races wherever found. With a determined will they have sought and pursued them in every quarter of the globe. The Anglo-Saxon **has** taken the lead in this work of universal subjugation. **But the** Anglo-American stands preëminent for deeds of injustice **and** acts of oppression, unparalleled, perhaps, in the **annals of** modern history.

We admit the existence of great and good people in America, England, France, and the rest of Europe, who desire a unity of interests among the whole human family, of whatever origin **or race.**

But it is neither **the moralist, Christian, nor** philanthropist whom we now have to meet and combat, but the politician, the civil engineer, and skilful economist, who direct and control the machinery which moves forward, with mighty impulse, **the na**tions and powers of the earth. We must, therefore, if possible, meet them on vantage ground, or, at least, with adequate means for the conflict.

Should we encounter an enemy with artillery, a prayer will not stay the cannon shot, neither will the kind words nor smiles of philanthropy shield his spear from piercing us through the heart. **We** must meet mankind, then, as **they meet us — pre**pared for the worst, though we may hope for the best. Our submission does not gain for us an increase of friends nor respectability, as the white race will only respect those who oppose their **usurpation, and** acknowledge as equals those who will not submit to their oppression. This may be no new discovery in political economy, but it certainly is **a subject** worthy **the con**sideration of the black race.

After a due consideration of these facts, as herein recounted, shall we stand still and continue inactive — the passive observers of the **great** events of the times and age in which **we live; sub**mitting indifferently to the usurpation by the white **race of every** right belonging to the blacks? Shall the last **vestige of an** opportunity, outside of the continent of **Africa, for the national** development **of our race,** be permitted, **in consequence of our** slothfulness, to elude our grasp, and fall **into the** possession **of** the whites? This, may Heaven forbid. **May** the sturdy, intelligent Africo-American sons of the Western Continent forbid.

Longer to remain inactive, it should **be borne in** mind, **may be to give an opportunity to** despoil us of every right and possession **sacred to** our existence, with which God has endowed us as **a heritage on** the earth. For let it not **be** forgotten **that** the **white race** — who numbers but *one* of them to *two* of us — originally located in Europe, besides possessing all of that continent, **have now** got hold of **a large portion of** Asia, Africa, all North America, a portion of **South** America, **and all of** the great islands **of** both hemispheres, except Paupau, **or New** Guinea, inhabited by negroes and Malays, in Oceanica; **the Japanese** Islands, peopled and ruled by the Japanese; Madagascar, peopled by negroes, near the coast of Africa; and the Island of Hayti, **in** the West Indies, peopled by as brave and noble descendants **of** Africa as they who laid **the** foundation of Thebias, or constructed the **everlasting** pyramids **and catacombs** of Egypt, — a people who **have freed themselves by the might of their** own will, the force **of their own power,** the unfailing strength of their own right arms, and their unflinching determination to be free.

Let us, then, not survive the disgrace and ordeal of Almighty displeasure, of two to one, witnessing the universal possession and control by the whites of every habitable portion of the earth. For such must inevitably be the case, and that, too, at no distant day, if black men do not take advantage of the opportunity, **by** grasping hold of those places where chance is in their favor, **and** establishing the rights and power of the colored race.

We must make an issue, create an event, and establish for ourselves a position. This is essentially necessary for our effective elevation as a people, in shaping our national development, directing our destiny, and redeeming ourselves as a race.

If we but determine it shall be so, it *will* be so; and there is nothing under the sun can prevent it. We shall then be but in pursuit of our legitimate claims to inherent rights, bequeathed to us by the will of Heaven — the endowment of God, our common Parent. A distinguished economist has truly said, "God has implanted in man an infinite progression in the career of improvement. A soul capacitated for improvement ought not to be bounded by a tyrant's landmarks." This sentiment is just and true, the application of which to our case is adapted with singular fitness.

Having glanced hastily at our present political position in the world generally, and the United States in particular, — the fundamental disadvantages under which we exist, and the improbability of ever attaining citizenship and equality of rights in this country, — we call your attention next to the places of destination to which we shall direct emigration.

The West Indies, Central and South America, are the countries of our choice, the advantages of which shall be made apparent to your entire satisfaction. Though we have designated them as countries, they are, in fact, but one country, relatively considered, a part of this, the Western Continent. As now politically divided, they consist of the following classification, each group or division placed under its proper national head : —

The French Islands.

	Square miles.	Population in 1840.
Guadeloupe,	675	124,000
Martinico,	260	119,000
St. Martin, N. part,	15	6,000
Mariegalente,	90	11,500
Deseada,	25	1,500

DANISH ISLANDS.

	Square miles.	Population in 1840.
Santa Cruz,	80	34,000
St. Thomas,	50	15,000
St. John,	70	3,000

SWEDISH.

	Square miles.	Population in 1840.
St. Bartholomew,	25	8,000

DUTCH.

	Square miles.	Population in 1840.
St. Eustatia,	10	20,000
Curacoa,	375	12,000
St. Martin, S. part,	10	5,000
Saba,	20	9,000

VENEZUELA.

	Square miles.	Population in 1840.
Margarita,	00	16,000

SPANISH.

	Square miles.	Population in 1840.
Cuba,	43,500	725,000
Porto Rico,	4,000	325,000

BRITISH.

	Square miles.	Population in 1840.
Jamaica,	5,520	375,000
Barbadoes,	164	102,000
Trinidad,	1,970	45,000
Antigua,	108	36,000
Grenada and the Granadines,	120	29,000
St. Vincent,	121	36,000
St. Kitts,	68	24,000
Dominica,	275	20,000
St. Lucia,	275	18,000
Tobago,	120	14,000
Nevis,	20	12,000
Montserrat,	47	8,000
Tortola,	20	7,000

BRITISH. (Continued.)

	Square miles.	Population in 1840.
Barbuda,	72	0,000
Anguilla,	90	3,000
Bahamas,	4,440	18,000
Bermudas,	20	10,000

HAYTIEN NATION.

	Square miles.	Population in 1840.
Hayti,	000	800,000

In addition to these there are a number of smaller islands, belonging to the Little Antilles, the area and population of which are not known, many of them being unpopulated.

These islands, in the aggregate, form an area — allowing 40,000 square miles to Hayti and her adjunct islands, and something for those the statistics of which are unknown — of about 103,000, or equal in extent to Rhode Island, New York, New Jersey, and Pennsylvania, and little less than the United Kingdom of England, Scotland, Ireland, and the principality of Wales.

The population being, on the above date, 1840, 3,115,000 (three millions one hundred and fifteen thousand), and allowing an increase of *ten per cent.* in ten years, on the entire population, there are now 3,250,000 (three millions two hundred and fifty thousand) inhabitants, who comprise the people of these islands.

CENTRAL AMERICA.

	Population in 1840.
Guatemala,	800,000
San Salvador,	350,000
Honduras,	250,000
Costa Rica,	150,000
Nicaragua,	250,000

These consist of five states, as shown in the above statistics, the united population of which, in 1840, amounted to 1,800,000 (one million eight hundred thousand) inhabitants. The number at present being estimated at 2,500,000 (two and **a half** millions), shows in thirteen years, 700,000 (seven hundred thousand), being one third and one eighteenth of an increase in population.

South America.

	Square miles.	Population in 1840.
New Grenada,	450,000	1,687,000
Venezuela,	420,000	900,000
Ecuador,	280,000	600,000
Guiana,	160,000	182,000
Brazil,	3,390,000	5,000,000
North Peru,	**300,000**	700,000
South Peru,	130,000	800,000
Bolivia,	450,000	1,716,000
Buenos Ayres,	750,000	**700,000**
Paraguay,	88,000	150,000
Uruguay,	92,000	75,000
Chili,	170,000	1,500,000
Patagonia,	370,000	30,000

The total area **of these states is 7,050,000** (seven **millions and** fifty thousand) square miles; **but** comparatively little (450,000 square miles) less than **the whole area of North America, in** which we live.

But one state in South America, Brazil, **is an abject** slaveholding state; and even here all free men are socially and politically **equal, negroes** and colored **men partly of** African **descent holding offices of honor,** trust, and rank, without restriction. **In the other states slavery is not known,** all the inhabitants enjoying **political equality, restrictions on account of** color being entirely unknown, unless, **indeed, necessity** induces it, when, in all **such** cases, the preference **is given to the** colored man, to put a check **to** European assumption and insufferable Yankee intrusion and impudence.

The aggregate population **was** 14,040,000 (**fourteen** millions **and** forty thousand) in 1840. Allowing for thirteen years the **same** ratio of increase as that of the Central American states, — **being one third** (4,680,000), — and this gives at present a popu**lation of 18,720,000 in** South America.

Add to this the population of the Antilles and Guatemala, and this gives a population in the West Indies, Central and South America, of 24,470,000 (twenty-four millions four hundred and **seventy thousand**) inhabitants.

But one **seventh of this** population, 3,495,714 (three **millions** four hundred and ninety-five thousand seven hundred and four-**teen**) being white, or of pure European extraction, there is **a** population throughout this vast area of 20,974,286 (twenty millions nine hundred and seventy-four thousand two hundred **and** eighty-six) colored persons, who constitute, from the immense preponderance of their numbers, the *ruling element*, as they ever must be, of those countries.

There are no influences that could be brought to bear to change this most fortunate and Heaven-designed state and condition of **things.** Nature here has done her own work, which the **art of** knaves nor **the schemes of** deep-designing political impostors can ever reach. This is a fixed fact in the zodiac of the politi-**cal heavens, that the blacks and colored people** are the stars which must ever most conspicuously twinkle in the firmament of this division of the Western Hemisphere.

We next invite your attention **to a** few facts, **upon which we** predicate the claims of the black race, not only to the **tropical** regions and *south temperate zone* of **this hemisphere, but to the** whole continent, North **as well as South. And here we desire it** distinctly to be understood, that, in the **selection of our places** of destination, **we do not** advocate the *southern* scheme as a concession, nor **yet** at the will nor desire of **our North American** oppressors; but as a policy **by which we must be** the greatest political gainers, without **the risk or possibility of loss** to ourselves. A gain by which the lever of political **eleva-**tion and machinery of national progress must ever **be held and** directed by our own hands and heads, to our own will and pur-poses, in defiance of the obstructions which might be attempted on the part of a dangerous and deep-designing **oppressor.**

From the year 1492, **the** discovery of Hispaniola, — the first land discovered by Columbus in the New World, — to 1502, the short space of ten years, such was the mortality among the na-tives, **that the** Spaniards, then holding rule there, " began to employ a few " Africans in the mines of the island.   The experiment was effective — a successful one.   The Indian and the African were enslaved together, when the Indian sunk, **and the African** stood.

It was not until June the 24th, of the year 1498, that the continent was discovered by John Cabot, a Venetian, who sailed in August of the previous year, 1497, from Bristol, under **the** patronage of Henry VII., King of England.

In 1547, the short-space of but fifteen years from the date of their introduction, Carolus V., **King** of Spain, by right of **a** patent, granted permission to a number of persons annually to supply the islands of **Hispaniola** (St. Domingo), Cuba, Jamaica, and Porto Rico with natives of Africa, to the number of four thousand annually.   John Hawkins, a mercenary Englishman, was the first person known to engage in this general system of debasing our race, and his royal mistress, Queen Elizabeth, was engaged with him in interest, and shared the general **profits.**

The Africans, on their advent into a foreign country, soon **experienced** the **want** of their accustomed **food,** and habits, **and** manner of living.

The aborigines subsisted mainly by game **and** fish, with **a few** patches of maize, or Indian corn, near their wigwams, which were generally attended by the women, while the men were absent engaged in the chase, or at war with a hostile tribe.   The vegetables, grains, and fruits, such as in their native country **they had been** accustomed to, were not to be obtained among the aborigines, which first induced the African laborer to cultivate " patches " of ground in the neighborhood of the mining operations, for the purpose of raising food for his own sustenance.

This trait in their character was observed and regarded with considerable interest; after which the Spaniards and other colonists, on contracting with the English slave dealers — Captain Hawkins and others — for new supplies of slaves, were careful to request that an adequate quantity of seeds and plants of various kinds, indigenous to the continent of Africa, especially those composing the staple products of the natives, be selected and brought out with the slaves to the New World.   Many of these were cultivated to a considerable extent, while those indigenous to America were cultivated with great success.

Shortly after the commencement of the slave trade under Elizabeth and Hawkins, the queen granted a license to Sir Walter Raleigh to search for uninhabited lands, and seize upon all unoccupied by Christians. Sir Walter discovered the coast of North Carolina and Virginia, assigning the name " Virginia " to the whole coast now comprising the old Thirteen States.

A feeble colony was here settled, which did not avail much, and it was not until the month of April, 1607, that the first permanent settlement was made in Virginia, under the patronage of letters patent from James I., King of England, to Thomas Gates and associates. This was the first settlement of North America, and thirteen years anterior to the landing of the Pilgrims on Plymouth Rock.

And we shall now introduce to you, from acknowledged authority, a number of historical extracts, to prove that previous to the introduction of the black race upon this continent but little enterprise of any kind was successfully carried on. The African or negro was the first *available contributor* to the country, and consequently is by priority of right, and politically should be, entitled to the highest claims of an eligible citizen.

" No permanent settlement was effected in what is now called the United States, till the reign of James the First." — *Ramsay's Hist. U. S.*, vol. i. p. 38.

" The month of April, 1607, is the epoch of the first permanent settlement on the coast of Virginia, the name then given to all that extent of country which forms thirteen states." — *Ib.* p. 39.

The whole coast of the country was at this time explored, not for the purpose of trade and agriculture, — because there were then no such enterprises in the country, the natives not producing sufficient of the necessaries of life to supply present wants, there being consequently nothing to trade for, — but, like their Spanish and Portuguese predecessors, who occupied the islands and different parts of South America, in search of gold and other precious metals.

Trade and the cultivation of the soil, on coming to the New World, were foreign to their intention or designs, consequently, when failing of success in that enterprise, they were sadly disappointed.

"At a time when the precious metals were conceived to be the peculiar and only valuable productions of the New World, when every mountain was supposed to contain a treasure and every rivulet was searched for its golden sands, this appearance was fondly considered as an infallible indication of the mine. Every hand was eager to dig. . . .
. "There was now," says Smith, "no talk, no hope, no work; but dig gold, wash gold, refine gold. With this imaginary wealth the first vessel returning to England was loaded, while the *culture of the land* and every useful occupation was *totally neglected.*
"The colonists thus left were in miserable circumstances for want of provisions. The remainder of what they had brought with them was so small in quantity as to be soon expended, and so damaged in course of a long voyage as to be a source of disease.
". . . In their expectation of getting gold, the people were disappointed, the glittering substance they had sent to England proving to be a valueless mineral. Smith, on his return to Jamestown, found the colony reduced to thirty-eight persons, who, in despair, were preparing to abandon the country. He employed caresses, threats, and even violence in order to prevent them from executing this fatal resolution."—*Ramsay's Hist. U. S.,* pp. 45, 46.

The Pilgrims or Puritans, in November, 1620, after having organized with solemn vows to the defence of each other, and the maintenance of their civil liberty, made the harbor of Cape Cod, landing safely on "Plymouth Rock" December 20th, about one month subsequently. They were one hundred and one in number, and from the toils and hardships consequent to a severe season, in a strange country, in less than six months after their arrival, "forty persons, nearly one half of their original number," had died.

"In 1618, in the reign of James I., the British government established a regular trade on the coast of Africa. In the year 1620 negro slaves began to be imported into Virginia, a Dutch ship bringing twenty of them for sale." — *Sampson's Historical Dictionary,* p. 348.

It will be seen by these historical reminiscences, that the Dutch ship landed her cargo at New Bedford, Massachusetts, —

the whole coast, now comprising the old original states, then went by the name of Virginia, being so named by Sir Walter Raleigh, in honor of his royal mistress and patron, Elizabeth, the Virgin Queen of England, under whom he received the patent of his royal commission, to seize all the lands unoccupied by Christians.

Beginning their preparations in the slave trade in 1618, just two years previous, — allowing time against the landing of the first emigrants for successfully carrying out the project, — the African captives and Puritan emigrants, singularly enough, landed upon the same section of the continent at the same time (1620), the Pilgrims at Plymouth, and the captive slaves at New Bedford, but a few miles, comparatively, south.

"The country at this period was one vast wilderness. The continent of North America was then one continued forest. . . . There were no horses, cattle, sheep, hogs, or tame beasts of any kind. . . . There were no domestic poultry. . . . There were no gardens, orchards, public roads, meadows, or cultivated fields. . . . They often burned the woods that they could advantageously plant their corn. . . . They had neither spice, salt, bread, butter, cheese, nor milk. They had no set meals, but eat when they were hungry, or could find anything to satisfy the cravings of nature. Very little of their food was derived from the earth, except what it spontaneously produced. . . . The ground was both their seat and table. . . . Their best bed was a skin. . . . They had neither iron, steel, nor any metallic instruments." — *Ramsay's Hist.*, pp. 39, 40.

We adduce not these extracts to disparage or detract from the real worth of our brother Indian, — for we are identical as the subjects of American wrongs, outrages, and oppression, and therefore one in interest, — far be it from our designs. Whatever opinion he may entertain of our race, — in accordance with the impressions made by the contumely heaped upon us by our mutual oppressor, the American nation, — we admire his, for the many deeds of heroic and noble daring with which the brief history of his liberty-loving people is replete. We sympathize with him, because our brethren are the successors of his in the degradation of American bondage; and we adduce them in evidence against the many aspersions heaped upon the African race, avowing that their inferiority to the other races, and unfit-

ness for a high civil and social position, **caused them to** be re-
duced to servitude.

For the purpose of proving their **availability and eminent fitness alone — not to** say superiority, and **not inferiority —** first
suggested **to** Europeans **the** substitution **of African for** that **of**
Indian **labor in the mines; that their superior** adaptation **to the**
difficulties **consequent to a new country and different climate**
made them **preferable to** Europeans **themselves; and their superior** skill, industry, **and general thriftiness in all that they did,**
first **suggested to the colonists the propriety of turning their attention to agricultural and other industrial pursuits than those
of mining** operations.

It is evident, from **what** has herein **been** adduced, — **the settlement** of Captain **John** Smith being **in the course** of a few months
reduced to thirty-eight, and that **of the** Pilgrims at Plymouth
from one hundred and one **to** fifty-seven **in six** months, — that
the whites nor aborigines were equal **to the hard,** and **to** them
insurmountable, difficulties which then stood wide-spread before
them.

An endless forest, **the impenetrable earth, — the one to be re-**
moved, and the **other to be excavated;** towns and cities **to be
built,** and farms to be cultivated, — **all presented difficulties too**
arduous for the European **then here, and entirely unknown to**
the native of the continent.

At a period such as this, when the natives themselves had
fallen victims to the tasks imposed upon **them** by **the** usurpers,
and the Europeans also were fast sinking beneath **the** influence
and weight of climate and hardships; when food **could** not be
obtained, nor the common conveniences of life procured; when
arduous duties **of life were to be performed,** and none capable
. of doing them, save those who **had previously, by** their labors,
not only **in their own** country, **but in the new, so** proven **themselves** capable, it is very evident, **as the most** natural conse-
quence, the Africans were resorted to **for the** performance of
every duty common to domestic life.

There were no laborers known to the **colonists,** from Cape Cod
to Cape Lookout, than **those of** the African race. They entered
at once into the mines, extracting therefrom the rich treasures

which for a thousand ages lay hidden in the earth; when, plunging into the depths of the rivers, they culled from their sandy bottoms, to the astonishment of the natives and surprise of the Europeans, minerals and precious stones, which added to the pride and aggrandizement of every throne in Europe.

And from their knowledge of cultivation, — an art acquired in their native Africa, — the farming interests in the North and planting in the South were commenced with a prospect never dreamed of before the introduction on the continent of this most interesting, unexampled, hardy race of men. A race capable of the endurance of more toil, fatigue, and hunger than any other branch of the human family.

Though pagans for the most part in their own country, they required not to be taught to work, and how to do it; but it was only necessary to bid them work, and they at once knew what to do, and how it should be done.

Even up to the present day, it is notorious that in the planting states the blacks themselves are the only skilful cultivators of the soil, the proprietors or planters, as they are termed, knowing little or nothing of the art, save that which they learn from the African husbandman; while the ignorant white overseer, whose duty is to see that the work is attended to, knows still less.

Hemp, cotton, tobacco, corn, rice, sugar, and many other important staple products, are all the result of African skill and labor in the southern states of this country. The greater number of the mechanics of the South are also black men.

Nor was their skill as herdsmen inferior to their other proficiencies, they being among the most accomplished trainers of horses in the world.

Indeed, to this class of men may be indebted the entire country for the improvement South in the breed of horses. And those who have travelled in the southern states could not have failed to observe that the principal trainers, jockeys, riders, and judges of horses were men of African descent.

These facts alone are sufficient to establish our claim to this country, as legitimate as that of those who fill the highest stations by the suffrage of the people.

In no period since the existence of the ancient enlightened nations of Africa have the prospects of the black race been brighter than now; and at no time during the Christian era have there been greater advantages presented for the advancement of any people than at present those which offer to the black race, both in the eastern and western hemispheres; our election being in the western.

Despite the efforts to the contrary, in the strenuous endeavors for a supremacy of race, the sympathies of the world, in their upward tendency, are in favor of the African and black races of the earth. To be available, *we* must take advantage of these favorable feelings, and strike out for ourselves a bold and manly course of *independent action* and *position;* otherwise, this pure and uncorrupted sympathy will be reduced to pity and contempt.

Of the countries of our choice, we have stated that one province and two islands were slaveholding places. These, as before named, are Brazil in South America, and Cuba and Porto Rico in the West Indies. There are a few other little islands of minor consideration: the Danish three, Swedish one, and Dutch four.

But in the eight last referred to, slavery is of such a mild type, that, however objectionable as such, it is merely nominal.

In South America and the Antilles, in its worst form, slavery is a blessing almost, compared with the miserable degradation of the slaves under our upstart, assumed superiors, the slaveholders of the United States.

In Brazil color is no badge of condition, and every freeman, whatever his color, is socially and politically equal, there being black gentlemen, of pure African descent, filling the highest positions in state under the emperor. There is, also, an established law by the Congress of Brazil, making the crime punishable with death for the commander of any vessel to bring into the country any human being as a slave.

The following law has passed one branch of the General Legislative Assembly of Brazil, but little doubt being entertained that it will find a like favor in the other branch of that august general legislative body : —

" 1. All children born after the date of this law shall be free.

" 2. All those shall be considered free who are born in other countries, and come to Brazil after this date.

" 3. Every one who serves from birth to **seven years of age, any of** those included in article one, or who has to serve so many **years, at** the end of fourteen years shall be emancipated, and live **as he chooses.**

" 4. **Every slave paying for his liberty a sum equal to what he** cost his master, or who shall gain it by honorable gratuitous title, the master shall be obliged **to give** him a free paper, under the penalty **of article one** hundred and seventy-nine **of the criminal** code.

" 5. Where there **is no stipulated price or** fixed value of the slave, it **shall be determined** by arbitrators, one of which shall be the public *promoter* of the town.

" 6. **The gov**ernment is authorized to give precise regulations **for the execution of** this law, and also **to** form establishments necessary for taking care **of** those who, born after this date, may **be** abandoned by the **owners of** slaves.

" 7. Opposing laws **and** regulations are repealed."

Concerning Cuba, there **is an old** established law, giving any slave **the** right of a certain *legal tender*, which, if refused **by the** slaveholder, he, by going **to** the residence of **any parish priest,** and making known **the facts,** shall immediately be declared a freeman, the **priest or bishop** of the **parish or diocese giving him** his **" freedom papers."** The legal tender, or **sum fixed by law,** we **think does not exceed two** hundred and fifty Spanish dollars. It may be more.

Until the Americans intruded themselves into Cuba, contaminating society wherever they located, black and colored gentlemen **and ladies of rank** mingled indiscriminately in society. **But since the advent of these** negro-haters, the colored people of **Cuba have been reduced** nearly, if not quite, to the level **of** the **miserable, degraded** position of **the** colored people of the United States, who almost consider it a compliment and favor to receive the notice or smiles of a white.

Can we be satisfied, **in this enlightened age of the world,** amid the advantages **which now present** themselves to us, with **the degradation and servility inherited** from our fathers in this country ? God forbid. And we think the universal reply will be, We will not!

Half a century brings about a mighty change in the reality of existing things and events of the world's history. Fifty years ago our fathers lived. For the most part they were sorely oppressed, debased, ignorant, and incapable of comprehending the political relations of mankind — the great machinery and motive-power by which the enlightened nations of the earth were impelled forward. They knew but little, and ventured to do nothing to enhance their own interests beyond that which their oppressors taught them. They lived amidst a continual cloud of moral obscurity; a fog of bewilderment and delusion, by which they were of necessity compelled to confine themselves to a limited space — a *known* locality — lest by one step beyond this they might have stumbled over a precipice, ruining themselves beyond recovery in the fall.

We are their sons, but not the same individuals; neither do we live in the same period with them. That which suited them, does not suit us; and that with which they may have been contented, will not satisfy us.

Without education, they were ignorant of the world, and fearful of adventure. With education, we are conversant with its geography, history, and nations, and delight in its enterprises and responsibilities. They once were held as slaves; to such a condition we never could be reduced. They were content with privileges; we will be satisfied with nothing less than rights. They felt themselves happy to be permitted to beg for rights; we demand them as an innate inheritance. They considered themselves favored to live by sufferance; we reject it as a degradation. A subordinate position was all they asked for; we claim entire equality or nothing. The relation of master and slave was innocently acknowledged by them; we deny the right as such, and pronounce the relation as the basest injustice that ever scourged the earth and cursed the human family. They admitted themselves to be inferiors; we barely acknowledge the whites as equals, perhaps not in every particular. They lamented their irrecoverable fate, and incapacity to redeem themselves and their race. We rejoice that, as their sons, it is our happy lot and high mission to accomplish that which they desired, and would have done, but failed for the want of ability to do.

Let no intelligent man or woman, then, among us be found at the present day, exulting in the degradation that our enslaved parents would gladly have rid themselves had they had the intelligence and qualifications to accomplish their designs. Let none be found to shield themselves behind the plea of our brother bondmen in ignorance, that we know not *what* to do, nor *where* to go. We are no longer slaves, as were our fathers, but freemen; fully qualified to meet **our** oppressors in every relation which belongs to the elevation of man, the establishment, sustenance, and perpetuity of a nation. And such a position, by the help of God our common Father, we are determined to take and maintain.

There is but one question presents itself for **our** serious consideration, **upon which** we *must* give a decisive reply: Will we transmit, as an inheritance to our children, the blessings of unrestricted **civil** liberty, or shall we entail upon them, as our only political legacy, the degradation and oppression left us by our fathers?

Shall we be persuaded that we can live **and prosper nowhere** **but under the** authority and power of our North **American white oppressors?** that this (the United States) is the country most, if not **the** only one, favorable to our improvement and progress? Are we willing to admit that we are incapable of self-government, establishing for ourselves such political privileges, and making such internal improvements as we delight to enjoy, after American white men have made them for themselves?

No! Neither is it true that the United States is the **country best adapted to** *our* improvement. But that country is the best in which our manhood — morally, mentally, and physically — can be *best developed;* in which we have an untrammelled right to the enjoyment of **civil** and religious liberty; and the West Indies, Central and South America, present now such advantages, superiorly preferable to all other countries.

That the continent of America was designed by Providence as a reserved asylum for the various oppressed people of the earth, **of all races, to us seems** very apparent.

From the earliest period after the discovery, various nations sent a representative here, either as adventurers and speculators, or employed laborers, seamen, or soldiers, hired to work for their employers. And among the earliest and most numerous class who found their way to the New World were those of the African race. And it has been ascertained to our minds, beyond a doubt, that when the continent was discovered, there were found in the West Indies and Central America tribes of the black race, fine looking people, having the usual characteristics of color and hair, identifying them as being originally of the African race; no doubt, being a remnant of the Africans who, with the Carthaginian expedition, were adventitiously cast upon this continent, in their memorable adventure to the "Great Island," after sailing many miles distant to the west of the "Pillars of Hercules," — the present Straits of Gibraltar.

We would not be thought to be superstitious, when we say, that in all this we can "see the finger of God." Is it not worthy of a notice here, that while the ingress of foreign whites to this continent has been voluntary and constant, and that of the blacks involuntary and but occasional, yet the whites in the southern part have *decreased* in numbers, *degenerated* in character, and become mentally and physically *enervated* and imbecile; while the blacks and colored people have studiously *increased* in numbers, *regenerated* in character, and have grown mentally and physically vigorous and active, developing every function of their manhood, and are now, in their elementary character, decidedly superior to the white race? So, then, the white race could never successfully occupy the southern portion of the continent; they must, of necessity, every generation, be repeopled from another quarter of the globe. The fatal error committed by the Spaniards, under Pizarro, was the attempt to exterminate the Incas and Peruvians, and fill their places by European whites. The Peruvian Indians, a hale, hardy, vigorous, intellectual race of people, were succeeded by those who soon became idle, vicious, degenerated, and imbecile. But Peru, like all the other South American states, is regaining her former potency, just in proportion as the European race decreases among them. All the labor of the country is performed by the aboriginal natives and the blacks, the few Europeans there being the merest excrescences on the body politic — consuming drones in the social hive.

Had we no other claims than those set forth in a foregoing part of this address, they are sufficient to induce every black and colored person to remain on this continent, unshaken and unmoved.

But the West Indians, Central and South Americans, are a noble race of people; generous, sociable, and tractable — just the people with whom we desire to unite; who are susceptible of progress, improvement, and reform of every kind. They now desire all the improvements of North America, but being justly jealous of their rights, they have no confidence in the whites of the United States, and consequently peremptorily refuse to permit an indiscriminate settlement among them of this class of people; but placing every confidence in the black and colored people of North America.

The example of the unjust invasion and forcible seizure of a large portion of the territory of Mexico is still fresh in their memory; and the oppressive disfranchisement of a large number of native Mexicans, by the Americans, — because of the color and race of the natives, — will continue to rankle in the bosom of the people of those countries, and prove a sufficient barrier henceforth against the inroads of North American whites among them.

Upon the American continent, then, we are determined to remain, despite every opposition that may be urged against us.

You will doubtless be asked, — and that, too, with an air of seriousness, — why, if desirable to remain on this continent, not be content to remain in the United States. The objections to this — and potent reasons, too, in our estimation — have already been clearly shown.

But notwithstanding all this, were there still any rational, nay, even the most futile grounds for hope, we still might be stupid enough to be content to remain, and yet through another period of unexampled patience and suffering, continue meekly to drag the galling yoke and clank the chain of servility and degradation. But whether or not in this God is to be thanked and Heaven blessed, we are not permitted, despite our willingness and stupidity, to indulge even the most distant glimmer of a hope of attaining to the level of a well-protected slave.

For years we have been studiously and jealously observing the course of political events and policy on the part of this country, both in a national and individual state capacity, as pursued towards the colored people. And he who, in the midst of them, can live without observation, is either excusably ignorant, or reprehensibly deceptious and untrustworthy.

We deem it entirely unnecessary to tax you with anything like the history of even one chapter of the unequalled infamies perpetrated on the part of the various states, and national decrees, by legislation, against us. But we shall call your particular attention to the more recent acts of the United States; because, whatever privileges we may enjoy in any individual state, will avail nothing when not recognized as such by the United States.

When the condition of the inhabitants of any country is fixed by legal grades of distinction, this condition can never be changed except by express legislation. And it is the height of folly to expect such express legislation, except by the inevitable force of some irresistible internal political pressure. The force necessary to this imperative demand on our part we never can obtain, because of our numerical feebleness.

Were the interests of the common people identical with ours, we, in this, might succeed, because we, as a class, would then be numerically the superior. But this is not a question of the rich against the poor, nor the common people against the higher classes, but a question of white against black — every white person, by legal right, being held superior to a black or colored person.

In Russia, the common people might obtain an equality with the aristocracy, because, of the sixty-five millions of her population, forty-five millions are serfs or peasants; leaving but twenty millions of the higher classes — royalty, nobility, and all included.

The rights of no oppressed people have ever yet been obtained by a voluntary act of justice on the part of the oppressors. Christians, philanthropists, and moralists may preach, argue, and philosophize as they may to the contrary: facts are against them. Voluntary acts, it is true, which are in themselves just, may sometimes take place on the part of the oppressor; but these are always actuated by the force of some outward circumstances of self-interest equal to a compulsion.

The boasted liberties of the American people were **established by a** constitution, borrowed from and modelled after the British *magna charta*. And this great charter of British liberty, **so** much boasted of and vaunted as a model bill **of rights, was** obtained only by force and compulsion.

The barons, an order of noblemen, under the reign of King **John, becoming dissatisfied** at the terms submitted to by their sovereign, which necessarily brought degradation upon themselves, — terms prescribed by the insolent Pope Innocent III., **the** haughty sovereign Pontiff of Rome, — summoned his majesty to meet them on the plains of the memorable meadow of Runnymede, where, presenting to him their own Bill of Rights — a bill dictated by themselves, and drawn up by their own hands — at the unsheathed points of a thousand glittering swords, they commanded him, against his will, to sign the extraordinary document. There was no alternative: he must either do or die. With a puerile timidity, he leaned forward his rather commanding but imbecile person, and with a trembling **hand and single** dash of the pen, the name KING JOHN stood forth in **bold relief**, sending more **terror throughout the world than the mystic** handwriting of Heaven throughout the dominions of Nebuchadnezzar, blazing on the walls of Babylon. A consternation, not because of the *name* of the king, **but** because **of the** rights of *others*, which that name acknowledged.

The king, however, soon became dissatisfied, and determining **on** a revocation of the act, — an act done entirely contrary to his will, — at the head of a formidable army spread fire and sword throughout the kingdom.

But the barons, though compelled to leave their castles, their houses and homes, and fly for their lives, could not be induced to undo that which they had so nobly done — the achievement of their rights and privileges. .Hence the act has stood throughout all succeeding time, because never annulled by those **who** *willed* it.

It will be seen that the first great modern Bill of Rights was obtained only by a force of arms: a resistance of the people against the injustice and intolerance of their rulers. **We say** the people — because that which the barons demanded for themselves, was afterwards extended to the common people. **Their** only hope was based on their *superiority of numbers.*

But can we, in this country, hope for as much? Certainly not. Our case is a hopeless one. There was but *one* John, with his few sprigs of adhering royalty; and but *one* heart, at which the threatening points of their swords were directed by **a** thousand barons; **while in** our case, there is but a handful of the oppressed, without a sword to point, and *twenty millions* of Johns or Jonathans — as you please — with as many hearts, tenfold more relentless than that of Prince John Lackland, and as deceptious and hypocritical as the Italian heart of Innocent III.

Where, then, is our hope of success in this country? Upon **what is it** based? Upon what principle of political policy and sagacious discernment do our political leaders and acknowl-**edged** great men — colored men we mean — justify themselves **by telling** us, and insisting that we shall believe them, and **submit** to what they say — to be patient, remain where we are; that there is a "bright prospect and glorious future" **before us in this** country! May Heaven open our eyes from **their Bartimean** obscurity.

But we call your attention to another point of our political degradation — the acts of state and general governments.

In a few of **the** states, as in New York, the colored inhabitants **have a partial privilege** of voting a white man into office. **This** privilege is based **on a** property qualification of two hundred and fifty dollars worth **of real estate.** In others, as in Ohio, in the absence of organic provision, the privilege is granted by judicial decision, based **on a** ratio of blood, **of** an admixture of more than one half white; while in many of the states there is no **privilege** allowed, either partial or unrestricted.

The policy of the above-named **states will be** seen and detected at a glance, which, while seeming to extend immunities, is intended especially for the object of degradation.

In the State of New York, for instance, there **is** a constitutional distinction created among colored men, — almost necessarily compelling one **part to** feel superior to the other, — while among the whites no such distinctions dare **be** known. Also, **in Ohio, there is** a legal distinction set up by an upstart judiciary, **creating** among the colored people a privileged class by birth! **All** this must necessarily sever the cords of **union among us,** creating almost insurmountable prejudices of the most stupid and fatal kind, paralyzing the last bracing nerve which promised to give us strength.

It is upon this same principle, and for the self-same **object,** that the general government has long been endeavoring, **and is** at present knowingly designing to effect a recognition of **the independence** of the Dominican Republic, while disparagingly re**fusing** to recognize the independence of the Haytien nation — a **people** four **fold** greater in numbers, wealth, and power. **The** Haytiens, it is pretended, are refused because they are *negroes;* while the Dominicans, as is well known to all who are familiar with the geography, history, and political relations of that people, are identical — except in language, they speaking the Spanish tongue — with those of the Haytiens; being composed of negroes and a mixed race. The government may shield itself by the plea that it is not familiar with the origin of **those people.** To this we have but to reply, that **if the** government **is thus ignorant of the relations** of its near **neighbors, it is the height of** presumption, and **no** small **degree of assurance, for it to set up** itself as capable of prescribing terms **to the one, or conditions to the other.**

Should they accomplish their object, they then will have succeeded in forever establishing a barrier of impassable separation, **by the** creation **of a** political distinction **between those** peoples, **of superiority and** inferiority of origin or national existence. Here, then, is **another** stratagem **of this most** determined **and** untiring enemy of our **race — the** government **of the United** States.

We come now to the crowning act **of infamy on** the part **of** the general government towards the colored inhabitants **of the** United States — an act so vile in its nature, that rebellion against its demands should be promptly made in every attempt to **enforce its infernal provisions.**

In the history of national existence, there is not to be found a parallel to the tantalizing insult and aggravating despotism of the provisions of Millard Fillmore's Fugitive Slave Bill, passed by the Thirty-third Congress of the United States, with the approbation of a majority of the American people, in the year of the Gospel of Jesus Christ eighteen hundred and fifty.

This bill had but one object in its provisions, which was fully accomplished in its passage, that is, the reduction of every colored person in the United States — save those who carry free papers of emancipation, or bills of sale from former claimants or owners — to a state of relative *slavery ;* placing each and every one of us at the *disposal of any and every white* who might choose to *claim* us, and the caprice of any and every upstart knave bearing the title of " commissioner."

Did any of you, fellow-countrymen, reside in a country, the provisions of whose laws were such that any person of a certain class, who, whenever he, she, or they pleased, might come forward, lay a claim to, make oath before (it might be) some stupid and heartless person, authorized to decide in such cases, and take, at their option, your horse, cow, sheep, house and lot, or any other property, bought and paid for by your own earnings, — the result of your personal toil and labor, — would you be willing, or could you be induced by any reasoning, however great the source from which it came, to remain in that country? We pause, fellow-countrymen, for a reply.

If there be not one yea, of how much more importance, then, is your *own personal safety* than that of property? Of how much more concern is the safety of a wife or husband, than that of a cow or horse; a child, than a sheep; the destiny of your family, to that of a house and lot?

And yet this is precisely our condition. Any one of us, at any moment, is liable to be *claimed, seized,* and *taken* into custody by any white, as his or her property — to be *enslaved for life* — and there is no remedy, because it is the *law of the land !* And we dare predict, and take this favorable opportunity to forewarn you, fellow-countrymen, that the time is not far distant, when there will be carried on by the white men of this nation an extensive commerce in the persons of what now compose the free colored people of the North. We forewarn you, that the general enslavement of the whole of this class of people is now being contemplated by the whites.

At present, we are liable to enslavement at any moment, provided we are taken *away* from our homes. But we dare venture further to forewarn you, that the scheme is in mature contemplation, and has even been mooted in high places, of harmonizing the two discordant political divisions in the country by again reducing the free to slave states.

The completion of this atrocious scheme only becomes necessary for each and every one of us to find an owner and master at our own doors. Let the general government but pass such a law, and the states will comply as an act of harmony. Let the South but *demand* it, and the North will comply as a *duty* of compromise.

If Pennsylvania, New York, and Massachusetts can be found arming their sons as watch-dogs for Southern slave hunters; if the United States may, with impunity, garrison with troops the court-house of the freest city in America; blockade the streets; station armed ruffians of dragoons, and spiked artillery in hostile awe of the people; if free, white, high-born and bred gentlemen of Boston and New York are smitten down to the earth,* refused an entrance on professional business into the court-houses, until inspected by a slave hunter and his counsel, all to put down the liberty of the black man, then, indeed, is there no hope for us in this country!

---

* John Jay, Esq., of New York, son of the late distinguished jurist, Hon. William Jay, was, in 1852, as the counsel of a fugitive slave, brutally assaulted and struck in the face by the slave-catching agent and counsel, Busteed.

Also, Mr. Dana, an honorable gentleman, counsel for the fugitive Burns, one of the first literary men of Boston, was arrested on his entrance into the court-house, and not permitted to pass the guard of slave-catchers, till the slave agent and counsel, Loring, together with the overseer, Suttle, *inspected* him, and ordered that he might be *allowed* to pass in! After which, in passing along the street, Mr. Dana was ruffianly assaulted and murderously felled to the earth by the minions of the dastardly Southern overseer.

It is, fellow-countrymen, a fixed fact, as indelible as the covenant of God in the heavens, that the colored people of these United States are the slaves of any white person who may choose to claim them!

What safety or guarantee have we for ourselves or families? Let us, for a moment, examine this point.

Supposing some hired spy of the slave power residing in Illinois, whom, for illustration, we shall call Stephen A., Counsellor B., a mercenary hireling of New York, and Commissioner C., a slave catcher of Pennsylvania, should take umbrage at the acts or doings of any colored person or persons in a free state; they may, with impunity, send or go on their knight errantry to the South (as did a hireling of the slave power in New York — a lawyer by profession), give a description of such person or persons, and an agent with warrants may be immediately despatched to swear them into slavery forever.

We tell you, fellow-countrymen, any one of you here assembled — your humble committee who report to you this paper — may, by the laws of this land, be seized, whatever the circumstances of his birth, whether he descends from free or slave parents — whether born north or south of Mason and Dixon's line — and ere the setting of another sun, be speeding his way to that living sepulchre and death-chamber of our race — the curse and scourge of this country — the southern part of the United States. This is not idle speculation, but living, naked, undisguised truth.

A member of your committee has received a letter from a gentleman of respectability and standing in the South, who writes to the following effect. We copy his own words : —

"There are, at this moment, as I was to-day informed by Colonel W., one of our first magistrates in this city, a gang of from twenty-five to thirty vagabonds of poor white men, who, for twenty-five dollars a head, clear of all expenses, are ready and willing to go to the North, make acquaintance with the blacks in various places, send their descriptions to unprincipled slaveholders here, — for there are many of this kind to be found among the poorer class of masters, — and swear them into bondage. So the free blacks, as well as fugitive slaves, will have to keep a sharp watch over themselves to get clear of this scheme to enslave them."

Here, then, you have but a paragraph in the great volume of
this political crusade and legislative pirating by the American
people over the rights and privileges of the colored inhabitants
of the country. If this be but a paragraph, — for such it is in
truth, — what must be the contents when the whole history is
divulged! Never will the contents of this dreadful record of
crime, corruption, and oppression be fully revealed, until the
trump of God shall proclaim the universal summons to judgment. Then, and then alone, shall the whole truth be acknowledged, when the doom of the criminal shall be forever sealed.

We desire not to be sentimental, but rather would be political;
and therefore call your attention to another point — a point
already referred to.

In giving the statistics of various countries, and preferences to
many places herein mentioned, as points of destination in emigration, we have said little or nothing concerning the present
governments, the various state departments, nor the condition
of society among the people.

This is not the province of your committee, but the legitimate
office of a Board of Foreign Commissioners, whom there is no
doubt will be created by the convention, with provisions and instructions to report thereon, in due season, of their mission.

With a few additional remarks on the subject of the British
Provinces of North America, we shall have done our duty, and
completed, for the time being, the arduous, important, and momentous task assigned to us.

The British Provinces of North America, especially Canada
West, — formerly called Upper Canada, — in climate, soil, productions, and the usual prospects for internal improvements, are
equal, if not superior, to any northern part of the continent.
And for these very reasons, aside from their contiguity to the
northern part of the United States, — and consequent facility for
the escape of the slaves from the South, — we certainly should
prefer them as a place of destination. We love the Canadas,
and admire their laws, because, as British Provinces, there is no
difference known among the people — no distinction of race.
And we deem it a duty to recommend, that for the present, as a
temporary asylum, it is certainly advisable for every colored

person, who, desiring to emigrate, and is not prepared for any other destination, to locate in Canada West.

Every advantage on our part should be now taken of the opportunity of *obtaining* LANDS, while they are to be had cheap, and on the most easy conditions, from the government.

Even those who never contemplate a removal from this country of chains, it will be their best interest and greatest advantage to procure lands in the Canadian Provinces. It will be an easy, profitable, and safe investment, even should they never occupy nor yet see them. We shall then be but doing what the whites in the United States have for years been engaged in — securing unsettled lands in the territories, previous to their enhancement in value, by the force of settlement and progressive neighboring improvements. There are also at present great openings for colored people to enter into the various industrial departments of business operations : laborers, mechanics, teachers, merchants, and shop-keepers, and professional men of every kind. These places are now open, as much to the colored as the white man, in Canada, with little or no opposition to his progress ; at least in the character of prejudicial preferences on account of race. And all of these, without any hesitancy, do we most cheerfully recommend to the colored inhabitants of the United States.

But our preference to other places over the Canadas has been cursorily stated in the foregoing part of this paper ; and since the writing of that part, it would seem that the predictions or apprehensions concerning the Provinces are about to be verified by the British Parliament and Home Government themselves. They have virtually conceded, and openly expressed it — Lord Brougham in the lead — that the British Provinces of North America must, ere long, cease to be a part of the British domain, and become annexed to the United States.

It is needless — however much we may regret the necessity of its acknowledgment — for us to stop our ears, shut our eyes, and stultify our senses against the truth in this matter ; since, by so doing, it does not alter the case. Every political movement, both in England and the United States, favors such an issue, and the sooner we acknowledge it, the better it will be for our cause, ourselves individually, and the destiny of our people in this country.

These Provinces have long been burdensome to the British nation, and her statesmen have long since discovered and decided as an indisputable predicate in political economy, that any province as an independent state, is more profitable in a commercial consideration to a country than when depending as one of its colonies. As a child to the parent, or an apprentice to his master, so is a colony to a state. And as the man who enters into business is to the manufacturer and importer, so is the colony which becomes an independent state to the country from which it recedes.

Great Britain is decidedly a commercial and money-making nation, and counts closely on her commercial relations with any country. That nation or people which puts the largest amount of money into her coffers, are the people who may expect to obtain her greatest favors. This the Americans do; consequently — and we candidly ask you to mark the prediction — the British will interpose little or no obstructions to the Canadas, Cuba, or any other province or colony contiguous to this country, falling into the American Union; except only in such cases where there would be a compromise of her honor. And in the event of a seizure of any of these, there would be no necessity for such a sacrifice; it could readily be avoided by diplomacy.

Then there is little hope for us on this continent, short of those places where, by reason of their numbers, there is the greatest combination of strength and interests on the part of the colored race.

We have ventured to predict a reduction of the now nominally free into slave states. Already has this "reign of terror" and dreadful work of destruction commenced. We give you the quotation from a Mississippi paper, which will readily be admitted as authority in this case: —

"Two years ago a law was passed by the California legislature, granting *one year* to the owners of slaves carried into the territory previous to the adoption of the constitution, to remove them beyond the limits of the state. Last year the provision of this law *was extended twelve months longer.* We learn by the late California papers that a bill has just passed the Assembly, by a vote of 33 to 21, *continuing the same law in force until* 1855. The provisions of this bill embraces *slaves who have been carried to California since the adoption of her constitution*, as well as those who were there previously. The large majority by which it passed, and the opinions advanced during the discussion, *indicates a more favorable state of sentiment in regard to the rights of slaveholders in California than we supposed existed.*" — *Mississippian.*

No one who is a general and intelligent observer of the politics of this country, will after reading this, doubt for a moment the final result.

At present there is a proposition under consideration in California to authorize the holding of a convention to amend the constitution of that state, which doubtless will be carried into effect; when there is no doubt that a clause will be inserted, granting the right to *hold slaves at discretion* in the state. This being done, it will meet with general favor throughout the country by the American people, and the *policy be adopted on the state's rights principle.* This alone is necessary, in addition to the insufferable Fugitive Slave Law, and the recent nefarious Nebraska Bill, — which is based upon this very boasted American policy of the state's rights principle, — to reduce the free to slave states, without a murmur from the people. And did not the Nebraska Bill disrespect the feelings and infringe upon the political rights of Northern *white* people, its adoption would be hailed with loud shouts of approbation, from Portland, Maine, to San Francisco.

That, then, which is left for us to do, is to *secure* our liberty; a position which shall fully *warrant* us *against* the *liability* of such monstrous political crusades and riotous invasions of our rights. Nothing less than a national indemnity, indelibly fixed by virtue of our own sovereign potency, will satisfy us as a redress of grievances for the unparalleled wrongs, undisguised impositions, and unmitigated oppression which we have suffered at the hands of this American people.

And what wise politician would otherwise conclude and determine? None, we dare say. And a people who are incapable of this discernment and precaution are incapable of self-government, and incompetent to direct their own political destiny. For our own part, we spurn to treat for liberty on any other terms or conditions.

It may not be inapplicable, in this particular place, to quote, from high authority, language which has fallen under our notice since this report has been under our consideration. The quotation is worth nothing, except to show that the position assumed by us is a natural one, which constitutes the essential basis of self-protection.

Said Earl Aberdeen recently, in the British House of Lords, when referring to the great question which is now agitating Europe, "One thing alone is certain, that the only way to obtain a sure and honorable peace, is to *acquire a position* which may *command* it; and to gain such a position, *every nerve and sinew* of the empire should be strained. The pickpocket who robs us is not to be let off because he offers to restore our purse;" and his lordship might have justly added, "should never thereafter be intrusted or confided in."

The plea, doubtless, will be, as it already frequently has been raised, that to remove from the United States, our slave brethren would be left without a hope. They already find their way in large companies to the Canadas, and they have only to be made sensible that there is as much freedom for them South as there is North; as much protection in Mexico as in Canada; and the fugitive slave will find it a much pleasanter journey and more easy of access, to wend his way from Louisiana and Arkansas to Mexico, than thousands of miles through the slaveholders of the South and slave-catchers of the North to Canada. Once into Mexico, and his farther exit to Central and South America and the West Indies would be certain. There would be no obstructions whatever. No miserable, half-starved, servile Northern slave-catchers by the way, waiting, cap in hand, ready and willing to do the bidding of their contemptible Southern masters.

No prisons nor court-houses, as slave-pens and garrisons, to secure the fugitive and rendezvous the mercenary gangs, who are bought as military on such occasions. No perjured marshals, bribed commissioners, nor hireling counsel, who, spaniel-like, crouch at the feet of Southern slaveholders, and cringingly tremble at the crack of their whip. No, not as may be encountered throughout his northern flight, there are none of these to be found or met with in his travels from the Bravo del Norte to the dashing Orinoco — from the borders of Texas to the boundaries of Peru.

Should anything occur to prevent a successful emigration to the south — Central, South America, and the West Indies — we have no hesitancy, rather than remain in the United States, the merest subordinates and serviles of the whites, should the Canadas still continue separate in their political relations from this country, to recommend to the great body of our people to remove to Canada West, where, being politically equal to the whites, physically united with each other by a concentration of strength; when worse comes to worse, we may be found, not as a scattered, weak, and impotent people, as we now are separated from each other throughout the Union, but a united and powerful body of freemen, mighty in politics, and terrible in any conflict which might ensue, in the event of an attempt at the disturbance of our political relations, domestic repose, and peaceful firesides.

Now, fellow-countrymen, we have done. Into your ears have we recounted your own sorrows; before your own eyes have we exhibited your wrongs; into your own hands have we committed your own cause. If these should prove inadequate to remedy this dreadful evil, to assuage this terrible curse which has come upon us, the fault will be yours and not ours; since we have offered you a healing balm for every sorely aggravated wound.

Martin R. Delany, Pa.

William Webb, Pa.

Augustus R. Green, Ohio.

Edward Butler, Mo.

H. S. Douglas, La.

A. Dudley, Wis.

Conaway Barbour, Ky.

Wm. J. Fuller, R. I.

Wm. Lambert, Mich.

J. Theodore Holly, N. Y.

T. A. White, Ind.

John A. Warren, Canada.